LIGHT
A GONE Novel

PRAISE FOR THE GONE SERIES

Gone

"This intense, marvelously plotted, paced, and characterized story will immediately garner comparisons to *Lord of the Flies* or even the long-playing world shifts of Stephen King, with just a dash of *X-Men* for good measure. A potent mix of action and thoughtfulness—centered around good and evil, courage and cowardice—renders this a tour de force that will leave readers dazed, disturbed, and utterly breathless."

—ALA *Booklist* (starred review)

Hunger

"Readers will be unable to avoid involuntarily gasping, shuddering, or flinching while reading this suspense-filled story. The tension starts in the first chapter and does not let up until the end. The story is progressing with smart plot twists, both in actions and emotions."   —*VOYA* (starred review)

Plague

"Grant's science fiction fantasy thrillers continue to be the very definition of a page-turner."   —ALA *Booklist*

Lies

"Grant continues to hurtle through an endlessly fascinating (and increasingly grim) story line; his chief achievement, though, is how the *X-Men*-style powers of his cast never overwhelm the mournful realization that their world is slowly degenerating."   —ALA *Booklist*

Fear

"Adding a layer of tension is the underlying feeling that judgment day is drawing near, but who will be judge and who will be jury? Fans can count on more excellent storytelling, multidimensional characters who continue to develop in unexpected ways, and some mighty fine eye-popping moments."   —*VOYA* (starred review)

KATHERINE TEGEN BOOKS
An Imprint of HarperCollins Publishers

GHT
A GONE Novel

MICHAEL GRANT

OTHER *GONE* BOOKS BY MICHAEL GRANT:

Gone

Hunger

Lies

Plague

Fear

Katherine Tegen Books is an imprint of HarperCollins Publishers.

Light: A Gone Novel
Copyright © 2013 by Michael Grant
All rights reserved. Printed in the United States of America.
No part of this book may be used or reproduced in any manner whatsoever without written permission except in the case of brief quotations embodied in critical articles and reviews. For information address HarperCollins Children's Books, a division of HarperCollins Publishers, 10 East 53rd Street, New York, NY 10022.
www.epicreads.com

Library of Congress Cataloging-in-Publication Data is available.
ISBN 978-0-06-144918-5 (trade bdg.) — ISBN 978-0-06-144919-2 (lib. bdg.)

Typography by Joel Tippie
13 14 15 16 17   LP/RRDH   10 9 8 7 6 5 4 3 2 1
❖
First Edition

For Katherine, Jake, and Julia

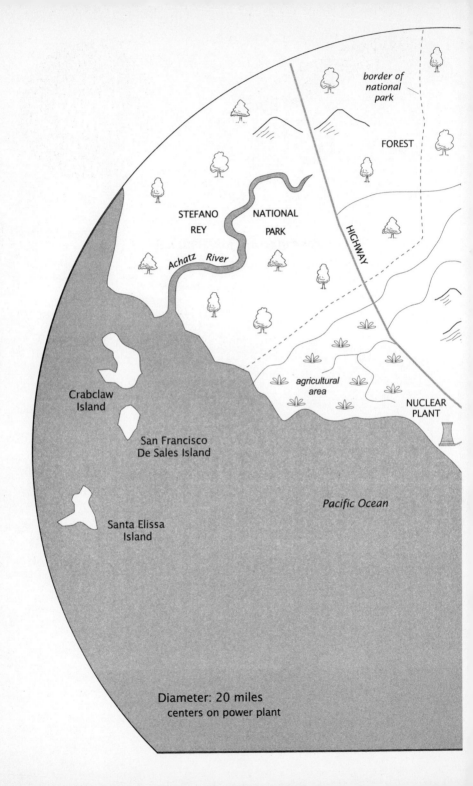

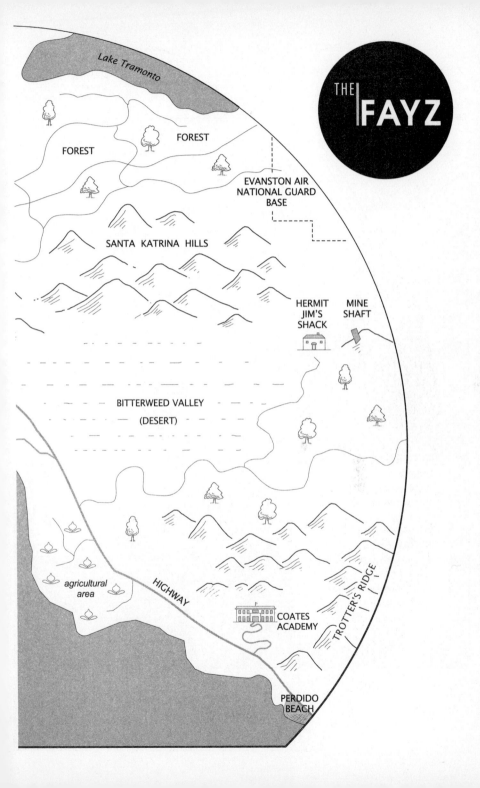

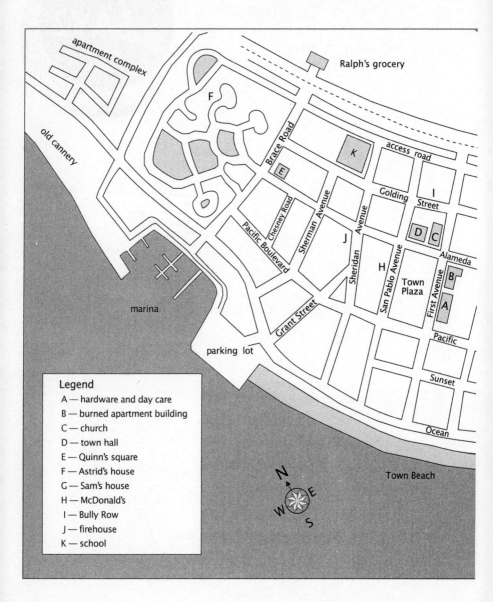

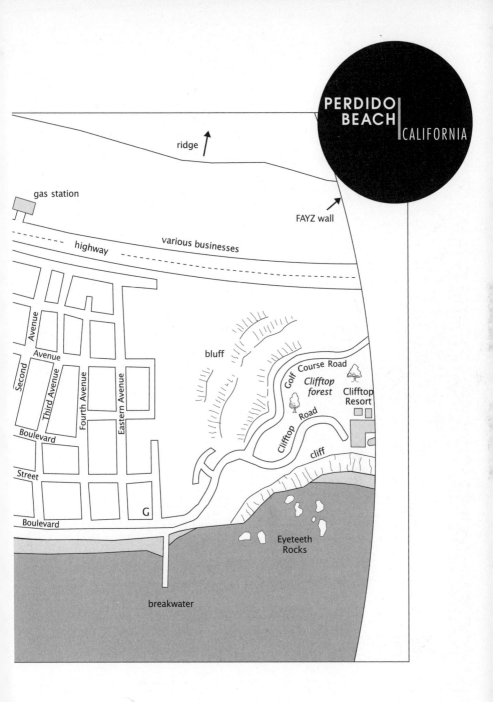

Darkness cannot drive out darkness; only light can do that. Hate cannot drive out hate; only love can do that.
—Martin Luther King Jr.

ONE

THE LITTLE GIRL'S hair caught fire. It flamed magnificently, for she had her mother's lush dark hair.

Sam fired again, and the little girl's flesh burned at last.

But all the while the girl, the gaiaphage, its face turned away from onlookers, stared at Sam in undiminished fury. The blue eyes never looked away. Her angelic mouth leered in a knowing grin even as it burned.

Gaia had started a fire in some twigs that Diana had gathered. It wasn't much of a fire. It would die out soon, and Diana would sleep, again, on the cold ground.

There had been a moment, two days earlier, when Diana might have gone to Caine. Caine had been with Sam, and she could have broken away from Gaia then and run to him.

Maybe Drake, Whip Hand, could have stopped her if she had tried that. Maybe Gaia could have as well. But for some reason Gaia had kept Drake from killing Caine, and then, seconds later, Sam had burned Gaia with his deadly light and . . .

. . . and right then, Diana could have run to Caine. She had wanted to.

Had she stayed with Gaia out of some new maternal instinct? Gaia had cried in genuine, terrifying agony from the burns. She could be hurt. She *had* been hurt.

Yes, Diana thought now, too desperate, hungry, cold, that had been part of it. Gaia was her daughter. What an impossible idea! Gaia had been created inside Diana's body, egg and sperm, Diana and Caine, the world's oldest story. And when Gaia was born in pain and blood, Diana had felt a connection. It had been good, that connection. It had been reassuring, because Diana had not been sure she would feel it. She had not been sure she was capable of feeling it. The connection meant Diana was human, that she was a woman, that she could feel something for the baby she had delivered.

That there was, despite everything, some hope for Diana.

But she had also felt fear. Gaia was a beautiful baby girl when she was born. She would be beautiful again, no doubt, when she finished healing herself of the deep and terrible burns that had turned her skin into something that looked like the top of an overcooked lasagna. (Gaia seemed unconcerned with all that.) But she would never be just a girl, the daughter of Caine and Diana. Because there was a third force, greater than egg and sperm and womb. Greater even than a mother's love.

Gaia was the creature of the gaiaphage. The gaiaphage had taken her. It had brutally suppressed whatever slight, tenuous personality the baby might have had, and it had imposed itself. Diana had seen it and had cried out against it, but the gaiaphage didn't care. It didn't care when it was a seething mass of green seeping across the floor of a deep cave, and it didn't care now that it was a girl with half-healed burned flesh and hair only now growing back, staring into a fire.

"Nemesis," Gaia whispered, not for the first time. Like she was whispering to a friend.

Diana's daughter was never going to love her. She'd been an idiot to even imagine it, to even dream of it.

But maybe . . .

Maybe what? Maybe what? Diana taunted herself, as pitilessly judgmental with her own self as she was with others. *What ridiculous hope are you holding on to, Diana? You know what she is. You know she's not yours, not really yours. You know she's not a "she" but an "it."*

But so pretty by firelight. Imagine, Diana tortured herself, imagine if she was really just a girl, your daughter. Imagine what a miracle you would see in her. Imagine how you would feel, Diana, if this beautiful girl was really yours.

Yours and his.

A beautiful, perfect little girl . . .

A dark and terrible creature.

"It won't hurt, my little Nemesis," Gaia said, but not to Diana.

Would Diana once again let herself be swept along in the

wake of an evil person, first with Caine, now with Gaia? Was impotent snark all that Diana had to offer in opposition?

During her abbreviated pregnancy she had allowed herself to fantasize about being a mother, a better mother than her own. She'd pictured herself becoming a good person. She could do that, she'd told herself. She didn't always have to go on being what she had been and what she had become.

She could have been saved.

"The end is the best part of any story," Gaia whispered, talking to no one that Diana could see. "The end."

Diana had imagined redemption, forgiveness, a new beginning as a young mother.

But she was mother to a monster who cared nothing for her.

"I don't make good choices," Diana whispered as she lay down in the dirt and wrapped her arms tightly for warmth.

"What," Gaia snapped, looking up at her.

"Eh," Diana said with a sigh. "Nothing."

Little Pete was getting littler. That's how it felt, anyway. He could feel himself sort of shrinking, and he wasn't so sure it felt bad. Maybe it was a relief.

Life had always been strange and disturbing for Peter Ellison. From the moment of his birth the world had attacked him with noise and light and scraping touch. All the sensations that were easy for other people to make sense of were terrifying and overwhelming for him. Other people could filter things out. Other people could turn down the noise, but

Pete could not. Not while he'd been in his body.

That body had been the problem. The severe autism that had crippled him had been in his body, in his physical brain.

It had been a relief to be out of that body and brain. When Astrid, his sister with the cutting blue eyes and the yellow snake hair, had thrown him to his physical death, he had been . . . relieved.

Pete had been able to create a new thing for himself, a new place that was not a body. He had carried his power with him, but with that power he had made terrible mistakes. He saw that now. He saw what he had done to Taylor. He could no longer do things like that; he could no longer play with the abstract patterns that were actually human beings.

Now he was fading, like a light with one of those special switches. There had been one in the house, the dining room of the house he'd been raised in, the one that had burned down. A dimmer switch, that's what his mother had called it.

Turn the dimmer down, let's make dinner seem romantic.

Little by little the light that was Pete was getting dimmer. He was romantic.

He had been like a rubber band stretched out. Like one end was attached to his body and the other end was . . . well, wherever he was now. But with his body gone the rubber band was contracting.

It wasn't so bad.

He could see the Darkness. The Darkness, too, could reach into this space of Pete's. It, too, had been dimming, the creature that named itself gaiaphage, but now it was stronger with a body to anchor it.

Pete could listen to the gaiaphage's mind sometimes. Pete knew the Darkness was watching him. Laughing at him as he weakened, but nervous, too.

So many times the Darkness had reached to him with its tendrils, sneaking up behind him, trying to find him, trying to make him believe things, do things.

The Darkness wanted Pete to dim. When Pete was all the way gone, all his power would be gone, too.

The Darkness whispered to him. *It won't hurt, my little Nemesis. It will just be the end, like the end of the stories your sister used to read to you. Remember how you always wanted them to end because her voice and her eyes and her yellow hair hurt you?*

Don't fight it, Nemesis.

The end is the best part of any story. The end.

Yea, though I walk through the valley of the shadow of death, I will fear no evil: for thou art with me.

Orc had memorized the verse. In his head he said it "yeah" instead of "yea," but that didn't change the meaning. What it meant was, if you're scared, don't be, because God is there. That much was clear. But the next bit about a rod and a staff... as far as Orc knew, a rod was maybe a stick and a staff was, like, all the guys who worked for you. My staff.

My staff will comfort you. Which made sense because if

you were God you'd need a staff of, like, angels or whatever to take care of comforting people and so on.

He had walked up Trotter's Ridge at sundown, up above the town of Perdido Beach. But as he'd reached the top of the hill where the barrier sliced it in two, he'd crouched lower and lower, afraid even to be outlined against the stars. He'd finished the last hundred feet on his belly.

You still couldn't touch the barrier, that hadn't changed; it would still zap you. But now you could see right through it. Like it was just plain old glass. Which meant people out there could see in.

That thought made him sick to his stomach.

He peered through a crispy, dead stand of tall yellow grass, and there it was. The other side. The out there.

No one was on the hill right where he was; they were all down on the highway and around there. It was so amazingly bright out there. The hamburger place was lit up like light cost nothing. The motels, so many lights. Like Christmas or something. He could see the lights of cars and vans and campers backed up in the world's biggest traffic jam. It went on as far as he could see. There were police lights flashing all over the place, near and far, the Highway Patrol trying to get things organized. Problem was, the highway just hit the barrier and stopped. Someone had bulldozed a turnaround, but with cars lining both sides of the highway as well as jamming the highway itself, that whole turnaround thing wasn't working. There was a slow-moving stream of red taillights.

Up against the barrier in the out there were a few big news trucks all covered in antennas and satellite dishes and crazy bright lights. A little past them it looked like some kind of army base, because earlier he had seen green uniforms and Humvees.

Above all there was the neon, red and gold and a little green—a Carl's Jr. His mouth watered. Fries. He would do just about anything for some fries and a chocolate shake.

From this angle he couldn't see the kids up against the inside of the barrier, but he knew they were there, because unlike the stuff outside he could hear the things inside. He heard voices, some yelling like they didn't believe no one could hear through the barrier.

A girl with a high-pitched voice was yelling, "Mommy! Mommy!"

Everyone seemed to think it was all going to end. They all thought the barrier had to come down now—sooner, not later. Caine, who called himself King Caine, had told Orc to help him get people back from the barrier, get them back to work, because here in the FAYZ every day was hungry, and starvation was never more than a couple days off.

But of course Orc had said no. No way. If he went down there, every camera would point toward him. People would scream: he wouldn't be able to hear them, but he'd see them, see their mouths making big Os and see them point at him.

Orc had always been a big kid, but he was more than big now. He was probably more than six feet tall and almost that wide just standing with his arms down at his side. And he was made of something that looked a lot like wet gravel, or maybe concrete that hadn't set yet.

He was a monster.

He wanted a drink of booze so bad. If he got really rip-roaring crazy drunk, then maybe he could go down there, down into the valley of the shadow. But not sober, no, he couldn't take that.

His mom might be there, if his dad hadn't killed her yet.

He tried to picture her and succeeded. Then Orc tried to picture his mother without a bruise on the side of her head or a cast on her wrist and he couldn't.

And his father . . . he didn't want to picture his father, but he couldn't help it, the pictures came: pictures of his father in a cold and evil drunk, sizing up his son, making sure that Charles Merriman, who had long been known as Orc, was hanging his head and looking away. Making sure his son was afraid.

His dad liked that part, the part where Orc was desperately trying to stay out of his way but was forced to sit down and do his homework while his father drank beer after beer and dropped the cans beside his chair, waiting until he had an excuse—almost anything would do.

His father sober was distant and indifferent. His father drunk was a monster.

Like Orc, but not as ugly.

He wondered if his father knew he could come here and

glare at his son again through the dome. And what would he say if he saw Orc now? Make that snorting sound of his, that sound that said, *You're worthless.*

If that happened . . .

His father was a big man. But Orc was bigger and had strength to match. Orc could snap him like a dry stick.

With one thick, stony finger Orc delicately touched the tiny patch of human skin near his mouth. It tickled.

If the barrier came down, everyone would see him in the bright TV lights. And sooner or later his father would, too. Orc was sure if he ever saw his father again, he would kill the man.

That was the death that shadowed the valley. That was the evil. And God's staff would have to move pretty quick to stop it happening.

"Don't let it come down, Lord," he prayed. "I know all them kids want to see their moms and all. But please, God, don't let that barrier come down."

Sam was asleep, finally, facedown, uncovered, naked, and turned slightly away from Astrid.

There was a light. Sam Temple, the hero of most of the kids in the FAYZ, had always been a little afraid of the dark. So he had created a night-light for this dark space.

It was not a normal light: a tiny ball, no bigger than a marble. It floated in a corner above the bunk. Astrid had taped a sheet of red paper in front of it so that its green, unnatural glow would be softened. The tape had come loose, so the imperfect lampshade blocked the light only intermittently as the paper twirled in the slightest breeze, drifted as the boat gently rocked.

When the light brightened, Sam would appear as bits and pieces—a broad back, a flicker of round, pale bottom, a length of muscular thigh in harsh shadow. When the light softened, he would be almost invisible just sounds of breathing, and a scent, and a warmth.

She should cover him. Really, she should. He'd get cold after a while and wake up and realize she wasn't sleeping and that would worry him.

But not just yet, she thought.

She was trying to read by the uncertain light. The book was on law, and Astrid had become convinced by the book that she would never be a lawyer, or even try. She could read most anything, but this was a very dull book, and it did very little to distract her from the view.

My God: she was *happy.*

The very idea that she should be happy was absurd. It was almost a crime. Things were desperate, but then they had been for a long time. Desperate had long since become the new normal.

If the barrier really did come down . . . if this really was the endgame . . . They were fifteen. Out there, out in the world, they had no legal right to be together.

They'd been through hell. They'd been through a whole series of hells, and they were still together. But none of that would mean anything in the eyes of the law. Her parents, or his mother, could snap their fingers and break what Sam and Astrid had built.

It was not the first time Astrid had had the thought that maybe liberation from the FAYZ would be no such thing.

TWO

THE BREEZE WAS famous.

She had been interviewed on the *Today* show.

The interview had been a bit unusual, because there was no way for Matt Lauer to actually speak to Brianna, and no way for Brianna to speak back. Communications with the outside world were purely visual. The world could see in. The kids in the FAYZ could see out. That was it.

Which meant that an interview was done with what amounted to a sort of primitive Twitter. The interviewer would write a question on a pad, or in the case of the *Today* show, since they were a little more high-tech, light it up on an HD monitor that had been set up to be visible within the dome. Then whoever was inside the dome could write the answer and hold it up to the cameras outside.

This made for extraordinarily tedious interviews. The interviewer could have a bunch of questions preloaded, but the kid on the inside would have to write his or her answer out, and that was slow. Very. Very. Slow.

For anyone except the Breeze.

Brianna had ripped a segment of chalkboard off from the school, and had found some chalk, and with her superhuman speed she could write faster than most people could talk.

Unfortunately, Brianna was not the most cautious or sensible person in the FAYZ. She was bold, fearless, very, very dangerous in a fight, and had a sort of reckless charm. But she was not a person who carefully thought out her answers.

So when Matt Lauer had asked whether kids had died in the FAYZ, Brianna's chalked answer had been: *A bunch. Kids have been dying all over the place. This isn't Disneyland.*

Which was okay in itself, although it sent shockwaves of fear through the parent community.

It was the follow-up question that caused the problem.

Matt Lauer: *Have you taken a life?*

Brianna: *Absolutely. I'm the Breeze. I am the most badass person in here except for maybe Sam and Caine.*

Then before Matt could put up his next question, Brianna went on happily scribbling and holding her chalkboard up for the cameras, then rubbing it with her sleeve and scribbling some more.

There's some more I want to kill but sometimes it's hard. I've cut Drake up with wire and a machete and blown his head off with a shotgun. He's still not dead! LOL.

And then:

What I'm thinking about doing is slicing him up and then zooming the pieces all around, like up in the mountains, out in the water. Let's see if he can put himself back together then. LOL.

So basically Brianna had confessed to several killings—despite the fact she hadn't actually killed anyone unless you counted bugs and coyotes—and bragged that she intended to go on killing and was in fact contemplating murder right then.

And grinning.

And striking poses for the cameras.

And adding a jaunty "LOL."

And demonstrating just how fast she could twirl a bowie knife, a machete, and a garrote. And brandishing the sawed-off shotgun for which she had modified a runner's backpack.

All of this got back to Sam.

Sam was not happy about it.

"Oh, my *God*. Are you out of your mind? 'LOL'? Really?" he demanded. "I thought I told everyone: no talking to people unless it's your parents. I told you *and* Edilio told you. And then, because I knew perfectly well that you would pay no attention to that and do whatever you wanted, I looked you right in the eyes"—he pointed at her eyes for emphasis—"right in those eyes, and I said something along the lines of, 'Breeze, don't go telling horror stories.'"

"He believes he said that."

That last was from Toto, the truth teller. The boy could not restrain himself from announcing the truth or falsity of everything he heard. And he was 100 percent accurate. And 100 percent annoying.

Sam, Astrid, Brianna, and Toto were on the top deck of the houseboat at the lake. Two days had passed since the dome went transparent. Two days since they had seen the outside world for the first time in almost a year.

Two days since Sam had burned Penny to ashes while his mother watched.

And two days since the evil child, Gaia, and her mother, Diana, along with the foul Drake/Brittney creature, had retreated in pain and confusion.

"In the eyes. Me looking straight at you," Sam said, insisting, even as Brianna adopted a transparently false *What, me?* look.

"Brianna, listen," Astrid said. "You're very useful at communicating with the world, but don't go confessing to major crimes."

"Crimes!" Brianna's eyes narrowed and her thin lip curled. "Hey, I only do what I have to do."

"We know that," Sam said wearily. "We know that. The world may not." Then he added, "LOL."

"Yeah, well they can all drop dead," Brianna said heatedly. "What are they doing to get us out of here? They tried to kill us all! Now they're going to judge us?"

Sam's face revealed his own private agreement, so he kept his eyes carefully averted from Astrid, as if that meant she wouldn't notice.

"They didn't try to kill us; they were trying to blow open the dome," Astrid said.

"With a nuke?" Brianna shrilled.

"She doesn't believe that," Toto said. Then he clarified: "Astrid doesn't believe what she said, Spidey."

Toto was talking less often to his long-since-destroyed Spider-Man bust, the object he'd spent lonely months with, but there were still occasional references. No one took notice: at this point no one in the FAYZ was entirely sane.

"Okay," Astrid said icily. "Let me restate that: They didn't set out to destroy us all. But they were willing to risk it."

Toto hesitated a moment. Then: "She believes that."

But now Astrid was angry, and not at Toto or Brianna or even Sam—to his relief. "They wanted their highway back. They wanted this to be over. And they sure didn't want people discovering that they'd been tracking mutations for months. So they set off a freaking nuke under the dome. Is that true enough, Toto? And maybe it would have overloaded the dome and crashed it like they hoped, and we'd be free. But quite possibly it would have incinerated all of us, the reckless, stupid scumbags who would kill us after all we've gone through, gone through hell trying to stay alive!"

There were other choice words, many, in fact, a long and erudite stream of them. Astrid had never been one for cursing, but she was very well-read and had obviously picked up a few phrases along the way.

When she was done and both Sam and Brianna were staring at her with a sort of wary amazement, Toto said, "She believes that."

"Yeah, I kind of think she did," Sam said dryly. "Do me a favor, Toto: go find Edilio, if he's free, and Dekka. We're wasting time."

Toto raised an eyebrow but did not comment. He climbed down to the dock. He was used to being sent on errands. It was almost as if people found him irritating.

"Breeze: you know what I need from you. I understand that you love to entertain the lookers, but I need you patrolling."

"I was just going," Brianna said huffily. She blurred, reappeared on the dock, and then, walking quickly backward, said, "By the way, they still want to interview you, Sam." Then she zoomed away out of sight.

"Why do I get the feeling we have a crazy twelve-year-old daughter?" Astrid muttered.

Sam looked at Astrid with affection so obvious a blind man would have seen it. The days of wondering whether they would be together were over. It wasn't that either of them had said it quite that way; it was just the way it was, it was there, it was a fact. It was chiseled in granite.

Astrid stood with legs apart, arms crossed, wearing a sleeveless T-shirt and jeans so torn and ripped they looked like they'd been tailored with a chainsaw, her once-long blond hair now hacked short, her cool, judgmental blue eyes still judging, still watching the world more closely than anyone else.

She was still Astrid the Genius, the girl who had so intimidated Sam back before the FAYZ that he hadn't even let himself think about asking her out, or even talking to her.

She had been so far above him—at least in his own eyes—that she was practically on a different planet.

The funny thing was that he was still in awe of her, but she was no longer unattainable. She wasn't the icy, distant Athena looking down at him from Olympus with affection mingled with disappointment. She had committed. She had bought in. And now it was as if an invisible FAYZ barrier of their own encircled just the two of them, defined them, and made each of them hate the idea of being apart.

They spent their days and their nights together, and they still disagreed, and they still argued, and they sniped, and they were absolutely bound together into one.

Unbreakable unless by death.

Which was a very likely outcome, and a thought that wiped the smug, contented look from Sam's face.

Endgame. That word had quickly become part of conversation in the FAYZ. He had tried to quash it. Edilio had tried to quash it. Down in Perdido Beach, Caine had tried to quash it. It wasn't good for people to start thinking things were coming to an end.

But Sam was thinking it himself, and he was trying to imagine that ending. Each time he tried, each time he ran the clock forward in his imagination, the fantasy would fall apart. He believed it was the endgame. He felt it in his bones. He just didn't think he was going to make it out.

When he saw the end, it was always a terrible one. And he always saw himself watching others leave the FAYZ while he did not.

When had that morbid thought first surfaced? Had it been there festering in the back of his mind for a long time? Had it only now broken through to conscious awareness because people were talking about the endgame?

Endgame. It can mean more than one thing, he thought.

But it was all nonsense, all speculation. None of it meant anything. None of it mattered, not really. It would end how it ended.

Edilio and Dekka arrived. They had very sensibly not brought Toto back with them.

Sam didn't get up, just gave them a wave as they climbed aboard the docked houseboat. Edilio plopped into a deck chair. He was weary and dusty. It would be wrong to say that he looked old—he was still physically a teenager, a sunburned, dark-skinned guy in jeans and boots, with a desperate-looking cowboy hat he'd found somewhere, over shaggy dark hair. He didn't look old, but in some way it was impossible to define, he looked like a man, not a boy.

That impression came only partly from the fact that he was carrying an assault rifle slung over one shoulder.

"Word from PB is that Caine is trying to get Orc to force people away from the barrier and back to work," Edilio said.

"Maybe not such a bad idea?" Sam said.

"Except it's not working," Dekka said. "Orc won't go near the barrier. He doesn't want anyone to see him. You know, the way he is. There's, like, no produce down in Perdido Beach, not even cabbages," Dekka went on. "If it wasn't for

Quinn still bringing in fish, they'd all be starving again. I'd almost say we need Albert back, if he wasn't such a backstabbing little worm."

Dekka had never looked young; she'd been born with a serious face that over time had become forbidding. When she was annoyed—as she was now—her expression could become downright intimidating. And an angry Dekka was a storm front coming.

"I guess you heard about Breeze?" Dekka asked, changing the subject. There was a mix of exasperation and affection in her tone. Dekka might not be over Brianna, but she had made peace with her rejection. The infatuation had burned out, but the love was still there.

"Oh, we heard," Astrid said. "You just missed her."

Edilio wasn't in the mood for small talk. Something was on his mind. "We're vulnerable here. We don't know where Diana and that freak-show baby of hers are. And we don't know what kind of power Gaia has—except that if she was really a normal kid, she'd be dead. We don't even know what they want, what they're after. Maybe they don't want anything, though most likely . . ." He shrugged. "But the bigger vulnerability is probably down in PB. We got, what, two hundred fifty kids all together, between the lake and PB? Give or take. At least half of them are down there right now where the highway hits the barrier. Waving and crying and writing notes. Especially the littles, man. It's not just no work getting done; it's that they're out in the open with no one protecting them."

"They're a target," Astrid said.

"Big one," Dekka said.

"That's Caine's territory down there," Sam said, shifting uncomfortably at the temptation to palm off responsibility on his alienated brother.

"Yeah, but a lot of them are our people. Lake people," Edilio argued. "You notice it's quiet around here? Half our people walked ten miles down to PB so they can cry looking at their family." He didn't say that with a sneer. Edilio didn't own a sneer.

Astrid said, "We have the same two top priorities we've had since the start: keep people fed and stop those trying to destroy us."

Sam smiled privately at the rather grandiose phrasing.

"We need a plan beyond hoping Breeze finds Drake and Diana and Gaia," Edilio said.

"I was kind of hoping you had one," Sam said. He was joking, but Edilio wasn't smiling.

Sam had the odd feeling that he'd just been caught goofing off in class. He sat up straighter and unconsciously lowered his voice half an octave. "You're right, Edilio. What is it you want to do?"

At some point, and Sam could not really pinpoint quite when, Edilio had stopped being his sidekick and become his equal, his full partner. The change had permeated the consciousness of the population at the lake, had become fact without anyone having to announce it. No one anymore told

Edilio they'd have to "check with Sam": in everything except for a battle, Edilio was in charge.

Sam could not have been more pleased. He had discovered about himself that he had no talent for details. Or managing. And it was a wonderful thing to be able to lie in bed with Astrid and not feel the whole world was depending on him. In fact, glancing up at her now, with her sleeveless T-shirt gapping at the side, and the amazing line of her legs, and . . . He forced himself back to Edilio.

"Okay, a couple things. First, while we have time, I want to prepare for the worst," Edilio said. "We don't have much extra food, but I want to stop people eating the last of the Nutella and Cup-a-Noodles. I want to put that stuff on a boat we'll anchor out in the lake. Also some of the vegetables that Sinder is growing, the stuff that won't spoil. I don't want us getting caught flat-footed again. From now on, people want to eat, they had better get their butts back to work."

Sam nodded. "Yeah." Up above, the sky was cloudy. But they were not quite normal clouds. They moved in a strange pattern, seeming to slide by, swifter close in, slower off in the far northern distance. Toward the southeast the sky turned dark blue. It was all part of the dome effect.

The newly transparent sphere that contained the FAYZ was twenty miles in diameter, with the nuclear power plant at its center. That meant that directly over the power plant the top of the sphere was ten miles up. At that point the top of the sphere approached the stratosphere, up beyond clouds, beyond much oxygen. It was quite a bit lower here at Lake Tramonto, which was near the northwest edge. This close to the barrier they could be seen from the outside by anyone with a decent set of binoculars.

Just forty-eight hours after the barrier had gone clear it was still very strange to Sam to be able to look across Lake Tramonto and see the rest of Lake Tramonto. There was a marina over there, probably not a mile from where he was sitting. There were boats, and people, too, though not more than a handful. Some had ventured out in the boats to nose right up against the barrier and look in, like people staring at the animals in the zoo. There was one over there right now with two guys pretending to fish but actually shooting video. Sam waved and felt foolish.

Life in the FAYZ had changed.

As if to make that point, Astrid shaded her eyes and looked off to the north. "Helicopter."

There was a helicopter with some sort of logo, maybe a news station or a police department, impossible to read from this distance. It was hovering above the "out there" marina, most likely aiming a camera into the dome. Perhaps focusing, as well as they could from that distance, on the four of them sitting there.

Sam fought a sudden childish impulse to give them the finger.

Edilio was still talking, and for the second time Sam felt like a distracted student in class.

"What we need most of all is simple information," Edilio was saying. "What are Drake and Diana and that kid going to do? And what can they do? Right now we're blind."

"Irony," Astrid said. When everyone just stared at her blankly, she sighed and explained, "For the first time we can see the real sky, and the world outside of this fishbowl, and we're still blind."

"Ah," the three said in unison. "Yeah, right."

"You know, it's not a witty remark if I have to explain it," Astrid said, obviously disgruntled.

"I want to talk to Caine," Edilio said. "I'm going to head down to PB. We need to work together."

"You want me to come?" Sam asked.

"If it's you down at the barrier trying to get kids motivated, it will just get Caine pissed off. And we don't have time for that whole enemies thing. To be honest with you . . . Well, I was wondering, Sam . . . I mean, just a suggestion . . ."

Sam smiled affectionately at his friend. "Dude: if you got a job for me, just tell me what it is."

"It's not just a job. It's . . . Okay, here it is: Even Breeze can't be everywhere. She searches, but she doesn't search smart. I love her, but she just zooms around randomly and doesn't let anyone tell her where to look."

Sam nodded. "You want me to go looking for trouble."

"Breeze is all over the area around PB, looking for any sign that Gaia and Drake are heading toward town—and of course making sure the TV cameras see her. But maybe Gaia is holing up somewhere, waiting. Getting stronger. Or maybe she's on the move."

Sam thought about it. "The mine shaft, the National Guard base, the Stefano Rey, or the power plant."

"Same as my list. And you can't take Dekka with you; I— we—need her here."

"Who can I take?"

"We don't know what Gaia can do. Sam, you may not be strong enough to take her, *it*, whatever. Not alone for sure, or even with Dekka." He nodded respectfully at Dekka. "No offense to you, Dekka."

Dekka nodded slightly to say no offense was taken. Dekka knew the limits of her powers.

"I don't think we should wait for Gaia to choose the time and place," Edilio said.

"She ran away with Diana and Drake," Astrid said. "She didn't come right back; she ran off. That doesn't make me think she's all that dangerous."

Sam looked down and smiled. "If Toto was here, he'd call BS on that, Astrid. The gaiaphage did not choose to take on a body thinking it would get weaker. You know that."

The mood, which had been light earlier, thanks to Brianna, had grown steadily darker. Edilio had brought reality with him. And reality had a bad feel.

Astrid was looking for something to say, some argument, but in the end all she had was, "I don't want you getting killed, Sam. If you go after Gaia . . ."

"Edilio isn't thinking I'll go alone, are you, Edilio?" Sam

said. He reached for her hand, squeezed, but she did not return the pressure.

"We should probably leave soon," Edilio said. "One hour?"

Sam nodded, a condemned man accepting the inevitable sentence. "One hour."

THREE

"I'M HUNGRY," GAIA said, and not for the first time that morning. Drake had come in the night and brought some artichokes and a dead rat, but it wasn't enough. Gaia had sent him right back out for more.

She was a very hungry girl. A growing monster.

At first Gaia had taken a little milk from Diana's breasts, but her development was way too fast to allow her to survive on mother's milk. And Diana's body was a wreck— malnourished, bruised, beaten. Her body had had only four months to adjust to what should have been a nine-month pregnancy. And the birth itself, crying out in pain in a hot, dark cave . . . Well, she wasn't in the best of shape.

For the last two days, as Gaia healed herself and grew, Drake had been sent off to forage for food. He had raided the fields; he had successfully attacked a cart heading from Perdido Beach to the lake; he had killed animals and brought them back to Gaia, who cooked them with a blast of light from her hands and ate them.

But her appetite was still growing. Her appetite was becoming dangerous. Diana no longer had even a small chance of taking any of the food for herself. And worse, more frightening still to Diana, were her daughter's long, speculative looks. Gaia was not good at hiding emotion: she was looking at Diana as a possible meal. At times the girl would drool like a dog at feeding time.

They were following the barrier still, stolidly walking along the circumference of the space that everyone had come to call the FAYZ. Fallout Alley Youth Zone, a mordant label that Howard Bassem had come up with. Howard: no longer alive. Himself eaten by coyotes.

So Drake was off foraging yet again, and Diana was in the unusual position of hoping her hated foe would succeed, and quickly.

Diana and Gaia had reached a high point, up in the hills above the gaiaphage's mine shaft. For the first time Diana could really see that beyond the dome the hills soared much higher still. They were standing on a series of foothills, really, but with enough altitude that in the other direction Diana could see the distant blue haze of the ocean. There were low, dark smears where the islands sat.

"Huh. I know where there's food," Diana said.

"You told me: Perdido Beach," Gaia said. "But I'm not ready to go there. Are you so stupid you don't remember?"

"I really am getting sick of being called stupid," Diana snapped. "You can call me Mother. Or you can call me

Diana. I'll take either one."

Gaia hesitated, stared at Diana, then blinked.

Diana screamed. "Aaaaahh! No, no, no!" She felt the hot knife in her head. The pain was terrible and terrifying, like some desperate animal inside her head trying to rip its way out.

The pain stopped as suddenly as it had begun. Maybe it had lasted three seconds, but it had felt much longer.

Had it lasted longer still, Diana would have gone mad. She was on her knees, trembling, fighting the urge to vomit up the nothing in her stomach.

"You don't make demands," Gaia said. She came close: just a child, but with a power no child had ever held. Her eyes were blue. Her hair was so dark, it was almost black. She ran her chubby child's fingers over Diana's back and neck, probing, feeling, like a cook assessing a piece of steak. "You serve me. You're a slave. My slave."

Diana nodded, unable to speak as the sense memory of that pain echoed in her skull.

Gaia relented. "But in using this spoken human language I have to call you something. So I'll call you Diana."

"Lovely," Diana said through gritted teeth.

"Food?" Gaia prompted.

"There's an island. You can see it, that gray lump out in the ocean."

Gaia looked. "I see nothing."

"You see the ocean, the bluish stuff out there."

"No."

Diana considered this for a moment, looked around for what she needed, and said, "Do you see the stand of trees on that ridge? How many trees?" There were three, quite distinct from one another.

"I can't count them. They blur together."

"You're nearsighted," Diana said. She laughed. "You've got to be kidding me? You're a nearsighted devil child? You need *glasses*?"

Gaia did not object to being called a devil child, apparently, as there was no stabbing pain. But she frowned at the term "nearsighted." "Do you mean that your vision is better than mine?"

Diana shrugged. "It has to do with the shape of your eyeball, I think. Bodies are like that: all kinds of imperfections. Also, you're growing at an amazing, unnatural rate. So who knows what's going on with your body?"

It occurred to Diana to wonder whether Gaia could control the aging process. She had assumed that the gaiaphage caused it, but was it just some bizarre effect of the FAYZ?

And she was still trying to figure out what Gaia knew and did not know. Gaia—the gaiaphage—had spent her life, if you could call it that, in a mine shaft. She could use language, but it always seemed forced. She knew many things, but there were also lots of holes in her knowledge. She was like a foreigner just coming to grips with a new society.

Diana's best theory—and she had not asked Gaia—was that Gaia knew what she had picked up from minds she had controlled or at least touched at different times. Minds like

Diana's. Like Lana's. Like Caine's, too, once upon a time.

She flashed back to the time after Caine had come crawling away from the gaiaphage. He'd been raving, paranoid, sick almost to death. She had nursed him through it. Was that why, despite everything, he had never betrayed her?

Gratitude? *Caine?*

"You'll need bigger clothing soon," Diana said. "At this rate you'll be healed and less, sorry, gross, soon. And you'll be . . . developing."

"Developing?" Gaia seemed unsure whether this was an opportunity or a threat.

"Never mind; I am so not ready for *that* conversation," Diana said. "Anyway, there's food on one of those islands out there."

"How do we get to this island?"

"Well, that depends, doesn't it?" Diana said.

"On what?"

"On what you can do, Gaia. On what powers you have. I saw you attack your fa—Caine. You moved him with your mind. Is that all you have? Telekinesis? What Caine has?"

"I have access to *all* powers, Diana. The speed, the ability to move things with my mind, strength. I can switch gravity on and off. I have the killing light. I can heal."

"Then you can bounce like Taylor. You could teleport yourself to the island, get us both some food, and be back in a flash."

Gaia looked curious. "I don't know Taylor."

Diana frowned. "Don't you?" Interesting, she thought.

"She's got the power to teleport. She thinks, and then, click, she's there."

Something that might almost have been embarrassment made a fleeting appearance on Gaia's face. She didn't like revealing her limits.

Maybe I can use that.

Use it for what? Are you her mother or her enemy?

All of the above?

Gaia closed her eyes and stood very still. Her expression was focused, questing for something, almost like she was praying. Finally she said, "That one, the one you called Taylor, she no longer exists as what she was. I cannot . . . reach . . . her power."

It took Diana a few seconds to figure out what she was hearing. Then it dawned. "You don't really have many powers of your own; you can only use theirs, the moofs', the mutants'. So you can't do what Penny could do, because she's dead. And Taylor?"

"The mutations that enable powers are physical, but the power exists beyond their bodies as well. I can reach into that space and use those powers." She spoke with acid condescension, like she was talking to a child, which was particularly strange coming from what looked like a child. "You wouldn't understand."

But Diana's breath caught, because she did understand one thing. "That's why you didn't let Drake kill Caine. It's why we ran away. You can't start by killing Caine or Sam or Brianna; if you do, you lose their powers."

Gaia looked smug. "All things are connected to me, stupid . . . Diana. My father's power exists because he mutated and formed a field with me. When he dies, one end of that field will fail. The power that stretches between us will fail. Eventually, though, I will cause others to mutate. It's my . . . my nature. It's what I am. What I may lose today, I can gain back later. Over time."

Diana wondered if she dared to risk a question. They started walking along again, almost like friends, if you could get past the fact that they were a fifteen-year-old half broken in body and spirit and a pretty child filled with the mind and will of a terrible monster.

Kind of a lot to get past there.

Gaia could kill her at any time. Gaia could torture her at any time. Gaia had done the second but not the first. Why? Did she feel something for Diana? Or was Diana useful? If so, for what? Certainly not for her own power, which was simply the ability to gauge others'.

"How do you know all this?" Diana asked, trying to make it sound admiring. In her mind she suddenly had an image of Astrid. Astrid would be furiously jealous if Diana understood the great mystery of the gaiaphage before she did.

"I was created knowing some things. And I have learned other things in the course of my life. I use this body, but this is not me," Gaia said. Her voice was still a child's voice. "I am greater than any form I may take."

The tiny part of Diana that still fantasized about this beautiful girl being her actual daughter noted that Gaia had a healthy ego. That was the kind of thing a parent should notice, wasn't it? She should beam with pride and say something like, *Yes, Gaia is quite self-assured.*

Gaia is advanced for her age.

Gaia is a gifted child.

Gaia is imaginative: she thinks she's a mass of green slime inhabiting a human body. Isn't that cute?

"It all happens because of me, Diana," Gaia went on. She was marveling at her own power, her own uniqueness. "A script written long ago and very far away. Not that they ever imagined that I would be born, but that script, that virus, got a diet of hard radiation and a trace of human and other DNA. That wasn't their idea; they were just trying to spread life around the galaxy."

"You're talking about the meteorite that hit the power plant," Diana said. This far Astrid had guessed. It didn't take a genius to figure out that the disaster that had given Perdido Beach its nickname, Fallout Alley, was connected to what had happened later. "Wait. *Human* DNA?"

"One human was in the power plant when the meteorite struck. His code and my code were melded together, fed by the uranium in the plant. And I was born. My *real* birth," she added quickly, with a disgusted look at Diana. "My true birth. Not the crude freak show of this body's birth, but the beautiful accident that made me."

Gaia's high-pitched voice sounded excited. But that voice held no true sense of joy or wonder. It was high because her vocal cords were still short: a biological fact, not a reflection of the mind behind the voice.

Or else she really was just a complete egomaniac.

Diana wondered if this creature felt anything real, aside from a high opinion of herself and a lust for power. And she wondered where Gaia had picked up the phrase "freak show." Whose mind had she ransacked to come up with that?

What exactly *did* she know?

Not *everything*, Diana thought, answering her own question. She hadn't known about Taylor. Maybe that's why she's keeping me around and alive: to fill in the gaps in what she knows.

"That crude freak show of a birth nearly killed me," Diana said a little bitterly. It still made her ache inside, and the trauma to her body sapped her strength.

This is not my daughter, Diana thought. That she looks like me, that she has Caine's chin and my eyes, all of that is an illusion. Whatever my daughter was, or might have been, this is the gaiaphage.

I am walking and talking with a monster.

"We are near the place where I spent my . . . my childhood," Gaia said. "I can feel it."

"The mine shaft? Yeah, I guess we are. We're not going there, are we? If Sam is looking for you, he'll go there."

"I'm hungry, stupid . . . Diana. I'll go there and call the coyotes, if any have survived. A single coyote would feed us for a while."

"I don't think there are many coyotes left. I think—"

"I'm hungry! I'm hungry! I have to eat!" Gaia bellowed like a spoiled child. "This body must be fed! All you do is tell me what I can't do! I can do whatever I want: I am the gaia-phage!" Her fists were clenched, and her face was white with fury.

Rage. So that's one emotion she has.

Diana backed away, afraid that Gaia would go after her. She cringed, awaiting the stab of pain. But it didn't come, because now Gaia was gazing past Diana.

"What is that?"

Diana turned and saw something so improbable it was hard to believe. They were in the hills, far from town, almost at the northernmost part of the FAYZ. But there, just outside the barrier, were two young men, both in their twenties, both outfitted in mountain-climbing gear with pitons hanging from webbing belts.

The men seemed surprised and excited to see them. Diana was suddenly aware of just how odd she and Gaia must look: a bruised, bloodstained teenager and a young girl still partly covered in third-degree burns.

The climbers stopped what they were doing—which was assembling a rickety aluminum ladder—and waved. The red-haired one took an iPhone out of his backpack and started to videotape.

Diana gave him the finger.

Red-hair laughed, a silent show.

"Let's get out of here," Diana said.

"No."

"They're just a couple of idiots trying to climb up the dome and get pictures."

"They won't get far," Gaia said. "They can lean things against the barrier, but nothing will stick to it, and they cannot drive in nails."

"So they'll fall down a few times."

"Stop talking. I need to concentrate."

"Concentrate on what?"

Gaia smiled grimly. "On *Nemesis*."

Gaia closed her eyes. Her little fists clenched, then released. Every muscle in her body tightened. Her skin took on a glow that Diana had seen before: a faint, sickly green glow.

The two men leaned their ladder against the dome. They didn't notice what was happening to Gaia. They were discreetly looking away.

Diana risked a small shake of her head: *No.*

No, you need to run. You need to get out of here.

But the redhead ascended with rope and pitons at the ready. At the top of the ladder he tried attaching a suction cup to the dome. It didn't work.

He shrugged at Diana, a little comically, like, *Hey, I was hoping it would work.*

Then he tried banging in a piton. This made no sound within the dome, and it also made no mark.

His partner handed up two more pieces of metal that Redhair fitted into the existing ladder. This allowed him to climb another twelve feet on a rickety, single-pole structure.

"Not exactly bright, are they?" Diana observed.

Probably Gaia couldn't do anything. Probably. But the little girl that was no little girl watched with teeth bared, eyes focused far away, seeming to enjoy whatever it was she was doing in that space that Diana could not enter.

"For just a moment, Nemesis," she whispered.

Despite the growing sense that something was about to go very wrong, Diana found herself fascinated at something she had not seen in what felt like a lifetime: adults. More than that, adults with clean clothing and clean, professionally cut hair. And they were unarmed, not even so much as a crowbar or a baseball bat. When was the last time she had seen any- one unarmed? Anyone over the age of four in the FAYZ had something, even if it was just a pointed stick.

"You're making me angry," Gaia whispered. "I'm hungry."

Gaia's eyes began to glow like someone had turned on a dim flashlight inside her head so that light bled just a bit around the rim of her eyes. Her fists were clenched tight. Her teeth made a cracking sound as she clamped her jaw.

The redhead was now well over Diana's height, but in no danger of making any progress. He had gotten himself into position to take some decent video, but he was at the end of his ladder. The dome was ten miles high in the center, and there was no ladder in the world that would cover even a tiny fraction of—

"*Ahhhh!*" Gaia cried, and the whole world wobbled. It was like a small earthquake, but more, as if the air itself had been stirred.

There was a blast of air in Diana's face.

A sound of rushing wind.

And the red-haired man fell.

He fell and hit the ground at Diana's feet. Inside. In the FAYZ.

The man lay stunned. He looked at them in amazement, looked back at his friend, who just stood with his mouth open, then grinned and said, "Whoa! This is cool!"

Gaia made her little teeth-baring smile and said, "Food."

It had hit Little Pete in a way that was impossible to explain to someone who lived in the normal universe. Pete had no body, but he had just been punched, very hard. It had hurt. It had sent his mind spinning.

He had never felt anything like it. It could only come from one person: the Darkness. The green, vaporous tendrils that had often reached to touch his mind had this time struck him.

The gaiaphage. Had punched him. Hard enough to make his consciousness blink out for just a fraction of a second.

It was shocking. He had not known such a thing was possible. No one could hit him! It wasn't okay. It was not okay to hit. His sister had told him that a lot of times. So had his mother.

It was not okay to hit. Even if you were mad or frustrated.

If it could happen once, it could happen again. The dark mind that had touched him very early on, that had shaped him in some ways, that had manipulated him at times, that had scared Pete at times—and feared him always—that constant if faraway companion had just *hurt* him.

Pete had begun to accept his own fading, the almost plea-surable sense of giving up and letting go of a life that had been short but painful. He was ready to go away. He was ready to fade out.

But that sudden attack . . . it was wrong. He hadn't done anything to deserve it.

It was wrong.

And it made Pete angry.

Don't hit me again, he thought.

Or else.

FOUR
76 HOURS, 52 MINUTES

THEY CLOSED THE door on the cabin. There wasn't room enough for them to stand, so they fell into each other's arms on the bunk.

Sam kissed her and tried not to think that it was for the last time.

He was happy. That was the hell of it. He was finally happy. Right here, right now, in this place, with this girl in his arms, he was happy. Was that why he felt the hammer about to fall on him? No, that was crazy. He was happy. Happiness didn't mean that tragedy was coming around the corner. Did it?

"He shouldn't ask you to do this," Astrid said.

"Sure he should," Sam said. "Who else is going to go if not me?"

"You've done enough. You've done more than enough. A hundred times more than enough."

They were only inches apart, so close that Sam could feel her breath on his face when she spoke. So close he could hear her heart beating too fast.

"It's the endgame, Astrid," Sam said softly.

"You're supposed to survive the endgame," Astrid pleaded.

"What am I going to do? Hide here with you and hope it all blows over?"

"Maybe, yes. Maybe just don't go out looking for a fight this time. Maybe just let it be on someone else."

"Gaia ran off with Drake and Diana, but I don't think it was because she was weak. If she is weak, great, let's find out now and maybe end this easily."

His words made sense. She wouldn't be able to dispute them.

"And if she's not weak? If she's exactly what we think she is and just as dangerous as we're afraid she is? Then what, Sam?"

"Then better to move on her before she's ready. Better not to let her choose the time and place." He tilted his head to rest against hers, sharing the pillow. "Edilio's right. You know he is."

He was a little disappointed when she didn't have a good counterargument. A part of him had been hoping that he was wrong. Her silence was his doom.

Another fight. Another battle. How many could he survive? He was living on luck. Was he supposed to believe that the world meant him to be happy with Astrid? That didn't sound like the world he knew.

"I love you," he said.

"I love you too, for all the good it does." She sounded bitter. Angry. Not at him, but at the universe. Then, in an intense whisper: "First, isolate her. Take out Drake. And Sam, if you need to, take out Diana."

That cold-blooded advice shocked him. "Diana?" Since when had Astrid used a euphemism like "take out"? And since when had she ever counseled him to be so hard?

"Gaia seemed to be relating to her. If you find Diana's still alive, it will be because Gaia needs her or maybe even cares for her. That's a vulnerability. Exploit that vulnerability."

He tried to treat it lightly. "You're kind of ruining the mood."

"I'll recapture the mood," she said. "But first, you promise me, Sam: whatever it takes to win, whatever it takes to survive."

"Astrid—"

Suddenly she grabbed his face with one hand and squeezed too hard. "You listen to me. I'm not losing you because you played fair. You're *not* getting killed. You're *not* dying. This *isn't* some doomed last mission. Do you understand me? This does not end with me crying and missing you every day for the rest of my life. This ends with us walking out of this nightmare together. You and me, Sam."

There was silence between them for a long moment. Sam didn't know what to say.

Astrid found the hem of his T-shirt and pulled it up over his head. She unbuckled his belt and shoved his jeans to the deck. She pushed him, gently but insistently, onto the bed. Then she undressed herself and stood in the faint light, looking down at him as he gazed up at her.

"You're giving me a reason to live," he said, half joking.

"I'm just recapturing the mood," she said, trying to make it sound light and sexy.

"You captured me a long time ago."

She climbed atop him. "We walk out of this together, Sam. Whatever it takes. You and me."

"You and me," he said.

She would not yet let him have her. "Whatever it takes," she insisted. "Say it."

"You and me," he said at last. "Whatever it takes."

"Swear it."

"Astrid . . ."

"Swear it. Say the words. Say 'I swear.'"

"I swear," he said, saying it too easily. Saying it even though he didn't feel it. Saying it because he wanted her and wanted to be happy right here and right at this moment.

He rolled a condom into place and she gasped as he entered her. "This is not the last time, Sam," she said.

"This is not the last time," he said, knowing that neither of them believed it.

Lana Arwen Lazar woke suddenly, and as she often did when startled, she grabbed for the big pistol beneath her pillow. She sat up and leveled the automatic, all in one easy motion.

Sanjit Brattle-Chance dropped to his belly and, in a surprisingly reasonable tone of voice, considering his face was in the ragged carpet, said, "If you shoot me, I can't tell you where I hid your cigarettes."

"You what?" Lana snapped. It was still fairly dark in the room. Clifftop Resort, where she had lived since the coming of the FAYZ, had excellent, thick curtains that blocked out the sun. The only light getting in came from a hole that had been burned in the curtains by one of said cigarettes.

"I think you need to cut back," Sanjit said, bravely getting back to his feet despite the fact that Lana had not dropped the gun.

Patrick, Lana's faithful dog, had an instinct for dangerous situations and took the opportunity to jump off the end of the bed and crawl behind the sofa.

"Cut back?"

"Quit, actually. But cut down for now."

"Give me my cigarettes."

"I can't do that."

"Do you see this gun?"

"I noticed it, yes."

"Give me my cigarettes."

"I don't want you getting lung cancer. You're very good at healing injuries, but you know as well as I do you aren't much use against disease."

Lana stared hard at him. "See this bed? Do you ever expect to be back in this bed? With me?"

Sanjit sighed unhappily. He was thin, not very tall, dark-skinned with dark hair and darker eyes, all of it generally lit up by a devil-may-care smile. However, he knew better than to smile at this particular moment. "I'm not going to even respond to that, because the day will come when you'll be ashamed of yourself for even suggesting—"

"Give me my cigarettes."

Sanjit reached into his pocket. He handed something to Lana.

"What is this?"

"It's half a cigarette."

Without putting down the gun she reached for her lighter. She lit the half cigarette and filled her lungs. "Where's the other half?"

"On a completely different topic," Sanjit said, "there's something kind of disturbing going on."

"This is the FAYZ, there's always something disturbing going on, and right now it's the fact that I'm calculating whether I can shoot you in the eyeball."

Sanjit ignored her and opened the curtains.

"Yes, daylight is disturbing," Lana said, blinking. She had smoked the half cigarette down to a length of about five millimeters and was still determined to get another puff, even if it burned her fingers.

Finally curiosity got the better of her, and she swung her feet out of bed, stood up with a groan, and walked to the sliding glass door. Sanjit opened the door and stood aside. Lana stepped out and froze.

The balcony provided an amazing view of the ocean. But since moving into Clifftop the left side had been nothing but the pearly-gray FAYZ wall. Two days earlier that wall had gone transparent, so she'd been able to see the rest of the ocean, and of course the rest of the hotel. But there had been no one in sight, and that was how Lana liked it.

Now, however, there were six people standing together on the balcony just to the left of hers. They were no more than six feet away.

Cameras—ranging from cell phones to full-on Canons with huge lenses—rose in unison and aimed at her.

Lana's hair was sticking out in multiple directions, she was wearing a ragged purple T-shirt that read "FCKH8" over boys' boxer shorts, and she was sucking a cigarette butt down to the ash.

And then there was the automatic pistol in her right hand.

Lana went back inside and said, "Okay: now where are my cigarettes?"

"How did that happen?" the red-haired man demanded. He looked at his friend, still on the other side. He reached over and banged on the barrier and got zapped in payment.

His friend was miming the same look: *How* did *that happen?* Then he whipped out his own phone and began to shoot video.

"How did that happen?" a stunned Diana asked Gaia.

Gaia did not look surprised. She did look troubled. "I hit Nemesis," Gaia answered, as though it was obvious. "But it wasn't good, really." She suddenly bit at the cuticle of her thumb, a nervous gesture Diana recognized: Caine.

"He was stronger than I expected," Gaia said. "I think I just made him realize . . . Never mind. I may have to move faster than I'd thought." She sighed and seemed surprised to have made the sound. Then she said, "But at least I have food to feed this body you made for me. Diana."

"I can't believe this happened," the red-haired man said. He stood up and extended his hand to Diana. "Amazing, right? Am I the first guy in?"

Gaia stepped in, grabbed the man's hand, then shifted her grip to his wrist, put her other hand on his bicep, and with one swift, sudden movement tore his arm off at the shoulder like she was ripping a drumstick from an overcooked turkey.

"Gaia!" Diana cried.

The man screamed, an eerie, awful sound.

"Ahhh! Ahhhh! Ahhhh!"

Blood sprayed from both the arm and the shoulder. The man fell onto his back, screaming, screaming, screaming as blood sprayed like water from a cut garden hose.

Diana dropped beside him, crying, "Oh God, oh God!"

Gaia casually slung the arm onto a flat rock. She raised one hand and played a terrible, burning light—just like Sam's light—up and down the arm.

She wasn't destroying, though: she was cooking.

"No, no, no!" the man screamed. "Ahhh! Ahhh!"

"He's going to die, Gaia!"

"Possibly," Gaia said, evaluating the cooked arm. "A lot of blood—"

"Gaia!"

Outside the dome the other man was screaming silently, his eyes wide, his mouth a horrified O. The phone in his hand tilted crazily.

Diana tore the man's small backpack open, found a T-shirt, and tried to stuff it into the gruesome, shredded wound that had been his shoulder. The man's eyes rolled up into his head, and he passed out as blood continued gushing, making mud of the dirt.

"Gaia! Save him!" Diana begged, and looked up to see Gaia ripping with her child's teeth at the charred and smoking bicep.

"Yes, I should save him," Gaia said through her chewing. "He'll be easier to move if he's alive." She ripped another chunk, a long, stringy piece of muscle, and while she chewed and sucked it into her mouth, she knelt beside the unconscious man and put her hand on the bloody mess of shoulder.

Diana scooted backward, pushing violently away.

Gaia held the cooked arm out toward her carelessly as she focused on the wound. "You should also eat. There is enough for both of us now."

Diana rolled to her knees and retched. There was nothing in her stomach to come up. But she retched, tears flooding her eyes.

The man's eyes fluttered open. He looked up at Gaia and screamed again, but more weakly. The one outside was banging on the dome with a piece of the ladder, yelling and threatening without making any sound.

Diana started crawling away. Her mind was spinning crazily: images, memories. Hunger and the smell of Panda's flesh, and the memory of the taste of it, and the memory of the sickening way it had flooded her with relief at the time, the way it had filled her stomach.

"No, no, no, no, no," she cried, over and over again, scraping scabbed knees over sharp rock.

Diana stood, so weak she could barely stay up, and tried to run away, but with a flick of Gaia's finger she was yanked back to land beside the brutalized man.

He screamed, but weakly.

His eyes focused on hers, confused, afraid. Betrayed.

Diana felt herself spinning down a long tunnel, wishing to hit bottom, wishing for death. And, mercifully, she fell unconscious.

FIVE
74 HOURS, 41 MINUTES

"WHERE THE HELL is everyone?" Caine demanded. But he was demanding it of no one in particular. He was king in Perdido Beach, but he was a king without a court. Literally the only person with him at that moment was Virtue Brattle-Chance, an African kid—not African American, but literally from Africa.

And literally a kid, though he was strangely solemn. In fact he was downright gloomy. He and his brothers and sisters, the adopted children of very famous, very rich movie-star parents, had once inhabited San Francisco de Sales Island. But when Caine had found his way to the island, they had found their way off it.

There was, to put it mildly, some history between Caine and the Brattle-Chance kids. Some violent, disturbing history.

But Virtue was efficient in his own morose way. Tell Choo, as everyone called him, to deliver a message, and it got delivered. Tell Choo to go see if anyone was working the cabbage fields, and you got a thorough and accurate answer.

But he was no Drake. He wasn't even a Turk. There was no chance of Choo beating someone up, let alone killing them for you. He wasn't a henchman; he was an administrative assistant.

Caine missed henchmen.

More, he missed Diana.

It was sad to think that he now looked back on the early days of the FAYZ as the good old days. Once, he had ruled Coates Academy. Once, he had ridden in a blaze of glory—well, an unsteady convoy of inexpertly driven cars—into Perdido Beach. Once, Orc and his bullies, and Drake, and Pack Leader, and even Penny had been his right arms.

Well, Penny had turned out to be a treacherous lunatic. Pack Leader had been killed, and the replacement Pack Leader, too. Drake had gone to serve the gaiaphage. And Orc had cleaned himself up and gotten religion.

If there was one thing worse than a bellowing, roaring-drunk Orc, it was Orc quoting—*mis*quoting, usually—scripture.

The hangers-on like Turk and that sniveling little creep Bug had ended up being more trouble than they were worth. Bug still crept around using his invisibility power to spy on people—yet without ever bringing Caine any useful intelligence—and when he wasn't watching people pick their noses, he was stealing food and causing pointless conflicts.

Slowly, inexorably, Caine's control had been diminished. His great ambitions had died. Now he had far more responsibility than power. Some kids still called him king, but it wasn't the same when they did it ironically rather than fearfully.

Oh, he could still use his telekinetic power to toss kids around randomly, throwing them through walls or out into the ocean, but what was the point? He didn't need dead kids; he needed someone to go and pick the lousy cabbages. Albert had always taken care of that, but Albert had jumped ship and sailed off to the island with a load of missiles.

Caine missed Albert.

Caine missed henchmen.

But most of all he missed Diana. He could see her if he closed his eyes. He could remember every detail of her body and face. Lips? Yes, he remembered her mouth. The smoothness of her skin? Yes, definitely, yes, he remembered.

"When kids get hungry enough they'll pick vegetables," Virtue said.

"Choo, you don't know people, do you? What they'll do is panic and freak out. Start robbing each other and most likely burn down whatever is left of town. People are idiots, Choo. Always remember that: people are faithless, backstabbing, weak, creepy, stupid, lazy idiots."

Virtue blinked and said nothing.

Caine looked around at his current lair—a desk Caine had levitated out onto the landing at the top of the church steps that looked down onto the town plaza. He had a rolling chair. And a desk.

He missed his previous lairs. This lair sucked.

He never should have left the island. He'd been there with

Diana and Penny. He could have tossed Penny off a cliff and been fine on the island. Decent food, a beautiful mansion, electricity, and a soft bed with Diana in it.

What had he been thinking, leaving the island?

He missed Diana busting him. He missed her snarky voice. He missed her eye rolls and that skeptical look she had where she'd half close her eyes and look at him like he was too dumb to merit her full attention. He'd have killed, or at least injured, anyone else who treated him like that. But she wasn't anyone else.

He missed her hair. Her neck. Her breasts.

She understood him. She loved him, in her own way. And if he had listened to her, he'd still be on the island. Somehow he would have found some fuel to keep the lights on there. Probably. And the food would have run out and then they'd have starved, but hey, this was the FAYZ, where all you could really hope to do was delay the pain.

Delay of pain: that was the meaning of life, wasn't it?

"I've made some bad decisions," Caine said, not really meaning to say it out loud.

Had Diana been there she'd have said something like *Duh* but cooler and funnier and meaner, and he'd have been annoyed but he'd have tried to kiss her and eventually she would have let him, and was it really possible that her lips had been that soft?

Virtue said, "Well, you're ruthless and narcissistic and totally devoid of morals."

Caine shot a look at Virtue, wondering if there was any

way all of that amounted to a compliment. Probably not. From Diana it would have been a perfect blend of snark and admiration, but Virtue seemed to have decided at some point to take his name seriously. The kid had no sense of humor that Caine could detect. He was a straight arrow. It was baffling.

"If I'm so ruthless, how come I don't walk down to the barrier and start slamming kids into the ground until they obey me?"

Virtue shrugged. "Because your birth mother or your adoptive parents might be out there watching?"

Caine bit at his thumbnail, a nervous habit when he was feeling thwarted.

"Also TV cameras," Virtue went on.

"Sam fried Penny's body in front of his—our—mother," Caine said, just to argue.

Virtue said nothing.

"What?" Caine demanded.

"Well . . . Sam is stronger than you are," Virtue said.

Caine considered throwing Virtue into the wreckage of the church. It would be satisfying. But if he did that, it would upset Virtue's brother Sanjit, and Sanjit and Lana were close, and the last thing Caine needed was trouble with Lana, the Healer. She had saved his life, and despite the fact that he was mostly incapable of gratitude, it wasn't wise to pick a fight with the closest thing they had to a doctor.

"We have visitors," Virtue said. Caine heard it, too: a car's engine. With gas as rare as food it was very unusual to hear an engine running.

A white van drove slowly—as slowly as only an inexperienced and frightened driver could go—down San Pablo Avenue. It came to a stop at a distance, and Caine found himself hoping it was trouble. Trouble he could handle. A fight would be a wonderful relief from the tedium.

Out stepped Edilio, and a second later, Sam.

So. Maybe it was a fight. Hah!

But Edilio was walking ahead with Sam hanging back and looking unusually reticent, even a bit abashed. Then Toto, the weird kid with the Spider-Man fixation, climbed out.

"We're not here for trouble," Edilio said, holding up his hand and crushing Caine's hopes.

"True," Toto affirmed.

Caine sighed. "Well, that's just great. Okay. Choo, go grab a couple of chairs."

"Caine," Sam said, and nodded.

"Sam. What do you want here? Is the surf up?"

Sam nodded to Edilio. "This is *his* party."

When the chairs came, they sat down around the large but rather forlorn desk. There was no chair for Toto. Caine didn't care.

"I'd offer you milk and cookies, but we seem to be out," Caine said. He put his feet up on the desk just to remind them who was boss here.

"It's true. He has no milk. Or cookies." Toto.

Edilio got right to it. "We can't have this. We need to get food production back up. We need to think through how to deal with the lookers. We need rules and organization."

"Yeah, brilliant," Caine said. "I wish I'd thought of that. Choo, make a note: need people to get back to work. That's genius. That's what you came to say? Are you asking me to go down there and start smacking kids around?"

Edilio pretended not to notice the sarcasm. "No. In fact, I don't think you can help, Caine. No one trusts you. No one will follow you."

"That's the truth," Toto said. Then, in response to Caine's withering glare, he added, "Spidey."

"Oh, I see," Caine said. "No one trusts me, but they will follow Saint Sammy here. Well, not to be impolite but—"

Caine's hand came up fast, and the telekinetic punch hit Sam right in the chest. Sam went flying. In fact he flew straight backward through the air. Ten feet. At least—maybe even a dozen feet. And when he hit, he landed on his butt, and the momentum carried him into a backward roll.

Caine laughed delightedly. This was so much better than just sitting around and—

Sam was up faster than Caine expected, and he managed to leap aside and dodge Caine's next blow. Sam's hands were up, palms out. Not ten feet away. And the real problem was that Caine was still seated.

It's not easy to move quickly when you're sitting and your feet are up on a desk.

"I'd actually rather not have to kill you," Sam said. "But if your hand so much as twitches . . ."

Caine let his hands hang in the air, carefully aimed just a bit off target.

He looked at Sam's face. His brother's eyes were focused narrowly on his own. Smart boy. Sam had gained experience since the old days when they were an even match. An inexperienced fighter watches the opponent's hands; a smart fighter watches the other guy's face.

Caine had to carefully control his eyes, not shift, not look toward—

Sam's right hand was still aimed directly on Caine's body. But from his left came the air-sizzling green light. It burned in a flash through the leg of Caine's chair.

The chair tipped; Caine slipped, landed on his side, rolled fast, and as Sam rushed him pulled one of his newer tricks: he blasted the concrete directly below himself, throwing his own body back with the recoil.

It worked! Sam rushed past, grabbing air. Unfortunately, Caine's new tactic was not a precision technique. It knocked the wind from him, and he banged the back of his head hard on a stair and saw stars.

"Ow."

Caine tried to roll to his feet, but something was jabbing him in the crotch. He shook off the stars and saw Edilio standing over him. Edilio had the business end of his automatic rifle in a very sensitive place.

"If you move, Caine, I will shoot your balls off," Edilio said. "Toto?"

"He will," Toto said. "Although he's not sure it will be just your balls."

Caine glared up at Edilio, murder in his eyes. "You'd get off one round—maybe—and then I'd knock your head right off your shoulders."

"He believes he could knock your head right off—" Toto began.

"No doubt," Edilio said. "I guess you have to decide whether one more killing will compensate for your . . . loss."

"What's the matter, Sam? You can't fight your own battles? You have to have your boy here cover for you?" Caine said.

Sam started to respond, then seemed to think better of it and remained silent. He even took a step back.

Edilio said, "Toto. I'm going to say some things to King Caine. You evaluate."

"I will, Spidey."

"One: I'm my own man," Edilio said.

"He believes it."

"Two: I am sick to death of this tired-ass sibling nonsense between you two."

"He believes it is tired-ass," Toto said.

"Three: the gaiaphage and Drake—your daughter and your former partner—"

"Partner? He was my henchman," Caine said. "Partner would be an equal. Drake was never my equal."

"Three," Edilio repeated, "the gaiaphage and Drake are out there, and I don't think they're just camping."

This made Toto hesitate. Then: "He does not believe they are camping."

"And now, I have a question for you, Caine: Do you believe you can take on Gaia alone? Yes or no?"

Caine's gaze slid toward Toto. Caine hated the very idea of a truth teller. Control was impossible without some dishonesty. But then his thoughts turned inward. He imagined fighting the gaiaphage alone. He could picture it all too clearly. Fear gnawed at the edges of his mind, and memories of terrible pain, weakness . . . despair.

"Yes or no?" Edilio pressed.

"You know the answer," Caine muttered.

Edilio pulled the gun barrel away. He extended a hand to help Caine up, but Caine just gave him a hard stare and climbed to his feet. He looked at his now three-legged chair. "That was a nice, comfortable chair."

He dusted himself off. The admission—even unspoken—that he couldn't take Gaia on alone left him feeling depressed. From the very start he'd been paranoid that a power greater than himself might emerge. In the beginning there had been only the two "four bar" mutants: him and Sam. Gradually they'd come to realize that Little Pete was somewhere off the scale, but that hadn't worried Caine too much, because Little Pete was just Little Pete, however god-like his powers.

Now here was Gaia, the physical embodiment of the gaia-phage, and Caine knew too much about that creature to believe it could be beaten by one guy with the power of telekinesis.

"So I'm supposed to stand aside and let Sam just walk in and take over," Caine said. "That's not—"

"Not me," Sam interrupted. "Him."

Caine looked in disbelief at Edilio. "What? The machine-gun wetback here?"

Sam stiffened at that, but Edilio with a small gesture waved it off. So Sam said, "There are exactly five people who are trusted by just about everyone. I'm one, but I kind of suck at running things—"

"True," Toto said, and this time caught a hard look from Sam.

"Lana is trusted," Sam went on, "but . . . well, she's Lana, and she has a job. And Dekka is trusted, but also . . . well, she'd be the first to say she doesn't want to run anything. The fourth person is Quinn."

"I tried to get Quinn to do something more than fish," Caine protested.

"I know," Sam said. "The other person everyone trusts is Edilio."

Caine barked out an incredulous laugh. "Are you seriously here to tell me you want Edilio to take over running Perdido Beach?"

"He's already running the lake."

"That's . . . ," Toto began, hesitated, and said, "mostly true."

"Yeah, well, I'm still king here," Caine said. It sounded

ridiculous, even to him. He pointed a finger at Toto. "No: don't say it."

Edilio said, "I can work well with Quinn. I get along well with Lana. I get along with Astrid and Dekka, who'll stay at the lake. Sam trusts me. And the fact is, even you trust me, Caine."

"I do?"

"Yes," Edilio said.

"He believes it," Toto muttered.

"You're still Sam's boy, Edilio."

"Sam won't be here, or at the lake. He's going after your daughter."

Caine chose not to argue that label, though it filled him with extreme and conflicting emotions. "Sam is going after Gaia and Drake alone? Hah. If I can't do it alone, neither can he."

"He believes this."

"Not *alone*," Edilio said.

It took Caine a few beats to get it. "No. Go kill yourself. Eat your own gun. No. No no no."

"You're happy here counting fish and nagging kids to work?" Edilio asked.

"He's not," Virtue said, beating Toto to the punch and earning an annoyed glance from Caine. "He's only done it for two days since the battle, and he's already bored."

"Here's the proposal," Edilio said. He had shouldered his assault rifle. "I come to Perdido Beach, work with Quinn and Sanjit and of course Virtue. And maybe bring Computer Jack down, too. Lana, well, she'll do whatever she wants to do, as usual."

"Wait, I thought Jack was dead."

"No. Lana got to him in time," Sam said. "But he's shook up, that's for sure. He could use a change and something to keep his mind occupied."

Caine shook his head no, but it wasn't as firm as it might have been.

Sam leaned forward, elbows on knees, and said, "Caine, you're not a king any more than I'm a mayor."

"No, then what am I?" Caine demanded, hating the pleading tone in his voice.

"You're a bully and a sociopath. You're a thug and a killer. You're also smart and powerful and you don't scare easy."

"True," Toto affirmed.

"And you love Diana," Virtue said.

"What? Shut up, Choo."

All eyes turned to Toto, who nodded and said, "He does."

"Probably the only person you ever did care for," Edilio said. "And surely the only person who loves you. And you're going to leave her out there? With Drake and that monster child of yours?"

Caine saw something then on Sam's face. An emotion he was anxious to conceal. Guilt? Sam suddenly had the need to rub his face. Caine's instinct was pinging, warning him of . . . well, he didn't quite know what. And Sam kept his mouth shut, which meant Toto was no help.

Caine swallowed hard and looked helplessly at Edilio.

Edilio nodded, accepting Caine's surrender.

"You know what?" Caine said. "You want Perdido Beach? It's all yours, my friend: it's all yours."

And thus ends my brief reign, Caine thought mordantly.

He had to fight down the urge to grin. He drew a deep, satisfying breath. His eyes met Sam's. Sam had a knowing smile, seeing and understanding, as no one else could, Caine's relief at giving up power.

"This is only because I'm bored," Caine said. "I'm not running off to rescue Diana. Or do the right thing or any of that."

"That is not—" Toto began, but Virtue reached over and put a hand over the truth teller's mouth.

Well, at least Diana would be grateful, Caine thought. And then smiled. Nah. She wouldn't be.

SIX

THEY HAD SOON discovered that Gaia needed to eat. So did Diana, but Drake didn't care about Diana: Diana could starve for all he cared. Diana could die a slow, painful death, hopefully caused by him, by Drake.

Gaia was a very different matter. Gaia could make him feel terrible pain, deep-down-inside pain. Drake's body, his unkillable body that somehow shared space with Brittney's, didn't normally feel much. Only the most intense pain broke through.

What Gaia did to him when she was displeased—that broke through.

Anyway, it wasn't like Drake could disobey Gaia. She might now look like a little girl, but Drake knew who and what she really was. Who else was he going to serve? He and Caine had parted ways. Caine had become weak. Drake had nowhere else to go if he wasn't with Caine. And in the gaiaphage he had found someone much tougher, more demanding. More powerful. Someone who would never be weak.

His sharp eyes detected movement on a rock. A lizard. He unwrapped his reddish, ten-foot-long tentacle arm from around his waist. He took careful aim, snapped the bullwhip arm, and sent the lizard flying.

He scooped up the dead thing and dropped it into the canvas bag slung from his belt. He'd so far nailed maybe a half pound of lizards—about all there was to be found out here in the desert emptiness. Should he carry it back to Gaia? Was it enough? Or would she punish him for bringing too little?

On the one hand, even here, a mile away from her, Drake could feel her hunger. Her hunger was his hunger. His only hunger since he—whatever he was—no longer felt the need for food. Or water. Or air.

But pain? He could still feel that, at least the pain she gave him. If he brought her too little, there was the thing the gaia-phage could do to him, that twisting inner agony, that little visit to hell.

Just then he spotted a roadrunner. The bird was about a foot and a half long from sharp beak to the end of its long tail. Of course that was mostly feathers and bone. But maybe a few ounces of actual meat, too, and if he nailed it he could head back to Gaia in the certainty of a pleasant, or at least pain-free, welcome.

They were quick little birds, though. Not as fast as the cartoon Road Runner, but quick and dodgy.

The bird had its head cocked. One eye was aimed right at Drake. He froze. He needed to halve the distance before he could strike.

The bird darted half a foot and suddenly had a lizard in its mouth. The lizard was still alive, thrashing in the bird's beak, and that distraction let Drake advance with, slow, silent steps.

Then: the unsettling feeling that presaged the emergence of Brittney. Since they had been buried together and resurrected they had shared . . . well, not a body, really. In fact they shared nothing except that they seemed to trade existences. He would be there, and then Brittney would emerge, and while she was present, he was simply gone.

"Not now!" he hissed, frustrated at the thought of losing his prey.

He snapped his whip arm, but it was already a foot shorter. The roadrunner was gone.

Brittney opened her eyes to see she was alone, in a very dry-looking place, nothing but brambles and sand and stone. She noticed the bag on her belt. Looking in she saw a wad of lizards, some in pieces.

The hunger that had motivated Drake filled her as well, the hunger of her god. The thought of Gaia eating well, growing stronger, made Brittney smile. What a miracle to have her god take on human form, become the baby Gaia! No, not a baby anymore, a beautiful little girl, and growing at an amazing rate. By the time Brittney got back to her, she could be a preteen.

Wouldn't that be exciting!

Food. That was the first thing.

She saw a roadrunner dart into a thornbush. She wasn't fast enough to catch the bird, but she wondered . . .

Brittney dropped to her hands and knees and crawled to the bush. She got as low as she could and shielded her eyes from the glare of the true sun beating down very hard here near the center of the FAYZ.

It was shadier beneath the bush, but she could still see clearly, and there was her reward: a circular nest and in the center of that nest three small, white eggs, no more than an inch and a half in diameter.

Brittney carefully lifted the eggs from the nest and put them in her bag. She pulled apart a bit of the nest and used it to pack the eggs carefully so they wouldn't break.

Now this would be a feast for Gaia!

She backed slowly, carefully, out of the thornbush, indifferent to the multitude of tiny cuts.

Brittney had no warning of the wire that went around her throat. No time even to flinch as the wire cut into her neck, severed the empty, bloodless arteries, and stopped tightening only when it had closed around her upper spine.

"Wish it was Drake, not you, Britt," Brianna said.

Then Brianna put her foot on Brittney's back and heaved as hard as she could. The wire sliced through cartilage and nerve tissue, making a sound like a knife cutting gristle, and suddenly Brittney's head rolled free and landed in the dirt with a thump.

Brittney could not move her head, but she had rolled to

an angle where she could see Brianna. Brianna was sweating from exertion. She wiped her brow with the back of her hand. The garrote—a two-foot-long piece of piano wire strung between steel grips that had once been part of someone's home gym—hung from her free hand.

Brianna looked down at her, quite satisfied, and said, "Now I'm going to chop you into little bits and spread the pieces all over the place. See if you or Drake can reassemble yourself then."

Brittney was not dead. Aside from no longer being attached to her body she didn't feel any difference, just a dull pain in her neck. When she strained her eyes upward, she could see her body. The body was attempting to stand up all by itself.

But when Brittney tried to speak, she found she could only whisper, and the sound of her whisper was partly drowned out by the gasping noise of air sucked into her severed esophagus.

"You can't kill us," Brittney whispered.

"Maybe not. But I'm sure going to try."

Brianna carried a sawed-off shotgun in her specially adapted runner's backpack, and a machete, also slung over her back. She pulled out the machete and swung it so fast Brittney couldn't see the blade move. She just saw the fact that her body was now minus a leg, which caused it to topple over.

Whump!

There was a whir of movement that raised the dust, and a sound of chopping, a rapid-fire *whap! whap! whap! whap!*

and what had been Brittney's body was in pieces—arms cut off and then cut in two. Legs off and then chopped into three pieces. Torso hacked into random chunks. There was no blood. It was as if Brianna were chopping up an embalmed corpse.

That thought bothered Brittney. How could she be alive with no blood? What was she?

"Want to watch?" Brianna asked.

She grabbed Brittney's hair, lifted her up, and set her on a flat rock. The first effort failed, and Brittney's head rolled off. But Brianna was finally able to settle Brittney's head atop the rock so that Brittney could see her body lying in a couple dozen bloodless pieces.

The pieces were already twitching toward one another, extending tentacles, attempting to rejoin. And things that had been female were becoming male as Drake slowly reemerged to discover he was in very bad shape.

With a look of distaste Brianna began to pick the pieces up and toss them a distance away. "I can't have you putting yourself back together, Brittney . . . Ah! Wait, is that Drake coming back?"

Brianna performed a short happy dance and stepped—perhaps accidentally—on a piece of flesh that Drake would miss.

"Perfect. So much better this way. Hello, Drake. So glad you could make it. I'm just going to start moving your pieces farther apart. Much farther apart. Then I'll have Sam go around and fry each piece. And then I believe that'll be it for you, Brittney slash Drake. I believe we'll have seen the end of both of you. And your little whip, too." She patted Drake on the head. Then she picked up a foot and a shoulder section, one in each hand. With a wink she was gone, leaving a trail of dust.

Quinn was rowing back to shore. It was a point of pride for him that he always carried his share of the hard work, in fact more than his fair share, because if you were boss, you started off by setting a good example. So even though he had gotten a hook caught in the back of his arm and had had to cut it out and as a consequence was bleeding through a salt water–soaked bandage held with a strip of duct tape, he pulled at the oars.

No one on his crews ever claimed Quinn was lording it over them or saddling them with too much work. Well, sometimes they did, but it was in the nature of long-running jokes.

"You're pulling to your left, Captain," Amber said.

"At least I'm pulling," Quinn said, and the two of them lifted the oars, leaned forward, dipped the oars, and pulled in long-practiced unison.

"You know, if you're feeling weak you could let Cathy take over," Amber said, grunting with the effort. "What with your boo-boo and all."

"I'd have to be missing an arm before I rowed as weak and spastic as Cathy," Quinn teased.

For her part, Cathy, seated in the stern and guiding the

tiller, said, "Just a good thing we didn't catch much or we'd never make the marina."

"Yeah, a good thing," Quinn said, unable to keep the worry from his voice. "Barely enough to feed us, let alone the whole town."

He glanced up at a cabin cruiser in the out there. He was a long way from getting used to the fact that he could see the outside. It was weird. Nothing had changed in his daily life except for the fact that he could now see out of his prison. Still a prison, but now the prison had a view.

Two women in bikinis were on the bow, and two much older guys were in the stern of the cabin cruiser, with their fishing rods in rod holders, chilling with bottles of beer. The captain seemed to be of a different breed, a thirtysomething man with salt-bleached clumpy hair and red skin and wrap-around glasses. He was watching Quinn's boats with interest.

The cabin cruiser was throwing up a bow wave Quinn admired and envied. What must it be like to fish from a power boat?

"Give 'em a wave, Cath," Quinn said. So Cathy did, and the captain gave them a sort of salute. And then one of the women on the bow took off her bikini top.

"Well, I didn't expect that," Quinn admitted.

"Drunk," Amber said.

The cruiser captain, obviously displeased, turned his boat sharply, which threw the woman off balance and would foul the men's lines if they weren't quick about reeling in.

Quinn could see the men yelling at the captain, and the

captain stoically ignoring them as he motored away. The last Quinn saw of him he was shaking his head in an *I can't believe these people* kind of way.

At the dock they unloaded the catch—not impressive—and hauled out their gear for mending. Salt water was hell on nets. By now Quinn knew just about every submerged rock or old wreck that could snag a net, but they still needed checking and mending every day.

He was excused by mutual agreement from this part of the day's work because he was the one who had to go and meet with Caine, a task no one else wanted.

He trudged up the slope toward the town plaza, torn between missing the businesslike and practical Albert and cursing him at the same time for being a treacherous, cowardly weasel. Dealing with Caine was always difficult. Caine was not a businessman: he had a tendency to believe that threatening Quinn would produce more fish. Other times Caine could be self-pitying or grandiose or even depressed. Until very recently Albert had managed Caine, but in these last couple of days Quinn was starting to fear that in some way the care and feeding of the temperamental "king" had fallen to him.

It was therefore with mounting joy bordering on giddiness that he made out the face of Edilio sitting at Caine's outdoor desk. Virtue was with him, and kids were coming and going, evidently getting instructions from Edilio.

Once, long ago in what felt like another life, Quinn had

derided Edilio as a wetback, an illegal alien. Now he could have kissed him.

"Tell me you're in charge," Quinn said after he had mounted the steps.

"I'm in charge," Edilio said, with a shy grin.

"If I were any less tired, I'd do the happy dance," Quinn said. "I still may."

Edilio stuck out his hand and Quinn took it.

"I hear you're having a hard time getting anything in exchange for your fish," Edilio said.

Quinn nodded. "Pretty much."

"Give me twenty-four hours to figure it out?"

"You got it. So, where's His Highness?"

Edilio, straight-faced, said, "His Highness is off with Sam."

"Are they killing each other?"

"Not as far as I know," Edilio said. "They're looking for Gaia."

That wiped the grin off Quinn's face. "Oh."

"Yeah. And I'm the one who asked them to do it, not that I had to twist their arms much. Have a seat, if you have the time."

Quinn took a seat. Virtue had a notebook. He was writing notes, like an administrative assistant taking minutes of a meeting.

"The island," Edilio said.

Quinn sighed heavily. Oh, man. "Yeah?"

"Have you seen anything going on there?"

"You mean like Albert up on the cliff watching us through a telescope?"

"Yeah, like that. And also like him trying to talk to you."

Quinn shook his head. "No, not that. Me and Albert are not friends, not anymore. And he's got those missiles out there."

"You think he got them up the cliff to where he can use them?"

"I know he did. I have a pretty good pair of binoculars. I've seen him and his girls training. He wanted me to see."

"Has he ever warned you off? Like threatened you?"

"He doesn't have to. No reason for me to go in there and look for trouble."

Edilio considered this and nodded. "It sucks. You guys used to work well together. By now Albert must realize he made a dumb mistake in panicking."

"Edilio, ask me anything, but don't ask me to go and try to sweet-talk Albert. He stabbed us all in the back."

"Caine's done worse, far worse, and Sam is out there with him now."

"Albert wouldn't listen to me anyway, Edilio. Albert thinks he's far above me. I'm just a working guy who smells like fish. He's the brains. He's the big organizer. He'd probably shoot me out of the water."

Edilio sighed and leaned forward, elbows on the desk. "Quinn, listen, man. We need stuff back to normal. We need the market open and we need people working, or we're all in big trouble. Kids are gonna die of hunger watching their mom or dad eating a pizza three inches away. Kids are acting like everything is all over; it's not all over. Just because they can see out doesn't mean they're getting out. Kids who ought to be harvesting and planting are sitting there up against the barrier watching TV shows because some network put up a big monitor with captions on. Those lookers out there don't know what damage they're doing here. They might as well be giving those kids drugs or something."

Quinn didn't disagree. He'd lost two of his own people that way. The rest stayed out of personal loyalty to him, not wanting to let him down.

Edilio didn't push the matter: he let it rest there. Which kind of irritated Quinn, because it meant Edilio was trusting him to step up. He had more than enough to keep him busy. He was tired, and he didn't even think Albert would listen. Plus Albert might well shoot him right out of the water.

"No fish, anyway," he muttered at last. Giving Edilio as peeved a look as he could, he said, "When?" He'd been hoping to find an excuse to visit Lana. It was painful seeing her with Sanjit, but less painful than not seeing her. And, after all, he did have a boo-boo.

Then he saw the *Sorry* look on Edilio's face.

"Great," Quinn said.

SEVEN

IT WAS EXHAUSTING work for Brianna. She would run two or three pieces of the Drake/Brittney thing off to far corners of the FAYZ, and by the time she got back to grab more, she'd find the body already partly reassembled. Then she'd have to chop it up all over again.

Still, the total pile grew smaller. Some of the pieces were now ten miles apart. That was a long way for a chunk of thigh to ooze and squirm. Other pieces would be swimming. If they could.

At some point in all of the back-and-forth, the head, still on its rock, had reverted to Brittney but then had gone right back to Drake, as if Brittney were weakening, no longer able to manifest for more than a few minutes.

This made Brianna much happier. Brittney had never been evil—a nut, maybe, a little weird, but then who wouldn't be, in Brittney's rather unusual situation? She'd been buried alive, after all, only to reemerge inextricably linked with Drake in a sort of weird immortality.

If that didn't mess you up, you were unmessable.

In any case it was Drake's head that now cursed her in a gasping whisper.

"I'm not quite sure what to do with you, Drake," Brianna said, squatting down to look him in the eye.

"The gaiaphage will kill you," Drake hoarse-whispered. Then he spit up a piece of gravel that must have been sucked up off the ground through his severed windpipe.

"I probably better take you to Sam; he can fry you up," she said. "By the way, why do you have a sack full of dead lizards and some eggs?"

Drake just hissed. Then he called her a dyke and made some extremely crude suggestions. Extremely crude. Crude enough that Brianna actually got angry. She raised her machete high and brought it down with all the strength and speed at her command. Which was considerable. The machete struck sparks off the stone after it had passed clean through the skull, face, and neck.

Drake's head split, top to bottom. The left side—which had almost all of his nose but only a quarter of his mouth—rolled off the stone. The other half—not so much nose and a lot more mouth—stayed in place.

Brianna had a strong stomach, but something about seeing the inside of Drake's head was almost too much for her. It retained all the same structures it had had when Drake was fully human. But it did not bleed. It was alive, but alive in a way very different from the way in which most people were alive.

The brain was gray. Brains are sometimes described as gray, but in reality they're pinkish—she'd seen brain spilled, so she knew. Drake's was genuinely gray with a tinge of green. It looked like an unhealthy cauliflower that had been split down the middle.

She could also see what she supposed were sinuses—open spaces above and behind the nose.

And she could see teeth.

The brain did not fall out all the way, but it did sag a bit and looked as if it might fall out if she shook the head sideways a little.

And it had an odd smell about it. It was the smell of the meat department at a supermarket. A smell that suggested slaughterhouses.

"About your little fantasies there, Drake? Your boy parts? They're in the glove compartment of an old, wrecked pickup truck that looks like it rolled down a ravine. Might even be Lana's grandfather's truck: I should ask her. And some are floating out in the surf. I mean, if you're ever looking for them."

What was left of Drake's mouth tried to speak, but his esophagus was no longer even slightly intact. The exposed tongue stuck sideways, licking air.

Brianna opened the bag of dead lizards and the little eggs. She lifted the right side of Drake's head and dropped it in.

Then fetched the left side and dropped it in as well.

The bag was surprisingly heavy, and the weight of it was awkward, so she couldn't run full speed. She set off at a slow thirty miles an hour, whistling happily but making no sound since even at thirty the wind snatched the tune away.

It took just ten minutes—she stopped to pee and drink some water at one point—to reach the lake. She sauntered down the dock toward the houseboat, swinging the bag with affected nonchalance, feeling a bit like one of those girls who likes to shop and can't wait to show off her purchases to her friends.

Astrid and Dekka were on the boat, apparently discussing something important. Astrid looked impatient, like she was restraining herself from saying something snippy. Dekka looked like a thundercloud that might spark lightning at any moment. So, basically, both girls were totally normal.

Astrid was the first to notice Brianna.

"Aren't you supposed to be patrolling?"

"Where's Sam?" Brianna asked.

"He's out. So is Edilio," Dekka said. "You going to tell us what's in the bag or do we have to guess?"

Brianna stopped. She was disappointed. In her imagination the big revelation would have been to an admiring Sam Temple. He was the one she wanted to impress. Failing that, Edilio, who was generally warm and sweet to her.

But she was tired and wanted to put the bag down. Also, she couldn't keep the secret any longer.

She climbed nimbly up to the top deck of the boat, grinned,

and said, "Is it anyone's birthday? Because I have a present."

"Breeze," Dekka warned.

So Brianna opened the bag. Dekka looked inside. "What is it?"

So Brianna upended the bag. Dead lizards, broken eggs, and Drake's head landed on the antiskid flooring.

"Ahhhh!" Astrid screamed.

"Ah, Jesus!" Dekka yelled.

"I know," Brianna said proudly.

"Oh, my God."

"Oh, that is . . ."

What lay there was something to strike envy into the heart of a horror movie special-effects expert. The two halves of Drake's head had started to rejoin. But because the halves had been tossed wildly together, the process was very incomplete. Very.

In fact at the moment the halves were backward, so that the left half was looking one direction and the right half another. Sections of neck and spine stuck both up and down. The part that held most of Drake's mouth was stuffed with hair from the back of his head.

And, somehow, bits of dead lizard were squeezed in between. But the dead lizards thus incorporated were no longer dead. And there was egg white smeared across one eye.

The mouth was trying to speak and not managing it.

A lizard tail whipped one eye—hard to tell if it was left or right—a parody of Drake's whip arm.

The three of them stared: Astrid with blue eyes wide, hand

over mouth; Dekka with mouth wide open and brow fur-
rowed; Brianna like a proud school kid showing off her art
project.

"Ta-da!" Brianna said.

Connie Temple had done three interviews, sitting in a chair
beside her trailer home on the bluffs south of the barrier.
They set up a monitor so she could see her interviewers—
MSNBC, the BBC, and *Nightline*.

She had noticed the sudden change in . . . temperature.
Even a week ago an interview with the media would have
been sympathetic. She would have been one of the brave band
of bereaved mothers.

Now she was the mother of not one but two killers.

The entire country had turned on a dime. One minute it
was concerned but bored—the whole thing had dragged on
too long. People were "over" the whole Perdido Beach Anomaly. Ho-hum.

Now the kids inside were a threat. Dangerous. Monsters.

The pictures were everywhere. Kids dressed like something
out of a Mad Max movie with knives and spiked baseball bats.
A sullen, bedraggled girl with a cigarette and a gun. Toddlers
wandering filthy and naked. Kids with the hollow eyes and
sunken cheeks of famine victims. A twelve-year-old who had
once been an altar boy but was now all-too-obviously drunk.

Video of Sam using some supernatural light to burn a
dead girl's crushed body. That played over and over and over
again.

Kids relayed stories by writing on scraps of paper and then holding them up to be read. This had yielded pictures and video of children relating terrifying accounts of hunger, murder, carnivorous worms, talking coyotes, a parasite that ate kids from the inside out.

And dark hints of someone called Drake and a creature called the gaiaphage.

The graphic that Fox News used was "Little Monsters" over a shot of Sam.

People drew comparisons to war criminals. To the killing fields of Cambodia. To the Nazis.

The outrage over the attempt to blast open the dome with a nuclear weapon had died very quickly to be replaced by the muttered suggestion that maybe next time the bomb should be bigger.

People were demanding the army be sent in to surround the anomaly—just in case the "containment" failed. The containment. Like these were dangerous wild animals in a zoo.

There were others who argued that the kids of the FAYZ— that word from the handwritten signs, "FAYZ," was quickly gaining currency—were victims, desperate survivors who could not be blamed for doing whatever it took to stay alive. But these people were fewer in number and not nearly as loud.

The president was avoiding the press. Many politicians were not, and were using every opportunity to talk about being tough, being firm, sending National Guard and army troops. One congressman from South Carolina had said flatly that the Perdido Beach Abomination, as he called it, should be obliterated. "A quick and easy death is the only way," he said. "Let God sort them out."

This, finally, led some to try and calm the building hysteria.

The pope had issued a statement calling for compassion. The movie stars Jennifer Brattle and Todd Chance, parents of the island kids inside, had issued an angry denunciation of the media, reminding everyone that these were children. Just children.

The American Civil Liberties Union had issued a press release with much the same message: children, just children trying to survive.

In a *Wall Street Journal* poll, 28 percent of respondents said that the FAYZ and everyone in it should be destroyed.

All of this had happened before the video that had crashed YouTube: a little girl ripping the arm off the first adult to somehow blunder into the FAYZ and then eating that arm.

The effect had been electric. Suddenly it was clear: this wasn't child's play. Whatever power was in there could kill adults as well. Connie had no doubt that the next poll would show many more people in favor of simply wiping out the FAYZ.

She carried a thick art pad and two black Sharpies and headed toward the barrier. It wasn't easy getting through the crowd that had grown despite the California Highway Patrol roadblock, despite all efforts to get people to back off.

It wasn't just parents now: it was every kind of nut who could wave a sign. It was people with their kids eating picnic lunches like this was a county fair. It was vendors offering flashing pins that said "FAYZ!" and T-shirts that said "Don't Let 'Em Out."

And the crowd had spread, north of the highway and south across the grounds of the abandoned, truncated half of Clifftop. Surfers rode beside the barrier, and in deeper water boats pressed close.

A no-fly zone had been established, but it didn't apply to news helicopters, or to the drones on loan from the army. Google had repurposed one of its satellites to watch. It was getting crowded in orbit as foreign powers also looked in to see whether this was all some American conspiracy.

Connie walked north at the edge of the crowd, looking for an opening. Over the heads of the lookers she saw the kids, maybe a hundred of them, peering out like suffocating fish from a badly maintained fishbowl.

She had to climb halfway up a dusty hill before she could achieve a little piece of privacy. There were no kids up there, but she thought if she waited, one might come. She wrote a sign:

I am Sam Temple and Caine Soren's mother.

Then she waited. What felt like ages passed before a girl who might have been fourteen or so noticed her and climbed the hill. She did not have paper or pen, but she had a stick, and the ground at that spot was bare dirt.

The girl used the stick to write:

Team Sam

Connie wrote:

What's your name?

Dahra.

Dahra Baidoo? I'm friends with your mom!

She told me.

Each time Dahra wrote she had to first wipe the ground clear with her hand.

I need to speak to Sam, Connie wrote.

Sam & Caine looking 4 Gaia.

Connie nodded. So her boys were working together. That certainly didn't sound like the stories of a deadly rivalry between them. She looked hard at Dahra.

Can I trust you?

Dahra smiled wryly. *People do.*

It didn't seem like a brag to Connie. Dahra, like all the kids Connie had seen, looked haggard and worn, with eyes that were way too old for the rest of her.

So this was the girl who had taken on the job of nurse, dispensing what medication she had, caring for the sick. Nurse Connie Temple had immediate sympathy for her. Good Lord, what must her life have been like? What terrible strains had this girl been under?

Things getting nasty out here.

Yeah. Dahra jerked her head toward the forest of signs down at the bottom of the hill.

You need to plan. Who can I talk to about that?

Dahra considered. *Edilio or Astrid.*

How can I get in touch with them?

Edilio very busy. Then, when she saw that Connie had read

that much, she added, *Astrid. They call her Astrid the Genius.*

Connie nodded. She knew the name. She knew most of the names of the kids in the FAYZ. This would be Astrid Ellison. Her parents were pains in the butt, the mother semihysterical and the father a tense, repressed engineer type, and they had contributed just about nothing to the group known as the families.

And judging by those early impressions when the barrier went transparent, Astrid was Sam's girlfriend.

I need to talk to Astrid. It is URGENT. How?

Dahra considered this for a moment, sighed noiselessly, then drew a circle. At the top of the circle she drew what Connie knew was a lake. Then she stabbed the stick into the lake. Then she drew a wavy line from where they were now to the lake and pointed at Connie. And a second line inside the circle and pointed to herself.

Dahra was telling her to get to the lake and she would meet her there and deliver Astrid.

Connie nodded.

Dahra dropped her hand to the two-foot-long lead pipe that hung from a leather strap and looked worried. Scared.

And Connie wavered. Was she sending this girl in harm's way? Was she meddling where she shouldn't? She was about to tell Dahra to forget it, but Dahra had already turned away.

"What's it all meant, Sammy boy? What's it all meant?"

Sam didn't bother to answer. Caine was just bored and looking to provoke him.

They each carried two water bottles and some dried fish in a backpack. They each carried a knife—a sheathed hunting knife for Caine and a big Swiss Army knife for Sam. They each wore a baseball cap. Caine slung a twelve-gauge shotgun over his shoulder, muzzle pointed up. Sam carried one of Edilio's automatic rifles over his shoulder, muzzle down.

The fact was that both of them had more powerful weapons in their empty hands. And with guns came ammunition, and both ammunition and guns were heavy. After about two miles on the road Sam was regretting the weight.

"Have you thought at all about what people out there are going to think about this bloody mess?" Caine asked.

Sam had thought of little else. But the day had not yet come when he would bare his soul to Caine. "We've got bigger problems on our hands."

Caine laughed, not believing it. "Nah, a dutiful son like you, surfer dude? You've thought about it."

Caine was walking a little ahead of Sam. Was that because Caine trusted Sam at his back more than Sam trusted the reverse? Maybe. Or maybe, Sam thought, Caine had longer legs. One of those things was probably true.

"No, you definitely thought about it," Caine went on, apparently not discouraged by Sam's refusal to engage. "You barbecued Penny in front of your mommy."

Sam felt a bit provoked. "Don't you mean *our* mommy?"

Caine shook his head. "No, I do not. She may have provided the egg and womb space, but she was not my mother. Yours. Not mine."

Sam winced a little. "You didn't miss all that much."

"Nurse Connie Temple," Caine said. "I knew she was spying on me back at Coates, you know. I never did know why until, well, until I knew."

"You figured she was just interested by you as a thug, a bully, and a manipulator?"

"Pretty much."

Caine was refusing to be provoked, whereas Sam was distinctly uncomfortable. This little mission could take days. It wouldn't do to let Caine work on him. He had to accept the fact that he was partnered with Caine. And that meant not calling up mental images of the plastering Caine had inflicted on kids who were now Sam's friends. And the burning down of half the town in a mad plot with Zil and his little bigot brigade. And about a thousand other felonies.

"Felonies." A legal word. There was a reason that word was popping up in his head.

Caine wasn't the only killer in the FAYZ. Of course, Sam had done only what was necessary to save lives and defeat Caine and Drake. But would courts see it that way?

To torture himself Sam ran through the laundry list of things he'd done that could be called crimes. Breaking and entering. Destruction of property. Assault and battery. Public drunkenness. Driving without a license. Burning a hole in a nuclear power plant. Theft.

Caine was looking back at him from the top of a rise. "You have a lousy poker face, Sammy boy. What's in your head is right there on your face. You're thinking about it, and it's not the first time."

"I am still underage," Sam said weakly.

Caine erupted in disbelieving laughter. "Yeah, that'll do it. 'I'm just a kid, Your Honor!' Hah. They'll have to find a few scapegoats, and guess who it will be? You and me, surfer dude. You and me."

"You act like we're getting out of here," Sam said.

"Do I? Funny, because I expect we'll all be dead. Because I'll tell you what: that girl, that Gaia? We both know who she really is. I don't think old green-and-gross chose to take on a body for fun. I think it expects to get out of here alive."

That was way too close to Sam's own thought process.

"Endgame," Sam muttered, not really expecting Caine to hear.

"Yep," Caine said. "That's right. Endgame. The FAYZ barrier is coming down; at least that's my bet. But there's also a ninety percent chance you and me both end up dead. Ten percent chance we both actually get out of here alive. In which case we end up sharing a cell somewhere." He laughed. "Kind of unfair, really, what with me being evil and all, and you just so darned virtuous and heroic."

"So why are we doing this?" Sam asked. "Why are we on this mission?"

Caine stopped, turned around, and walked back to him. Sam was struck by the undeniable fact that even now, even after being beaten and humiliated by Penny, his brother could project that hard-to-define thing called charisma. Evil, yes, but a tall, handsome, charming kind of evil.

"Why are we doing this?" Caine asked him. "You know damned well why we're doing this. Because it's a fight. It may be *the* fight. It may be the final fight. And what else are we good at, you and me? What are we going to do if we ever get out there anyway? You going to sign up for some AP classes? Get your college essay started? Take driver's ed?" Caine laughed, laughing at himself, it seemed. "Yeah, I'm pretty sure Harvard will want me. I mean, how many former kings do they have applying?"

Sam tried to stop himself asking, but in the end he blurted it out. "And Diana?"

"Great body," Caine said breezily. "And a very open mind."

Sam didn't buy it. "It's more than that, you and her."

Caine didn't answer, which was all the answer Sam needed.

"Less talk, more walk," Sam said.

"Ta-da?" Dekka echoed, staring at Brianna because it was much better than looking at Brianna's trophy. "Ta-da?"

Astrid knelt down to look at the monstrous object. The temptation to taunt Drake was powerful. Drake had been the bogeyman in her life. Drake had made clear that he intended to kill Astrid, slowly and with every humiliation his diseased mind could conjure up. Astrid had spent almost four months in the forest, and fear of Drake had been the constant. She had spent hours practicing the smooth unlimbering and aiming of a gun just so that when the time came she would at least get in a useless shot.

There was a second effect of seeing Drake helpless: Sam would face one less enemy. His odds of survival had just ticked up.

Dekka was obviously thinking the same thing. "One down," she said.

As she watched, the object moved, oozed, coming slowly together. The lizard tail remained.

"What are we supposed to do with him?" Dekka asked.

Just then Roger, known as the Artful Roger for his skill in drawing, came up the side. "Is Edilio around? Because— ahhhhh! Oh no. Oh no."

"Hey, Roger," Brianna said. "Have you met Drake?"

"Oh, God, no. Oh . . . Oh . . ."

"I know!" Brianna said proudly. "We're just trying to fig- ure out what to—hey, you know what? You should totally draw him so we can always remember what he looked like."

Dekka, in as dry and nonchalant a tone as she could man- age, said, "Roger, can we help you?"

"Can you . . . ?" He had definitely forgotten why he was there.

"You were looking for Edilio, right? He's down in PB."

The Drake head was almost back to being Drake with the addition of the lizard tail, and the larynx was mostly repaired, so he was able to produce a windy, wheezing sound while his tongue and mouth worked furiously.

"I figured Sam would fry him up," Brianna said.

"Sam's not coming back right away," Astrid said. She was

trying to mimic the light tone, but failing. She was worried about Sam. And she was a little sickened by the emotions that swept over her in waves: bitterness, rage, triumph. How much of her life had been about fearing this psychopath? And now he was in her grasp. Now he was without his famous whip hand. Now he was helpless.

The urge to kick him was almost too much to resist.

"Go ahead," Dekka said, as if she'd read Astrid's thoughts.

It took Astrid a while to react, to slowly shake her head no. She hated Drake; there was no denying it. But she couldn't give in to that. She had to use what she had been given.

"Tell us about Gaia, Drake," she said.

His answer was voiceless but easy enough to decipher.

"Yeah, you don't seem to have the body parts to do that," Dekka said.

"Hah! I told him the same thing," Brianna said with a happy grin.

"I'm just going to, um, not be here anymore," Roger said, and beat a retreat.

"You had a bag of dead lizards and a couple eggs," Astrid said. "Why was that?"

Drake cursed foully. But softly.

"Where are Diana and Gaia?" Astrid asked Drake.

"Better just chop him up," Brianna said. "I can spread the parts of his head all over like I did the rest of him. I only brought him to show Sam."

Astrid and Dekka exchanged a look. They were in charge at the lake. It was their call. But neither wanted to decide without Edilio. This was not exactly one of the contingencies they had discussed beforehand.

A thought occurred to Astrid. "He morphed from Brittney back to Drake. He'll sooner or later go the other way. Brittney may be easier to talk to."

Dekka nodded. "Yeah, that's right. She might be of some use if we can get her to talk."

"We can't be careless, though," Astrid said. "We don't know what his capabilities are. Maybe he can regenerate beyond just his head. For all we know the separate parts can regenerate." She glanced uneasily at Brianna. "Do you know where you put all the parts?"

"Yes," Brianna said, but with definite uncertainty in her tone, accentuated by the way she stared up and off to one corner as if trying to remember.

"If he can regenerate . . . ," Dekka began.

"Then we could have a bunch of Drakes, one from each severed part."

"Are you guys going to turn this into a bad thing?" Brianna asked shrilly. "I *got* him! I got him and I sliced him up. And I brought you the head."

"You did great, Breeze," Dekka said. "But do us a favor and check on some of those parts. Make sure they're where you left them, huh?"

"Okay, I just have to eat something first. I ran a hundred miles, probably." She zipped away, leaving Astrid and Dekka, and the head, which was still making faint vocalizations of an unpleasant nature.

"I have an idea," Dekka said. "There's a cooler in my trailer. I get it, I poke some holes in it, put the head in, weigh it down with rocks, and we sink him at the end of a long rope. Maybe it'll even kill him."

Astrid sighed. "This would be a story not to tell the *Today* show. I'll start getting some rocks."

EIGHT

DRAKE COULD HEAR perfectly well, although there was something of an echo effect. But pretty well given that his head was separated from his body and split in two still-somewhat-mismatched halves.

He had heard what they were planning. And he was afraid. It was an odd kind of fear, disconnected from his body: there was no stomach-churning, no shortness of breath, no quickening of his pulse.

But he was afraid. He had spent long weeks buried underground—it had had an effect on him. He was not quite human, but he could still feel fear.

And pain. Not like he would have in the old days, but still . . . he could feel the body that was no longer attached to his head.

He itched for his whip hand. God, he would make these two witches pay. Oh, definitely. He could picture it. He had pictured it, many times, especially Astrid. How long had he hated her? Probably from their very first meeting. She was just that kind of girl: hate at first sight.

But now . . .

Dekka, the dyke, was using a Phillips screwdriver to poke holes in the plastic cooler. It wasn't easy—she was slamming it again and again, like some crazy killer. She'd already put a couple of dozen holes in it.

Astrid was just standing there, watching her, and looking back at Drake. He knew she wanted to say something to him. She wanted to tell him, *Hah, see, now it's me on top. Now it's me looking down at you.* She couldn't hide the look of triumph, not from Drake.

"Ready," Dekka said.

Astrid squatted down. She grabbed a handful of his hair, and suddenly he was up and swinging through the air.

He saw the cooler with its top open. He wanted to scream, but he couldn't manage that much noise, and he wouldn't give them the satisfaction.

Astrid set him down—didn't drop him, set him down—in the cooler.

"I have a bike chain I can wrap around it," Dekka said. "Then I'll tie the rope around the whole thing, in case we need to haul him back up."

"Drake," Astrid said. "Last chance: tell us where we can find Gaia and Diana."

For a terrible moment Drake considered it. But he knew

that whatever these two could do was nothing next to the pain the gaiaphage could inflict.

He cursed weakly.

The two of them set heavy chunks of broken concrete in beside him. Astrid closed the lid. Darkness stabbed through with beams of light from the holes.

The cooler rocked back and forth with much scraping noise as they wrapped the chain and then the rope.

"That'll hold," Dekka said.

Drake felt the cooler being lifted. It teetered precariously as they almost lost their grip.

Then: A short drop. A splash.

Water began seeping in through the screwdriver holes as air leaked out. Water came in from all directions, like some kind of awful multihead shower. Soon there was an inch of water in the bottom, and when Drake tried to curse, it was lake water that he sucked up into his severed throat.

The descent seemed to take forever. Then: a bump as the cooler landed on the lake bottom.

It took ten minutes for the box to fill completely with water as it rose over his mouth, his nose, his eyes, and finally swirled his hair.

But he was not dead.

Tiny fish, guppies, came sneaking in through the holes. They nibbled at him, but stopped once they'd had a taste. Still, they swirled around him, faintly luminescent in the dark water, like dull fireflies.

They looked into his ears. They poked curious heads into his nose. They swam up into his esophagus and from there up into his mouth.

They were still there when Drake began screaming without sound as he changed into Brittney.

The idea of facing Taylor without a cigarette was bothering Lana quite a bit. Not that she was addicted to cigarettes, she told herself; it wasn't anything like that. Only a very weak person would become addicted, and she was not weak.

The fact that she'd been shaking and even more snappish than usual all day absolutely did not prove that she was addicted. Neither did the fact that she'd spent much of the day searching for smokes or cursing Sanjit.

And yet she was thinking of cigarettes even as she turned the key in the lock. The old electronic key system at the hotel didn't work, of course, but she hadn't wanted to leave Taylor free to just walk away—like she could anyway—so Lana had told Sanjit to screw a lock onto the door. He was handy that way. It was almost a pity she would have to shoot him.

Strange the idea of locking Taylor up. Before her recent— well, it wasn't quite a mutation; no one knew what it was—anyway, before all this, she'd had the power to teleport. To "bounce," as she called it, from one place to the next with just a thought. Maybe she still could, but she'd have a hard time standing up when she got wherever she was going.

Lana slid open the bolt.

"Taylor. It's me."

She opened the door. No one had ever closed the curtains in the room, so it was bright with the slanting rays of the setting sun. Different light now. Hard to say what made it different; it just was. The old sky and the old sun had had a seasonless sameness to them. This sun—the real sun—set a little earlier, and a low cloud bank out beyond the barrier bent the light into shades of yellow and gold.

It was a different gold than the gold color of Taylor's skin: Taylor was more metallic. Almost as if she really was made of actual gold. She sat propped up in the hotel bed, leaning on her one stump arm, the other complete arm in her lap. Her legs had been placed on the bed with her, but one had fallen off and was on the floor.

Taylor was completely nude, but it didn't matter. She had none of the signs of gender. She was a golden Gumby with one arm and a long, green, reptilian tongue.

The best theory anyone had was that it had been done by Little Pete. Little Pete was not thought to have done it maliciously—Petey was incapable of malice. Or any intention, really. He might be the most powerful person in the FAYZ but he was still, despite it all, a five-year-old autistic kid. Couldn't blame him. He'd probably just been playing. A heedless, unaware little god.

With great power comes great responsibility, Lana thought, recalling the line from the Spider-Man movie. But Little Pete had all kinds of power and no responsibility.

"Let's try the hand again, Taylor," Lana said. "Where is it?"

Maybe Taylor understood what she was saying, maybe not. Her ears looked normal, but who knew what went on down inside them? And who knew what went on in her brain? Or if she still had a brain?

Lana couldn't find the hand, which was disturbing. She'd had no evidence that Taylor could move off her bed. Then she found it all the way across the room and behind the permanently off television. Were the parts moving on their own? Once, Brianna had told Lana that Drake could do that: reassemble. As if the parts had lives of their own. Was Taylor the same sort of thing Drake now was? Or at least similar?

No. Drake still looked like Drake. Taylor . . . well . . . But maybe there was some kind of similarity. It was a puzzle. A creepy, creepy puzzle.

Lana carried the cold thing back and pressed it against Taylor's stump. She focused her thoughts on healing the stump. Had Taylor been a regular human, it might well have worked. It wouldn't be the first appendage Lana had reattached. But it wasn't working, just as it hadn't worked on earlier efforts.

"What do I do with you?" Lana asked Taylor. "What are you? You're sure not human. Or even mammal, obviously. Or . . ."

A thought struck her. Was she sure Taylor was even an animal?

A second more perverse thought popped into her head: what would happen if she dragged Taylor out to the balcony to wave to the lookers out there? *Hey there, tourists, check this out! That should keep your nightmares fresh for a while.*

She wondered how much The Powers That Be in the FAYZ—Sam, Caine, Edilio, and Astrid—had thought about the outside world's view of what was going on. The reality in the FAYZ was way weirder than the lookers could imagine. This wasn't just a bunch of kids trapped in a bubble; it was an unprecedented event in the history of the planet. The barrier wasn't the only thing separating inside from outside—things could happen here that just flat *could not exist* out there.

For example: a girl able to heal with a touch.

"Yeah, let's not even start thinking about that," she told herself. She looked at Taylor, a pretty girl with dead eyes and golden skin and black hair like a sheet of rubber. "Are you more like a plant?"

No answer.

"Are you made out of Play-Doh?"

There came a soft knock at the door. "Can I come in?"

"Why not?" she answered sourly.

Sanjit stepped in. "Any change?"

Lana shook her head. "What if she isn't an animal? If she was a plant, what would we do if we wanted to try and reattach a broken stem or whatever? Bring me a knife. The big sharp one."

"A plant?"

He fetched the knife.

"Now, hold her stump," Lana said.

Sanjit shuddered. "You know, Lana, that's one of those phrases I could have gone my whole life without hearing.

'Hold her stump.'" He had seen a lot in his life and dealt with some serious weirdness, but Taylor gave him the willies. Nevertheless, he came around the bed, stepping over Lana's legs, and took hold of the stump.

Lana took the knife and began to shave off a thin slice of the stump. Taylor turned her head to watch, but there was no evidence it was causing her any pain or concern. Sanjit, on the other hand, was turning green.

Lana removed an oval slice and picked it up like a piece of bologna. She held it to the light, inspecting it critically. Then she laid it aside and took a similar slice from the hand. Then she pressed the two newly cut pieces together.

"Get me some duct tape," Lana said.

"Some what?"

"Some tape," she said impatiently. "Tape. Staples. Whatever."

It took Sanjit twenty minutes, and he came back with a roll of white Velcro.

"How am I going to Velcro this?"

"It's adhesive-backed. It's like tape. I couldn't find tape. I found a stapler, but this will be better. Also less disturbing."

"Wimp. Get me a cigarette."

He pulled another half cigarette from his pocket, stuck it in her lips—she was busy holding the hand and the arm together—and lit it.

Then he rolled out a foot of Velcro, cut it, and carefully taped the body parts together.

An hour later they carefully unwound the tape.

"Huh. It's adhering," Lana said. "A little, anyway. Huh. Wow. You think you could manage a trip into town?"

"Why? So you can try to find your smokes with me out of the way?"

"Yeah, that, too. But mostly I was thinking you could bring Sinder back here. I saw her in town, down from the lake. Or she might be out at the barrier playing wave-at-the-'rents. Either way, get her: she has a green thumb."

"I don't feel it," Sam said.

Caine shook his head. "Me neither."

They were at the entrance to the mine shaft. They hadn't even discussed their first stop; they'd both just known that it had to be here. This mine shaft was where the gaiaphage had lain for years, growing and festering. This had been the nexus of the evil, its home.

"Should we go in and check?"

"No," Caine said. "I've been in. It wasn't enjoyable."

"I can imagine."

"No, you can't," Caine said flatly.

Caine felt Sam watching him, impatient, ready to move on. But Caine was mesmerized by that dark, blank opening. Once, it had been neatly framed with timber, but now it was more of a gash in the ground, a twisted mouth with stone teeth.

The memory of it . . . Dread had left a permanent mark on him. Pain. Fear.

Loneliness.

"Lana knows," Caine said at last. "And I guess Diana does now, too." That thought, that realization, something he should have long since acknowledged, rocked him.

When he had come crawling away from this terrible place and found his way home, shattered and insane, Diana had helped him. Who had helped Diana?

"Once it touches your mind, see . . . ," Caine said, "once it really reaches inside you, it doesn't let go. It doesn't just stop. It's like a, you know, like a wound, like you got cut real badly, and you stitched it up, but it won't really heal."

"Lana fought it," Sam said.

"So did I!" Caine snapped. Then, more quietly, "So did I. I still do. It's still in my head. It still reaches out to me sometimes." He nodded, now almost seeming to have forgotten Sam. *"Hungry in the dark."*

He had fought it. But he hadn't fought it alone.

What the hell? He felt tears in his eyes. He tried to shake it off. Diana had spoon-fed him, and protected him, and cleaned him. And what had he done? He'd been sitting in Perdido Beach feeling sorry for himself while she was out there. With *it*.

"Is that what you're going to tell people if we get out of this?" Sam asked. "That the gaiaphage made you do it? Because I don't buy it."

If Sam expected a furious answer, Caine disappointed him. He wasn't going to let Sam bait him. At the moment he didn't care about Sam.

The failing light was casting long shadows. They would need to think about finding a place to spend the night.

"Won't make any difference what I say," Caine said softly. "Won't be me telling the story. It'll be a hundred kids if we get out of here. All those kids who mostly just kept their heads down all through this, they'll be the ones telling the story."

"Why do you say that?"

Caine laughed. "Sometimes you are so naive. You think you and me and the other big deals are going to be the only ones talking to whoever? The cops? The FBI? Don't be stupid. You think the adults are going to listen to us? They'll be afraid of us."

"You think we'll still have our powers? Even if we did—"

"It's not about that, Sammy boy." Caine turned his back on the mine shaft. It seemed to take a great deal of effort for him to do that, and once he'd accomplished it he nodded like yes, yes he could do it. "It's not about the powers, man; it's that we aren't kids anymore. Look what we've been through. Look what we've done. Look at yourself, surfer dude. We've done something none of our parents have even come close to. We didn't take over their boring world; we took over a world about a thousand times tougher. If we walk out of this alive, we won't have to bow our heads to anyone. There'll be guys who were in wars hearing what we did and thinking, 'Whoa.' You and me, we can say, 'You got yourself some medals, soldier? Yeah, well, I lived through the FAYZ.'"

"I haven't thought much past wanting to get out of here

and have a pizza." Sam was trying to lighten the mood, probably because what Caine was saying made Sam squirm.

But Caine wasn't done. "They'll be afraid of us, brother, not because we can shoot light out of our hands or throw people through walls, but because we'll be the living proof that they're nothing special just because they're old. They'll fear us and they'll hate us. Most of them, anyway. And they'll try to use us, make money off us." He sighed. "You don't know much about human nature, do you?"

At last Caine smirked and nodded his head, satisfied with himself and satisfied as well with the troubled expression on Sam's face.

Sam said, "Yeah, well getting back to reality here, we should make sure the gaiaphage doesn't come back this way. Let's shut this place down once and for all."

Caine spun on his heel, looked back at the mine shaft. "Now, that is an excellent suggestion." He raised his hands, palms out. Loose rock from all around the mine entrance hurtled into the pit. Boulders rose and suddenly veered, fast as jet fighters, to crash into the hole. Pebbles and rocks and bushes and dirt and bits of broken timber all flew at the entrance.

The noise was a screaming hurricane.

"That outcropping up there, that big rock?" Sam pointed to a sun-bleached boulder about the size of a house. "If I get it to break loose, can you handle it?"

"Let's find out."

Sam aimed green beams of light at the rock and held them

on target for several minutes. The rock went from orange-by-sunset to a deep, glowing red. There was a loud cracking sound, and half of it broke away, a single very big, very hot boulder.

Caine focused and stopped its slide down the hill. He swung it left and let it drop just to the side of the cave entrance.

"Break it up a little more," Caine said.

Sam focused the killing light again and held it until the face of the rock began to melt. It fell into two uneven pieces, which Caine easily drew back and then hurled into the mine shaft entrance, blocking it completely.

Sam once again focused energy and held it for a very long time, lighting the mountain's face with the green glow, until the rock softened into magma and crumbled wetly into the shaft entrance.

Finally he stopped. The boulder formed a welded plug that would have to be blasted out with a great deal of dynamite should anyone wish to dislodge it.

Without looking at Caine, Sam said, "Something we're good at."

"Yep. Something we're good at. But listen to me, Sammy boy, I have one rule for when we throw down with the gaia-phage: Diana doesn't get hurt."

It took Sam completely by surprise. "We may have no choice."

"You're not listening. I'm going with you to kill what some would call my daughter, although I don't think she's anyone's daughter. But if I suspect you're going to hurt Diana, our peace treaty ends. We clear on that?"

Sam nodded. "We're clear."

"Deep down, she's a good person, Diana is," Caine said, and sighed. "Deep down, I'm not. But she is."

NINE

AS SOON AS the lights came on, so to speak, Albert had known he had made a mistake. He had seen doom, nothing but doom coming as the dome went dark. But then, like something out of the book of Genesis, it was "Let there be light."

And there *was* light.

Now as he stood sourly recalling his own failure of judgment, the sun, the actual sun, was setting out over the ocean, and Perdido Beach was touched with gold.

In this light Albert pretty much looked like he'd panicked. In this light he didn't look like the prescient, cold-eyed businessman. He looked like a coward.

Standing on the southernmost point of San Francisco de Sales Island over these last three terrible days he'd seen that the wild, terrified mobs of kids had not, as he'd expected, burned Perdido Beach to the ground just to provide light as he'd expected. In fact, he was looking now through a very good telescope he'd found in the Brattle-Chance home, and while he could certainly not make out faces, he could see people in town. And he could see beyond town to the motels that had been built, and the fast-food restaurant, and the news trucks. Out there.

And now all was being revealed to that wider out-there world.

Had it happened just a week earlier, he, Albert Hillsborough, would have been one of the great heroes of the FAYZ. Who had kept the McDonald's running while there was still electricity? Albert Hillsborough. Who had created the market up at the school? Albert Hillsborough. Who had created a stable currency—the 'Berto—using gold and McDonald's game pieces? Albert Hillsborough.

He had put people to work.

He had saved them all from starvation. Everyone knew it.

My God, had it all ended then, he could have written his own ticket. He was barely in high school and he would have had university business schools lining up to give him a full scholarship.

Albert Hillsborough—Harvard MBA.

Recently graduated Albert Hillsborough offered vice presidency at General Electric.

Albert Hillsborough named youngest president ever of Sony Corporation.

All of it lost in a moment of panic. The story might already be out there. Half the country might already despise him.

Albert Hillsborough buys waterfront villa in the south of

France. Says, *"I needed some place to dock my yacht."*

Albert Hillsborough hosts party aboard his yacht. George Clooney, Denzel Washington, Olivia Wilde, and Sasha Obama in attendance.

But he really had done all those good things, and he'd done them without ever raising his hand against anyone, and without any so-called powers he had saved everything.

Just by being smart. Not a genius like Astrid, just smart. By working hard. By not giving up.

Albert Hillsborough dating supermodel. "Marriage not in the plans," Hillsborough says.

Albert Hillsborough declines to run for president despite huge poll numbers. Says, "That job doesn't pay enough."

A boat.

There it was, black on a rippled yellow sea: a boat.

One of his missiles was lying under a tarp held down by rocks on what had once been a lush green lawn and was now an overgrown, dried-out weed patch. He had read the instructions carefully. The missiles weren't hard to fire, really, but then, why would they be? They were used by soldiers in the heat of battle—they'd have to be fairly simple.

It was a rowboat. One of Quinn's.

He turned the telescope toward it and after a few jumpy misses finally centered the boat in the circle and saw the broad back straining against the oars. It would be at least another hour before Quinn could reach the island.

Albert had never before felt shame; it was an alien emotion for him. But of all the people to have to see: Quinn.

At the start Quinn had been Sam's best friend. But he had been weak while Sam was still uncertain and had fallen in with Caine. Caine had been too violent, too overtly evil for Quinn to stomach, which had left Quinn neither here nor there, not someone Sam trusted, not someone of any use to Caine.

But over time Quinn had found his place. And then he had slowly, imperceptibly, grown from the unreliable, foolish boy he'd been into, well, into the Fisherman. People called him that, just as they called Lana the Healer. The Fisherman, with a capital "F."

His crews were absolutely devoted. He outworked anyone in the FAYZ. More than any other person except for Albert, he fed Perdido Beach. He had stood up to Penny and to Caine, although Quinn was not the hero type.

And at the end it had been Quinn who'd stayed to see things through when Albert ran away.

No, he did not want to speak to Quinn.

Albert glanced at the missile. It wouldn't be hard. But beyond the missile, out at sea, out in the open sea beyond the FAYZ barrier, there was a glistening white cruise ship passing slowly. Probably, what, four miles away? Five? But not so far that binoculars and telescopes trained in his direction would miss the flame and the explosion.

"And there's the fact that I don't kill people," Albert admitted almost sadly. "I'm a businessman."

He walked slowly back to the mansion to tell Alicia and Leslie-Ann that they would be having a guest.

"Oh, God, it hurts. It hurts!" He was staggering and shrieking, pausing to stare in horror at the stump of his arm, crying, babbling. His shirt was saturated with blood, now mostly dried.

The red-haired man was not used to suffering, Diana thought.

Well, welcome to the FAYZ, mister. This is a hard place.

Gaia was walking along at a sprightly pace, still following the barrier as the sun fell into the distant sea and the shadows deepened. They were very near the northeastern point, where there was a wrecked train: a dozen boxcars tossed around the landscape, some plowed into the sand, others piled up against each other.

Their shadows were long. Night was rapidly approaching. It was possible to imagine goblins and spooks in this desert train wreck.

"The Nutella train," Diana said. She of course knew about the bisected train that Sam, Dekka, and Jack had found. The freight had been mostly useless, everything from toilets to wicker furniture. But there had also been a huge amount of Nutella, Cup-a-Noodles, and Pepsi. The discovery remained one of the great days in FAYZ history.

Diana would have given anything for a bowl of noodles.

Everything edible had been removed, hauled to the lake, and either eaten and drunk or bartered to Perdido Beach. Baby Gaia had been nurtured in Diana's womb on a diet that included a lot of Nutella. Sam and Edilio had been generous with her for the sake of her baby. For the sake of what could be their own destruction.

"What is this thing called?" Gaia asked.

Again Diana noted the fact that there were holes in Gaia's knowledge. She knew a lot. She didn't know everything.

Weakness.

Vulnerability.

"It's called a train."

When exactly had Diana started thinking in those terms of weakness and vulnerability? When had Diana stopped feeling she had some duty to Gaia and begun to think of ways to stop her?

Gaia had slung the cooked arm over her shoulder. The bicep was mostly consumed, as was the tender meat of most of the fingers. The thumb still remained untouched.

Diana knew the taste of human flesh. That was the terrible crime for which she had been punished by a God who could see even into the FAYZ. Gaia was that punishment, the curse that now mocked her mother's horror at cannibalism with jaunty, careless amorality.

"Why won't you let me go to a doctor?" the red-haired man moaned.

"There's no doctor," Diana said. "Where do you think you are?"

"She . . . oh, my God!" the man cried.

"You'll be better off if you don't spend too much time thinking about it," Diana said. "The wound isn't bleeding any—"

"She's eating my arm!"

Diana spotted a long stick, an umbrella pole, she thought, part of the wicker mess from the train, perhaps. She hefted it experimentally. It was about six feet long and not too heavy, broken jagged and sharp at one end, brass-bound at the other. A very nice walking stick.

"Stab her with it!" the man hissed.

Diana almost laughed. "You don't want to attack her."

"She's a monster!"

"Yeah. We have monsters here. She's one. The worst. But you won't kill her with a stick."

His face was gray, the look of a man in terrible pain and shock. The look of a man who had lost a lot of blood. But the wound had been cauterized, if not really healed. Gaia didn't care much about cosmetic things; she hadn't even completely healed her own face. He would live long enough to feed her again. That's all Gaia cared about.

"I have a knife in my pack."

This time, Diana did laugh. "Go ahead: give it a try."

That hard, cynical laugh brought him up short.

"Are you . . . like her?"

"I'm her mother," Diana said.

"Jesus."

"Yeah, we haven't seen *him* around here much." Diana liked the stick. It helped her plow ahead through the sand, following in Gaia's footsteps.

"Who are you people?" It was like he'd been in too much shock to ask these basic questions before now.

"My name is Diana. She's Gaia. She's . . ." How to explain Gaia? "Well, not exactly what she looks like. Less girly. More Satan-like. What's your name?"

"Alex. Alex Mayle. I feel like I'm going crazy. I don't know what—"

"What were you doing out there?"

"Just trying to get some cool video. You know. YouTubes."

"Still have your camera?"

"My phone! I have my phone." With his one hand he managed to draw his iPhone from his pocket. He dialed a number.

"911? Seriously?" Diana laughed.

"There's no signal."

"Hmmm. That's a surprise. Because none of us ever thought of making a phone call to 911 and saying 'get us out of here.' Should have thought of that." It wasn't that Diana was enjoying this, exactly. But it was a reminder of just how much she had endured, how much she had survived.

Still here, she thought. Still alive. Still sane, mostly.

He opened his camera app and aimed it at Gaia's back. Then he slid the phone back in his pack. He had to use his knees to hold the pack.

"I'm going to die," Alex moaned.

"Not yet," Diana said darkly. "Not until she finds another food source."

The implication stopped him in his tracks. He hung back, and then Diana heard the sound of his footsteps scrambling away.

Without even looking back Gaia simply raised a hand, and

Alex flew through the air to land hard at her feet.

"Leave me alone!" Alex cried up at Gaia.

"I could kill you and carry the nutritious parts with me," Gaia said. "But that would be harder, carrying all that meat. So you'll carry yourself until I find better food. If you try to run away, I'll do something very painful to you. It won't kill you, but you'll wish you were dead."

"What are you?" he begged, rising to his knees. "What are you?"

"I am the gaiaphage," Gaia said proudly. "I am your . . . your master. Obey me."

Gaia found that amusing, obviously, as her young face broke out in a grin that she shared with Diana, as though the two of them were coconspirators in dismembering Alex. As though Diana would see the humor in it all.

Gaia walked on, and Diana helped Alex to his feet.

It was strange. The first adult she had spoken to in almost a year. Sometimes she had pictured this moment. The fantasy had usually involved firemen and cops rushing in, offering help and food and comfort. Safety.

But this adult wasn't here to rescue her. He was just another lost, desperate fool, more scared than she was.

"I just want to go home," he moaned. He started crying again.

Diana's stomach clenched with a hunger pain. That familiar pain reached into her memory and dragged out images she could not stand to look at. It was a terrible feeling. So was the fact that she was eyeing the cooked arm and salivating.

No, she told herself. *Not again. I'll die first.* She thought of Alex's knife, supposedly in his backpack. Not the wrist—that could be too easily fixed by Gaia if she chose to. It would have to be an artery in her throat. A quick, deep, assured, stabbing thrust. And death before the evil creature, her daughter, could stop her.

But then hope, that cruel thing, came to taunt her. Caine would come for her, wouldn't he? He would know she needed rescue. Because deep down he cared for her, didn't he?

But when he did come, if he did come, Gaia would kill him, wouldn't she?

And then I'll do it, Diana told herself. Then the quick, deep, assured thrust. Not before.

Albert had taken three people to the island with him. Leslie-Ann was his maid, a mousy little thing. She was mostly useless, but she had saved his life once upon a time.

Pug—she had an actual name, but Albert didn't recall what it was—was a big girl, strong and not very bright, and loyal to Albert, though he wasn't quite sure why. She was not clever enough to make trouble.

And finally, Alicia. Alicia had been trained by Edilio to handle a gun. She'd been part of his security force until he'd caught her extorting bribes. At which point Albert had hired her, informally, as a spy. She was clever, a good observer, and had done a good job of keeping him aware of everything.

She was also tall, about five inches taller than Albert, which he liked, and she had large breasts, which Albert also liked. But she was not loyal like Leslie-Ann or Pug; she was too unstable for loyalty. She had been one of the first Coates kids to abandon Caine and come over to the Perdido Beach side. Later she had rejoined Caine for a time, and later still had lurked at the edges of Zil's Human Crew.

She was on the island because Albert had lately begun to develop an interest in girls. When it had seemed that the FAYZ would be plunged into permanent darkness, Albert had thought that under the circumstances . . . well . . . But, no. None of that had happened.

And now he was stuck with her.

At present, she was shining a flashlight down, watching Quinn come up the rope hand over hand, climbing the cliff with the agility and ease of an ape.

"He's strong," Alicia said.

"He rows a boat all day long."

"Huh." Pause. "You know, you should work out, Albert. We have a gym. You and those stick arms of yours."

Albert was looking for a suitably cutting retort when Quinn came up over the side of the cliff, stood up, brushed himself off, and said, "Albert."

"Who sent you, Quinn?" He was not interested in small talk. Alicia had a gun, and so did Pug, who was standing a few dozen feet away, watchful, ready.

"Yeah, good to see you, too, Albert," Quinn said.

Albert hesitated, nodded, and said, "I guess come inside and we can talk." He turned on his heel and stalked up to the house, not waiting for Quinn. Alicia fell back so she could walk just behind Quinn.

There was an electric light on inside, something no one had seen for months in Perdido Beach. But just a single bulb: fuel was in very short supply, and Albert's priority was keeping the water pump running and having enough energy to at least take some of the chill out of his showers.

They went inside and to the living room with vast bowed windows that provided a horizon-to-horizon view. Perdido Beach was a silhouette now, a dark space against the bright lights of out there.

Leslie-Ann brought in a pitcher of iced tea and glasses. Glasses filled with actual ice. Quinn stared at the ice like he was seeing the gates of heaven.

"So?" Albert pressed as Quinn poured himself some tea, added sugar—a second impossible luxury—and took a drink.

"So, Albert, I noticed you didn't fire a missile at me."

"No."

"Which means you want to know what's going on. So maybe stop acting all high and mighty. I don't work for you anymore, Albert. I'm only here because Edilio asked me to come."

"Edilio?" Albert frowned. "Not Caine?"

"Well, you wouldn't know this, Albert, since you ran off when things looked bad, but with the barrier transparent things have changed."

"Yes. It's lighter during the day," Albert said dryly.

"Lookers—people, adults, people out there, I mean—are all up against the barrier where the highway goes. TV cameras, parents, nuts. It's a mess because—"

"I can see them," Albert cut in. "Let me guess: no one's working, they're all waving at their family members, and pretty soon everyone will be very, very hungry."

Quinn didn't bother to confirm.

"Caine?" Albert asked.

"Caine is off with Sam looking for Gaia. Edilio is running things now, thankfully."

Albert drank some tea and thought it over. He could work with Edilio. Edilio was much more sensible than Caine. For one thing he wouldn't go around proclaiming himself king and then let his psycho allies terrorize everyone.

"Edilio wants me to come back and get people working," Albert guessed.

"Yep."

"How about you, Quinn?"

"Me?" Quinn looked him right in the eye. "I think you're a selfish little coward."

The insult did not particularly bother Albert. Selfishness was a virtue, and if self-preservation was cowardice, so be it. "I've got everything I want right here," Albert said, holding up the glass of ice as proof number one, then nodding at Alicia as proof number two, then sweeping a hand around the elegant room, barely visible in the meager fifteen watts.

Quinn set the glass down and ran his hand through his hair, a gesture that flexed his considerable biceps and well-defined triceps, causing Alicia to edge a little forward on her seat and thereby definitely annoying Albert.

"I'll tell you, dude," Quinn said, "I think the way things stand right now, you'll go down in history as a slimy little creep who ran off and left everyone to starve."

"History?" Albert mocked.

Quinn shrugged. "Everyone seems to think the barrier is coming down. Just before I left, we saw some TV footage outside of some guy, some adult guy, falling through. *Into* the FAYZ. Yeah. Into. Anyway, the gaiaphage obviously thinks we're getting out; otherwise why move into a body? Right?"

Albert couldn't argue with that.

"So, yeah: history," Quinn said. "We're all being watched now. And judged. Up until a few days ago you were a big hero. Now you're dirt. The only way you fix that is by coming back and doing what you do."

TEN

THAT NIGHT SAM and Caine camped out within a mile of Gaia and Diana.

Quinn slept in a bed with actual sheets while Albert walked the halls of the mansion on San Francisco de Sales Island and wondered if he had made a mistake agreeing to go back.

Astrid lay in the cabin she usually shared with Sam and tried to think about life after, about how they could be, how . . . but ended up thinking of Drake, twenty feet below her in a water-filled box. She tried then to turn her thoughts to memories of Sam, but again Drake intruded. So she gave up on sleep and read a book.

Diana curled on the ground near a pile of stones Gaia had consented to heat and prayed not to dream but did dream, a dream of an overly lit hospital room, and an incubator, and herself approaching that incubator, only to see a bloody beast inside beating violently at the Plexiglas sides. Nurses stared at her.

Edilio crashed on a ratty mattress in the corner of what had once been the town magistrate's office. He started to try and organize his plans for the next day but fell asleep so suddenly and so completely that when he woke up in the morning he would find he had only removed one shoe.

Lana lay with Sanjit and thought of many things. Of Taylor, and what she might be, and whether Sinder—who had agreed to stop by tomorrow—would be able to make any difference. And she thought for a while of Quinn, and wondered if he would care enough to try and force her to stop smoking. This made her feel disloyal, so she veered her thoughts away and tried to imagine what she could ever do, how she could ever survive out there.

Dekka dreamed of Brianna.

Brianna dreamed of running, and she smiled in her sleep.

Little Pete didn't notice the passage of time in the usual way. He drifted and for a while seemed almost to stop thinking, to stop being. But then he was again, focused, aware, and still repeating to himself that it was not okay to hit.

Where the highway passed through the barrier, eighty-seven hungry, traumatized, heavily armed kids wrapped in filthy sleeping bags or blankets lay bathed in the eerie light of the out there and saw that the price of a Carl's Jr. Memphis BBQ burger was just $3.49.

ELEVEN

BY MID-MORNING ORC was on the move. He had decided once and for all he would go into hiding. There was forest off to the west somewhere. Dark trees and good places to hide. Astrid had told him about being there, about wild berries but with thorns all around them—oh, he was hungry. And how she had laid traps for squirrels and things. But mostly about berries. Thorns didn't bother Orc.

That was where she had lost God, out in the forest for four months alone. She said that, anyway, so Orc was worried a little. Since finding God he had become a better person. He didn't drink anymore. And he didn't hurt anyone. And he wasn't angry inside like he'd been all his life.

Well, angry a little, still. He missed Howard. He could see now that Howard had used him. And Howard was a sinner, too, that was for sure. But Howard had still been his friend. Not his good friend, maybe, but his close friend.

Howard had been killed by Drake. And eaten up by coyotes.

Once, he'd read a story in the Bible about a woman who was eaten by wild dogs. There was some bad stuff in that book.

But Orc was not afraid of coyotes.

He planted huge, bare, stony feet on rock and dirt and thorny brush and none of it mattered. He just wanted to find a place, like Astrid had found, where he could be alone. In the wilderness.

Once, Jesus had gone into the wilderness. He had talked to the devil there and outsmarted the devil by making the devil get behind him.

It's a metaphor, you idiot, Howard had said once when Orc had read it to him. *Or a whatever. A simile. Something like that, I forget. What it means is if someone is trying to get you to do something bad you say, "Get away. Get thee behind me, dude."*

Orc had grinned. Well, he had tried to grin, which usually scared people. And he'd said, *I guess I better tell you to get behind, huh, Howard?*

Howard had had a nice way, sometimes, of kind of cocking his head and looking up at Orc and smiling with just half his mouth. *I'm always behind you, big guy,* he had said.

It made Orc almost cry, remembering.

Anyway, his own Satan, who was also his only friend, was gone, and now Orc was alone.

He looked up and thought of the day ahead and was

not afraid. Whatever bad stuff was ever going to happen to Charles Merriman had already happened. Probably. And anyway, there were bigger hands even than his own gravel hands, and it was those big hands that held his fate.

"Berries and thorns," Orc said to himself, trying to picture what Astrid had told him.

Quinn had spent the night on the island. He ate cheese— actual cheese that Albert's careful survey of the house had found in a special cheese-aging room. It had apparently never occurred to Caine and Diana, or to Sanjit before them, to look for cellars and subcellars, but Albert, being Albert, had located and cataloged everything of any use in the mansion, and had done it all in just the few days he'd been there.

Quinn had to admit: it never would have occurred to him, either. The concept of a special cheese room was not part of his experience.

Someone had also been growing pot in a small, under-ground greenhouse, but it had all died off when the power was cut back.

In the morning Albert had Leslie-Ann and Pug help lower a massive wheel of Parmesan cheese in a net down to Quinn's boat. Alicia would be going back to the mainland with Albert, but Leslie-Ann and Pug would stay behind. Pug had been taught to fire the missiles and use a gun and had strict instructions to fire on anyone who was not Albert.

Anyone.

It took Albert a while to get ready. It was lunchtime when

they finally got moving—after crackers and peanut butter, lovely, lovely peanut butter. Quinn was trying hard not to regret the fact that it would now be back to the regular grind of work. It was a long, hard row back to town—harder since Albert and his giant cheese were dead weight and Albert clearly was not going to take a turn at the oars. Neither would the cheese.

Alicia rowed for a while, but she was almost more trouble than she was worth. In the end she just put her feet up on the cheese and added to the dead weight.

"The thing is," Albert said, "I did the logical thing with my business. Right?"

Albert was in an unusually talkative mood, which just annoyed Quinn. Generally when Quinn rowed, he slipped into a contemplative mood, often pondering the meaning of life, but also less overwhelming questions like *Star Trek* versus *Star Wars*, and why people would spend a fortune on some fancy car when any car would get you where you were going.

"I'm used to being criticized, everyone resenting me because I'm successful," Albert said. "It's probably inevitable."

And sometimes, despite himself, Quinn thought about Lana.

Those thoughts never ended well. The thing was, Quinn liked Sanjit. And he was glad that Lana was happy, or at least as happy as Lana could get.

"They don't really have a right to hate me, you know: it's not like I owe anyone anything. Actually, they owe me.

Without me they'd all have starved to death by now."

There had been a time when Quinn had thought he and Lana would end up . . . what, going out together? Hah. Those sorts of ideas were just strange in the FAYZ. "Hanging out." The phrase made Quinn smile. If they were getting out of here, he would have to adjust to a world where people hung out. A world where there wasn't really any such thing as a full-time job for a fourteen-year-old kid.

"If they'd all been reasonable instead of panicky and emotional, I wouldn't have had to offshore."

That finally penetrated Quinn's reverie. "You're going with 'offshoring'? Good luck. Some people might call it treason, or cowardice, or abandoning ship like a rat, but give 'offshoring' a try."

Albert waited until he was finished, then said, "Obviously none of it is my fault so long as I behaved in my own best interests."

"Douche."

"What?"

"I was coughing," Quinn muttered.

He looked up, avoiding Albert's suspicious gaze, and saw the same cabin cruiser he'd seen the day before. The captain didn't look in his direction.

They passed Quinn's outgoing crews and received some good-natured catcalls for Quinn—mostly on the theme of him shirking work. And there were some less good-natured remarks for Albert.

Edilio must have spotted them coming in, because he was

waiting on the dock to receive Albert like some kind of visiting celebrity.

Edilio reached down, took Albert's hand, and hauled him up onto the dock.

"I'm glad you could come, Albert," Edilio said, perfectly diplomatic. "We need your help."

"I'm not surprised," Albert said. "You want people back at work and you've already figured out that begging and reasoning don't work."

"Also threatening," Edilio said.

"You just used the wrong threat," Albert said. "I brought some paper and a Sharpie. I need a stick. No, make it several sticks."

Half an hour later, Albert marched to the barrier with Edilio in tow. It was now a rather desperate-looking encampment. At least a hundred kids, all filthy and bedraggled, sat staring out. Out at parents, out at siblings, out at the Carl's Jr. just a block away, out at TV monitors, out at news reporters trying to interview them. It was like some kind of desperate refugee camp, except all that seemed to separate the well-fed, even overfed, people from the starving people was basically a sheet of glass.

No one had bothered to even dig a slit trench, so the entire place stank of urine and human excrement.

Albert focused on the largest cluster of TV cameras. With Edilio carrying half a dozen signs stapled to wooden poles, Albert strode purposefully to a slight rise, unceremoniously chased off the kids sitting there. He swung a backpack off his shoulders and opened it.

"Attention! Attention, everyone! I have cheese!"

Then he began throwing chunks of Parmesan cheese out into the crowd.

The result was instant pandemonium. Desperately hungry kids rushed for the cheese, pushed, shoved, shouted, threatened, waved weapons, beat, kicked, clawed, cried, and cried some more. And as soon as any of them had a hand on some morsel of cheese, they began to stuff it into their mouths like hyenas rushing to eat a wildebeest before the lion came back.

"I'm going to—" Edilio began.

Albert cut him off. "No! Do nothing!"

Then, as the cheese ran out and the riot calmed, and kids were left to stanch the flow of bloody noses, Albert began setting up his signs, one by one.

The first one read:

These kids are going to starve if they sit here watching you.

The second one read:

They need to get back to work. If you keep them here, they will die.

The third one read:

I can feed them if they work. Go away or stay and watch them die.

The fourth:

You can visit from 5 p.m. to 8 p.m. daily. Now leave.

The last sign read:

Alberco: Feeding your kids. Albert Hillsborough, CEO.

To the stunned and now bruised and bloodied crowd of kids Albert said, "I'm going to make this simple. I'm shutting Quinn down, so no more fish. You just had the last food you get unless you get back to work. Everyone will resume their old jobs. If you've come here from the lake, either go back to the lake or see me for a work assignment."

It would work right now, Albert thought, or it wouldn't work ever.

A single voice muttered something about Albert trying to push everyone around. Albert ignored it.

"Now, wave good-bye to your families or whatever, and let's get back to work."

Kids started to move. A few at first, then more. Some of those on the outside, some of the parents and siblings, started to retreat tearfully.

The TV cameras did not retreat. Instead they swiveled toward Albert. Albert looked impressive. He wasn't a big kid, he was still a bit of a shrimp, but he was wearing clean and pressed khakis and a somewhat too large, pink, immaculate Ralph Lauren button-down shirt.

Albert pulled a six-inch-long tube from his pocket, unscrewed one end, and tapped out a fat cigar. Among the things he had discovered on the island was a humidor. He used a small chrome blade to snip one end of the cigar, stuck it in his mouth, lit it with a matching cigar torch, and puffed out a cloud of smoke.

Albert knew two things at that moment. First, that his signs, and the image of him right now, standing as tall as he could and playing the role of arrogant businessman, would be on every newscast in the world.

And second, he knew that from this moment forward his recent error would be forgotten and if he lived to get out of the FAYZ he would be a millionaire before he even went to college.

"You did the right thing sending for me, Edilio," Albert said.

Edilio sighed.

Along with many other things from the old days, bikes had become a luxury in the FAYZ. Many had been destroyed out of sheer vandalism or stupidity—attempting the kinds of stunts that were harder to do with adults around, such as riding down the steps of the town hall or setting up a ramp to jump over a car.

Dahra had helped some of the kids who'd tried that last one. And at least one kid who had tried to ride a bike through a window. And another who'd thought he could ride a bike off his roof. Lana had refused to heal them at first on grounds that they were idiots.

And there had been blown tires, broken chains, all the mishaps that occurred, along with parts being stolen and bikes being repurposed to make wheelbarrows. So Dahra's own bike—a relic of better days that she had kept hidden underneath a tarp in her garage—was a rarity. It had been kept in one piece. But the tires had long since gone flat and Dahra had wasted much of the day before looking for a pump before finally finding one in a neighbor's garage. She was concerned that she was now too late and Astrid would miss meeting Connie Temple. But hey, this was the FAYZ, this was not the world where all you had to do to get someplace was nag your parents into driving you. She would do her best. That's all she could do.

There had been times in the history of the FAYZ when she would have expected to be set upon by gangs or by coyotes as she rode out of town, but at the moment most of the population was up against the barrier and not paying much attention. And most people thought the coyotes had been finished off by Brianna anyway.

The highway was an eerie graveyard of cars wrecked at the moment the FAYZ occurred, and of course others that had been vandalized or burned out since. Every single one had been broken into by kids searching for food or drugs or alcohol. The batteries were all long since dead, gas tanks evaporated or drained off.

Dahra weaved her way through the wrecks and around debris and drifting trash. From Perdido Beach to the lake was just about the maximum distance you could go in the FAYZ. A full day's walk for sure, but not quite as bad by bike, although sticking to the roads made it less direct.

She passed the turnoff to the power plant, the center point of the FAYZ and more or less the halfway mark for her. The Santa Katrina hills rose off to the right, shadowed by the rising sun, and now she had to choose which road to take. The nearest was gravel and dirt, which would be hard with a bike.

If she rode on into the Stefano Rey National Park she'd find a better-paved but steeper road—at least that's what kids said; Dahra had never been. The wooded part would be shadier, too, and that sounded good. It was hot and she was out of shape. She had spent most of the last year in the basement of the town hall, down in the so-called hospital, reading medical books and doling out the dwindling supply of medicine.

She had taught herself to bandage, to attach splints, to suture wounds—Lana wasn't always available. And she had with great misgiving taken on a bit of dentistry. At least as much dentistry as could be accomplished with a pair of needle-nose pliers and a small vise grip.

Well, maybe if they ever got out she could look into medical school. Of course, first she'd have to go back to being a kid. Three more years of high school, then college, and then medical school, maybe.

She had "spoken" with her mom at the barrier. Her mother had wondered if she was keeping up with her school subjects. How were you supposed to even answer a question like that? She hadn't slept a full night since . . . forever. She had been up just about every night of the last year applying cold compresses to bring down fevers, holding puke buckets, wiping up diarrhea . . . until the great plagues had come, the killing cough and the murderous insect infestation.

That had broken her. For a while. But she had come back. Yes, she had.

Dahra rested, drank some water, wished she had some food, told herself they'd feed her at the lake, and rode on.

The sign for the Stefano Rey was still in place. Not enough people got up this way to properly vandalize it, like every other sign had been. There was even an unvandalized stop sign, a rarity in the FAYZ, where bored kids with spray paint had painted suggestions for just what you should stop: breathing, wetting yourself, and things a bit cruder.

Why was she doing this? Dahra asked herself. She was taking a risk, why? Because she hadn't before? Because she'd stayed out of the battles, out of the wars, except to tend the wounded? Because she wanted, just once, to play the hero and not the person who bandaged the hero?

Stupid.

It was cool under the trees, but the steepness of the road soon brought back the sweat. She—

She hit the branch before she saw it. The bike yanked out from under her, and Dahra went flying. She hit the pavement hard, facedown, hands too slow to cushion more than a little of the impact.

Dahra lay there, stunned, panting into the blacktop. She tasted blood. Gingerly she checked her extremities. Legs moved. So did her arms. Her palms and knees were bloody but not broken; that was a relief. Her jaw felt funny, like it was off center, but it moved okay. She climbed slowly and only then felt the stab of pain in her ankle. She tested it, and yes, oh, definitely, it hurt.

The bike's front tire was no longer round. It wasn't going to be any use—not that she could have ridden it with a sprained ankle.

She fought down the panic. She was still at least four miles as the crow flies, more like five in reality, from the lake. That was a long way to hop on one leg.

She glanced around for a stick to use as a crutch. "You'd think there would be more sticks in a forest," she said aloud, wishing the sound of her voice made her feel braver instead of emphasizing her aloneness. Her abrasions stung, and she'd have liked to wash the wounds at least, although she doubted there were too many terrible bacteria living on the surface of the road.

"You'll be okay," she told herself.

The dark trees and her own inner voice said otherwise.

She had felt it when she'd panicked, when she'd broken down in the aftermath of the plagues. When the plagues hadn't killed her, she had felt then as if she had used up the last of her luck. Yet now she had tempted fate again, and now, with the end of the FAYZ perhaps in sight, here she was.

Why?

"Just to deliver a message?" Dahra asked herself, bewildered.

She sat by the side of the road and cried.

TWELVE

GAIA HAD SLEPT in, seeming to both age and heal while asleep. She had gone to sleep still burned and perhaps seven or eight years old, and had awakened healed and closer to ten.

Diana had not tried to wake her.

Let sleeping monsters lie.

Alex had raved through much of the long night, had awakened several times after sunrise to cry out in pain, and then had fallen back into a restless, disturbed sleep.

Diana had tried not to look at the cooked arm, now mostly eaten but not entirely, which lay by the softly snoring Gaia.

Finally, with the sun already past its peak, Gaia had snapped awake, stood up without preamble, and stepped behind a tree to take care of necessary business. Then she had eaten the rest of the arm, down to bare bone, while Alex watched in some disturbing mix of awe and horror and hatred.

He's going off the deep end, Diana thought. She could see it in his eyes. Too much, too fast.

"I'm hungry," Gaia said. "Growing this body at an accelerated rate demands a lot of nutrition."

"Gaia, no," Diana said.

Alex made a gurgling sound and tried to run. Gaia raised a finger, and he found himself running in place, feet slipping helplessly on stony earth. "I have a . . . I . . . Wait! Wait! I have a granola bar!"

"What is a granola bar?" Gaia asked.

"It's food! Food!" Alex cried. He let the backpack slip from his intact shoulder.

The mere mention of a granola bar made Diana's mouth water. Hunger pains stabbed at her insides. If Gaia took Alex's other arm, she would let Diana have the granola bar.

Take it, kill him, eat him; I don't care.

Diana lifted the pack. It was small, more a runner's pack than anything meant for camping. She spilled it out on the ground. A small tube of lotion. A knife. A water bottle. An iPhone with headphones and some sort of solar charger. The granola bar. A map.

Gaia moved in. "Which is the food?"

Diana stared at the bar. Unimaginable luxury in the FAYZ. Oats and raisins and dates, it brought tears to her eyes. All she had to do was say, "Take *him*!" and the bar would be hers.

"There it is! Eat it!" Alex cried.

Gaia stooped, picked it up, frowned at it, and finally realized it was meant to be unwrapped. She ate it like Cookie Monster scarfing a chocolate chip cookie.

Diana breathed. Decision made.

"What is that?" Gaia pointed at the iPhone.

"It's his cell phone," Diana said. "They don't work in here."

"I've got my tunes on there," Alex said eagerly. "Want to hear some, Gaia? Do you want to hear some music?"

"Music," Gaia said. "What is it?"

"See, you listen to it. You stick the white things in your . . ." He had grabbed the headphones with his remaining hand and was trying to proffer them to Gaia.

Gaia took them.

"Gaia, I know how to get to the lake from here," Diana said. "I can get you food there." *And some for myself.*

Gaia laughed as she toyed with the white earbuds. "Once we go to the lake we'll have plenty to eat."

"You're going . . . I mean, wait," Diana said, confused. "You're going to the lake? I mean, we're deliberately going there?"

"Of course, stupid Diana," Gaia said. Her blue eyes were merry. "Once it's dark. How else can I kill them all?"

"Kill them all?" Diana echoed blankly.

"Any human that *Nemesis* can use. I thought that was obvious, Diana. I can't allow *Nemesis* to find a host; do you know how powerful he would be? No, he must die. First the people at the lake. It will be easier. Then Perdido Beach. There are many hiding places in Perdido Beach. I know." She nodded smugly. "How many humans are alive in this small universe of ours?"

"Gaia, you can't—"

Diana felt herself slammed to the ground, hard enough to

knock the wind out of her. Then she was hurled straight up into the air, flying, arms windmilling, screaming in terror.

She began to drop. The drop onto hard stone would surely kill her.

Please, yes, let me die.

But Gaia stopped her fall just two feet from impact. Gaia's child's face was twisted into a sneer. "Don't tell me what I can't do, Mother."

She let Diana go so that she would fall the last two feet.

"See, she's the one causing trouble," Alex cried, pointing at Diana with his one hand. Spittle flew from his lips. His eyes were wild. "Eat her! Eat her! Hah hah hah! Yeah!"

Diana wasn't even offended. The red-haired man was traumatized. He'd fallen into a nightmare, unprepared. His eyes were rimmed in red. Madness was moving in to claim him.

Wait until he's hungry enough that the smell of his own cooked flesh begins to . . .

Gaia laughed. It was a jarring sound, strange and out of place. "You don't want to feed your god?" she asked Alex. She moved close to him, and as he recoiled in fear she took him by his ear and drew him close. It was an act of pure sadism, Diana realized. Gaia wasn't simply ruthless; she enjoyed causing fear. Gaia whispered to Alex, "You have hope still. You think you might escape me. Stupid man. Don't you understand? You only live to feed me. You have to *hope* you can feed me. Beg to feed me. Because when you can't, you die."

Alex shook so badly he fell to his knees. Urine stained his pants.

Gaia laughed, delightedly. "See?" she asked Diana. "Now he worships me on his knees."

"Are you killing them all or humiliating them?" Diana asked bitterly.

"Can't I do both?"

"Why do you need to do this, Gaia? What . . . Just, why? Why?"

Gaia was suddenly matter-of-fact, businesslike. "Nemesis may take a body for himself. And then where will I be? I need Nemesis to die, Diana. When he dies, the barrier will fall. When he dies, I will be free to emerge. I am ready. I am seeing this place and realizing that it is small. Look at the world out there." She waved her arm grandly toward the transparent barrier, toward the desert beyond. "It goes on and on, doesn't it? How big is it, Diana?"

"What, the whole country? Earth?"

"All of it. Is the earth all of it? Then the earth. How big is the earth?"

Diana shrugged. "I don't know. I'm not exactly honor roll. Astrid would know, down to the mile, I'm sure."

Gaia turned to her, eyes lit with excitement. "But it's big. How many humans?"

"Billions."

That seemed to take Gaia aback. Her mouth dropped open.

"Even you can't kill them all," Diana said, enjoying Gaia's look of consternation.

But Gaia had absorbed the new information. "I won't need to kill billions, Diana. When Nemesis is gone, there will be

no other like me. Just me alone. I will grow and spread, one
body and then another, and soon there will be so many of me
that it will be impossible to eradicate me. Eventually all will
be me, and I will be all."

"Won't that be boring?" Diana asked. "You'd be dating
yourself. You'll have no one to discuss your evil plans with.
No one left to terrorize."

Gaia nodded thoughtfully. "Yes. Yes, you make sense. I
will leave some free so that I can teach them fear and pain."

Diana stared at her, seeing not the fast-growing girl but the
monster beneath. Only now did she truly understand. How
had she not realized it before? The sadism. The game playing.
The irrational fears and grandiose visions of godhood.

Diana had seen enough of it in the FAYZ; how had she not
seen it in this creature? Madness. Lunacy.

The gaiaphage was insane.

Gaia was going to kill everyone: that was her plan. Kill the
good and the bad, all of them. Diana grasped the truth of it
now. That was Gaia's mad endgame. The gaiaphage couldn't
allow Little Pete to find a body and survive, and that meant
killing every living person in the FAYZ.

And it wouldn't be a simple act of survival. She would
enjoy it. She would enjoy watching people run from her. She
would enjoy hunting them down and killing them. Gaia
wasn't ruthless and self-serving like Caine; she was evil, like
Drake. A psychopath. A mad and terrible beast.

For some reason Diana's mind went to Orc. Not a regular
kid by any stretch. He'd been a bully, a thug, a drunk, and a

killer. Then he'd been a penitent. Like Diana he had come to regret what he'd done. He had irritated her with his Bible reading and his endless questions, but he had found a way to redemption.

Could Orc's life story simply end in Gaia's flames, just to feed Gaia's psychotic ego?

Sinder, who was so devoted to her garden.

Dahra, who had worked herself into a breakdown caring for sick kids.

Computer Jack? He'd been confused and aimless, and in her time Diana had used and manipulated him, but to actually die? To be killed by this . . . this abomination?

Astrid, that sanctimonious bitch . . . and Brianna, who Diana had actually come to like. And Dekka, who had never liked Diana but had forgiven her in her own snarling way. And Lana.

And Caine.

Yes, above all, Caine.

All their battles, hers and Caine's, all their rages? All of it to end in death so this evil creature could walk out to trouble the wider world?

She remembered the touch of Caine's skin on hers. Who would have guessed that egomaniacal, power-mad Caine would have such a gentle kiss?

Yeah, and that worked out so well. Pregnant with a mutant child who was sacrificed at the moment of her birth to the needs of the gaiaphage.

It wasn't like Caine could ever walk free from the FAYZ,

Diana knew that. He was a criminal ten times over, a rotten, charming, worthless sociopath, and they would lock him up.

And she would visit him and make fun of him behind the security glass at the prison. And then she would wait for him. Years, if necessary. All her years, if necessary.

You make bad choices, Diana, she told herself. *So: one more won't be a shock.*

At that moment Diana felt a change in herself. It surprised her. At some level she had, like Alex, held on to hope: she had somehow still wanted to believe that this was her daughter, that she was a mother, that . . .

But this was no little girl. This was a beast with a pretty face and beautiful blue eyes.

Gaia had let the earbuds and the phone fall as Alex wept and whimpered and implored her. Diana picked them up off the ground.

"Music," Diana said through gritted teeth.

"Music?" Gaia said, confused.

"You wouldn't like it, Gaia. It's only for humans."

Gaia knew a lot of things. She did not know about child psychology.

"I *will* hear it!"

It would be close to dark by the time they reached the lake. Diana didn't think much of her chances: what she was thinking of doing was hopeless, futile, and certainly stupid. But what the hell, was there really anything left for her to lose?

Wasn't there an old song that went "Freedom's just another word for nothing left to lose"?

Gaia was fumbling with the earbuds now, frowning as she mimicked what Diana showed her.

And, to her own dark, private amusement, Diana was planning to play hero.

Many hours had passed, night was falling, and Dahra had managed to hobble maybe three hundred yards. It was painful work. Her hands were bloody from the bike crash, and she kept tripping and landing on them again, leaving red handprints on the road behind her.

Maybe, she thought, the barrier would come down and there would suddenly be cars driving down this road. If so, it had better happen fast. Night came dark and intense in the forest. She could barely make out the tree trunks on either side of the road. Looking up, she could see that the sky was the darkest possible blue before going black. Far up above and well off to the east she saw the blinking lights of a passenger jet. A plane full of people, regular people, not captives of the FAYZ, on their merry way from San Francisco to Los Angeles.

Ladies and gentlemen, if you look out the right side of the aircraft, you can see the Perdido Beach Anomaly.

Maybe if it all did come to an end, there would be tours of the former FAYZ. *And here is where Dahra Baidoo starved to death by the side of the road.*

That made her start to cry again. What had she done to deserve—movement! She raised her head, and there, not twenty feet away, stood a coyote. Its head was low. Its eyes glittered in the gloom. It was bedraggled, filthy, skin and bones. Dahra knew that Brianna had played grim reaper to the coyote population, chasing them down one by one. After the terrible coyote attack on panicked kids just south of the lake Sam had made it part of Brianna's job to eliminate the mutant canines once and for all.

But here was one who was not dead.

The coyote sniffed the air, ears cocking this way and that, on the alert for the sudden death brought by the Breeze. It was nervous, but it was more hungry.

"Go away!" Dahra yelled. "The Breeze is coming to meet me. She'll be here any second!"

The coyote didn't buy it. "Not here," it said in its strangle, glottal voice. It advanced, still cautious. Saliva dripped from its muzzle.

An awful terror took Dahra then. The coyote wouldn't just kill her; it would eat her. It would eat her alive, and she would watch it happen until blood loss deprived her of consciousness. She knew. She had heard the stories; she had seen the bloody, mangled survivors dragged into the so-called hospital to await salvation at Lana's hands.

She began to pray. *Oh, God, save me. Oh, God, hear me and save me.*

Then, aloud, she said, "Kill me first. Kill me before you . . . before . . ."

Oh, God, don't let him . . .

The coyote closed to within two feet. His nostrils were filling with the scent of her; his mouth was foaming in anticipation.

"No," she whispered. "No, God, no."

The coyote froze. Its ears swiveled to the right. It hunched low, and now Dahra could hear it, too, a slow crashing of underbrush and fallen leaves.

"Help! Help!" she cried, having no idea who or what might be in those woods, only knowing that whatever it was, the coyote didn't like it.

The coyote made a low growl.

The crashing sound came closer, and with a furious, frustrated whine the coyote trotted away.

"Help me!" Dahra cried.

At first she couldn't make sense of what she was seeing in the shadows. It looked like a person, but built on too thick a scale, with outlines all blurred and indistinct. Then she recognized him and almost fainted with relief.

"Orc!"

Orc easily climbed the incline up to the road, then squatted beside her.

"Dahra? What are you doing here?"

"Praying for you to show up," she gasped.

Orc couldn't make much of a smile; it was only the human part of his mouth that could do that. "You prayed to God? Like in the Bible?"

Dahra was about to say she would happily have prayed to any and all gods and the devil, too, but she stopped herself and instead said, "Yes, Orc. Just like in the Bible."

"And he sent me." This seemed to give Orc great satisfaction. His huge chest swelled. "He sent me!"

"I crashed my bike. One leg is twisted. Can you help me get to the lake?"

"Shouldn't you go see Lana?"

"Lake first, if you don't mind. I have an important message to deliver. I have to talk to Astrid."

Orc nodded. "Be sure and tell her God saved you. He brought me here, just to save you. Maybe then Astrid will . . . Anyway, I can carry you."

He lifted her up like she was a doll. He had always terrified her. He was as strange as if he was from another planet.

But she felt safe in his arms.

He chuckled to himself, giddy, as he carried her.

THIRTEEN

40 HOURS, 3 MINUTES

FOR ASTRID IT was another night apart from Sam. How quickly his presence had become necessary to her. Sam in her bed: an addiction that had swiftly taken hold. Fifteen years of sleeping alone now seemed like it had involved some other person entirely. Hadn't she always had him beside her? Hadn't she always awakened to his touch?

Astrid was trying to think. And not about Sam. But she was in the cabin she shared with Sam, and everything about the place reminded her of him.

She was also not trying to think about the fact that Drake's head was in a cooler twenty feet below her at the bottom of the lake.

Heavy tread on the dock, followed by someone large and very heavy stepping onto the boat. Astrid snatched up her shotgun and headed out. One of Edilio's guards should have challenged the intruder. She heard the sound of someone peeing—that would be the guard.

With shotgun leveled Astrid went the length of the passageway, then carefully climbed the steps out onto the deck. She found her sights aiming at Dahra Baidoo, improbably in the arms of Orc.

"Don't shoot," Dahra said through gritted teeth.

"God sent me to save her!" Orc blurted.

"What happened to you?" Astrid asked, setting her gun aside and helping Orc lower Dahra onto the padded bench.

"I was coming to see you, riding my bike," Dahra said. "Twisted ankle."

"Your ankle is three times its normal size," Astrid observed.

"Yes, Astrid, I noticed that," Dahra said. Sarcasm was not usually in Dahra's repertoire, but Astrid could hardly blame her.

"What can I do to help you?"

"Get me to Lana as soon as I tell you what I came here to tell you," Dahra said.

"Maybe I can have you driven down," Astrid said, wondering if this was enough of a justification for using some of their dwindling gas supply. If so, she'd have to make the trip useful in some other way as well. Maybe she could go to Perdido Beach . . . see if Sam was around . . .

"What is it you have to tell me?" Astrid asked.

"Food," Dahra said. "First, something to eat."

"Well, since you're injured, I can give you a Cup-a-Noodles. I guess you can each have one."

Heating the water for the noodles—there was a small hibachi on deck and a few dry twigs—took some time, and while the water was heating Dahra relented and told her tale.

"Sam's mother, Connie Temple, I ran into her at the barrier. She wants to talk to you."

"To me?" Astrid frowned. Was this about her relationship with Sam?

"She says things are getting very nasty outside. Out in the world. And she's right, by the way. I saw a sign that said 'Kill Them All, Let God Sort Them Out.'"

"That is not Christian," Orc huffed.

"No, it isn't," Astrid said dryly.

"I guess Nurse Temple wanted someone to talk to about it. Sam was gone, Edilio is busy, so it was you, Astrid."

"Third choice?"

Dahra shrugged, but the motion made her wince. "She'll meet you at the barrier. Probably thought it would be earlier, sorry, slightly delayed." She was talking through gasps of pain. "Tomorrow maybe, right? You'll need paper or something. You know, to communicate."

Astrid thought about it. "Thanks, Dahra. And thank you, Orc."

"It wasn't me," he said solemnly, and pointed one thick finger upward. "Maybe he has a use for me. You know? Like a plan."

Astrid smiled at him. "You have become one of the good guys, Orc. If there was ever an example of redemption, it's you."

She hesitated only a moment out of fear of touching him, but then gave him a hug. How strange he felt. How alien.

Orc seemed too overcome to say anything. Which was nice, Astrid thought as she drew back, but her thoughts moved quickly on to what she and Sam had been calling the endgame. It wasn't enough to survive a war: you had to plan for the aftermath.

She was pleased Connie Temple was reaching out to her. Getting ready for the aftermath was possibly the most important thing left to do. It was something Astrid could handle very well, she thought.

Gaia was singing. She wasn't singing well—her voice was thin and reedy and she had no experience of music—but with the earbuds in she was singing.

She was singing "Mainlining Murder" by Lars Frederiksen and the Bastards.

"Great playlist you've got there, Mr. Alex," Diana said.

They were just beyond a low hill, very near the lake. They had a small twig-and-branch fire going, lit easily by Gaia. Diana had suggested it, hoping the light would be seen from the lake. Hoping that Sam was even now planning a surprise attack that would end this.

Gaia was staring into that fire and singing: "Mainlining Murder" followed incongruously by "Girls Just Want to Have Fun." If she was at all concerned by the proximity of the lake settlement, she showed no sign of it.

"Is that the Miley Cyrus version or the original Cyndi Lauper?" Diana asked Alex. He didn't seem to know. He was not in a talkative mood; at least, he was not talking to her. He muttered unintelligibly sometimes, and had taken to mumbling, "Melted, man. Melted." Whatever that meant in crazy town, where Alex had apparently taken up residence.

Diana was hoping he would pass out or fall asleep. She didn't trust him: he could easily rat her out to curry favor with Gaia.

Diana had seen people break before, just collapse, lose it. But never this quickly. Was he already a mess before he ventured into this particular level of hell? Was he already fragile? Or was it that he was an adult?

She pondered this for a moment. People always said kids were resilient, so obviously adults were less so. She wondered how much differently things would have gone if it had been three-hundred-plus adults trapped in the FAYZ with the gaiaphage and dangerous mutants—human and nonhuman.

But now she was stalling. She had to act before Gaia could. She was convinced Gaia was just waiting to attack until the sky was completely dark, and it was dark.

Enough. Time was up.

Time to die, most likely.

Oh, well. Bad decisions. My secret power: bad decisions.

"I have to go pee," Diana said through a tense, clenched jaw. She heaved herself up, knees popping, muscles aching, and scabs stretching with the effort.

Gaia didn't even glance up, and Diana realized her eyes were closed. Somehow she looked less . . . well, evil, with her eyes closed. She could almost be asleep except for the fact that she was back to singing about murder. Or rapping, maybe.

Diana walked away with all the nonchalance she could manage. She was stiff-legged, but she was always stiff now. Nothing new.

Gaia didn't seem to even notice, and Diana was most afraid Alex would take this as a sign that he, too, could walk away. That would ruin everything. But the man was busy pretending to enjoy Gaia's singing, obviously in the ridiculous belief that Gaia would like him. And muttering, "Melting, melting."

Poor one-armed fool, Diana thought. *Pray Gaia doesn't get hungry again. Or bored. Or just wants to see you scream.*

They were in an area of low, rolling hills. Boulders jabbed up out of the hard dirt. Desiccated grass edged up to small stands of nearly dead, stunted trees. Diana knew the area: Sinder's garden was just over the hill. The lake was not a quarter mile away.

As soon as she was out of sight she started to run. The moon—the actual moon, not the simulation they'd seen back in the old days—had just risen, and its light was faint. She stumbled, tripped, but kept running. It hurt each time she fell, but Diana had endured worse, far worse. And she ran now hoping, believing, that Sam and Dekka and Brianna and maybe enough force to fight off Gaia were just over the next hill.

Sam liked her; he'd been kind to her; he could save her. She had to believe that. Absent Caine to play knight in shining armor, Sam could save her.

She heard her own feet on sand. She heard her own gasping breath. She felt the heart pounding in her chest. Running brought hope, and hope was a cruel trick, but she ran anyway.

She spotted a human silhouette and ran to it.

"Hey, who's there?" a young voice cried out.

"It's Diana," she said, not yelling, but urgent. "Keep it down!"

"Show me who you are!"

She forced herself to slow—not much point in getting shot by her rescuers—and waited until the boy recognized her. She did not recognize him, but she'd never made a lot of friends at the lake.

"Listen, kid, do you have some way to sound an alarm?"

"What?"

"Don't 'what' me!" she snapped. "Do you have a way to sound an alarm?"

"I'm supposed to fire in the air."

"No, she'll hear that. Come on, let's run! Run!"

Her fear was contagious, and the nameless boy set off after her, his automatic rifle banging against his back. Ahead were the lights of the lake, just a few pitiful candles, a few faintly illuminated trailer windows and boat portholes.

"What's happening?" the boy asked, breathless behind her.

"The devil's on her way," Diana said. She glanced back: still no pursuit. Of course when Gaia came she'd be a whirlwind with Brianna's speed. Diana wouldn't even have a warning.

She pelted into the settlement, which was a dozen or so trailers and motor homes, some bedraggled tents, a few boats at the dock, and a few more boats anchored out in the water.

Diana had lived here for a while; she knew her way around.

She ran onto the houseboat and yelled, "Sam! Sam!"

Silence.

"Sam's gone," the out-of-breath guard said.

"*What?*"

"He's gone to Perdido Beach."

Diana felt like she'd been kicked in the stomach. Without Sam there was zero chance of beating Gaia.

Ah, hope: you tricked me again.

Dekka came running down the dock. "What's going on?"

"Dekka! Thank God. Gaia is just over the hill. Listen to me: she's going to kill everyone."

Dekka stared. Diana thought it was as close as she'd ever come to looking truly frightened. Then to the guard, Dekka said, "Get Jack. Right now!"

"Who else is here?" Diana demanded.

"That can do any damage in a fight? Me and Jack. Breeze may have come back. Breeze! Breeze! If you're down there, wake up!" Nothing. "She may be asleep down below, but she went out on patrol earlier, I think. Breeze!"

Someone very large was climbing up from below, and Diana was relieved to see the mudslide that was Orc's head.

"Orc!" Dekka said. "Thank God you're here! Is Breeze down there?"

Orc shook his head. "But I am because the Lord sent me."

"Glad to have you however you got here." Dekka grabbed Diana's arm. "What powers does she have? What can Gaia do?"

"She says she has everyone's powers. But if you die, she loses that power. That's why she didn't take on Sam and

Caine. She'll kill the moofs last."

"Why is she . . . Everyone? Never mind. Where is Astrid?"

"She was in the outhouse. Here she comes," Orc said.

Astrid and Jack were running toward the boat with the guard leading the way. "Gaia may be here any second," Dekka explained quickly. She repeated what Diana had told her.

"We have to evacuate into the boats," Astrid said.

"We can fight!" Dekka said. "Me, Jack, Orc, we can take her on!"

"Fine, but the rest have to get on the water. That's the plan," Astrid said coolly.

Dekka nodded and ordered the guard to run and ring the alarm bell.

"No!" Diana cried. "Quietly! If she hears anything . . ."

"You're right."

Into the boats, out into the water. Once, they had defeated a determined attack by Drake using that simple tactic. The water was their defense.

"Dahra's downstairs, injured," Astrid said. "She can't run. Dekka?"

"The three of us, Jack and Orc and I, need to get between Gaia and the lake. If we head up onto the ridge, top of the bluff there—"

"Agreed," Astrid said, cutting her off.

"I wish Sam was here," Diana muttered.

"We all do," Astrid snapped, "but this is what we've got. Dekka, Jack, Orc. That's a start."

"No," Jack said.

"No what?" Dekka asked, honestly confused.

"I'm not fighting. Don't you know what happened to me the last time? I nearly died!"

"You'll die for sure if you don't fight," Diana said. "Listen to me: This is the gaiaphage. It's going to kill anything with a human body that might act as a host for Little Pete."

Astrid's eyebrow shot up. "Interesting."

"Really, Mrs. Spock? Not *fascinating*?" Diana made a strangled noise of frustration. "Does anyone have any food? If I'm going to die, I'd like to eat first."

"I'm not fighting," Jack said stubbornly. "Just because I'm strong doesn't mean I'm a fighter."

"You'll fight or die, most likely both," Diana said. "Do you not get what you're dealing with here?"

But Jack shook his head. So much for the resilience of youth, Diana thought. He's as broken as Alex.

"Let's get the houseboat started up and cast off," Astrid said. "Dekka? Orc? Good luck. Jack, you can at least help people get to the boats."

Diana felt Astrid's fingers wrapped around her bicep and realized she was being pulled away. Everyone else was running to their assigned tasks, but Astrid led Diana to the railing and looked hard into her eyes. "Keep your mouth shut about the powers. And about Petey."

"What are you grabbing me for? Get off me!"

Astrid released her but leaned in even closer. "That information? That gets Sam killed. It gets Caine killed, too. You understand me?"

Kids were already streaming out of their motor homes and tents, racing to cram onto the boats. Boats moored farther out saw that there was an evacuation under way and fired up engines or dipped oars to come in and pick up their friends.

The evacuation had been practiced many times, thanks to Edilio's persistence. It was working.

And then, in a blaze of swift-moving light that practically flew over the hills: Gaia.

FOURTEEN
39 HOURS, 40 MINUTES

TWIN BEAMS OF green light, so bright you couldn't look at them, swept from right to left, from a motor home that burst instantly into flame to a tent near the dock that seemed to simply disappear in the heat.

"Jump!" Astrid yelled, and took her own advice.

Orc saw what was happening, flashed on Dahra, and dived down the steps. Dahra was up, hobbling, and he just had time to wonder how he could turn around with her in his arms in the narrow passageway when the houseboat blew up.

It did not burn; it blew up.

Orc was thrown against a bulkhead, which dissolved before he hit it. Fire was everywhere and, an instant later, water. He sucked in a lungful, gagged, and vomited into the lake.

He windmilled his hands and legs, fending off debris from every direction—shattered plywood, a toilet, blankets and bits of clothing like poltergeists floating and swirling and tangling. The only light was the yellow of the fire that now burned directly above him.

He looked frantically around, searching for Dahra, but nothing. His lungs burning, he kicked his massive legs and only then realized: gravel is much heavier than flesh.

Orc sank toward the lake bottom. Air bubbles rose from the thousands of crevices in his body.

Below him he saw a picnic cooler, bound with chain, and wondered what it was. And whether it mattered. And whether he was truly, finally, going to be comforted by God's staff.

Dahra never knew what was happening. She heard noises and agitated voices up above. It all sounded important, so she climbed painfully out of the bunk Astrid had let her use. Then she saw Orc coming toward her in a rush.

And then she was torn apart by the explosion.

Diana and Astrid had already hit the water.

When Astrid clawed her way back to air, she saw Diana in the water beside her, facedown, seemingly unconscious. Three quick strokes and Astrid was beside Diana. She twisted her around and tilted her head back to face up toward the sky.

Diana coughed water and opened her dark eyes, reflecting moonlight outshone by sudden green lasers.

Fifty feet away a sailboat at anchor did not explode—there was no fuel on board. It just erupted in a ball of fire that ran from stem to stern and swirled up around the mast. It seemed to burn it to the waterline in seconds.

"Dekka! Jack!" Astrid yelled. "Orc!"

Dekka dropped from the sky, sinking down through a waterspout. She had suspended gravity and risen above the explosion, but the flames had singed her shoes and jeans. There was smoke coming from the soles of her shoes, and she let herself sink down into cooling water before saying, "Give me your hands, both of you!"

"No, find Orc! He can't possibly swim!"

Another bolt of green light, and another boat and then another burned like torches. The shore was all aflame, tents simply gone, motor homes exploding at the touch of the light. One of the burning motor homes rose into the sky, paused, suspended, then was slammed against a minivan, crushing it, burning it, killing the screaming occupants.

Dekka sucked air and dived under.

A boy named Bix ran screaming, stopped suddenly, and was thrown into the air. The green light found him there, and he burst into flames.

Like skeet shooting. Gaia wasn't just killing: she was playing.

Edilio's boyfriend, the Artful Roger, tried to grab some of his pictures before the light reached the boat he called home, but the end was too swift. The killing light was interrupted by a trailer between the boat and Gaia, so only half the boat burned.

Roger recoiled, shouting for Justin, who he had cared for for months. Roger was two feet behind the kill line. Justin was two feet on the other side, and was incinerated as Roger cried out in horror. He tried to yell, but the heat sucked the air from his lungs. He stumbled back with fire spreading toward him, climbed the ladder, fell onto the tilting deck of the sailboat, and rolled into the water, unconscious.

"Wake up," Caine said, shaking Sam roughly.

"What the—"

"Get up. You want to see this," Caine said, and trotted away, up out of the dip where they had decided to spend the night after a long day searching from the mine shaft down to the burned-out remains of the hermit's shack.

They had decided to leave the power plant for last and had been on their way to the Stefano Rey when night rolled over them.

Sam threw off his thin blanket and followed Caine to the high point. He instantly saw what Caine was pointing at. Far in the north there were flames throwing yellow light against the sky.

"The lake!" Sam cried.

"I think we just found Gaia," Caine said. "It's probably, what, five miles away? The road's out of our way, but it might be faster in the long run. Cross-country like this it'll take us—"

But Sam was already running.

Caine dashed after him. They ran in the dark, keeping the forest to their left, until Sam tripped and realized he was going to kill himself if he didn't watch where he was going. He formed a ball of light in his left hand and held it at shoulder level. It didn't cast much light, but it was better than relying on the faint moon.

If they could keep up the pace—a moderate running speed—they could be there in an hour. Maybe a little more.

Both of them knew it would be too late.

Gaia strode through the burning camp, earbuds still in, music still on, with the terrified Alex cringing like a Harry Potter house elf behind her.

Each time she saw movement she aimed and fired. The killing light was quite effective, she thought, not as messy or as slow as using her father's telekinetic power. But the lifting and throwing and smashing were more fun, somehow. There was a certain pleasure in grabbing a human, throwing it high in the night air, and letting it fall with a scream that ended in a satisfying crunch of broken bone. Or bashing a car down like a hammer on a fleeing person and seeing the way two tons of steel would collapse a human body and burst it like a water balloon.

A group of maybe twenty was racing away on foot, running at top speed. Gaia turned on her own speed and was on them in a flash, running beside them effortlessly.

She lit her hands, not to kill, but to see the looks on their faces. Terror. They were like terrified herd animals running from a predator, eyes wide, mouths open, gasping, weeping. She was the tiger and they were, what, sheep?

She decided to play with her other powers. She canceled

gravity beneath the fleeing people. They stumbled and rose into the air, twisting, unable to get their balance.

She looked up at them and laughed. She raised one hand, picked out a first victim, and fired. A girl burned like a torch in the sky.

It was wonderful.

The others screamed and begged and floated even higher, unable to escape, unable to hide.

She fired and missed, which was embarrassing. The moonlight was too dim to see them clearly, even when Gaia squinted. So Gaia lowered them until her nearsighted eyes could make them out in detail. Then she lit them up, one by one. They burned prettily, casting a lurid orange glow over the ground below.

She pulled out the earbuds to hear more clearly. The sound of burning was—

Gaia toppled over. She hit the ground, face in the dirt, and realized she was staring over at her own leg, lying by itself, the severed knee bleeding.

The second blow was from a knife that seemed almost to come out of thin air, it happened so fast. An invisible force had left it planted in her belly.

Agony!

With Gaia's focus destroyed, her burning human torches plummeted and splattered in greasy flames on the ground all around her. Someone—a girl, Gaia thought, a blur—was momentarily caught in the light, and Gaia saw her yanking something off her back.

Gaia rolled to one side as *BOOM!*

Shotgun pellets tore up the ground where Gaia had been. She kept rolling, each turn forcing the knife deeper into her stomach.

Gaia yanked the knife out, amazed by the pain, and pressed one hand on the wound. Her severed leg was now several feet away.

BOOM!

She was too slow this time, and some of the pellets hit her arm, lacerating her bicep and spraying blood everywhere. Blood was pumping from the hole in her belly and her leg, and Gaia could already feel herself weakening dramatically.

She felt fear. Pain. And worse, a sort of humiliation that she might be beaten.

"Who are you?" Gaia gasped.

The girl froze for a moment. Looked at her. Smiled and said, "Who am I? I'm the Breeze, bitch!"

This person, this blur of a girl, this *Breeze*, was a mutant. She was the source of the speed. Gaia couldn't kill her. And yet, if she didn't . . .

Gaia swept her killing beam in a wide arc, low to aim for the girl's legs, and so fast she almost caught her with it. But quickly, so quickly, her target leaped to let the beam pass beneath her, and even as she jumped, Gaia could hear her slamming in another shotgun round.

Gaia struck then with telekinetic force, and the mutant girl went flying backward through the air.

Gaia pressed one hand on the deadlier wound, the one in

her midsection, and caused her leg to fly to her. It came a bit too fast and hit her in the head, knocking her on her back again, and now Gaia was really afraid, because if the speed demon attacked again, Gaia would be helpless.

But the telekinetic blow against the Breeze must have been effective, because Gaia had time to shut off the loss of blood from her stomach before the counterattack could come.

This time her tormentor was not moving so fast: she had been hurt, too. Gaia had time to aim and fire her deadly light. The aim was poor and the girl was still quick enough to sidestep the worst of it, but the light caught the side of her head, and she screamed in pain and dropped her shotgun.

Just like I was burned, Gaia thought.

Justice.

Gaia shoved the leg stump in place and focused all her healing power, ignoring the fires and screams, the burning bodies, all around her. She waited only until the skin had reattached at the most tenuous, superficial level—she could not walk on the leg, let alone run—and stood on her remaining good leg and hopped away.

It was an undignified, pain-racked retreat, but no one came after her.

FIFTEEN

THE LAKE SETTLEMENT burned.

Astrid swam to shore, chilled to the bone by the freezing water, and in something like a state of shock.

She climbed heavily from the water, dragging herself up over the wet pebbles and into the sand. Dekka was already on the shore, and Diana was just behind Astrid.

Other survivors were swimming ashore or had just climbed out of the water. No one was talking. Many were crying.

The water of the lake rose suddenly, a massive waterspout that seemed to carry Dekka and Orc in its flow. Astrid saw Orc move. He was alive.

Computer Jack was on his knees, sobbing, hands over his face. Astrid had no time for that. "Jack, get a dinghy, go pick up survivors."

"Everyone's dead," he moaned.

"No, they aren't. If you don't want to fight, then you get ambulance duty. Go! Put that strength to some use."

Brianna was hobbling toward them, cursing loudly with every step. Half her hair was gone. One side of her face was cherry red.

"Brianna!" Dekka cried. She reached land, dropped Orc unceremoniously on the shore, and ran to Brianna.

Brianna sagged into her arms, showing weakness in a way Astrid had never before witnessed. But then Brianna had never had to fight someone like herself.

"She's hurt! She's hurt bad!" Dekka cried.

Other kids were gravitating toward the three, now four, girls on the beach. Orc got slowly to his feet and looked around in confusion.

Astrid gave orders with a calm she did not feel. See what cars or trucks we have that will still run. Look for survivors. If anyone's too hurt to move, come tell me where they are. See what food you can round up.

Brianna's left ear was gone, and the skin around it and all the way down to her neck looked like melted wax.

"Orc," Astrid said. "This is a terrible thing to ask, but we need someone on the perimeter—the edge out there—to see if Gaia is heading back. Or maybe she's injured and—"

Suddenly she felt weak and her head spun. Shock. She recognized it. It was Diana who steadied her.

Astrid sank into the mud, head between her hands, trying to think, trying to not think. *Big picture, Astrid: what do we do?*

I won't be meeting Sam's mother, she thought. The endgame is not yet ended. The after is a million years away.

The game is to stay alive. The game is survival. For the next minute, hour . . .

Facts. The van they sometimes used was intact, and it had a quarter tank of gas. The Winnebago they sometimes ran as a charging station had an eighth of a tank. That would still leave a couple of dozen people by the look of it. So most people would have to walk, but the severely wounded would be able to ride—assuming that anyone could be found who could drive a motor home without running it into a ditch.

She would have to stay with the ones on foot.

They would die.

The noise level was rising as the shock slowly wore off. Kids were crying more now, sobbing, yelling for lost friends or relatives. People shook with fear. No one was foolish enough to believe Gaia was done or that they were safe.

Jack was rowing out in the lake while someone with him played a flashlight around and shouted, "Is anyone alive?"

Diana, haunted, stood looking after Orc as he trotted in the direction Gaia had taken. "She's going to kill everyone. She's going to kill us all."

"I'm getting Breeze in the van," Dekka said. She had her friend in her arms, was holding Brianna like a child. "Her and another kid who is in real bad shape."

Astrid nodded, understanding there was no way to stop Dekka from going with Brianna. She looked into Brianna's bleary eyes and tried not to stare at the awful burn. "You saved a lot of lives, Breeze," Astrid said. "You're a hero."

"Damn right she is," Dekka said, her voice rough with emotion.

"Lana will fix her up," Astrid said. "Get everyone you can in that van. If you run into Sam . . ."

Ten minutes later the van pulled away.

Computer Jack rowed three shocked survivors—just three—back to shore. "There's more kids floating," he said.

"Then go get them!" Astrid said.

Jack shook his head. "There's no hurry," he said, and Astrid understood what he was saying. She sent him to help carry the injured to the Winnebago.

Orc came back to report a blood trail heading almost due west, in the general direction, if Gaia followed the barrier, of the tall trees of the Stefano Rey.

Oily smoke billowed from some of the vehicles as the fire burned out the last of the gasoline and plush interiors and plastic dashboards and now down to the tires. On the lake the boats had sunk except for bits and pieces of debris. Everything smelled of fire and charred meat.

"Okay, everyone, listen, please," Astrid said, but her voice wasn't loud enough against the rising babble of cries and complaints and the chattering of teeth. There were only about thirty healthy kids left. Another twenty or so were either in the van or in the Winnebago, which was now making its shaky, lumbering way toward the road with Jack at the wheel.

At least seventy kids had been killed. A quarter of the population of the FAYZ. Later she would be filled with rage, but for now just sadness and defeat. These kids had endured so much. . . . To die with the end perhaps in sight . . .

Astrid realized that she and they were now almost completely defenseless. They had Orc, some guns, and some bladed weapons and baseball bats. Two dozen kids with an average age of nine, against a monster with all the powers of the FAYZ.

"Listen!" she yelled at the top of her lungs. "Listen!"

Most quieted. They turned terrified faces to her, faces lit by the fires of their homes.

"We're going to Perdido Beach."

"It's dark!"

"Coyotes!"

"It's too far!"

"Listen," she repeated. "That thing, the gaiaphage, Gaia, she's hurt but she's not dead, at least I don't think so. We have to join up with the others in town. We have to have all of our people together."

"Is Sam there?"

"I hope so," Astrid said fervently. "But anyway, Dekka and Brianna are there, or will be soon, and Lana will heal Brianna." It struck Astrid that just yesterday she'd snarked to Sam about Brianna being their difficult child. Without that child they would all be dead now.

"Orc is coming with us to protect us on the way. If we walk fast, and we help each other out, we'll be there by morning."

"We have to bury the people who got killed," a little boy said.

"Yes, we do," Astrid said softly. "But not tonight."

"My sister's dead," the boy said. "She's burned up."

"Your brothers and sisters and friends want you to live," Astrid said, her voice quivering with emotion. "We have to live. Later we can bury people, but right now, tonight, we have to live."

In the end, three kids stayed behind. Astrid didn't have the energy or the certainty to compel them. And she was fairly sure that she herself, and her little band of wanderers, would also be dead before they ever reached Perdido Beach.

There would be no meeting with Connie Temple. It seemed Astrid had been wrong: it was not time to plan for after. It was still time to run, to cower, to beg for life.

To fight.

A tent pole stood stark, its surrounding nylon all burned away. Astrid looked for something, anything, and found nothing. So she bit the hem of her shirt, ripped at the small tear, and with some difficulty tore off a six-inch-wide swatch of fabric.

She yanked out several strands of her hair, twisted them into a knot with the fabric, and jammed it onto the tent pole like a pathetic flag.

It would have to do.

Sam and Caine reached the lake, their lungs screaming for air, muscles twanging with exhaustion. Neither was fit for what had turned out to be an hour-long run punctuated by pratfalls and scrapes.

As they pelted down the slope they could see that it was too late. The devastation was total.

Sam fell to his knees. "Astrid! Astrid!"

There was no answer.

"Give us some light, Sam," Caine said grimly.

"Astrid!"

"Hey, keep it together, surfer dude, you're no good to her freaking out."

Sam got to his feet again, but it was all he could do to stand up. The houseboat was a hull, improbably still floating, but burned down to the waterline. She was dead.

She was dead. The monster had killed her.

"Hey: I said, turn on some light!" Caine yelled, and shook Sam by both shoulders. "Light!"

Sam dragged himself back to reality. The smell of cooked grease and smoking tires was in the air. The fires burned low, consuming the last of their grisly fuels. The lake itself was black. Sam focused and formed a ball of light.

He moved the light up in the air, ten, twelve feet, then sent it drifting across the settlement, like a weak searchlight. Burned cars, burned tents. Burned bodies.

Sam rushed to the nearest body. No, too short to be Astrid.

"You don't want to do that, man. Because if it is her you don't want to see it."

It bordered on compassionate. At another time Sam might have appreciated it. Now he stared down at a kid who looked like a plastic toy soldier that had been put in the microwave.

Caine directed him to move the light out over the water. A sailboat—no, half a sailboat—rocked crazily in the gentle swell.

Suddenly, there was movement. Sam and Caine both spun toward the sound. A person, walking.

"Who's that?" Caine demanded.

No answer.

"I count to three and if I reach three you die," Caine said tersely.

"Don't!"

There was something odd about the voice. It sounded too deep. Caine grabbed Sam's floating light and brought it closer.

Sam and Caine both stared.

"You're an adult!" Sam said.

"Who are you?" Caine demanded. "How did you get here? Is the barrier down?"

The man was a wreck, that much was clear. He had a stump of an arm with dangling bits of meat half healed. No surgeon had done that.

"What's your name?" Sam asked.

"Alex."

"Where did you come from, Alex?"

"I . . . I fell through."

Both stared. It was weird. Both still felt some automatic deference to adults, but at the same time it was clear that they were the ones in charge here. This particular adult was not exactly ready to take charge.

"Hey, Alex, you need to start talking," Caine said. "What do you mean you fell through?"

"The goddess . . . she drew me through the barrier so that I might feed her." He clenched his remaining fist, but the expression on his face was almost reverential.

Sam and Caine exchanged a glance. They'd both seen their share of kids in shock, kids deranged by trauma. This was their first adult. Their first adult of any kind in a very long time, and he was crazy.

"What happened here? Did you see?" Sam asked.

The man pointed to the bluff overlooking the east end of the lake and the settlement. "She came from there. The goddess of light. She swept down upon them . . ."

"Gaia?" Caine asked.

"You know her?" Alex asked eagerly. "Do you have food?"

"Did anyone survive?" Sam asked, his voice catching, afraid to hear the answer.

"Yes, some. Children. They went off . . ." He searched around, then nodded. "That way. I saw some trying to get a body from the lake. I think maybe they drowned. Judgment day. Hey? Like judgment day."

"They're heading toward Perdido Beach," Sam breathed.

"There was a big RV. Maybe a truck," Alex said. "I don't remember. Others walked. I don't think it will matter. She's going to kill them all, you know. She's going to melt their brains. Hah! It's the seventh seal, it's the opening of the book, the judgment, you know, like . . . like in . . ."

"Gaia just let them walk away?" Sam asked. The man was crazy, but he was still responding.

Alex seemed suddenly very uncomfortable. "She was . . . While she was about her killing and burning, what do they call it? A reaping? While she . . . there came a whirlwind and hurt her. I saw it. Like a devil whirlwind!"

"A whirlwind?" Caine demanded.

"Brianna," Sam said.

"The goddess was hurt. Oh, she'll be hungry," Alex said, his voice an odd mix of fear and anticipation. "I . . . She's a goddess, the gaiaphage. Her name is Gaia. But shhh. Don't speak it."

"She's not a she; she's an it," Sam snapped. "And it is no one's god."

"If she's hurt, that may be her blood trail we saw going toward the southwest," Caine said. "Which leaves us a choice. Perdido Beach to see if your girlfriend is alive, or go and hunt down this lunatic's so-called goddess?"

Sam peered at Alex. He had a moment of sickening insight. "She took your arm, didn't she?"

Alex closed his eyes. "She was very hungry. She must grow and . . . very hungry."

Sam asked, "Was anyone else with you? A girl? A guy with an arm like a kind of snake? Like a whip?"

"A girl, yes. She was the goddess's mother, so she said."

"Diana?" Caine frowned, then bit angrily at his thumb.

"She betrayed us and came to warn the people here." He grinned. "But she was too late! You should have seen it! Hah! Light show, man, like a heavy metal concert."

Sam saw something then that was out of place. He peered into the darkness, formed a ball of light in his hand, and walked over to the stick with its pathetic flag.

He drew the blond hairs out, looked at them, and put them

in his back pocket. That moment was the worst of it. Feeling that she had been so close. That he had not been there when she needed him. The tears came, and he extinguished his light so that Caine would not see.

But she was alive. Astrid was alive and most likely on her way with the other survivors to Perdido Beach.

Sam steadied his voice and without turning around said, "Mister? Alex? I'm sorry all this has happened to you. This is a very . . . terrible place, sometimes. But we can't help you. You're going to have to fend for yourself."

"So we're going after Gaia?" Caine asked.

Sam nodded. "We're going after Gaia."

SIXTEEN

SINDER HAD SPENT the afternoon, evening, and now into the night with Lana working on Taylor. It seemed to take both of them, together, to reattach the missing bits of Taylor.

She was not quite a vegetable, which would have made Sinder's powers sufficient. And she was not quite an animal, which would have allowed Lana to heal her alone.

She was . . . she was a bloodless, gold-skinned, lizard-tongued, rubber-haired, dead-eyed freak, and she pretty obviously gave Sinder a case of the unholy willies.

Lana had to admit that even in a place where there was a kid named Whip Hand and a kid made of wet gravel, Taylor was weird.

"Can you stand?" Lana asked Taylor.

It had not been established that Taylor could understand what they said. Or that she really had control over her body. Whatever awful thing Little Pete had inadvertently done to her, it was quite a job.

Taylor did not stand. She flicked out her long tongue and sat, no different from before.

"I don't know what to make of her," Sinder said.

"How's Taylor?" Sanjit asked, coming in from taking Patrick on his evening potty run.

"Well, she's been put back together," Sinder answered when Lana refused to do anything but glare at Sanjit. The truth was, she was craving the smokes just a little less than earlier. And yet she still wanted one.

Suddenly the bed was empty. Taylor was gone.

The three of them stared at the spot where she had been.

"Okay," Sanjit said. "That was unexpected."

Then, just as suddenly, Taylor reappeared.

She flicked out her reptilian tongue, slowly moved her head from side to side, and then disappeared again.

"She's got her bounce back," Lana said.

Taylor did not return in the next five minutes, and they were about to give up and go about their other business when she popped back, this time standing in a corner of the room. In her left hand she had an irregularly shaped, pale-yellow chunk. She threw this on the bed.

Sinder picked it up gingerly. It was the size of half a loaf of bread.

"It's cheese," Sinder said.

The object in Taylor's other hand was a half pack of Marlboros.

Lana grinned and accepted it, ignoring Sanjit's despairing cry.

"Finally," Lana said. "All this healing stuff finally pays off."

Taylor bounced away and did not bounce back.

A minute later the door was literally kicked in by Dekka with an unconscious Brianna in her arms.

Alex remembered waking up in his bed, in his room in his grandmother's house in Atascadero. He had turned on the Cartoon Network and started the day with a Coors Light and a couple hits off a very stale bong. He had called in sick to his job at Best Buy and texted Charlie Rand to see when he'd be coming by.

Then he'd updated his iPhone to make sure he had plenty of free memory for the taping, and grabbed rope, the ladder, his pitons, and a granola bar.

He'd told his grandmother he was heading out to do some rock climbing, which was close to the truth. She'd asked him to take her to Costco on Saturday. He had groaned inwardly but agreed.

Life had been not spectacular, maybe, but okay. Normal, anyway. Then, with a suddenness that he never would have believed possible, everything had changed. Now he was broken in body, and even more broken in mind. Last week he had been a lapsed Methodist; now he worshipped a cannibalistic girl monster. He was self-aware enough to know that this was madness. There was no way to put a good spin on that fact.

Alex wandered the shores of the lake. It was an eerie place as the sun rose. It smelled terrible, and yet his mouth watered from the same scent that had come from his burned arm.

"Food of the gods," he said, and almost laughed and instead sobbed.

Not what he'd expected when he'd headed out to climb the barrier wall and get some cool video.

"But hey, life, man."

This was a whole new experience. Pain surged from his shoulder. It did that. It came and went. Mostly it was just there, but every now and then it would rise up like a demon and he would feel a terrible rage at his mutilation.

He looked at it, at the stump. It was horrifying and awesome all at once. She had eaten his tattoo, the one that he'd gotten in San Diego, the one that showed a guy hanging from a rock face.

With it she had eaten his soul, he was pretty sure of that. He could feel that his soul was no longer with him. It made him cry. Also, who would take Gran to Costco? And she had an appointment at . . . Well, wherever, it didn't matter now. He was a broken toy, and he'd been so easy to break: that's what would be sad for him. If he'd still had a soul.

"Gaia!" he cried. "Gaia!"

No answer. He himself was hungry now. His body had suffered and he was desperate. But at least he could drink. The lake was freshwater. He waded in a couple of feet and bent to cup water to his mouth. It tasted of ashes and oil.

Then he saw the rope. It floated on the surface, curved like a water snake.

Sometimes he went boating over on Lake Isabella, waterskiing and drinking beer. They often trailed nets full of beers over the side to keep them cool. Maybe . . .

Alex began pulling on the rope. There was definitely something attached, and it was heavy, but it was coming. Hah! A cooler punched full of holes. Water drained out as he hauled it out of the lake. It was heavy, heavier than if it was just beers.

Alex had some trouble untying the rope with just one hand, but his teeth helped. The bicycle chain nearly defeated him, and he almost gave up. But a search of the camp, ignoring as best he could the dead bodies and parts of dead bodies, turned up a crowbar. The crowbar broke the chain lock.

At last he pried open the lid and gasped.

It was a head. Mostly a head. But there was something like a lizard's tail protruding, whipping back and forth between the pale blue eyes.

The head spit water from its mouth and seemed to be whispering. Looking up at him with cold blue eyes, so like the goddess. This awesome horror had to be a sign from her.

Alex leaned close, pushing past repugnance and fear, to hear a wet, gurgling voice say, "Who the hell are you?"

Computer Jack was next to arrive at Clifftop. Jack hauled the horribly burned, mauled, broken kids with soot-stained faces and bloody clothes, one at a time, up to Lana's room.

The motor home had broken down, too, and Jack had hauled it with sheer, brute force, pushing from behind, shoving it back onto the road with the incredible strength that had never mattered to him.

In the end they hadn't been far ahead of the kids who had walked.

One kid had died en route. The rest had cried and wailed and shouted their pain with every lurch and jolt. And all the while Jack had been clenched, waiting for the next attack.

Sanjit ran to get his brothers and sisters to haul water and offer comfort. Sinder did a sort of rough triage, deciding who needed the most immediate help, but Brianna was first, that much was clear. There was a war on, and Brianna was a soldier.

Lana laid her hand on Brianna's scarred, half-destroyed face, and Brianna cursed feebly.

"What happened, Breeze?" Lana asked while she stretched to also touch a four-year-old whose leg had been burned down to the white bone.

"Gaia," she said. "The gaiaphage. Trying to kill us all. I—" And that was it for Brianna for a while as her eyes rolled up and she slipped back into the relief of unconsciousness.

Sanjit stepped behind Lana, stuck a cigarette in her mouth, and lit it.

"How many dead?" Lana asked.

Sinder answered, "One of the kids said . . . she said it was all burned down. All the boats, all the vans . . ." Sinder brushed tears from her eyes. "Like more than half the kids up there."

"Sam?"

"He wasn't there," Sinder said.

"Then we're not beaten yet," Lana said.

*   *   *

Gaia had dragged herself and her parts away and into a stand of trees. It was all a terrible shock. She had felt pain, terrible pain when Sam had burned her in the battle at Perdido Beach, but she had never before felt such fear. It had never occurred to her that she really had anything to fear from anyone aside from Little Pete.

Weak humans, even mutants, should be no threat to her. The fact that she'd been very nearly destroyed by one girl— one girl!—was disturbing in the extreme. Obviously she had miscalculated. Worse: What did this mean for the outside world?

Could she be defeated? By mere human creatures?

The fear seemed to have the effect of tightening her throat, a strange aspect of having a body. Her body actually reacted in ways other than what her mind dictated. A weakness, that was. Her heart had hammered; her senses had become disoriented; her muscles had tensed. All of that was apparently beyond her control.

And the way the pain twisted her awareness, the way it forced her to pay attention to it, to the pain, and only to the pain. Weakness. There was a downside to having a body.

You see, Nemesis? Is this what you want for yourself? Are you seeing?

Now there was water leaking from her eyes. And where was the stupid Diana? She should be here. Not to mention the food. She had killed dozens and yet she was hungry, driven off before she could renew her energy. That was injustice. It was unfair!

As soon as she had healed herself she would go after them again and finish them. Had to, especially now, especially if they could actually conceivably *defeat* her.

A complicated problem, though. She couldn't kill the mutants, but she needed to. If she didn't kill them, they might kill her. If she did kill some of them, she might lose the power necessary to defeat those left.

It took hours of focused attention to grow her leg back. She stood at last, but it still felt too shaky to handle super-speed. Assuming she even had that speed. Had the girl who called herself Breeze died? Part of Gaia hoped so; part of her feared so.

The sun was rising, the sun of the outside world shining down on her, revealing the woods around her, tall trees and fallen pine needles, exposed roots and fragile saplings.

And then she saw *them*. Her distance-blurred vision did not reveal faces, but one she recognized immediately. She knew Caine, yes. She knew him without seeing his features. It had been a while since she had reached into his mind, but she could still touch him.

Can you stop me, Nemesis? Will you?

The other was probably Sam, the one who had turned his killing light on her and burned her, caused her such pain. She had not reached into him, not really, though she had brushed against his mind more than once.

So: the brothers united against her again. Well, well, old family ties.

Never mind: none of that mattered. What mattered was

that one possessed the telekinetic power and the other the power of light. She couldn't kill either of them without depriving herself of her most powerful weapons. But she could cripple them. She could terrorize them.

She could *break* them.

Gaia couldn't tell if they had seen her. Were they looking right at her? They seemed to be moving apart, going in different directions. She squinted at the forest and flexed her fingers, ready for—

Only the swift-moving shadow alerted her. She leaped to one side, hit the ground, and rolled away as a huge section of fallen redwood dropped from the sky to smash the ground where she had stood.

Caine!

She reached for his mind, stabbed at him, and, from much nearer than she'd expected, heard a cry of pain.

"Caine!" Gaia yelled. "Yes, I can still hurt you!"

"Aaaaahhh!"

"Scream for me, *Father*!"

She heard running feet, someone crashing through bushes and brambles. There! He was running straight at her. She raised her hand to fire the killing light, aiming for his legs, but he struck first. A bolt of green light shot past her, striking a fallen tree and setting a rotted branch aflame.

She fired back, but Sam had already dropped to the ground.

Gaia hobbled toward him, closing the distance so she could see more clearly. She felt stabbing pain from her unready leg, stumbled, and felt Caine's mind pushing back against her with surprising force.

"Aaaarrrgh!" she yelled in sheer fury.

A beam of light aimed blindly nearly cut her in half. She jumped aside and burned the hem of her pants leg.

The beam had cut most of the way through a hundred-foot-tall redwood, which now swayed too far to recover. A loud crunching, cracking sound was followed by a rush of snapped branches and torn canopy as the tree crashed down through the woods, blocking Gaia's line of retreat.

Gaia fought down a moment's panic. No, she was still the stronger. She was the gaiaphage.

Caine was the weak point. Gaia dropped to the ground, literally trying to dig herself into the dirt, make herself invisible, as she focused all her malevolence on Caine.

Scream! she ordered him. *Scream!*

And he screamed. Oh, yes, he screamed.

He screamed like he was being torn apart. He screamed like he was dying.

Sam would go to him, knowing he couldn't defeat Gaia alone. Now, while Sam was trying to rescue Caine! She scrambled away through the dirt, scraping her belly like a snake, forcing her way through the branches of the fallen tree, hair tangled and torn, and filled with the hatred that can only come from humiliation.

Gaia was having a bad morning after a very bad night.

She couldn't win a battle when she had to pull her punches. Which meant that her course was clear: She had to attack Perdido Beach and get the major killing done with. Then she could take her time torturing the defiance out of Caine and finally deal with the eternally troublesome Sam Temple.

In the meantime, she needed a game changer.

She saw a thin spiral of smoke rise from the dead tree Sam's light had touched.

Well, why not? Fire. Yes, perfect. Fire would drive everyone toward Perdido Beach. And it might cover her rear from a sneak attack.

Gaia raised her hands above the cover provided by the fallen tree and began to fire randomly, long, sustained bursts hitting a forest that had experienced no rain since the coming of the FAYZ.

Then Gaia fled, pursued by smoke as fire took hold in the Stefano Rey National Park.

SEVENTEEN

ASTRID, DIANA, AND Orc arrived in Perdido Beach at the head of a strung-out procession of exhausted kids, an hour behind Dekka and Jack. Most collapsed upon reaching the town plaza, just dropped where they were.

Edilio had already checked with the wounded at Clifftop. Now, with barely controlled panic, he raced to each person, looking into each face.

"Have you seen Roger?"

Most didn't answer. Edilio wasn't sure they even heard him. But one little said, "His boat got burned up."

"Did you see him, though? Did you see him?"

Head shake. No.

Edilio's heart ached. No way Roger had been killed. That wasn't fair. It wasn't right. He and Roger had just, finally, been able to acknowledge how they felt about each other, how they had felt for secretive months.

Edilio's searching eyes met Astrid's.

She didn't need to hear his question. "We didn't see him, Edilio. Jack rowed around the boats . . . there were bodies in the water. Roger and Justin were probably both on their boat. It was cut in half, burned."

"But you didn't . . . Did you bury . . ." He couldn't finish the thought.

"Listen, Brianna kept Gaia from finishing us all off, but we couldn't stay there. We had to run. We had wounded kids. Everyone was scared; we couldn't stay and search."

Edilio nodded dully. He had to put this reality in a box, like he had done so many times with so many tragedies.

But this was too big: it wouldn't go; it couldn't be put aside for quiet grief at a more convenient time. A sound of anguish rose from Edilio. Astrid put her arms around him, and he cried into her hair.

"I should have been there," Edilio whispered.

"You couldn't have stopped her," Astrid said. "Did Brianna and Dekka and the rest make it here?"

Edilio pulled away, wiping tears from his cheeks. "Brianna's hurt bad, but she's alive. Her and Dekka are up at Clifftop."

"Don't ever let me say anything bad about that girl again," Astrid said. "Everyone who made it out alive owes their life to Brianna. Edilio, it was . . . Gaia would have . . . She was enjoying it . . . floating kids into the air and then . . ."

Edilio nodded bleakly. "What do we do now, Astrid? Did

you see Sam? He should be here, but I . . . didn't work. It's my fault."

"Edilio, nothing is your fault." Astrid called Diana over. Orc had taken it upon himself to fetch water in a big five-gallon plastic tub. Kids were drinking greedily while Orc watched in satisfaction.

"Listen to me, Edilio." Astrid took his face in her hands, forced him to see, to pay attention. "We don't have time to grieve. There are things you need to understand."

Edilio nodded, but he wasn't there: he wasn't tracking.

"Diana, tell Edilio what you know about Gaia."

Diana did, but Edilio needed it repeated. It was impossible to focus. Mental images of Roger dead . . . floating on the lake. Or maybe only terribly injured, lying somewhere.

Had Roger even had a chance to think? Had he seen it coming? Had he seen Justin die before his eyes? That by itself would have killed him. Justin had become a little brother to Roger.

"Listen, Edilio. Gaia's going to kill everyone," Astrid said. "The only good news is that we took Drake down. Well, Brianna did. Again, Brianna."

"What?" Edilio asked, confused. He hadn't followed anything they'd told him.

Astrid and Diana exchanged a look. "Diana . . . ," Astrid said, and nodded at Edilio.

"Come with me, Edilio; we're just going to have a seat over on the steps," Diana said.

•   •   •

"What was the scream about?" Sam demanded, checking Caine for injuries. "Are you hurt?"

Caine was breathing hard, bent over, like he'd been kicked in the belly. "She got me."

The air smelled of smoke. Something was burning.

"Where?" Sam asked. "Where did she get you?"

Caine straightened slowly. His face was grim. "Here," he said, jabbing a finger angrily against his temple.

"What's that supposed to mean? We had her!"

"We had nothing!" Caine yelled. To Sam's amazement it almost seemed he had tears in his eyes.

Sam decided to take a less confrontational tack. He didn't need a fight with Caine. "Listen, dude, whatever is going on, you need to tell me. You're supposed to watch my back."

Caine brushed dirt from his knees and avoided looking Sam in the eye. "The gaiaphage owned me, okay? Back a long time ago, back after our first big fight, the one in Perdido Beach. I imagine you remember."

"Yeah, I remember," Sam snapped. "You and Drake tried pretty hard to kill me."

"After that I went to the mine shaft. You know all this. And the gaiaphage . . . Look, it's not something I can explain, okay, or at least not something you can understand."

"But you fought against the gaiaphage later."

"It was already weakening. And it was focused on Lana and Little Pete. It's stronger now. Much stronger."

Sam frowned. "Why Lana? Why would it care about Lana?"

"It . . . she . . . hates Lana. Lana lost it, Lana was taken, same as me, but Lana shut it down. I don't know if it's because of Lana's healing power or what, but Lana . . . the girl is tough and strong. The gaiaphage doesn't like that."

"Okay," Sam said, not knowing what else to say. It had cost Caine to admit vulnerability. It cost him more to admit that Lana could do what he couldn't.

Smoke stung Sam's eyes. All this smoke couldn't be from the one rotted limb he'd torched.

Caine was trying to explain. "It's like, like, we're all here in this world, but there's some other place, some other connection. I can't see it, but I can kind of see it. Like something you see out of the corner of your eye, only when you turn to look at it, it's not there. And the gaiaphage can reach me through there."

"What happens when it reaches you?"

"Pain."

"Bad?"

Caine gritted his teeth and had to squeeze the words out. With his hand he held an imaginary knife and slowly twisted it into the side of his head. "Like someone took a white-hot knife and stabbed it into your head and twisted it back and forth, again and again."

Sam had felt pain. He had wept and cried under Drake's lash. He had felt helpless. He had lost control of himself. He understood what it meant and what pain like that did to you. He was about to reach out and put a hand on Caine's shoulder but caught himself. The gesture would not be appreciated.

Instead he jumped up onto a low branch and pulled himself up to get a better view. Fire had definitely taken hold in the trees. At least three were burning. A year without rain had left the forest dry and vulnerable. It would spread, Sam had little doubt. And there wasn't anything they could do about it.

"Any time we throw down with Gaia she can do this to you?" Sam asked, dropping back to the dry pine-needle floor.

Caine shrugged. "It's been a long time. I thought I had it beat. Like Lana. But the gaiaphage is growing more powerful now in this body. It's up out of the mine shaft. And Little Pete, well, he's dead or whatever the hell he is."

"Astrid thinks he's still alive in some form."

"Some form." Caine laughed bitterly. "Seems like one minute we were talking about getting out, all hugs and burgers. Now we're back deep in the crazy."

Sam looked curiously at his estranged brother. They'd been born minutes apart to the same mother. Sam had never been a hundred percent sure how that had happened. Did they share a father? Or was their mother a bit more . . . *adventurous* than he wanted to think about?

And why had she kept him and not Caine?

The crazy had started earlier than all of this: that much was clear.

"I don't think I can beat her without you," Sam said after a while. "And now I'm not sure you aren't just a big weak spot."

Caine did not react angrily; he knew it was true.

"Don't try to save me if she hits me again," Caine said. "She'll expect you to; that's why she did it this time. We had her in trouble, so she lashed out at me and got you to back off."

Sam nodded. "Yeah. Fair enough. But what's her next move? That's what I don't see."

Caine thought it over for a minute. Then his face went slack. "She'll attack. She didn't get everyone at the lake; Brianna got in the way. And we're on her tail, and now she knows she's not invulnerable. So she has to force us into defending; she can't have us just chasing her, because we might get lucky." He nodded at the smoke that now stung their noses and throats. "That's why the fire. She's done being cocky. She's fighting scared, which is bad, really bad for us. She's accelerating things. Whatever time we thought we had? It's used up. You want to talk endgame? This is it."

"Yeah," Sam said tightly. "She's going for Perdido Beach."

The head named Drake had spoken to Alex.

The head had told him that it served Gaia.

Gaia would reward Alex if he brought Drake to her. Gaia would give him back his arm, better than ever.

So Alex had taken out all the heavy stones but left the head in its convenient carrying case. The cooler was heavy, but he could just manage it with his one arm.

As they traveled to find Gaia, Drake and the other person,

the one called Brittney, taught him all about Gaia, so that Alex would understand where he fit in. He would understand the truth. He would understand that he served a true goddess.

And when Gaia emerged triumphant—and could there really be any doubt?—Alex would walk triumphant beside her. So Brittney said. So Drake later agreed.

They were the three apostles, Brittney said: Drake, Brittney, and Alex Mayle.

Alex set out after Gaia to bring her the head of Drake Merwin. He didn't think much about what Gaia would do with the head of her lieutenant.

Drake, however, seemed to have a pretty good idea.

Connie Temple had arrived the previous afternoon at the place Dahra had sent her. There was a lake, there was a marina, and across the lake, over in the FAYZ, there was a similar marina, almost a mirror of the one she was in.

She had seen kids over there, but none had approached the barrier. And Dahra had not shown up. So Connie had stuck on a note on a sapling that was quite near the barrier and found a motel for the night. She had worried that Dahra might show up late and wonder where she was, but it was almost dark and she didn't know the area at all well. She found a motel ten miles away, made a dinner of convenience-store fare—crackers, cheese slices, a bottle of wine, and a 3 Musketeers bar—then fell asleep watching Jon Stewart.

The next morning, not at all well rested, and somewhat hungover, she made her way back to the rendezvous armed with convenience-store coffee and donuts. She had little hope that Dahra or Astrid would show up.

Connie climbed from the car, armed with stale coffee and staler donuts. She found the note she'd left, crumpled it, and looked toward that distant, unreachable shore.

Thin trails of black smoke rose from several spots around that second, barely visible marina. In the distance, off to the south, a larger pillar of smoke rose, an ominous sight.

She walked into the marina and out onto the dock to get a closer look, wishing she had a boat to take her closer still.

"All hell broke loose over there last night."

Connie spun and faced a tall man, slightly stooped, older, with white hair and a weathered face.

"What do you mean?"

The man nodded toward the distant shore. "I been watching since the thing cleared up. I have a grandson in there. At least, I hope he's still in there, somewhere."

"Are there kids staying over there?" Connie asked.

"Seemed like there was a camp or settlement or whatever you might choose to call it. They didn't have any electricity, so there weren't many lights, but at night you'd see glimmers of candles. And the other day some of them brought one of the boats close up and traded messages with us." He shrugged. "Didn't say anything about my grandson; everyone said they didn't know him. But there were some grim expressions when I mentioned his name."

Connie nodded sympathetically. "I'm Connie Temple. My son—"

"I recognize you, Ms. Temple. From TV. My name is Merwin. The boy is named after me: Drake."

Connie did her best to conceal her reaction. She had heard the name, and not in a good way. There were stories . . . terrifying stories. "What happened last night?"

The elder Drake Merwin shrugged again; it seemed to be a habit with him. "Well, it's going to sound crazy."

Connie waited.

"It was like someone shooting lasers around. And there were explosions. This morning I kept expecting someone from over there to row over and explain. No one showed up. I've been watching. I have a good set of binoculars on my boat; the problem is my eyesight isn't that great anymore. Good till I hit sixty-five, then . . ." Another shrug.

"Can I look through your binoculars?"

He led her onto his boat, docked at the end of the pier. The binoculars were big and mounted on a stand. She had to crouch to see through, and then it took a few tries to get them focused.

Suddenly the scene leaped into view.

"If you'd tell me what you see . . . ," Merwin suggested apologetically.

"There's a sailboat, all upended. There's a burning trailer, like a camping trailer . . ." She swallowed hard. "There are more burned things, cars, boats . . . Can we take your boat closer?"

Merwin looked grim. "I've been worried what I might see up close."

She understood that, and without thinking put a comforting hand on his arm.

She cast off the lines while he manned the wheel. It was a big boat for the lake, and with the lake much reduced in size it seemed almost absurd. But he maneuvered it with practiced skill and brought it within ten feet of the barrier.

The two of them were on the flying bridge with the binoculars.

"Are those . . . ," he asked in a pained and fearful voice.

"Yes." Yes, there were bodies in the water. They were bumping softly against the barrier.

She spotted movement, a single individual. She swung the binoculars toward him and saw what looked like a man, not a child, carrying a blue-and-white container, a cooler, and moving away from the lake, threading his way through coals and tendrils of smoke.

No one would be meeting her here today.

"You said you saw what looked like lasers?" Connie asked, fighting the tremor in her voice.

"I know what you're thinking, Ms. Temple," he said. "I saw the video of your boy with that light coming out of his hands. But best not to draw any conclusions about any of this."

"No," she agreed.

"There's a coffeemaker down in the galley. A little cream is all for me."

Connie went below, grateful for the suggestion. She started the coffee and then found herself gripping a cup so hard the handle broke. She found another and filled a cup for each of them and carried them back up.

Merwin took his and drank, easily holding the boat on its station with slight turns of the wheel and little thrusts of the engines.

"I'm seventy-four years old," he said, and shrugged again, this time like he was trying to get that fact to roll off his shoulders. "I was drafted into Vietnam. Way before your time, but it was a nasty war, that one."

"I guess wars usually are."

He smiled and laughed a little. "Yes, they are, generally. Well, there was this kid, just been bumped to corporal on account of the regular corporal was dead. Nice enough fellow. Only one day, after he'd had no sleep for three days, and no hot food in five days, and had two buddies shot . . ." He stopped then for a moment, breathed hard, and looked away.

She waited.

"As it happened, they captured an NVA—sorry, North Vietnamese Army regular. This NVA was injured, so he couldn't keep up when his compadres retreated. So, corporal decides to question him. The NVA spits in the corporal's face. Long story short, the corporal shot him in the neck."

Silence.

"War crime, that was, shooting a helpless prisoner.

Court-martial offense. At least it would have been if anyone had ever reported it."

"You didn't report it?"

Merwin shrugged, heavily this time. "No, ma'am. No one reported me for shooting that man in the neck. Because we were all of us hungry and tired and scared and very, very angry. And the oldest of us was just twenty years old."

"Sam wouldn't . . . ," she started to say.

"Oh, well, Ms. Temple, there are genuine saints in this world: I married one. But there aren't many. I like to think Drake—my grandson, Drake, not that old corporal—I like to hope, anyway, that he found the strength to . . . But he was always a troubled boy. Especially after my son died. The step-father . . . young Drake's stepfather . . ." He blew out a breath. "But I don't know and you don't know."

"What happens when we do know?" she asked in a small voice.

"I suppose we'll behave like a bunch of holier-than-thou hypocrites. Because the alternative is to look at ourselves in the mirror and know that we are capable of dark and terrible things."

They were quiet on the ride back to the dock. Connie shook his hand.

"Thanks for taking me and for talking with me. That must be a very hard thing to carry all these years."

The old man smiled, and there was a glint of steel in his eyes. "Not the way you think, though, Ms. Temple. See, what's hard is knowing I took pleasure in that act of revenge. And knowing if I had to do it all again, I'd still pull that trigger."

She slowly released his hand and stared, stricken, into eyes that were cold and cruel, as he said, "Dark and terrible things. And the joys they bring."

EIGHTEEN

GAIA WAS MOVING faster, almost at a normal walking speed. The leg was healing. It would have healed altogether if she'd been able to sit and focus on it. But the two mutants were on her trail, and in addition to that she had to keep moving to stay ahead of the fire, which had quickly burned to the edge of the forest and merely awaited some encouragement to spread farther.

It had occurred to Gaia that inhabiting a body meant she, too, was vulnerable to smoke and fire. She had run through her mental inventory of powers that would save her from smoke inhalation. Nothing.

At least the pain was under some control now. The music in her ears helped distract her. The song was called "When All the Lights Go Out." There was a lot of yelling. Gaia decided she liked yelling music best.

She walked straight down a gravel road, counting on the fact that she had a small lead and was in open ground now where she would see Sam and Caine before they caught up to her. They were a manageable threat. What worried her far more was the knowledge that Little Pete was looking at her. She could feel him watching her. And while Nemesis was fading fast, he wasn't dead yet.

Bodies were definitely a mixed blessing—they kept you alive, they focused power, and they allowed you to move about. But they felt pain, and they could be killed.

What would happen to the great and glorious creature called the gaiaphage if this body died?

The truth was, she didn't know. She might end up like Little Pete, a disembodied ghost. Or she might actually, truly, die. Cease to exist.

They hungered, these bodies. Constantly. It was like an insistent, nagging voice in her head: *Feed me. Feed me now!*

She found a dead body by the side of the road, a boy. At first glance he didn't seem to be injured. But when she used her foot to push him over, she saw a chunk of wood protruding from his back near his spine. He might not even have known it was there, and had simply bled to death as he walked from the lake toward Perdido Beach.

Well, one less to kill.

She quickly stripped off his clothing and put it on. It was filthy and stained with blood, but her own clothing was worse and now too small as well. It might confuse her pursuers. She ate some of his thigh, then quickly moved onward. In a while she would try out her speed again. This slow walking was boring.

She reached the highway just as a yellow school bus half covered in graffiti came rattling toward her. It stopped by the side of the road, and a dozen kids climbed out. They were carrying implements and buckets. Two of them manhandled a wheelbarrow out through the back door.

One of them, a girl with black hair, looked up, saw Gaia, and frowned uncertainly. Other kids stared past Gaia and pointed not at her but at the forest fire, which was certainly generating a lot of smoke. Even here, far from the trees, Gaia could smell it.

Gaia walked straight to the group, who were now heading into the field, tossing what looked like fish heads and bones ahead of them. The fish heads were instantly devoured by seething masses of worms, which then allowed the kids to pass unharmed into the field, dragging their buckets with them.

Gaia pulled out one earbud.

"Better get to work," a boy said to Gaia.

But the black-haired girl, who had been watching her narrowly, said, "I don't know you."

"No, you don't," Gaia agreed. She didn't want to alert and panic the others, so she avoided a light show and simply swung a backhand that crushed the girl's head and killed her instantly.

The bossy boy said, "What the—"

He dodged her first punch; her second one caught him a glancing blow that shattered his arm. He opened his mouth to scream, but he never had the chance. Her hand found his throat and crushed his larynx as easily as crushing a grape.

She tossed his body behind the bus, where it wouldn't be seen by the kids now moving slowly across the field.

There were ten in all. She followed them at a quick walk, stepping between rows of plants heavy with green pods. She caught up to the nearest girl and punched her once in the back and snapped her spine.

Nine.

The second one had time to yell, however, before Gaia knocked her head cleanly off her shoulders and set it flying to land between cabbages.

Eight.

The shout, cut short, alerted the rest of the workers, who spun and died, died, died as she easily killed three with blasts of green light.

Seven. Six. Five.

BLAM! BLAM!

One of them had a weapon. He fired fast and panicky. Gaia swept her beam and cut him in two.

Four.

No, there was a second gun. Too late!

BLAM! BLAM! BLAM!

Gaia spun around, not so much knocked by the impact as by the spasm of pain. She fell on her back.

"Get her! Get her! Get her!"

BLAM! BLAM!

"I'm out of bullets!"

Gaia tried to sit up, but something inside her was badly

damaged, and the pain was extraordinary.

In one ear Social Distortion sang "Story of My Life." It was a song both upbeat and melancholy.

A girl with a knife rose up beside her. Gaia threw an invisible punch that sent the knife wielder flying.

Sudden noise behind her, feet on soft dirt: Gaia twisted to see and was hit in the chest with a spiked baseball bat.

She grabbed the bat with lightning reflexes, held it, and with her other hand burned a hole through her assailant.

Three.

Gaia pushed herself up and shook her head. She was woozy. Her head was pounding; her eyes didn't want to focus; her chest hurt. Blood was leaking from her in too many ways.

Unable to see clearly, she swept a beam of light three hundred sixty degrees. Again. Again. A scream cut short.

Two.

She had to prioritize. What should she heal first? What was killing her?

She lifted her new shirt and saw that the nail wound in her chest was small compared to the bullet hole. And worse still, far worse, was the exploded exit wound where the bullet had come out of her side. She pressed her hand on that and focused.

She blinked tears from her eyes and saw two people running away, already back at the highway, racing toward Perdido Beach. She aimed a beam after them, but there was no aiming now: they were fuzzy in the distance, and she hit nothing.

Killing everyone in the FAYZ was proving more difficult than she'd expected.

Staying alive was proving more difficult.

Why did everything have to be difficult? It was unfair. It was wrong. She was the gaiaphage, and what were they? Weak things made of meat and blood and bone.

Like you, Darkness, just like you.

Gaia gasped. The voice was in her head. His voice. Nemesis. He was seeing. He was learning from her mistake in taking on a body.

That's right, Nemesis. See how weak a body makes you?

That would confuse him, she hoped. That would delay him. But at any moment Nemesis could make his move, and things would go from difficult to very hard indeed. She didn't have time to lie here and recover. And Sam and Caine . . .

It began to occur to her then that the outside world might also be difficult to conquer, especially if they were ready for her. Stealth would be demanded. She must escape from this place without the humans outside realizing who and what she was. Once outside she would gain in power. She was, after all, a sort of virus that would propagate. She would attract followers. She would take control of other humans. She would . . .

Conquer.

Gaia, the gaiaphage-made-flesh, lay on her back and stared up at the blue sky.

"Story of My Life" was just ending.

Somewhere, way out there, past the thin shell of atmosphere, past this tiny solar system, somewhere out there in the unimaginable distances of the galaxy, was the place where the gaiaphage had first been conceived.

All that way, all that time, millions of years, to arrive here. To feel blood leaking from a human body into the dirt beneath her.

It could not end like this. The gaiaphage was destined for more, meant to transform. Its mere existence had begun to alter the laws of physics that ruled this planet.

Today the FAYZ, tomorrow the planet.

But right now she . . . it—whatever—was very tired.

"You're back," Astrid said to Albert. "I heard you were."

"Yes. And we're getting a trickle of food in from the fields already. Some teams have come back in, but I've pushed some others back out."

Astrid nodded. "Probably a good thing."

"Just probably?" Albert demanded.

"Gaia will come after us. It could be in a day; it could be in ten seconds. Having some of the people in different locations might make it harder for her to kill us all."

She had called a hasty meeting in what had once been the mayor's office. It struck her that if the barrier really came down there would once again be a real mayor in Perdido Beach. A week from now, or a month, or whenever, some responsible adult would be sitting here deciding important issues of trash collection and water and curfews and assorted other things that would not be life and death.

Albert was there; so were Edilio, Dekka, Quinn, and

Diana. She'd have liked to have Jack there as well: he was not especially useful, but he was smart. Lana, too, might have been helpful, but she was busy, to put it mildly.

More, much more, Astrid wished Sam was there. Even Caine would have been welcome. They were facing what was probably the final battle, and she had no soldiers except Dekka and Orc. Dekka was strong and brave, as was Orc, but they were nothing to Gaia.

Astrid had begun to believe that the time had come to plan for after. And now she was afraid there would be no after. The barrier would come down, and the only person walking out into the world would be Gaia.

There was one person she wished wasn't there: Diana.

It was Astrid's meeting, but it was Albert who asked Diana the question. "Diana, you've been with this gaiaphage-Gaia thing. Everything you know."

Diana glanced at Astrid, and Astrid saw that Albert had intercepted that look. So had Dekka.

There was a painfully long silence. Now even Quinn and the distracted Edilio noticed.

"Hey," Quinn said. "No secrets."

Astrid, as calmly as she could, said, "Tell them everything you know, Diana."

For once Diana did not see the need to be difficult. "Gaia's body is growing fast. She needs food constantly, and she doesn't care where she gets it. She doesn't seem to have powers of her own, really, except for what she had as the gaia-phage: the power to reach directly into minds, especially of moofs, people with powers, and especially those she's been connected to in the past. She can cause them terrible pain and fear and—"

"Caine? She can hurt Caine?" Dekka asked.

Diana nodded. "Probably, yes. And me. Everyone but Lana."

"Lana?" Astrid pressed.

"Gaia hates Lana. Somehow Lana was able to shut her out. Another thing," Diana said, carefully avoiding Astrid. "Gaia's powers are borrowed, or derived, or whatever big Astrid word you'd like to use. They aren't hers. She said if she kills Sam she won't have his power anymore. Or maybe it's just that it's easier if . . . if Sam is alive; I don't know. I don't know."

"That's why she didn't kill him, or Caine, when she might have," Astrid said. If she could shut Diana down now, she might still be able to manage the conversation. "So, suggestions? Ideas?"

"Astrid," Diana said. "Little Pete."

"What about him?" Albert asked.

Diana started to stand up, obviously felt the pain in her battered body, and remained seated. "He's Nemesis. That's what Gaia calls him. He's the one the gaiaphage really fears. That's why she's killing everyone: to keep him from being able to take a host body, like she did."

"Well, I don't know how helpful that is," Astrid snapped. "I don't know how we'd . . . I mean, that's useless information." She sounded shrill, even to herself.

Dekka said, "What is Little Pete? Are we sure he still

exists? Maybe Gaia's just nuts."

Again, every eye was on Astrid. She could feel it. "What about Gaia's feelings for you, Diana?"

There was an uncomfortable silence. Dekka broke it. "Astrid, this isn't the time for you to be Pete's protective big sister."

"I want to know what Gaia feels about Diana," Astrid shot back. "It might be a vulnerability we can exploit."

Edilio had said nothing. Now he spoke. "That creature murdered dozens of kids, including Roger. We need to know everything. No secrets, no evasions, no lies."

Astrid glared at him, but she couldn't make it work. She ended up turning away.

"Diana's told us what she knows," Albert said coolly. "Your turn, Astrid."

"I threw Petey to his death," Astrid said quietly. "I did what I had to do; it was the only way to force his hand, to make him destroy the bugs. I killed him once. Now you're asking me to . . . to . . ."

"We've all lost people," Quinn said softly. "We've all been through hell. And we've all failed at times. Everyone in this room has scars on their body and worse ones in their . . . well, souls, I guess."

"We're a bunch of sheep waiting for the tiger," Albert snapped. "There's only one question: are any of us going to walk out of here alive?"

"Maybe you should run back to your island," Astrid said with a vicious edge. She glanced up to see something she'd never seen before: Edilio, his face transformed by dark anger. She took a step back.

He said, "Talk, Astrid. Now."

Astrid swallowed hard. She tried to think of something to say and failed. She was not strong enough to say no to him. She felt her resistance crumble. She felt her own surrender. The coolly logical part of her mind noted almost sardonically that Edilio had a superpower after all: being Edilio.

"Yeah," she whispered. "Okay. Little Pete is alive. I can't explain it; believe me, I wish I could. When I was with Cigar, in the dark, waiting for the end, hearing Cigar scream from what Penny had done to him, Petey talked to me."

"Your imagination?" Albert suggested.

Astrid shook her head. "I can feel him sometimes. Poor Cigar could see him, a little, at least."

"Gaia sure thinks he's alive," Diana said. "She says he's weaker being separated from a physical self."

"So we need Little Pete to pull a Gaia, take a body," Albert said. "Fine. How do we do that?"

Now it was Edilio's turn to flinch. Astrid had already followed that line of reasoning to its obvious conclusion; he had not. And now that he understood it, he didn't like it any more than she did.

Not surprisingly it was Diana, with some of her old snark back, who clarified. "So we're saying Astrid should tell her little brother to go all exorcist on some sacrificial lamb, then get him or her to kill the kid I gave birth to."

This was followed by another long silence.

Astrid almost didn't dare to think, lest someone somehow read her thoughts. Because there was another way. If Caine and Sam should die . . .

She focused to see Edilio making eye contact with her. He gave the slightest of nods.

Yes. He had seen the other path.

The silence in the room was profound. The choices were sinking in. Find a sacrifice for Little Pete. Or kill Sam and Caine.

Still looking at Astrid, Edilio said, "Dekka, Quinn, come with me. I'm getting anyone who can shoot. I'll put everyone who has a gun into a window or doorway around the town square. We'll fight her here."

"Without Sam and Caine and Brianna, too, you won't win," Diana said.

"Yeah." Edilio nodded.

"Listen to me," Albert said, placating, knowing he was speaking the unspeakable. "None of us likes these choices, but that's what we have. Right? We have what we have."

"Maybe," Edilio said. "But there are things I'll do, and things I won't do. I'll die trying to keep people alive. But I won't do murder."

He slung his rifle and marched from the room with Dekka and Quinn in his wake.

NINETEEN

SAM AND CAINE saw the school bus. It wasn't a particularly unusual thing, really: the last of the gas was occasionally parceled out to get kids to this, the farthest out of the farming areas.

But there was something too silent about the bus and the field. If the bus had brought kids out here, then they should be seeing them.

They found the first body lying facedown, leg stretched out into the dirt, face on blacktop. Something very, very powerful had smashed the body and then ripped off one leg. The remaining leg wore a red sneaker.

"She's not that far ahead of us," Caine said. "She's probably going straight down the highway."

"If we run . . . ," Sam said, though he felt too tired to last long running.

"You go right ahead and run. I'll take the bus," Caine said.

"Ah. Yeah, that would be better. Have you ever driven a bus?"

Caine shook his head. "No, I have not."

"Strangely enough," Sam said, remembering the long-ago moment of terror and competence that had earned him the nickname School Bus Sam, "I have."

Lana heard the sound of the door opening and someone clearing their throat. Without looking up she said, "I can't take any more messed-up kids!" She had been running in a sort of desperate relay race, going from person to person in the room, out in the hall, in the room next door, laying on hands, trying to keep the worst hurt from dying, parceling out a minute here, five minutes there. It was working. Except for the two who had died because she hadn't gotten to them in time. No one else had died. Yet.

The throat clearer at the door turned out to be Astrid. Lana looked sourly at her. "You want something?"

"Do you have a minute?"

"Do I have a minute? Sure, who do you want to have die while we chat?"

Patrick came padding up to Lana and nuzzled her, as though sensing that his master was on the edge.

Lana had a hand each on a boy, maybe twelve, and a three-year-old girl. The boy was burned over half his body, the clothing melted into the bubbled and cooled flesh. The girl had lacerations on her face that would ensure she would never be a pretty girl again unless Lana healed those wounds.

Astrid squatted down in front of Lana, who was herself cross-legged on a big cushion she dragged from casualty to casualty.

Lana had great respect for Astrid's loyalty to Sam. She had great respect for her intelligence. And she had even come to respect her toughness. She had never quite decided that she liked Astrid.

"The gaiaphage," Astrid said.

"What about it?"

"Diana says—"

"Is that witch in town? Great. Are you trusting her?"

"She brought us useful information. She's been with Gaia. Her *daughter*."

Lana snorted derisively. "There is no Gaia; there's only the same Darkness there's been since day one."

"Diana says she—okay, it—hates you."

Lana barked out a laugh. "Yeah? The feeling's mutual."

Astrid was wearing her patient face as she said, "The gaiaphage can't reach you anymore. That's why it hates you."

"Whatever. Not really my problem right now."

"The question is, can you reach it if you need to?"

Lana's face was hard as stone. "Why would I want to do that?"

"Because it's coming. And I'm looking for any weapon we can use."

"I'm the weapon," a voice said. Brianna sat up on the couch. Her face was still burned, though was no longer blood red. There were patches that looked almost normal. But one eye was swollen shut.

"You're half blind, you idiot," Lana said, but not angrily, affectionately.

Brianna jumped up, wiggled her legs like the world's fastest tap dancer, shook her arms fast enough to create a breeze.

"*Sit!*" Lana roared. To Lana's amazement, Brianna sat. So did Patrick. "Listen to me, Brianna: that burn is bad, and if I don't heal it now you may be stuck with a half-melted face and no hair. Do you understand that? After a while it's a chronic condition, not an injury, and I won't be able to heal it any more than I can make someone not be ugly."

"Ugly may be the least of our worries," Astrid said. "You have any idea how dangerous a creature we're talking about? It's Sam, Caine, Dekka, Brianna . . . all rolled into one."

Lana felt as if the ground was opening beneath her. But also like she had known it would. Like she'd been expecting it for a long time.

She had fended off the evil; she had not defeated it. She couldn't. She knew that. It had taken all her strength to shut her mind to the Darkness. It felt almost as if the gaiaphage had infected some physical part of her brain and Lana had healed that damaged bit. But the scar tissue remained and was still sensitive to the slightest touch.

She could feel it reaching for her. It had been out there probing for a moment of weakness for a long time. The gaiaphage did not like defiance. It especially did not like successful resistance. It demanded submission.

Now it had at last brought total war to the FAYZ, and Lana couldn't sit on the sidelines.

Could she? Could she? Please?

In a dull, lifeless voice Lana said, "Help Sanjit give these kids water."

"I'm not here to—"

"I'm taking five, Astrid," Lana said, glaring up at her, and Astrid nodded.

Lana's knees cracked as she stood up, and it was a few steps before she could straighten all the way. She went out into the hallway, past the crying, scared, and traumatized kids lying under blankets on the floor, past Sanjit's little brothers and sisters, each trying to offer comfort or prayers.

Down the stairs and out onto the long-dead lawn. Here she was shielded from the eyes of lookers, but she could see the ocean. She soaked in the air, which should have been fresh but tasted of fire.

Then she closed her eyes and turned her thoughts to the Darkness.

Hello, Darkness, my old friend. The words of an old song. *Hello, Darkness.*

The effort was through a space Lana could not see but could feel, manipulating limbs she didn't have, listening for soundlessness, looking for an object she could only see by looking away.

But then: the contact. The gaiaphage felt her touch. It

reacted violently, lashing out, trying to push her away. Sensing a trap.

Lana cried out in pain. No one heard her.

She wept a little—memories, mostly—then wiped the tears away.

She went back inside, felt rather than really saw Astrid's expectant gaze.

"It's coming. But it's hurt. It's trying to heal. It's coming straight down the highway."

"How soon?" Astrid asked.

"It can be killed, I think. It thinks so, anyway," Lana said, in a wondering whisper. Her hand moved reflexively to the automatic pistol still stuck in her belt. "It's afraid."

"Edilio's setting up an ambush."

"No!" Lana said furiously. "Do it now. Now! Kill it now while it's weak. If it heals that body, we're all dead."

Lana grabbed Astrid by both shoulders and looked her in the eye. "Listen to me. I had a chance to kill it once and it beat me. This is a second chance. There won't be a third. Kill it. Kill it! Tell them all, whatever it takes, Astrid. Kill it!"

"There she is!" Caine said. He was in the front seat of the bus, which Sam was driving with painstaking care, weaving across the highway.

Gaia was a quarter mile away, just passing a pair of burned-out cars. She was dragging what looked a lot like a human leg. The foot wore a tattered red sneaker.

"Floor it!" Caine said.

"She'll hear us," Sam countered.

"Look again. She has earbuds in. We're only about two miles from town. Now or never, surfer dude. Floor it! Floor it!"

Sam did. The engine didn't exactly leap to respond. It accelerated at a slow, stately pace, only gradually picking up speed. Caine watched the speedometer needle.

Twenty.

Twenty-five.

Thirty.

Sam weaved madly around an overturned van, and the bus squealed on two wheels.

Thirty-five.

"She doesn't know we're here; hit her, *hit* her!"

Forty.

The distance was eaten up in a rush.

Thirty-five.

"What are you doing?" Caine demanded. He was gripping the chrome pole with white fingers.

"I don't know!" Sam yelled. "It's not me!"

The engine sputtered. Coughed. And suddenly they were freewheeling.

"We're out of gas!"

The bus slowed but did not stop.

Fifteen miles an hour and a hundred feet left. Gaia was smack in the middle of the road.

The engine caught! It found a last sip of gas and the bus jolted forward, and the instant before it reached Gaia she leaped nimbly aside.

The bus seemed to be moving in slow motion now. Caine saw Gaia twist, her face older, no longer quite a little girl, her eyes mad with fear and fury.

She raised a hand, and a beam of light stabbed through the bus, not a foot away from Caine, then burned right through seats, sidewall to sidewall. Acrid smoke filled the bus.

But Gaia was off balance and tripped. Sam slammed open the door. Caine swung to hang off it, raised one hand, and threw Gaia back. The bus veered, clipped a car, slowed further still, and Caine was out, running, stumbling, fighting for balance, trying to close the distance with Gaia when a punch of invisible force knocked him down flat on his back.

Through misted eyes Caine saw Sam jump from the bus, roll, jump up, and fire with both hands at once.

The beams were nowhere near Gaia: they fired without effect over her head.

Gaia raised both hands, laughed, and lifted Sam up and up into the air. Sam fired at her and burned furrows in the concrete.

Suddenly Sam fell.

He did not cry out. He didn't stop firing. But he hit the concrete with a loud crunch. He cried out in pain, struggled, but did not rise.

Gaia walked calmly toward them, and Caine raised his hands to hit her with everything he had . . . and the inside of his head exploded. Caine fell to his knees, clutched his head, and screamed in unbearable pain.

"Gaaaahhh!"

Like knives. Like a wild beast tearing its way into his skull through his eyes. Like being crushed in some massive vise. It was impossible to believe nothing was touching him.

He shrieked. "Stop it! Stop it!"

But the pain did not stop.

Through a swirling migraine distortion Caine saw Sam pulling his broken body around to face Gaia. Gaia used her telekinetic power to lift the crashed van and drop it just in front of Sam, cutting him off from view, blocking his field of fire.

"Stop it!" Caine begged.

Gaia stood over him, glowing faintly green, feet planted wide, and watched as he writhed in agony, as he bent double, holding his head in his hands, and screamed.

On it went, and his voice was hoarse from screaming. On and on it went as his entire body went into spasm, as he lost control of himself, slavered and drooled and wet himself.

If he could have taken his own life . . .

And still it went on.

Then the pain stopped.

Caine lay on the concrete road. He gasped air through a raw throat. His heart jackhammered in his chest. His entire body was slicked with sweat.

"Father," Gaia said.

"Don't hurt me," Caine whispered. He didn't have the will to look up at her.

Gaia laughed. "Have you seen Mother? I seem to have lost her."

"Don't do it again. Just don't do it again."

"I asked a question." Steel in her voice.

Caine couldn't recall a question. Words? Had she spoken words? His body still shook. He still clutched his head, as if somehow his hands could shut her out.

"Have. You. Seen. Mother?"

"No. No. Diana . . . I thought she was with you. Did you . . . ?"

"Did I kill her? Is that what you want to know?"

Caine was afraid to nod, afraid that she was toying with him, afraid she was looking for a pretext to hurt him again.

"Not yet," Gaia said. "Soon. Probably."

That slight uncertainty gave Caine a glimmer of hope. But still he did not look up, afraid to give any offense.

"I dropped my food," Gaia said. "Pick it up and carry it for me."

"Your—aaaaahhhh!"

This time the pain only lasted a second. A reminder. A whip snapped at a difficult horse.

Caine saw the leg. It had been gnawed.

"Take it and walk in front of me. If you even turn around, I'll hurt you and make it last until your mind is gone. My power grows, Father. You can no longer defy me. No one can. Not even *her*."

Caine did not know who she meant by "her." Did she mean Diana? Gaia glared toward Perdido Beach.

Caine took the leg by the ankle. It was heavy. It smelled like a barbecue grill that needed cleaning. Shaking, he lifted it and headed toward town.

Would Sam be able to kill her as they passed by?

Please let him kill her.

They walked around the van, and there was Sam. His body was twisted at a comical angle. He was propped on one elbow and raised the other to strike. But he couldn't keep his hand elevated. Something was wrong in the bones of his shoulder, the bones of his back. His face was white.

Gaia calmly lifted Caine and held him suspended ludicrously between herself and Sam. Sam would have to burn through Caine to reach her.

As they drew nearer, Gaia flicked a finger and knocked Sam onto his back. His head hit pavement with a sickening crack.

"Lie there until I'm ready to come back and kill you," Gaia said. "It won't be long."

She put her earbuds back in and walked behind a beaten Caine.

TWENTY

THE ISLAND, WHERE she looked at a startled Leslie-Ann.

The power plant, where she saw no one.

The forest. Same. No one. But lots of fire. She bounced out of there quickly.

The beach, where she saw a dead fish and some driftwood.

The so-called hospital, where one sick girl was wandering, calling for Dahra.

The lake. Dead bodies bloated in the water. Others like fish washed up onshore.

Taylor paused there.

What. Was. What.

What was she?

She had memories. Like old predigital photographs curled with age. She looked at them and understood them. But they weren't really hers. They belonged to Taylor. She was Taylor, but she was not that Taylor.

A random spot in the desert. No one.

A wrecked train. No one.

A field of artichokes. Worms seethed from the ground, touched her, and retreated.

What. Am. I?

Taylor saw that someone was following her, but not someone she could quite see.

No one could move like Taylor. But he could.

She bounced to the ruined ghost town by the mine shaft. He bounced with her.

What. Are. You? Invisible bouncer?

She had an idea then. She bounced twelve times instantaneously, spending only a half second in each place.

He was there.

Following her.

What are you? he asked her.

I don't know, she answered.

Maybe I can help you, the invisible one said. I made you this way. I didn't mean to. Maybe I can fix you.

Taylor felt. She hadn't felt lately, but now she felt. Something. Like she was water and someone was plunging a hand into her. She gave way: she formed around the probing.

For a moment she was gone. Then back. For a moment she felt disturbed, and then not.

Suddenly she gasped. She drew air into her mouth. It was surprising. She hadn't breathed lately, though she remembered breathing before. That other Taylor.

"I can't remember what I did to make you this way."

She heard the voice, though she saw no one here.

"But I'm trying."

She reached up and touched her hair with a golden hand. "My hair," she said, the words a shock to her. The voice coming from her thoughts felt alien. "It's wrong."

"Like this?" Little Pete asked, because now she knew it was him.

She touched her hair, and it was no longer a single rubbery sheet. It was black hair. Her hair.

"This is better," she said.

"Your eyes," he said.

"Yes?"

"Is this better?"

She felt that strange touch, that solidity where she was somehow liquid. And suddenly she saw him. He didn't look like Little Pete. He looked like a swirl of light, like a thousand fireflies swarming together.

"I can't do more right now," Little Pete said. "I am weak, and the Darkness will notice. It looks away from you now. It has forgotten you."

Some part of Taylor, some reawakened part of her, some fragment of the old Taylor, realized that she was not back to what she had once been. Her eyes saw things and her ears heard things differently than in the old days, before. But there was breath in her lungs. And a heartbeat in her chest.

And she had hair.

"I hurt you, even though I didn't mean to. I can't ask you to help me," Little Pete said.

"You don't have to," Taylor answered. "I know the Darkness. I know it hates the Healer. I know what side I am on."

TWENTY-ONE

EDILIO HAD HEARD Lana's warning by way of Astrid. But attack? With what? With who? People were just now coming back in from some of the fields. Brianna was still down. Sam missing, Caine missing, Jack reluctant, Orc willing but exhausted.

Attack? Where?

No, that might be good advice in other circumstances. Not with what he had available. Besides, he had an instinct. If Gaia wasn't already here, it was because she was waiting for darkness. She might be a monster, but she was a monster used to darkness, not to broad daylight. She had attacked the lake at night, despite having Brianna's speed. She had waited for night.

She would wait for darkness again.

Edilio was well aware that he was playing a hunch, and playing with all their lives. Like every general since the dawn of time, he was assessing his forces, trying to understand his enemy, putting his bet down and rolling the dice.

He had made his arrangements. He was on automatic now, not thinking about Roger, not thinking about the images of corpses floating on the lake.

If he'd been there, maybe . . .

"Dekka, how long can you maintain a gravity-free zone?"

"As long as you want, Edilio."

She was being too nice, feeling sorry for him.

"I want you to be out of sight," he said.

"But anytime I do my thing, everything floats up. Dirt, plants, rocks . . . It's not exactly invisible."

"I know. I was thinking if you kept it just to the concrete on the road. Just like a narrow slice. Nothing to float there. Also, it's starting to get dark, and the ash from the fire . . ."

Dekka nodded. "I can do it."

Edilio had chosen a spot right at the edge of town, near Ralph's grocery store. Open ground was his enemy: he needed places to hide shooters, he needed a complex terrain, and he needed to be concealed.

There was an overturned moving van. It had long since been looted, of course, and the household goods were strewn all around the area: leather easy chair, cracked by the sunlight; a dining-room table with wood bleached by exposure; a mattress in plastic wrap; boxes of books and boxes that had once held clothing. Knickknacks, lawn furniture, a bundle of brooms and mops, all of it tossed around on the road and the shoulder. The van itself was two-thirds empty, and what was left was just a jumble of small tables and chairs and cardboard. It was dark inside.

"Are Orc and Jack here yet?" Edilio called over his shoulder.

"Just walking up," Dekka said.

"Okay, Dekka, find your spot, do your thing. About twenty yards down the road. You can hide behind that burned-out Volkswagen."

Orc and Jack—one lumbering, the other stepping cautiously—appeared. Edilio pointed at the roof of the moving van, which was now a wall. "I want six holes punched in here, just big enough for a shooter to see through and shoot from."

He walked away and heard six hard blows.

Did he have six capable shooters? He looked around. He'd started the day with twenty-four of his trained people. Somehow he was now down to seventeen. Some had gone to pick food, driven by hunger more than cowardice. Ten were lying in wait around the town plaza—plan B. More might join when the field hands came back. He had seven here. Six for the van, one to use as a sharpshooter with a scoped rifle fifty feet down the road.

"Don't shoot until you see Gaia stumble or start to kind of float, right? When she walks into Dekka's field. Once that happens, you shoot." He held up a cautionary finger. "Shoot smart, like you've practiced, right? Aim every shot. Don't stop until you've run out of ammo. Don't assume she's dead. Don't forget, she can heal like Lana."

Orc and Jack emerged from the van and Edilio said, "You get some sleep, Jack?"

"A little."

"A little is all anyone got."

"Yeah, but I—"

"Jack, I know you don't want to fight."

"I just—"

"I don't care," Edilio said flatly. "It's no longer your choice. I'm drafting you."

"You can't—" Jack started to say.

"The one person I care most about is floating dead in a lake," Edilio said. "Pretty soon everyone will be dead. That includes you, Jack. Everyone you know."

Jack's defiance withered as Edilio met his eyes and didn't let go.

"Good," Edilio said. "Here's the way this goes."

He laid out his plan, which hinged entirely on Gaia not spotting the ambush. Diana had told them all she could about her daughter, so they knew Gaia was nearsighted. Maybe that would help. Maybe, too, the fact that Gaia only had bits and pieces of human knowledge, so she hadn't seen a hundred ambushes laid in a hundred movies and TV shows.

It was a pitiful plan. Gaia would burn through them like a hot knife through butter. They would be forced to run for it and they wouldn't make it. Any who did survive would be caught in a panicky cross fire in the town plaza, where ten shooters hid in windows and doorways.

Well, ten minus however many had run off.

Edilio walked up the road to the very edge of Dekka's gravity cancellation. He checked the clip in his automatic rifle. He slowly slid back the bolt to see the round already chambered.

He stroked the safety with his index finger.

Where were Sam and Caine?

Where was Brianna? Would she be able to come?

How had Edilio ended up as bait?

That idea sent a wave of nausea through him. Bait. Like a body floating in a lake.

Mother Mary, take care of him. Please take him to heaven and let him be happy.

Tears filled his eyes. No. No time for that.

A figure appeared in the middle distance, walking down the road, red in the last slanting rays of sunset. Now two figures. One walked in front of the other.

Well, at least now he knew what had happened to Caine. Had he gone over to her side?

They had little enough chance against Gaia. Against Gaia and Caine together?

Well, Edilio thought, *I'll be seeing you soon, Roger.*

He wished he had his rosary with him. *Santa María, Madre de Dios, ruega por nosotros pecadores, ahora y en la hora de nuestra muerte. Amen.*

La hora de nuestra muerte. The hour of our death. . . .

Edilio raised his automatic rifle and fired six shots at Gaia.

Sam had endured pain before. This was not as bad as the whipping Drake had given him, but it was bad. And each time he hauled himself another few inches down the road it made him cry out. He couldn't even be sure what had been broken. But he knew that he could not feel one leg and the other tingled like a banged funny bone. And he felt a twisting, grinding agony in his back and shoulder.

He didn't even know how long he had been like this. There were periods of unconsciousness of unknown duration. He seemed to fade in and out, nightmare sleep followed by pain-racked awakening.

At this rate he would get to Perdido Beach . . . never. He had at least a mile to go just to get to Ralph's, six inches at a time. He would die of hunger or thirst long before he reached help. Gaia had turned Caine, or maybe just tortured him into submission. It didn't matter which, because if Caine helped her, or even if Caine just stayed out of the fight, the odds would grow impossible.

"Unh!" he cried as he pulled himself forward.

He could get up on one foot and hop, maybe that would be faster, but if he fell, the pain would be awful.

Maybe he shouldn't think ill of Caine. He had no idea what agony Gaia could cause his brother. He was unwilling just to risk a fall onto a broken leg; maybe Caine feared something worse.

Astrid. At least Gaia would not stretch out her death. Gaia would kill everyone as quickly and efficiently as she could. She would burn the town down to do it. Force everyone from hiding and kill them with a light like his own.

"Unh!"

He was useless, here at the end, useless. The great and

powerful Sam Temple, crawling like a mutilated insect down a road as the sun set out over the ocean. The final sunset of the FAYZ.

It was unfair. They had all believed the end was in sight. To be slaughtered like those poor kids at the lake, all of them just cut down, crushed. All those lives . . .

Astrid.

He'd actually had fantasies of the two of them walking out of this place hand in hand. He had run endless scenarios, wondering how they could stay together outside, out there.

And she had been worrying about the aftermath, how they would all be seen by the world. Well, maybe this was better. Maybe it would just be better to—

No, to hell with that. No, they deserved to live. They all had paid and paid and paid their dues a thousand times over. They deserved to live.

Someone.

He looked up, flinching, fearing it was the gaiaphage.

The creature before him was bizarre, a golden-skinned, eerily smooth-looking thing.

"Taylor?"

Her eyes blinked. They had changed, somehow. She had changed. She still had that impossible golden skin, but her hair . . . and her mouth was different, somehow more human.

"Taylor! Don't bounce! Stay!"

Did she understand? Lana must have finally found a way to heal her. Although she was no longer the old Taylor who had flirted and teased him so often: unreliable, flighty, gossipy Taylor.

"Taylor, help me," he said.

"I will," she said.

"You can talk!"

"Yes," she said, and she seemed a bit baffled by it.

"Okay, listen, Taylor. I need something to write on. Paper, a pen, a pencil, anything you can get me to . . ."

And she was gone. No nod of the head, not a word.

He dragged himself again, but his arms and shoulders were aching from the effort, cramping from the unusual work demanded of them.

He stopped.

They were all going to die. And he, the big protector, the warrior, wouldn't even be there for the final battle. Eventually Gaia would come back down the road, find him, and finish him off, kill him as easy as stepping on a bug.

Why hadn't she already?

Wait a minute, why hadn't she killed him? It made no sense. She should have.

Taylor was suddenly in front of him. In her hand she had a single Post-it note. Orange. And a pencil.

"Thank you."

Who should he write to? A last "I love you" for Astrid? She would sneer if he used this final opportunity for a stupid romantic gesture. No, no good-byes. Not yet.

He tried to think clearly. Edilio would have a battle to

fight. Dekka would be in it, too, and if Sam asked her, she would come to save him, no matter what. He couldn't do that to her and the others. It had to be someone resourceful. Someone with no powers necessary for the battle. Someone he could trust.

He began writing. The first word was "Quinn."

Edilio was in the road, holding an automatic rifle.

It was an ambush. Caine saw it immediately. Not that he saw anyone out there aside from Edilio. But Edilio wouldn't be standing there in the middle of the road if it wasn't an ambush.

The leg was in Caine's arms.

Gaia was behind him.

She was singing. Badly. The song was hard to decipher, not something he had ever heard before, or at least nothing he recognized. Gaia sounded as if she was singing, "Mmmm. Bop. Bop. Bop."

"Mmmmm. Bop. Bop. Bop. There's a person up there," Gaia said. She took out her earbuds.

"Yes," Caine said. He didn't dare speak another word unasked. He tried to think, but inside he was cringing, waiting in mortal terror of the pain.

What was Edilio up to? Did he think he could outfight Gaia?

Only Edilio was visible. They didn't have Sam over there, obviously, which meant they probably had Dekka and

Brianna, Jack and Orc. Could they really take on Gaia?

Maybe. If he helped them.

Maybe. If at the right moment he committed: all-in. And if they failed? What she would do to him . . . She wouldn't let him die; he would beg for it, but she would just go right on and he would—

"Who is it?" Gaia asked.

Would she know if he lied? He couldn't hesitate. "I think it's Edilio."

"What are his powers?"

"None," Caine said. And thought, Unless you count having the courage to stand out there facing the gaiaphage.

"Then keep moving, Father," Gaia said.

"He does have a gun."

"Do you think I fear a gun?"

You should, you arrogant . . . "No, but I do," Caine said.

"Ah. I see. I can't have you killed yet," Gaia said.

Suddenly shots rang out. One, two, three, four, five, six.

Gaia laughed gleefully as the bullets buzzed by. "My leg is sufficiently healed. Stay down, Father, I still need your power. You can't die just yet!"

She blurred away like Brianna.

Quinn.

Hurt bad. On highway. Reach me from that little cove if u can.

Sam.

Quinn read the note twice. The truth was, this Taylor—this weird Taylor 3.0 standing here—creeped him out. She wasn't in as bad a shape as when he'd last seen her down the hall from Lana's room—Taylor 2.0—but she was still pretty strange.

The truth was also that the note moved him. Sam was calling on him. *Him.* After all the ups and downs he'd been through with Sam. Of course it was because the others were more important for the fight. Of course. Still.

"Worth using a bit of diesel," Quinn said, trying to sound all cool about it. "Thanks, Taylor. I hope you—" But she was gone. And frankly, he was relieved. Quinn had come a long way since the first days of the FAYZ, but he was still not fond of weird, impossible creatures.

"How is it I got more normal and everything else got weirder?" he asked the night air.

Somewhere fairly far away there was the sound of gunfire.

Dekka waited, heard the sudden burst of gunfire, and saw Edilio running past in staged terror—well, not entirely staged terror; it had to be at least partly very real terror. She herself was quivering with fear. She dared not even peek around the side, could not give away the ambush. One chance to get it right.

Then suddenly gunfire from half a dozen guns.

She popped up and yes! Yes! Gaia had hit her force field. Gaia was still running, but running in the air, flailing, getting nowhere.

The gaiaphage—she refused to think of it as a little girl—
was about head height now, orange in the rays of a setting
sun. She still hadn't realized what had happened to her.

BLAM! BLAM! BLAM!

She saw a chunk of flesh blown from Gaia's arm. But the
bullets were missing. Gaia was rising too fast and too high
now to make an easy target. Dekka had to moderate the field,
drop her again, bring her back down into range.

Twin beams of brilliant green light stabbed from Gaia's
hands, and the firing from the moving van faltered. No one
had been hit, but now Gaia was using the altitude to her
advantage: she was able to spot the shooters and was firing
back.

It was like some terrible parody of a rock concert laser
show. Bright beams of light melted runs in the road surface,
then reached the moving van and sliced it neatly into three
uneven pieces.

Dekka heard an unearthly scream and saw people bolting
from the van. Blinding light followed them as they ran.

Edilio had stopped and now stood, legs apart, rifle steady,
taking aim.

BLAM!

And Dekka saw the bullet clip Gaia's ear. Blood sprayed.

The monster cried in pain, and Dekka shouted in fierce
joy.

"Yeah! Yeah!"

But Gaia was not seriously hurt. And now down came
Gaia, dropping too quickly toward the ground. Gaia

had used her own mirroring of Dekka's power to restore gravity.

Dekka strained, focused with all her might, but Gaia was too strong. Bleeding and howling in rage Gaia touched down and leveled a shocking telekinetic blast at the moving van, which knocked the three segments apart, exposing the remaining shooters. They broke and ran.

Gaia stretched out a hand, raised a car from the pavement, and used it almost like a bowling ball: rolled it down the road and crushed three of the runners. There was no time for screams. They were bugs squashed on the highway.

Edilio still stood, firing, defenseless, almost daring Gaia to kill him.

"Jack! Orc!" Edilio shouted over the sound of his own gun.

A wooden telephone pole, thirty feet long, trailing telephone lines, flew like a javelin. Gaia ducked and the blunt end missed her, but as the pole flew, it dropped and caught her shoulder, slamming her hard around.

She pushed the pole away and it rattled onto the road, rolled a few feet, and stopped.

Edilio still kept up his fire, but now Gaia hit him with an invisible fist and knocked him a hundred yards off the road into the dark.

"No!" Dekka roared, and went for Gaia with nothing but her fists as weapons.

Gaia grabbed her face in one hand and laughed as Dekka punched air.

"You're the one with the power over gravity, aren't you? I

could almost do without you," Gaia said. Blood still spurted from her ear. Almost absentmindedly, Gaia reached her free hand to touch it and stop the flow. "So don't annoy me." She twisted Dekka's face and sent her sprawling.

Suddenly Gaia was a blur. Picking herself up Dekka saw a boy simply explode from the force of a blow he'd never seen coming. A girl, screaming, was tripped and then thrown with a sickening crunch into a wrecked car. The last of Edilio's shooters.

Gaia paused then, blurring back into sight, and held a hand against the bullet wound on her ear. The chunk taken out of her arm had already stopped bleeding.

From out of the darkness at the side of the road, Edilio fired again.

BLAM! BLAM!

Gaia snarled and swept a telekinetic fist like a haymaker punch and the firing stopped.

"Edilio!" Dekka cried.

"Ah, so that was Edilio," Gaia said. "I've heard of him. I should have killed him, but I thought he might be a mutant." Gaia did not blur out again; she was clearly focused on healing herself.

Dekka looked around for a weapon, anything. "Jack! Jack!" she cried, but no answer came.

She saw Caine, still carrying a human leg, coming down the road, uncertain.

"Caine!" Dekka cried, her voice ragged. "Help us!"

Caine looked like a different person. A zombie version of

himself. He dropped the leg and looked down at his hands as if they were not his.

All firing had stopped. Gaia stood alone, triumphant.

Then from the shadow stepped a living slag heap.

Gaia did a double take. "What are you?"

"Orc."

"You're not human," Gaia said dismissively. "I don't even need to kill you. Run away."

"No."

Gaia cocked her head, curious, as she chewed her food. "Aren't you afraid?"

Orc shook his massive head. "The Lord is my shepherd."

Gaia walked right up to him, peering carefully at his gravel skin and taking special interest in the patch of human skin that remained on his face. "Interesting effect. I don't quite see how you happened."

Orc swung a ham-sized fist at her.

Gaia sidestepped with Brianna's speed. She dodged Orc's next three blows as well.

"Not at all the usual mutation," Gaia said, fascinated. "You could join me; I doubt Nemesis could use you."

Orc was panting from the effort of missing Gaia.

"No," Orc gasped.

"Mmmm. Well, then, I guess I'd better kill you, just to be safe."

"That's gunfire!" Brianna yelled.

Lana said, "Brianna, no! You're not done healing."

"What, this?" Brianna pointed at her disfigured face. "Pff. Just a flesh wound." She winked with her good eye. "Where's my stuff?"

Lana nodded toward a pile in the corner: the familiar modified runner's backpack with the sawed-off shotgun and machete.

"Kick ass, Breeze," Lana said, but she was talking to air.

Down the hall in a second. Down the steps in less. Through the lobby. And now she could really turn on the speed as she blew down the hill, tripped, and went tumbling head over heels.

Brianna did not get up with super-speed. She stood slowly. Both knees were bleeding, as were the palms of her hands.

Brianna touched her swollen eyes.

"Depth perception, Breeze," she chided herself. "Depth perception."

She slowed through town, doing no more than sixty miles an hour down Ocean Boulevard past a darkening sea that was just swallowing the sun. She hung a hard right on San Pablo, blew through the town plaza, slowing just enough to hear the fierce cheers of "Breeeeze!" from shooters positioned in windows and on rooftops. She gave them a jaunty wave.

She hit the highway and cranked a left toward the sound of gunfire, passed a fleeing kid, noticed that the entire north-west was on fire and the air smelled of smoke, yanked out her machete, and had merely enough time to think, This could go bad, before she saw Gaia and Orc.

Gaia had a hand on Orc's throat, and Orc, forced to his

knees, was punching air as Gaia twisted her head this way and that to dodge blows. Gaia was laughing. Her blue eyes were alight.

Brianna blurred to a stop.

"Hey. Gaia. Remember me?"

Gaia tossed Orc aside as though he weighed no more than a toy.

TWENTY-TWO

THE FIGHT LASTED six seconds.

In that time Brianna rushed, swung her machete, and missed.

Gaia swung a fist as powerful as Jack's and caught just a corner of Brianna's shoulder, spinning Brianna away to sprawl on the concrete.

Brianna was up in a flash, snapped her shotgun up, fired, and hit Gaia in the chest with a load of buckshot that knocked Gaia staggering back with seven small holes in her.

Brianna rushed, yelling, "Die!" stuck her shotgun into the stunned Gaia's mouth, and pulled the trigger.

And there was no explosion. Dud shell.

Brianna's one good eye widened and Gaia's hand was on her neck. Impossible to get away. Brianna swung her machete, but the angle was all wrong, so she caught Gaia's neck, too low and too weak. Blood was everywhere.

But Brianna's head was woozy. The weakness was spreading through her.

She struck again, and Gaia easily blocked this blow, ripped Brianna's machete from her hand, and threw it aside.

Gaia's face, those cold blue eyes, were all Brianna could see. But she felt Gaia's hand pressing palm-out against her heart and knew . . .

"NO!" Dekka screamed.

But there was a hole burned right through Brianna. A smoking hole where her heart should be.

Brianna's body fell limp. Suddenly so small.

Gaia fell back, touched the buckshot wounds, but then realized the arterial spray from her neck was the bigger problem. She was bathed in her own blood.

"NO!" Dekka screamed again, and charged, with Orc at her side, with Jack suddenly yelling, rushing up from the side of the road, all straight at Gaia.

Gaia fired the killing light but missed, and now retreated in confusion, her already weak vision blurred by her own blood.

She tried to turn on her speed, but she felt it ebbing. Of course: she had just killed the girl with the power of speed! She'd had no choice: another few seconds and she herself would have been dead.

Gaia turned to run, but the gray monster would be on her in seconds. She kicked wildly and hurled herself through the air, canceled gravity to slow her descent, touched down, and kicked off again into the darkness, trailing an arc of blood behind her.

"No, no, no! Brianna!" Dekka sobbed, cradling the burned head in her arms. The obscene hole in her chest did not even bleed; it had been cauterized.

Brianna's eyes were still open. In a hundred movies Dekka had seen the survivors shut the eyes of the dead, but no, she couldn't do that. Those were *Brianna's* eyes. She couldn't be gone. She couldn't be dead, not the cocky, funny, terrifyingly brave little girl Dekka loved.

"Get Lana!" Dekka raged. "Get Lana!"

"We'll get her," Edilio said softly, but Dekka knew better. Lana healed the injured; she did not raise the dead. Brianna's lioness heart had burned from her body.

Dekka looked up at Edilio, tears streaming so she could barely make out his features. He knelt beside her and put his arms around her.

Still holding Brianna, Dekka buried her face in Edilio's shoulder and sobbed uncontrollably.

Orc did not stop chasing Gaia. But he couldn't see her, and after a while he couldn't hear her. Maybe she was hiding. Maybe she was just too fast. Jack caught up with him.

"Where did she go?" Jack cried.

"I don't know."

They stopped running. They stood side by side on the dark highway. Neither knew what to do. Neither could bear the thought of going back and seeing Dekka cry. And seeing the body of the girl who had more than once fought their battles and saved their lives.

Anything but that, anything but that.

"I changed my mind, Lord," Orc said to the night sky. "It don't matter if people see me. Please let us out of here. This place is too sad."

Sam had passed out, or maybe it was just sleep. Hard to differentiate. He expected to wake up at any moment to find Gaia gloating down at him.

Instead when he woke it was to realize that Quinn and one of his crewmen were lifting him up off the pavement. Taylor stood a short distance away, saw, then disappeared.

Sam said something brilliant like, "Huh?"

And then either passed out or went back to sleep. Hard to differentiate.

He wasn't quite conscious enough to put names to the sounds of a low-power motor or waves slapping the bow, but they were comforting.

He woke once more as they were bundling him up onto the dock. He said, "Astrid?"

"She was okay last I saw her," Quinn said.

"Then evr'thin' 'kay," Sam slurred.

"I wish that was true, my friend," Quinn said.

TWENTY-THREE

"WHERE ARE YOU in all this, Caine?" Edilio asked him.

They stood on the road, staring out into the dark. Dekka still wept. No one had tried to take Brianna's body away from her.

Orc had come back from a futile attempt to find Gaia. Jack was standing a few feet away from Brianna. There were tears running down his face, but he hadn't been able to find a way to go closer. Jack and Brianna had had a complicated relationship. He had flirted with her in his own awkward way; they had made out once or twice, neither of them really enjoying the experience much. Brianna was too fierce for Jack, and he was too geeky for her. But he had cared for her. Just not with the intensity of Dekka.

So he just stood, awkward, bearing silent witness.

"Me?" Caine said. He sounded exhausted. Defeated. He was staring at Brianna. "We fought side by side once, me and Breeze. Against the bugs. She was badass."

Edilio made an impatient sound. His voice was ragged. "Listen, Caine, I have no time. For all we know that monster will be back in five minutes."

Edilio saw pride flare in Caine's eyes, but then it died. "The truth is she . . . it . . . it has its hooks in me," he said. "It's stronger now. Or maybe I'm weaker. Either way, the pain she hits me with . . . you don't want to know what it's like."

Edilio could see the truth of it in his haggard expression.

"Without you and Sam both we probably can't beat her," Edilio said.

"Yeah, well, Sam's lying out there busted up. Maybe dead for all I know."

"Then we have to get him," Edilio said urgently.

"Walk down that road right now?" Caine asked. "Are you out of your mind?"

"I'm not sitting here while—"

"Go out there and she'll pick you off easy," Caine said. "Take anyone with you and you're just getting them killed, too."

Caine looked around, lost. "If I try to fight her, she'll make me crazy. You don't know . . . Anyway, Sam and I already tried . . ." He shook his head. "We can't beat her. We can't beat the gaiaphage; we never could. It was always going to end this way with all of us being hunted down, one by one. We were always the sheep and it was the wolf."

"Shut up, Caine," Edilio said in a voice so soft it was almost a whisper.

Anger, a dangerous anger, flared in Caine. "Who are you to talk to me that way?"

"You've been the problem, Caine. From the start. You're the one who kept us from ever really being able to unite, to fight this thing. You and your ego and your stupid need to control everyone. Don't you come here now all sheepish, all head hanging down and tell me you're scared." Edilio stabbed a finger in Caine's chest. It was such an un-Edilio moment it surprised both of them.

Edilio knew his own fear was pushing him now, because he knew Caine wasn't wrong about the likely ending. Still, he needed Caine's power on his side to have any slight hope. And he definitely needed hope.

"I lost someone I loved at the lake," Edilio said, his voice full of emotion. "Maybe seventy kids died up there. Just now, six, eight more. Now, Brianna dead. More to come. Well, some of that is on you, Caine. So you are going to step up. You hear me? You are going to step up."

Edilio had nothing else to say, and Caine seemed to have no answer. So Edilio turned back to Dekka and Jack and said, "That's it for grieving. We do more grieving later if we're alive. Right now we fall back and get ready for plan B."

"There's a plan B?" Jack asked.

"You're another one," Edilio snapped. "You're not going to tell me again that you won't fight, because I swear to God I'll shoot you myself." Then in a more measured voice he said, "Yes, there's a plan B. We fight that evil creature every step of the way. Caine, Orc, Jack, Dekka, follow me."

He didn't look back to see if they were following him.

He didn't need to.

It was just luck that Sam was gone and Alex was not when Gaia rejoined the highway, fuming, and crying in pain and frustration as she dealt with her wounds and confronted the fact that in killing Brianna she had deprived herself of a power.

Stupid!

No, not stupid: necessary. They were stronger than she'd thought. They were more dangerous.

And then she heard movement in the darkness. She had her hands up, ready to kill, when it occurred to her who it might be.

The adult human, the food, stepped into view. He was carrying something in his one remaining arm. A head.

Drake!

"Come here!" Gaia demanded.

Alex came up in a mix of hesitancy and sudden, rushing steps. The sight of him made her salivate. She was very hungry.

But Drake, ah, he could be useful. Had she had him in these last few fights, she wouldn't now be skulking this way.

"What happened to you?" Gaia demanded of the head. "You were supposed to feed me."

"Brianna happened," Drake whispered.

"Ah. Then you'll be happy to learn she's dead."

Drake's shark mouth twisted into a ghastly grin. For some reason there was a lizard's tail protruding between his eyes.

"I wonder . . . ," Gaia whispered to herself. She had Drake, she had Alex, she had the healing power, and she was hungry. It was a puzzle. The solution that occurred to her in a flash of genius was imperfect, but it might work, given time. And if it worked, she'd have a faithful and dangerous ally.

And a meal.

She stepped closer to Alex, who bobbed his head and grinned a sickly, cringing, frightened smile.

Gaia smiled back to calm him. Then with a single swipe of her deadly light she cut the head from his shoulders. It hit the ground with a surprisingly loud thump.

The Drake head dropped from Alex's dead fingers.

And, finally, Alex's body collapsed in a heap.

There wasn't much blood: his heart was no longer pumping.

Gaia dropped to her knees, lifted Drake's head, and pressed it against the stump of Alex's neck.

Drake tried to speak, but now his airway was blocked.

"Transplant," Gaia explained. She held the head in place and focused her healing power. Would it work? Drake was no longer fully human, and Alex was dead, but only just.

At the same time, her own wounds had been barely patched, not healed. She was pushing at the very limits of her great powers now, fighting pain and the weakness of her damaged body. And she would never get through it all without something to eat.

So she stretched out her leg and awkwardly rolled Alex's head closer to her.

Diana knew things had gone badly as soon as she saw Caine walking into town behind Edilio with his head down. She was running to him before she could stop herself. Like a fool, like a stupid tween rushing some pop star. Right across the plaza.

But even when she was standing right in front of him, right where he couldn't fail to at least see her legs, he wouldn't look up.

She reached to touch him on the arm, hesitated, did it anyway. "Caine."

"Hey, Diana. How's it going?" It was the worst of commonplaces. It wasn't even words, really, just sound.

"How's it going?" Her sarcasm didn't seem to affect him. "You mean, aside from giving birth to a monster who is going to try to kill us all and will probably succeed?"

He nodded. "Yeah, aside from that."

"Aside from that, things are pretty bad, Caine."

He nodded. "Yeah." Then he raised his face but only to look away, to the left, to the right, everywhere but at her, behind to the town hall and the ruined church, as if he couldn't quite figure out where he was and desperately wanted to be somewhere else.

Well, Diana thought, she also wanted to be somewhere else. Pretty much anywhere would do.

"How long have we got?" Diana asked him.

He shook his head. "I don't know. She can be hurt. She's not invulnerable. But in the end she'll get us. Sam's crippled. Brianna's dead. Orc and Jack are—"

"Brianna's dead?" Diana interrupted. Now she was squeezing his bicep, fingers digging in. He didn't seem to notice.

"Yeah. I actually, uh, admired her, you know. The two of us—"

"Caine, Gaia's powers are borrowed from other moofs. She gave me some big story about fields and connections or whatever, but the thing was, that's why she didn't go after you and Sam in that first fight, why she didn't stay and finish you: she needs you alive."

Now Caine met her gaze with an expression of disbelief and dawning horror. "That's why she didn't kill Sam; she just left him helpless. Why she didn't kill me. So why did she kill Brianna?"

"I don't know. Maybe she had no choice. Maybe she was confused. I don't know." Then, her mouth twisting into a bitter smile, she added, "It's not like I really know her. She's not . . . I know I gave birth to her, but . . ."

At last he looked at her and really seemed to see her. There had always been a guardedness between them, a layer of dishonesty, of show. Caine was not a person who could let himself be vulnerable.

To her surprise, Diana realized that was gone. For the first time, Caine wasn't wearing a mask. For the first time, when she looked into his eyes she saw undisguised sadness.

He drew her to him. For once, maybe for the first time, it had nothing to do with either power or desire. They were two people at the end of the world. They were two losers waiting for their final defeat.

Diana went willingly to him. He put his arms around her and she refused to cry, refused because how would that make anything better? Their time was over: their chances had all been used up.

"We have to make sure Edilio really understands all this," Diana said. "About Gaia . . . about the gaiaphage, and these powers. Edilio's been shaken up. Maybe too much to really . . ."

She looked at him and saw his eyes shutting her out. His withdrawal wasn't total, but it was undeniable.

"Diana, you want to make sure Edilio understands this? Do *you* understand it? Diana, if I'm dead and Sam's dead and Dekka and Jack are dead, the gaiaphage isn't very dangerous." He made a disbelieving sound. "It will be 'kill the moofs' all over again. It'll be that moron Zil and his Human Crew all over again."

"So we do nothing? We wait until Gaia's killed everyone but you? And then, at the end, she comes for you?"

"Maybe by then the barrier's down," Caine said.

"But maybe it's not, and you and Sam are the last ones

standing, surrounded by nothing but dead bodies."

It was as if a cold wind had blown through the space between them. He was Caine again.

"Isn't that the game we all play, Diana? We all try to stay alive. Even though in the end we all die."

Diana turned away and only then realized that Astrid had been standing just a few feet away, quiet, listening.

Caine saw her, too. "What's your advice, Astrid the Genius? When she comes, when that monster child of ours comes to kill us all, it will be Sam's little laser show she does the most damage with. So what do you have to say, oh great fountain of morality?"

Diana stared at Astrid. Caine was right, and Astrid knew he was right. Of course, Diana thought, Astrid had seen the implications quicker than anyone. That's why Astrid had tried to derail the big meeting in the mayor's office.

Astrid, still manipulating, Diana thought bitterly. And yet, wasn't she just defending the boy she loved? Was that so terrible?

A little kid came rushing up and pulled Astrid away.

"See?" Caine said, as though Astrid had proved his point. "When it gets down to it, when it gets down to the endgame, everyone just wants to buy another five minutes for themselves and their . . . and the people they care about."

It was Sanjit's little sister, Bowie, who had found Astrid and pulled her away. "Lana says you should come."

"Why?" Astrid asked.

"Sam. Quinn just brought him to Clifftop. And he's hurt."

Astrid ran from the town plaza to Clifftop with her heart in her throat. She burst in, breathless and red in the face, and nearly stepped on one of the injured in the hallway.

Lana looked up as Astrid came tearing in and, before Astrid could speak, said, "He'll live."

But Lana was not with Sam: Sam was in a corner, on the floor, practically shoved underneath a coffee table. Quinn was with him.

"Hello, Astrid," Quinn said.

She ignored him, knelt beside Sam, and took his face in both hands. "Sam. Sam!"

"He's been out for a while," Quinn said.

"What happened?"

"It seems he ran into Gaia outside of town. Broke him up pretty bad."

Astrid twisted her head around and yelled at Lana, "Why aren't you helping him?"

"Because he's not going to die and this one is!" Lana snarled back.

"We need him!"

"You all needed Brianna, too. How did that work out for you?"

Astrid jumped to her feet and for a moment was so out of control she nearly swung at Lana. Lana did not flinch. Sanjit moved smoothly between them.

"Hey, hey, hey, come on. Come on."

"You want to do something useful, Astrid, talk to your brother," Lana said.

Astrid recoiled.

"I know all about Nemesis," Lana said. "I know what's on the line. You asked me to reach out to the gaiaphage—well, let me tell you, Astrid, that touch goes both ways. It's not pleasant, Astrid." She was barely squeezing the words out through gritted teeth. "It's not fun sliding up next to evil . . . hearing in your head the voice of a thing that tried to enslave you. To kill you. It hates me. It's practically salivating at the idea of crushing me. Do you get that, Astrid the Genius?"

Astrid was taken aback by the venom in Lana's voice, the pale fury on her face. Lana had aged in just the short time since Astrid had seen her last. Astrid knew she was seeing the face of some kind of suffering that she couldn't really understand. But the fear, the fear on the face of this tough girl . . . that she understood.

"Lana, we can kill Gaia," Astrid said.

"And Little Pete can kill the gaia*phage*," Lana said. "Little Pete is the power: you know it, I know it. The gaiaphage is desperately afraid; that's why it's attacking. It's afraid of Pete. It's slaughtering people out of fear of Little Pete."

"You know what Little Pete *needs*?" Astrid demanded. "Do you know what you'd be asking?"

Lana fell silent. She looked at the child she'd been touching. With her free hand she felt his neck, searching for a pulse.

Then she laid her head on his chest, ear to his heart. Finally, she sat back. "I didn't realize how damaged . . . I should have started sooner."

It took Astrid a moment to realize what she had just seen. She stumbled back, stopped herself, met Lana's haunted gaze.

"Yeah. That's my life now," Lana said. She raised a trembling finger to touch her own temple. "And now with *it*. With it back in my head. Extra fun."

Lana stood up, nearly lost her balance, stretched to crack her back. "Well, *now* I have time for Sam. Plenty of time for Sam." She accepted a glass of water from Peace and dropped down beside Sam.

"See those scissors?" Lana pointed to a pair of heavy shears on a table. "Bring them here and cut away his shirt. We have to start with his back."

Astrid did as she was asked. She gasped seeing the bone protruding stark and white through Sam's shoulder. But when they rolled him tenderly onto his side she saw the twisted jumble of his spine and almost lost hope.

"Yeah, that's not good," Lana said. "You're going to have to help me. We need to straighten him out a bit, get the spine lined up. It goes a whole lot quicker if you at least get all the pieces back in place first. Where is Dahra? I could really use . . ." Then she remembered. "Two down, both hurt on lonely roads," she said softly. "One dies. One lives, at least for now. The God you don't believe in anymore rolls the dice."

Sam groaned in his sleep when Astrid cut the last of the fabric away.

"She was a good person, Dahra," Lana said. Her lip trembled. "She was a good person, that girl." She looked around the room, at kids softly crying, moaning, asking for water. "Bunch of good dead people." Then, shaking her head as if trying to throw something off, she yelled, "Sanjit! Send Peace to find some kind of a board. Like a shelf would do."

Lana lit a cigarette, sucked in deep, and blew it out in Astrid's direction. "You ever notice something, Astrid? No two moofs have the same power. There's not two kids with super-speed, just one. Not two or three or five or ten with Sam's laser thing, just him. One Jack, one Dekka."

"Yes," Astrid acknowledged cautiously.

"One healer."

"Yeah, we all noticed that," Astrid said, making no secret of the fact that she wished someone less volatile was that one healer.

"But this Gaia monstrosity seems to be able to heal itself, and to shoot light beams, and to do the whole telekinesis thing. Interesting, isn't it? Kids have been telling me stories while I lay my little magic hands on them. Okay, now take Sam by the waist. Grab on, because this is going to be really bad."

Astrid did as Lana directed. *Don't start crying,* she told herself. But it hurt seeing the body she loved broken this way.

"You're going to pull, see, so I can try to push the bones back into line. And you're going to keep pulling until I tell you different. Got that?"

"I do," Astrid said.

"Pull."

Astrid pulled and Sam thrashed and Lana yelled at Astrid for loosening her grip so Astrid tightened her grip and pulled hard and Sam opened his eyes and yelled and flailed with his hands so Sanjit ran over and grabbed his hands, fast, because Sam's hands could be very dangerous, and Quinn came around to help Astrid pull.

Lana pushed vertebrae back into place with a sickening wet crunch, then slid a wooden shelf beneath him and let Quinn and Sanjit work together to wrap strips of sheet around and around, locking Sam into place.

Sam quieted and lapsed again into unconsciousness.

"He may have internal injuries," Lana said. "I can fix the back and the shoulder, maybe. We'll see about anything else."

"I should get back to Edilio, see if he needs . . . ," Astrid said and stood to leave.

"Yeah. You should go," Lana agreed. "And then you better figure out which is worse, smart girl: That we give someone up as a living sacrifice to Little Pete. Or the other thing."

Lana was smirking now, angry and challenging. Astrid didn't want to ask, because she knew the answer. But she couldn't not ask.

"What *other* thing, Lana?"

"The thing where we kill Sam, and Caine, too, if we can find him, to disarm the gaiaphage."

Astrid stood stock-still.

Lana laughed her cynical laugh. "Yeah, you're the genius, but that doesn't make me an idiot."

Astrid nodded. Her focus went to the big pair of shears, and beyond to the automatic pistol at Lana's waist. She bit her lip hard and then said, "Sam?"

"I'm not going to hurt him," Lana said. "That's not what I do. Remember? I'm the Healer."

"I WANT MY whip back."

Drake's head had melded perfectly well to Alex's neck, although there was a definite red line, like . . . well, like surgery had been done and not quite healed.

Alex's own head, now a fleshless, tongueless, and empty skull, lay in a ditch.

"Be glad you have a body at all," Gaia snarled.

"I am glad," Drake said, trying to sound obsequious. "But I can't fight beside you like this." He pointed with his remaining hand at the stump of his other arm. "It happened once before. It could happen again."

Gaia seemed uncertain. It was a strange expression for the face of a goddess, Drake thought. But then Gaia herself was strange for what she was. He knew better than to take the beautiful, olive-skinned, blue-eyed face at face value. He knew he was still looking at the creature formerly represented by a seething carpet of green particles. But she was a beautiful girl now, almost his own age by all appearances.

As beautiful as Diana had been before starvation took its toll. As beautiful as Astrid and just as smug and arrogant.

It confused him. Because he instinctively wanted to hurt her. Fantasy images came to his mind and shocked him. She would kill him if she knew.

It was not a good idea to lust after a god. Even worse to imagine the whip coming down on her—

No, he ordered himself. *Stop.* She was not Diana or Astrid. She was nothing like them. She was still it. She was still the Darkness. Still the evil that had welcomed him, given him a place, given him a purpose.

"I need my arm," Drake said, willing to push on this point at least because without his whip hand he was weak. Without his whip hand, what weapon did he have? Without it he was just Drake, not Drake Whip Hand.

"Why do you want it so badly?" Gaia asked. "What would you use it for?"

"To fight beside you, defend you, protect . . . To . . ."

Her face was blank, but her eyes bored into him. "Tell me the truth."

If he lied . . . she could destroy him right here, right now. How much did she guess? He had to answer. Truth or lie. "Diana first," Drake hissed. "Astrid more slowly."

Gaia shook her head. "Later. If."

"If?"

"If you bring me the Healer," Gaia said. "She is . . . She resists me. She looks for a way to deprive me . . ." Suddenly she seemed to think better of opening her thoughts to him. "Just bring her to me. Then you can do what you like."

She put her hand on the stump of an arm. "I don't know what will grow," she said.

"It will come back," Drake said. "It has to."

Astrid stood at the top of the cliff that gave Clifftop its name.

There were boats out there, out in the dark ocean. She could see the lights going by.

When she craned her neck to the left she could see the glow coming from the camp, from the Carl's Jr., the lights of the new hotels.

It was all so desperately, terribly near. How far to cheeseburgers and fries and cars that weren't burned out and policemen to call when danger threatened?

Not a quarter of a mile.

Electricity and freedom from fear. Food and warmth. Her mother and father, cousins and aunts and family friends, and all of them saying, *So what was it like?* And *I bet you're glad to be out of there.*

Were you afraid?

So afraid.

I guess you saw some bad things?

So many I can't even tell you. So many I can't remember them all. And some that I can't get out of my head.

I have scars. Want to see my legs and arms and back? Scars.

Want to see my soul? Scars there, too, but you can't really see them.

I'm sure you did your best.

Did I? Are you sure I did my best? Because I'm not.

I lied. I manipulated people. I hurt people at times. I was cruel at times. I betrayed trust.

I threw my brother to his death. Yes, to save my life and other people's lives; does that make it okay?

"In the old days I would have talked to you, God," she said. "I would have asked for guidance. And I would have gotten nothing, but I'd have pretended, and that would have been almost like the real thing."

Lana would heal Sam. And then he would march out to fight Gaia.

And Gaia would kill him. But only after she had killed Edilio and Sinder and Diana and Sanjit and Quinn and and and . . . *Then* she would kill Sam, but before that she would kill Astrid, so that Sam would see, and he would cry out in despair, and only then would Gaia kill him.

Sam would die, and he would die knowing he had failed to save Astrid.

As if summoned from her thoughts Astrid saw Sinder passing around the side of the hotel, heading perhaps to join the desperate crowd huddled down by the highway. Was Sinder's mother there? Astrid hadn't really ever talked to the girl about her life before the FAYZ.

A lot of them she had never come to know. A lot she would never now be able to know. She closed her eyes and saw the terrible light from Gaia's hands. She smelled again the burning of tires and varnished plywood, canvas and flesh.

If Sam died right now, right this minute, it would weaken Gaia, and the rest of them might survive.

"I made that choice once before," she said to the dark sky. "I did that with Petey, didn't I?"

The sky had no answer. The sky was bright to the south with burger lights, and to the west the ships glided by, carrying cars, iPads, and oil, and old people who wanted to see whales.

To the north the red glow of fire. It was brighter each minute. It must have spread beyond the forest now. Was it racing across the dry grassland? Was it burning across the fields that had fed them?

Fire? She wanted to laugh. Well, why not? Why not fire? This was the FAYZ, after all.

Somewhere out there the monster plotted their deaths. And if Astrid was going to do anything at all to stop it, it would mean sacrificing someone, either some nameless victim or Sam.

What was the lesson? What was all this teaching her? That sometimes there were no good choices?

"I learned that a long time ago," Astrid said.

She had told Sam—insisted on it—that he had to do whatever it took to win, even if it meant attacking Diana, even if it meant burning down the world, but only survive, only live, Sam, because I can't do it without you.

Live.

I can't walk out of this place without you.

Astrid closed her eyes, shutting out the ships and the stars and the burger lights and the distant fire.

"Petey . . ."

Caine made his way down to the dock. The answer was obvious: if he was going to survive, he had to get to the island. Out of here. Away from Gaia. Not that Gaia couldn't find him there, but as he'd told Diana, the trick wasn't to live forever, but to be the last to die.

And to never suffer that pain again. He couldn't think about it; he couldn't or he would feel an echo of it, and even that was agony.

There was a kid on guard, one of Quinn's people, posted there to make sure no one tampered with any of the fishing boats.

Caine didn't hurt him, just used his power to smack him against the wooden planks until he stopped yelling. Then he tied him up and stuffed a rag in his mouth to keep him quiet. Gaia would find him, too, and kill him in due course. But his death might come a bit later just because he was incapacitated.

Hey, that was a good thing. Right?

Caine saw the boats that had been reserved for emergency use. There should still be a little gas left. It wouldn't be much—they'd been running on fumes just a few days ago when Caine had been king.

The memory brought a grim smile to his lips. King Caine.

Things changed, didn't they? Now he was ready to try and creep away to hang on to a another few hours of life. Run away.

King Caine to Rat Caine in a heartbeat.

Well, Penny had already knocked the crown off his head, hadn't she? He recalled the humiliation of waking up to find his hands cemented and a crown stapled to his scalp. Pain, too. But he'd had pain, he knew pain, and while staples in your scalp were no picnic, they were nothing to compare with the agony of having that hard concrete chipped slowly away with a hammer.

Yeah, that had been bad. Change-your-whole-outlook kind of bad. Still, the humiliation of powerlessness had been worse.

But not worse than what Gaia had done to him. Nothing to what she had done.

In his arrogance he had thought he was free of the gaia-phage. But he never would be, would he? As long as that monster existed, it would have a back door into his brain and could make him crawl and cry and beg for death . . .

He made a whimpering noise. Like a scared child. Well, he was a scared child, wasn't he?

He hopped down into the boat. There was no gauge on the tank, so he looked around for a while, wishing he had Sam's power of light. It took him a few minutes to find what he needed, something thin enough and long enough to stick in the fuel tank and check the amount. It was a broken piece of fishing pole, a one-foot length of dark fiberglass. It came back up showing about an inch of gas sloshing in there.

Out in the ocean Caine saw something large going by—a tanker, maybe, carrying hundreds of thousands of barrels of gas.

"Must be nice," he said.

"What must be nice?"

She had snuck up on him without his seeing or hearing her. Diana, a dark shadow above him, outlined by stars.

He started to say something to her, but nothing came. She was on the dock. He was in the boat below her.

Diana.

Finally he said, "What are you doing here?"

"Finding you," she said. "You took off."

"You didn't find much," he said bitterly, and immediately regretted it. It sounded self-pitying. Well, it was, wasn't it?

"This is where we landed, coming from the island," she said.

"Yes. In triumph. The conquering hero," he said. "King Caine. I was just remembering that."

"With that monster in my belly," Diana said.

"Not your fault," he said tersely. "Not mine, either."

"I wonder."

"We had . . . Listen, we made love, right? Isn't that what we're calling it? No one warned us we were conceiving a body for the gaiaphage."

"Did we make love?" Diana asked him.

"Jesus, Diana," he pleaded.

"Tell me, Caine. Did we make love or did we just have sex? It's a simple question."

"No, it isn't," Caine said.

He heard Diana's sardonic laugh, and at that instant he knew the answer to her question. He heard that snarky, almost cruel laugh and he knew, and it filled him so suddenly full of emotion that he almost cried out.

"No, it's not an easy question between us," Diana admitted. Then: "Did we make love, Caine?"

"Okay. Okay, yes, Diana, we made love."

"Say it to me, Caine," she said.

"What's the point?" he pleaded. "I'm running away. I'm saving myself and leaving you behind. I'm a rat deserting the sinking ship. I'm a coward holding on to his pathetic life for an extra hour or two. I'm scared to death; I can't stand up to it anymore. I'm done. Why do you want me to say it?"

She didn't answer.

She had bathed him when he was lost in madness, had spoon-fed him, had been there each time he woke to rave, to rave about the hunger in the dark.

She had backed him in all his wild plans. She had stood by him, despite, oh man, despite so much. So much.

He couldn't see her face, just her outline, but he could picture her face in detail. In his mind he saw the full lips and the smirk and the way she sometimes pressed her lips together as if physically repressing laughter. And he saw her cheeks and the perfect line of her jaw and the neck that no male had ever seen without wanting to kiss.

And he saw her dark eyes.

And he saw her breasts.

And he saw her thighs and . . .

And somehow Diana, being Diana, knew every thought going through his mind, and she said, "I've had a baby. Things aren't quite the way you left them. And it's going to be some time before I'm ready for what's going through your evil mind."

"Okay," he said.

"'Okay,' he lied," she mocked.

He shook his head. She had him. Again.

"Just what are you ready for?" he asked.

"I'm a bit stiff," she said. "Hard to climb down there."

He raised one hand, and she rose slowly from the dock and then slowly descended, sliding down just inches from his face. He let her feet touch down in the boat, felt the weight of her as the boat rocked.

She tripped a little, or maybe she didn't but only pretended, who cared: he took her in his arms. Yes, she felt different. Her belly was larger. Her breasts larger as well. The rest of her felt pitifully thin.

"How's your mouth?" he asked, wanting badly to kiss her.

"Why, what do you have in mind?"

He laughed.

"Say it. But . . ."

"But what?" he asked.

She whispered it, sounding too vulnerable. "But only if

it's the truth, Caine. Only. If."

"I love you," he said.

"Yes," she said, satisfied.

He kissed her, and yes, her mouth still worked.

Then, serious, he said, "So we don't go to the island?"

"Why were you going?"

He sighed. "I had two answers in mind. One, I was running away like a rat. That was the main answer. I can't . . . I'd rather die. I can't let her do that to me again. So I was running away."

"Two answers?" Diana asked.

"Look, number one . . . no, numbers one through nine were running away. But the other answer, the one that was much less at, sort of, the forefront of my mind, but that was a possibility . . ." He ran out of steam after all that evasion. "Look, part of me was thinking about those stupid missiles of Albert's."

"You think they would kill her?"

He shrugged. "It's all I could think of that would surprise her. Catch her off guard." He sighed. The truth welled up inside him. The fact that he loved her. And the fact that it wouldn't save him.

"We don't make it out of here, do we?" he said.

Diana shook her head. "No, my love."

They stood for a long time in each other's arms. Then, at last, Caine fired up the motor and the boat headed toward the island.

And Diana, with Perdido Beach falling away behind her,

with tears rolling down her cheeks, with the light of the onrushing fire reflected in her dark eyes, whispered another boy's name.

"Little Pete . . ."

His name was Peter Ellison, but everyone had always called him Little Pete.

Sometimes Petey.

And now he heard his name. Like prayers floating up to him from the ghosts.

A voice he knew.

A voice he did not know.

A third voice that reached to him in a way like the Darkness sometimes did, silently, through that emptiness that connected all who had been touched by the Darkness.

In different words, in different ways, they each said, *Take me.*

Take me, Petey.

Take me, Little Pete.

Take me, you little freak.

TWENTY-FIVE

PUG, THE CRAZY thing, had actually fired one of the missiles at them as Caine and Diana neared the island.

The missile was not much good against a person with the power to move things with his mind—something Caine knew he would have to remember later. Maybe the element of surprise . . . maybe Gaia wouldn't know what they were . . .

Yeah. Maybe. And maybe not. In which case, plan B.

Caine did not much like plan B.

But as he lay beside Diana in the big bed, the same one where they had conceived Gaia, he knew he had, finally, no alternative. He was trapped between pains: the pain that Gaia could bring, and the pain that would come if he lost Diana.

Why had she forced him to admit his feelings? Women. Didn't they know that emotions were meant to be suppressed?

"Love sucks," Caine muttered.

Diana nuzzled against him, her lips on his neck, sending chills all through his body.

A line of night-blue between separated curtains became a line of gray. Dawn, and time to go.

He slid carefully, silently, out of the bed. Where were his clothes? He'd left them right here, right on the floor, knowing he would have to dress silently to escape undiscovered.

"I hid them," Diana said.

He turned to face her. "And why would you do that?"

"So you couldn't sneak away. Really, Caine: how long have I known you? Also . . ."

"Uh-huh?"

"Also I like you like this."

He swallowed hard, feeling strangely vulnerable and a little silly. "You said we couldn't . . ."

"Mmmm. True. But I still like looking at you. It's a good thing you're so rotten," she said with a long sigh. "Scares off most girls. I never would have had a chance with you if you'd been a decent human being."

"I wasn't running away," he said.

"I know. I know what you were doing, Caine. And thanks for the thought. But I want to be there to see the end. I want to see you stop her."

"Yeah," he said, straining to put some slight shred of optimism into the word. "If you're coming, then we have to go."

"Or the reverse of that . . . We have a few minutes," she said. "Come here. It won't take more than a few minutes."

Connie Temple had given up waiting for Astrid to arrive at the rendezvous Dahra had arranged. She had spent the night

at a motel, then come back in the morning, just in case. She
wrote a note and stuck it on the end of a stick where the
northeastern shoreline of the lake met the barrier. The note
said, *Sorry I missed you. Connie Temple.* There was a PS. Just
the single word "Sam," followed by a question mark.

It seemed somehow ludicrous. Like putting a Post-it on the
refrigerator door for Sam, back in the old days.

As she was leaving, she noticed a body on the beach that
she had not seen before. Maybe someone sleeping, maybe
some survivor, most likely a body washed ashore. She watched
until she was sure it was not Sam.

Boats were heading out from the outside marina, more
lookers drawn by rumors of a slaughter at the lake. She
couldn't bear to think of mothers like herself possibly seeing
the bloated body of a child floating just inches away, unreachable. A TV truck had come in the night. She saw cameras
with long-distance lenses.

She climbed into the borrowed SUV and drove back down
south. She tuned the satellite radio to a news station.

"The fire is clearly now spreading beyond the Stefano Rey.
California fire officials are rushing firefighting teams to the
perimeter of the anomaly. They are concerned that should
the containment fail, the fire would spread immediately to
the large forest outside the so-called FAYZ."

Connie switched stations.

". . . monstrous and evil children, and the idea that they
should be allowed to walk out of that satanic place and infect
decent God-fearing people with—"

On the third try she got a calmer voice. NPR. But the subject was still the same. The anomaly. The FAYZ. It was all anyone was paying attention to.

". . . physics. As has been long theorized, especially by Dr. Jacobs at the University of California, Berkeley, these phenomena demonstrate that in some way we do not begin yet to understand, the laws that define our universe have been altered. What's troubling, of course, is that if it can happen once, it can happen again. We can never again be entirely confident—"

Enough. She'd had her fill of clever people with impressive degrees trying to explain what was happening. People like that had convinced the government to try and implode the sphere with a bomb.

Finally she found the nineties-rock station and let that play the rest of the way while she tried to think. She was sleepy and nearly running off the road, so it wasn't easy.

If the dome fell, if Sam and Caine walked freely out into the world, there was a better-than-even chance that they would be arrested shortly thereafter.

There wasn't much, if anything, she could do about that except to warn the kids inside to start getting their stories straight. The local district attorney had soft-pedaled the matter of arrests and investigations, but other state officials were grandstanding, and Congress looked as if it would stick its nose in as well.

The idea that the kids inside should come through all they'd survived and then go to prison was intolerable. But with something like three hundred kids—fewer now—it would be child's play for prosecutors to get some, at least, to testify against others.

And truth be told, didn't some of those kids need to be locked up?

She pushed that thought aside, but the image of Sam with his deadly light blazing from his hands . . . the little girl he'd tried to kill . . . the other one he had incinerated . . . The fact that before all this ever started, he'd lashed out and burned the hand off her ex-husband, his stepfather . . .

She'd watched YouTubes of all the interviews with kids inside. Those that mentioned Sam described him as a leader, a fighter, someone who had saved them more than once. Inside the FAYZ he was a hero.

But one interview had stuck with her. It had been given by a young boy who called himself Bug and could almost disappear, or at least fade into the background to become nearly invisible. He'd said Sam was a killer.

He almost killed me once, Bug had said.

The stories of her other son, Caine, were much darker. Kids looked nervously over their shoulders when they talked about him.

But he's not the worst, the super-speedy little celebrity who called herself the Breeze had said. *He's evil, absolutely. But he's not psycho like Drake.*

Yes, maybe some really would need to be locked up. Like rabid dogs or rogue tigers.

What could she do? Get a lawyer for Sam? She didn't have that kind of money.

But wait, others would have that kind of money. Wouldn't they? The kids in the FAYZ needed lawyers; they needed friendly politicians; they needed celebrities to speak for them. All that nonsense, they needed it. Public relations. Advisers.

All of which meant money. Lots of money.

Connie arrived back at the small trailer she'd shared with Abana Baidoo for almost a year. She found Abana sounding optimistic.

"I talked—well, you know, wrote notes to—another kid inside who said Dahra is loved by everyone. Running the hospital, a good girl."

"Yes," Connie said.

"Where have you been?"

Connie knew she should tell Abana that she had sent Dahra to the lake. But it would just worry her, probably needlessly. Most likely Dahra had not made it to the lake. Most likely she'd sent word or sent someone else or . . .

And she couldn't. She couldn't tell her friend she'd sent her daughter to a massacre.

"I went to the lake. I heard Sam was up there and I . . . I went up there."

Abana looked closely at her, head tilted quizzically, sensing something wrong. "There's some video of a crazy old woman saying she saw fires up there."

Connie shook her head. "Not crazy. Something awful happened up there."

That much she had to tell Abana. It would all come out anyway, but she didn't have to tell Abana that she, Connie Temple, had sent Dahra there. So she told her what she had seen, and Abana started crying and then so did Connie.

They drank a fair amount of wine after that. The TV was on but muted. Connie saw a video of what they'd been talking about earlier on the radio: images of what was clearly a massive forest fire raging in the Stefano Rey and now spreading beyond it.

Then the news switched to long-range camera shots of the lake. The anchor was somber, obviously warning people that they were about to see something disturbing.

And then the picture shifted to a body floating facedown in the lake.

Abana was not looking at the TV; she was laughing over something funny that Connie didn't really understand. So it was not then, not at that moment, that Abana would see her daughter, Dahra, floating facedown in the lake.

The sun rose and Edilio was still alive. It surprised him. He had spent the last part of the night on the steps of the town plaza. He'd gotten a little sleep, hunched over, head between his knees, but not much. He looked around owlishly, wondering how many of his people were still in place. How many had bailed? The thought of walking down to the barrier depressed him, because he was afraid he'd see all his soldiers there.

Albert was just striding up, looking peeved, which was more or less his regular expression.

"I've done an inventory on food," Albert announced without preamble. "It's not good. I don't suppose you have any idea how long we have to hold out?"

Edilio blinked. "No, the gaiaphage has not given me the schedule either for how long until the barrier comes down or how long until she attacks again. Sorry."

Albert sniffed. "You've learned sarcasm, Edilio."

"I've learned a lot of things, Albert."

Albert nodded at a pair of kids wandering past the long-destroyed fountain. "See that kid? Hair's falling out. We already have pretty severe malnutrition."

"Why do you think I brought you back?" Edilio snapped.

Albert held his hands out in a *See what I mean?* gesture. "You've drafted everyone to play soldier. I know business isn't your thing, Edilio, but I need labor. I need people picking the crops. If they're holding guns, they're not picking crops. If they're not picking crops, they're not producing food, and if they're not producing food, they're not eating. And not eating is what causes malnutrition."

Despite the pedantic and obnoxious way he said it, Albert was not wrong, so Edilio bit his tongue and took the lecture.

He nodded. "Yep."

"The point is, don't blame me," Albert said. "I did my part."

"They're not playing soldier, Albert. They're scared to death. They've gone down to the barrier to be with their families when they die."

"Well, that's stupid, isn't it?"

"Is it? We had a busload of field-workers not come back, remember? Anyway, the fire's coming."

Albert shook his head impatiently. "Actually, if you send them into the fields, they're probably safer than here. Concentrating them here in town, or worse yet down at the barrier, just makes it easier for the gaiaphage. Plus everyone starves. Including me. I'm already sick of Parmesan cheese. It smells a little like vomit, if you think about it."

The thing was, Albert was right. Starvation was a sure thing. "You're right," Edilio conceded. "Get anyone you can to the fields. Tell them I said so. Bribe them. Threaten them. Do your thing, Albert."

It was bizarre, but the truth was that the most useful thing people could do was go to work. Even with the beast stalking Perdido Beach, someone had to pick the cabbage.

Sinder could put her finger on the moment when she broke.

She had come to help Lana with Taylor. And she'd been feeling honored, somehow, by the request, and by the opportunity to work alongside the Healer.

Once upon a time, a million years ago, Sinder had been a Goth girl, very into dark fantasies, very into the clothes, the makeup, the look, and most of all the *I don't care about the rest of you people; I'm living my life* feeling.

Yeah, I'm weird: deal with it.

Then: the FAYZ. And black fingernail polish was no longer available. Neither was food. Or water. Or safety.

She had seen terrible things. She had lost friends.

Eventually she had found a place at the lake, and dis-covered that she had a power, maybe the best of all powers. What she touched grew. So, of all the strange, impossible-to-imagine outcomes, the FAYZ had given Sinder a whole new life. As a gardener.

Even now it almost made her smile.

Carrots, cabbages, radishes, anything they could find seeds for, she could grow. Not like *pop!* overnight. Not like some special effect. Just like she had a really amazing green thumb, and when she spent time in her vegetable patch with Jezzie, she could grow some serious veggie. Some unusually big, fast-growing veg.

She had left the patch in Jezzie's care. They had been farm-ers together, hoeing, weeding, watering. Talking about life.

Then had come the burned, wounded, terrified survivors of the lake. And Jezzie was not with them. None of Sinder's friends were with them. Everyone she was close to had been slaughtered.

And that was when Sinder broke.

She had crept away in the night—no one cared. She had walked toward the bright lights of *out there*. They were magic, those lights. The FAYZ was so dark. Like being in some ancient village, back in the Middle Ages, or maybe in some forgotten jungle. It was always so dark.

But out there! The motel signs, the Carl's sign, the cam-era lights, the flashing police lights, the headlights and taillights . . . She half closed her eyes and it became a single beacon of light, like a pulsing searchlight aimed right at her.

As she had headed down the hill, she had seen all the rest of them, all the kids. How many? More than a hundred, surely. The light from out there was like a cold sun shining on their faces.

Mostly people weren't bothering to try and communicate. Most had seen their parents and written notes and waved and all of that.

Sinder had not. Sinder hadn't thought she could bear it. But now in the light of day she searched the crowd out there. So many faces, some looking in, some looking away. They all looked so clean. They all wore clothing of the correct size. They were unarmed. And they all had food. They were having breakfast sandwiches and donuts and coffee.

Sinder's stomach churned. But she was so much better nourished than most of these kids. They were skin and bones, a lot of them. Kids at the lake had been eating better than those in town.

Yeah, well, most of them were dead now, so what good had it been, feeding them?

Was her mother or father there? She searched the crowd, hundreds of faces. Then she saw the HD monitor that advertised "Reunion Center." She went to it.

A bored-looking twentysomething out there looked at her quizzically, then, seeing the question in Sinder's eyes, held up a placard. Searching for Loved Ones?

Yes, Sinder thought. I am. Loved ones. Living loved ones. I have plenty of dead loved ones.

Your Name?

Sinder had no paper. She wrote it in the dirt. The woman made the universal symbol for phone call. Then she pulled out a phone and started texting.

Sinder nodded her head gratefully. The woman signed that she should sit and wait patiently.

Sinder did just that. Then, to kill time while she waited, and to take her mind off the nervousness that came with the thought of seeing her parents again, she searched for some living thing she could help grow. Unfortunately the area had been trampled pretty thoroughly. Not even an intact blade of grass.

"How are you feeling, Sam?"

He opened his eyes, looked up at Astrid, seemed momentarily baffled as to where he was, looked back at her, and smiled. "Better now."

He struggled to sit up.

"No, no, take it easy. You're better, but you're not well yet." She stroked his hair, and he let her. "Also you're strapped to a board."

Suddenly he was alarmed. "Gaia?"

"She's hurt. She ran off."

"But not dead."

Astrid shook her head.

"Something's burning," he said, sniffing the air.

"Yes," Astrid said. "Yeah. The forest is burning. I don't know how far it's gone."

Sam closed his eyes and nodded. "Me and Gaia. I wasn't even thinking, I just fired . . ."

"Trying to stay alive?"

"How about Caine?"

Astrid began to unwind the shreds of cloth that held him to the board. The way he was straining to get up it was obvious his back was working.

"Are you ready for all this?" Astrid asked him.

"Lay it out for me," he said, and smiled wanly at her and sat up. "You're so beautiful. And my shoulder still hurts."

Astrid filled him in on what had happened. She avoided talking about the fact that Sam, by his very existence, was empowering Gaia. Nor did she talk about her futile and now seemingly ridiculous attempt to contact Little Pete. She stuck to the facts: Caine and Diana reportedly run off to the island; Edilio bracing for Gaia's next attack; fire visible in the northwest; kids in the fields but scared to death.

She waited until he had absorbed all of that before telling him the last fact.

"Sam. Brianna is dead."

He just stared at her. Then, in a soft, almost childlike voice, he said, "Breeze?"

"She stopped Gaia. It looked like Brianna almost killed her. The second time she . . . But this time . . ."

There were tears in Sam's eyes. "My God. How is Dekka?"

"Like you'd expect. Destroyed. Roger's dead, too, so Edilio . . . It's been really bad, Sam. Really bad. It's like we're in a war."

"We are," he said. "I don't understand why Gaia didn't kill me."

Astrid said nothing.

Lana came over then, so Sam didn't notice Astrid's silence. "How do you feel, Sam?"

"Better than I should," he said. Then: "I know you did all you could for Breeze."

Lana shook her head. "I never had the chance to. The gaiaphage hit her point-blank through the heart with your light. Burned a hole six inches across. That's not something I can heal."

"What do you mean, my light?" Sam asked.

Astrid shot a dirty look at Lana, but it was too late. Sam wasn't going to be put off.

"You need to tell him," Lana said. Her voice wasn't unkind, but it was uncompromising.

Astrid said, "It seems Gaia has some connection to your power. There's a . . . I don't know what to call it . . . no one knows what to call it, because it doesn't exist in the world out there . . ." She was stalling. He saw it. So Astrid said, "Diana says Gaia let you and Caine live because if you die you take the power with you."

Sam's face turned to stone, completely immobile. Astrid wanted to say something, but the words wouldn't come. Lana flicked a dead cigarette butt into the corner of the room.

Sam held up his hands, looking at them as if he might find some meaningful answer in his palms. Finally he spoke in a near whisper. "My light killed those kids at the lake, all those kids? And Breeze?"

His gaze went inexorably to the big automatic pistol hanging at Lana's waist.

"I know what you're thinking, Sam," Astrid said finally, "but no. No."

"I'm not thinking anything," Sam said softly, lying.

"You cannot take your own life," Astrid said, putting steel into her voice. "It's a crime. It's a sin."

"I thought you were done with all that religious belief," Sam said.

"It's worse than a sin *or* a crime; it's a mistake," Lana said. "At least for right now." She knelt down to be closer to eye level. Patrick sidled up beside her. "Let's say Gaia suddenly doesn't have the light thing. Right? She still has Dekka's power and Jack's power and Caine's power. Caine's bailed. Which means how do you think we're going to kill this monster? Jack's not very useful lately, Caine's gone, so it's Gaia versus Dekka and Jack? How does that come out?"

Astrid didn't like the *At least for right now* part at all. But she kept quiet and let Sam think it over.

"Then I have to take her on right away," Sam said. "Before she can go after anyone else. I have to do it now." He stood up and staggered a step. Breathed deep, steadied himself, and headed for the door.

"Best I can do for you," Lana said privately to Astrid.

Astrid knew she wasn't talking about the healing but about what she had said to Sam. She nodded in respectful acknowledgment and followed Sam out.

Where are you, Petey?

Why won't you talk to me?

"Maybe because I killed you?" she whispered mordantly. Yeah. Maybe that was it.

TWENTY-SIX

THE DAY WORE on. Edilio arranged to send water and a mouthful of food to his troops in their concealed firing positions.

The farmworkers began drifting back without reports of attack and bearing at least some meager crops—insect-eaten cabbages, not-quite-ripe artichokes, even a few delicious beets.

With the church steeple ruined, the highest point in Perdido Beach was Clifftop, but Dekka could do better. She lifted herself high into the air over, directly over, the town hall steps so as to avoid a whirlwind of trash and dirt, and surveyed the scene with a pair of binoculars.

When she came back down, Sam and Astrid had arrived.

Sam hugged Dekka, and the two of them stayed that way for a long time, saying nothing. Both had loved Brianna.

To Edilio, Sam said, "I'm so sorry, man. I wish I'd . . . You know what I wish."

Edilio fought back a fresh rush of tears, nodded, waited until he was sure he could speak, and said, "I'm glad you're back, boss." He pivoted to Dekka. "What did you see?"

"The fire, mostly. It's big. It's nothing but smoke up north. Like a wall of smoke."

"It's not exactly clear here," Astrid said. The fire smell was stronger, and the sky was already silvery with ash and smoke that had drifted to town. "Do you think it's moving beyond the forest?"

"I'm not Smokey the Bear," Dekka said with a shadow of her old peevishness. "I don't know about forest fires. But it seemed like I could see a line of smoke closer in. It's like darker, heavier smoke behind and more of a light-gray smoke closer in. Don't ask me what that means."

To Sam, Edilio said, "I've got shooters all around the plaza. With Brianna gone . . ." He glanced at Astrid to see whether she had told Sam. Then, "Okay, you know. Supposedly with Breeze gone it means Gaia won't have the speed. So we'll see her coming. We should be able to shoot. And she doesn't like bullets; we know that much. I saw at least one bullet hit her."

"Wait," Astrid said, frowning. "Wait, who are we forgetting?"

"What do you mean?" Sam asked.

"You, Caine, Dekka, Jack . . . who else has a power that she might exploit?"

They stood staring blankly at each other for a long minute.

Then Edilio snapped his fingers. "Paint!" He yelled orders to some of his people, who, glad for the excuse to temporarily abandon their posts, went scurrying off across town.

And at that point Quinn appeared, walking up from the beach and carrying a backpack.

"Catch anything?" Sam asked him. The two boys embraced.

"Dude," Quinn answered, shrugged modestly, and added, "No big thing."

"Very big thing, brother. Very big. I'm here because you brought me here. Now: why is your backpack squirming?"

"Oh, that," Quinn said nonchalantly. "I believe we fished up Drake's foot." He dumped it on the ground, causing a definite sensation. It was a foot that had grown a dozen writhing tentacles.

The thing flailed and squirmed, and the tentacles tried to go centipeding away, but it was directionless, mindless, and ended up just making Edilio jump out of the way.

"Kill it," Dekka said.

Sam held his hands, palm out, toward the bizarre remnant of the unkillable Drake. Light blazed. A sickening cooked-flesh smell rose.

The thing, the foot, squirmed madly. But it burned. It burned first like a steak dropped into charcoal. And then it caught fire and burned like a marshmallow held too close to a campfire. Then it burned like a house that is near collapse.

Then it fell into a pile of ashes.

And still Sam burned it. Until the waves of heat scattered the ashes.

"Well," Sam said. "At least we know that would have worked had it been necessary."

"Too bad it wasn't Drake himself," Dekka said. "But my little Brianna did him in. Yeah. Breeze took down Drake and saved our butts, twice. Oh, man. I thought I was cried out."

"Dekka," Sam said, putting his arms around her, "we will never be cried out."

"We have a lot of people to bury," Edilio said. He was looking at the crude grave markers in the town plaza. The first had been a little girl who died in a fire just a few feet from this spot, when Edilio had taken on the job of burying the dead.

"Brianna wouldn't want to be in the ground," Dekka said. "She'd want to, I don't know. Cremation, maybe. You could do it, Sam."

"He's thinking," Gaia said. "Nemesis. He's thinking. I can sense it. He's weak, weakening, so close. But he's thinking, and hiding his thoughts from me."

She swallowed hard, and Drake was frankly contemptuous. It was crazy that the gaiaphage should be afraid of Little Pete, the Petard. He wasn't going to say that to the gaiaphage, that was for sure, but still he could hardly conceal his disappointment.

It was the gaiaphage that had gone weak since inhabiting this girl's body. She, it, seemed almost paralyzed by fear. Drake's arm was back! Back, baby! Gaia had given it back to him, better than ever. He snapped it and broke a branch from a bush. Time for war. Time to kill. He was back!

Back! Hah hah hah! But his master was healing, and slowly. And worst of all, complaining. Like a typical female.

"She's fighting me," Gaia said. "I can feel her blocking me."

Shook up, that was it. The mighty gaiaphage, all shook up. Well, that's what came of turning yourself into a girl.

"When do we go?" Drake demanded. "They're waiting to die."

"When it's dark," Gaia said sullenly. "When the barrier comes down I have to walk out of here. In this body. I can't be recognized by every human out there. I will need time. I will need to gather my powers . . . find a new form . . . a place to hide, out there."

A place to hide? Drake coiled his arm around his new body. He was stronger than before. His whip was longer, quicker. A better, badder Whip Hand. And ready to go!

"I get Astrid to myself," Drake said.

"You don't make demands of me!" Gaia raged.

Drake laughed. His voice was strange now, with portions of Alex's throat melded to his. He sounded older than he had before. "You're afraid of the people outside?"

"This body keeps me alive. This body allows me to concentrate my strength. But this body is weak. I had not realized how weak. It makes its own demands. It needs food. It excretes. It hurts." Gaia shook her long black hair. "It bothers me."

"You look like her, you know. Like Diana. The way she looked before. Back when she thought she was hot."

Gaia frowned.

"Yeah," Drake said. "Yeah. You look hot and nasty. Like her."

He knew immediately that he had gone too far, said too much.

Gaia's blue eyes were like lasers. "You want to hurt me," she whispered.

Drake shook his head violently. "No. No, that's not what I—"

"You. Want. To *hurt* this body."

"Not *you*," Drake said, desperately. "Not the real you."

"You think you know the real me?"

Drake shook his head again. He didn't want to go any deeper into this. He just wanted to feel the satisfying slap of his whip hand on flesh. That was all. He just wanted to hear the cries of pain and terror. He wanted to find that blond witch, that smug so-called genius, and watch her fear grow, watch her—

"It comes closer, the fire. In the smoke . . . that's when we attack." Gaia looked off toward the wall of smoke in the north.

"I thought you were worried about Nemesis."

"I worry about nothing," Gaia said, but there was impatience in the toss of her head, worry in her eyes.

"He has a sister. Someone he cares about. Your Nemesis. Her name is Astrid. She could be a hostage. She could give us leverage over the Petard."

Gaia's eyes widened. "A loved one? Does he?" She smiled. She had very white teeth, almost perfect but for a single too-far-forward canine. "But if you kill her she's useless as a hostage."

"She's no fun dead," Drake said, and then laughed. "Let me go after her. I'll bring her to you."

"A hostage," Gaia said thoughtfully. "A hostage." She looked at Drake suspiciously. He could feel her dark mind brushing against his, probing for some trick. But there was no trick. He would bring Astrid alive.

Barely.

Eventually.

Drake saw her reach the decision. He saw a frown, a worried look. And then Gaia glanced around as if looking for someone. Then back at Drake.

It struck him that she didn't want him to go because she didn't want to be alone. He struggled to conceal his growing contempt. This girl's body had given the gaiaphage the emotions of a girl. The weakness of a girl.

When he was done with Astrid . . . and done with Diana . . . Gaia?

"Go then," Gaia said finally. "Bring her to me."

Astrid found Sam in the church. What was left of the church. He was sitting on an overturned pew, gazing toward the shards of a stained-glass window in a ruined frame. The cross had been propped up yet again by someone, so it wasn't lying on the floor but was rather leaning in a corner, its base stabilized by rubble piled there.

He must have recognized something about the sound of her movements, because he didn't bother to turn around.

"Anything?"

"Nothing," she said. "Edilio's losing his mind waiting, I think. He's got Orc and Jack and Dekka all doing the rounds to try and get kids to stand fast, trying to get some more kids to come back from the barrier. I don't think it's working. And Albert's actually riding a bike out to the fields to try to get kids to keep working."

They both smiled at the picture of Albert in his chinos and button-down shirt exhorting kids from atop a bike.

"He's looking for redemption," Sam said.

"That's unusually observant of you," she said.

He smiled. "Occasionally I observe."

She sat down next to him. "Well, he needs redemption."

"We're in the right place to be talking about it, huh?" He looked around the church as if just noticing where he was. "That was the story, right?" He nodded toward the cross.

"Don't, Sam," she said.

"You think you can read my mind, don't you?"

"You don't need redemption," she said.

"So what do I need?" he asked, trying to make a joke of it.

"One more win," she said.

"One more win." He hung his head. "I've had more than my share, haven't I? I've been way luckier than I should have been. I mean, how many times should I have died? I can't even count them all."

"Don't do this, Sam."

"What was I doing it for? Just so I would survive?" He

shrugged. "Mostly, huh? But also sometimes so other people would live. Not meaning to make it sound all self-sacrificing or whatever."

"Yes. You also kept a lot of other people alive. Yes. So enough, all right? You promised me, remember? You promised me you'd do whatever it took to stay alive."

He sighed. "Here's the thing, Astrid. It's like . . . like a math problem or something, you know? Like if you're doing an equation or whatever, and there's an answer, and there's only one answer, and so you're stuck with that, aren't you?"

"This isn't math. Besides, you're a math ignoramus. Remember?" She was getting angry because the alternative to feeling angry was to feel desperate.

"I am a math ignoramus, aren't I?" He smiled as if at a distant memory. Or at something that would never matter again. "But I've won a lot of battles. I've gone in a lot of times and I've figured out the winning move. And that's worked pretty well so far, right? Well, the problem is that I see the winning move here. I see it just as clear as your very perfect nose."

"It's not a winning move if you end up dead."

"Ah, it hasn't been before, no. But I keep running the equation, Astrid. And each time I see that maybe we can beat the gaiaphage. But not if she has my power. That's the trick here. Would that be irony?"

"No, damn it, that would not be irony, Sam. That would be throwing your life away. That would be suicide."

"I know you're kind of over the religion thing, but what he

did"—he nodded toward the cross—"that was still a big thing to do, wasn't it? Was that suicide?"

"Really?" she asked with acid sarcasm. "You're Jesus now?"

He laughed softly.

"You want to know the truth, Sam?" She pulled his face to her. "No, it wasn't suicide when Jesus did it. It was fake. If he really was the son of God, then he was risking nothing and he *knew* it. He knew he had a couple of bad hours but then it was going to be all over and he'd pop back into heaven and have a really amazing story to tell all his friends."

"He has friends?"

She would not be distracted with jokes. "You? If you die you're dead. We've seen dead now, Sam, we've seen a lot of it, and it's ugly and permanent."

He turned to her and she saw the tortured look on his face. "That light, Astrid? That light I shoot out of my hands? It's like it's mine. It's like I invented it. Or at least I own it. And that light killed Brianna. And it's going to kill a bunch of other kids. You know it and I know it." He ran a hand back through his hair, slowly, like it mattered that he felt each hair.

"No," she said. "They're going to die because Pete won't talk to me."

There was a long silence after that.

"I wondered if you would try that," he said at last.

"Don't worry about it," she said, brushing it off. "Nothing. I was talking to air."

Now Sam was mad. "You should have talked to me about it first. What if he had done it? What if Little Pete had taken over your body and your mind?"

"He didn't, so—"

"What do you think happens if he does it? Whoever does it ends up like her, like Gaia, except that Gaia was just a baby and didn't even know. What do you think happens if Little Pete does this? What do you think happened to that baby girl when the gaiaphage—"

"We don't know if it would be like that."

"You don't know it wouldn't," Sam snapped. "You're a hypocrite, you know. You tell me to keep myself alive. Well, for what? So I can know that you gave your life instead?"

His words brought no answer. A silence fell between them. A rat ran by. It didn't scare either of them. In fact it made their mouths water just a bit. Both had eaten rat and been glad for the chance to do it. The bad old days of the FAYZ, back before Albert took over.

"Like these are the good times," Sam said without explanation. But Astrid knew what he was thinking.

"Don't go out in a blaze of glory, Sam."

"Don't nail yourself to a cross," he said.

"Listen to us," Astrid said, and laughed.

He shook his head. "I lost Brianna, Astrid. And she wasn't the first."

"Who made you responsible?" He didn't answer, so she said it. "I did. Didn't I?"

"Astrid . . ."

"I did," she said more definitely, accepting the truth of it. "I pushed you to lead. I made it your business. I used you to

protect my little brother, and then in the end I was the one
who sacrificed him. Now I'm trying to make good on all that.
I'm trying for redemption, too, Sam, and instead there you
go, once more unto the breach, Sam to the rescue even if he
dies doing it."

"You didn't make me responsible. You don't have that
power. This"—he held up his hands, and light glowed from
his palms—"this made me responsible. Having power made
me responsible. I had the power and you had the brains. So
we were chosen. That's the way it works, isn't it? People who
can have to help those who can't. The strong defend the weak
from the strong. I don't think you invented that, Astrid; all
you did was make me see it. Well, I see it. There it is. The
FAYZ gave me this light, and the FAYZ made it necessary.
And now the light isn't helping, is it? Now that monster is
going to walk into town and kill people I care about and people I love."

Astrid stood up. She was shaking. "I can't . . . ," she said.

Sam stood and tried to hold her, but she pulled away. "If
one of us is getting out of here, it has to be you, Astrid. If I get
out, it's trouble anyway, you know that. The world out there
is waiting for a scapegoat."

"You promised me," she said. "You've always kept your
promises to me, Sam. Keep this one. I'm holding you to it.
You swore. You swore to me."

From outside there came the sounds of yelling. Someone
was crying, "Fire! Fire!"

"Go," Astrid said, dismissing him. "And keep your word to

me, Sam, or you're a damned liar."

He left, not sure how to respond to that. He was relieved to have something tangible to do.

It felt good to be running free down the beach. Lying in a box at the bottom of the lake Drake hadn't expected to ever have it all back. A body. Not his, but his now, and it was in good shape and strong.

And so much more important, he had his whip. He had his whip hand!

Whip Hand!

No one was watching the beach. They were all huddled in terror in town. And the best thing was, they weren't expecting him, were they? Astrid would have bragged all over town how she had looked down at a helpless Drake and laughed and laughed. She must have thought she was safe from him at last. No more Drake. All Drake's threats were nothing now, hah hah.

What he would do to her.

The longing for that moment almost made him weak. He wanted it so badly. Had he ever wanted anything as badly as he wanted to hear Astrid beg for mercy?

But no, he couldn't kill her. He had to keep her alive, which was better. Life meant pain. If there was one thing Drake had learned his entire life—well, at least since his mother had remarried—it was that life was pain. And there was such joy in causing pain.

He had seen the pleasure his stepfather had taken in

beating Drake's mother. And his mother must have almost enjoyed it, too, right? She kept doing things that pissed her husband off. Like she expected it. Like she wanted it. Law of the jungle, his grandfather told him once. The big and strong kill and eat the small and weak. And Drake knew his grandfather was speaking from experience. He could see it in the old man's eyes. That old man had brought the pain in his life.

Drake climbed over the rocks that separated Town Beach from the much smaller Clifftop beach. He would climb the cliff, sneak past Clifftop, and come into town from the last direction Astrid would expect.

As he climbed, he felt the strength in this new body. He felt the power in his regrown whip hand as it lashed up, finding bushes and ledges and hauling him upward as swiftly as any rope.

Spider-Man! Hah!

Whip Hand!

As he climbed, he looked north and saw the fire. The fires of hell. Hah hah! Perfect. Let it all come down in pain and fire! He felt his ambitions broaden.

He was resurrected. He was resurrected to kill.

He was Jesus with a whip, an unkillable Satan coming with smoke and fire to destroy! In his mind it was a lurid comic-book panel: Drake Whip Hand, wreathed in fire, with Astrid and Diana cowering, whipped and begging for mercy.

And at some point he forgot all about Gaia.

TWENTY-SEVEN

ASTRID WATCHED SAM go and tried to calm the wild emotions she felt.

He wasn't wrong. That was the hell of it. He wasn't wrong. It would be his own light that killed. It was his light that had burned a hole in Brianna's heart.

But this could not be the answer. Not after everything that had happened. This could not be the answer.

It *is* the answer, Astrid. You know it.

She followed him out as far as the door—well, the wreckage of a doorway—and saw him rushing across the plaza to where a fire had caught somehow in a drifted pile of trash.

A couple of kids were already taking care of it, and Sam wasn't necessary. The truth was, the cries of "Fire!" almost served as a distraction, something to—

The whip was around her throat. She screamed but no sound emerged. She tried to breathe, but nothing came.

She reached for a standing pillar of stone; her fingernails

clawed at it. She kicked at a piece of wood, hoping it would make some sound to draw Sam's attention. The buildings around the plaza were supposed to be full of Edilio's people: one of them must see!

Sam had only to turn around . . .

Astrid dropped, putting all her weight on the tentacle arm, hoping to pull him off balance. But he was too strong.

Drake drew her back into the shadows of the church. She was kicking, trying to scream, her lungs already burning from lack of oxygen.

"Hello, Astrid," Drake said.

And she lost consciousness.

"We need a bucket brigade," Sam said to Edilio. "There must be some kind of air current up high in the dome. It's picking up sparks from the forest fire and dropping them all around."

"I'll get all my spare people on it right away," Edilio snapped. Then, "Sorry."

"I know you're stretched thin, man."

"Thin? I'm stretched invisible, Sam. There are maybe two, three dozen kids in the fields. I have maybe twelve left actually holding guns. And the rest? You know where they are."

"It's the waiting," Sam said, looking to the northwest, the direction of the highway. "Why doesn't she just attack?"

"Maybe she knows we're panicking. Or maybe she's waiting for the fire to do her work for her."

Sam looked up. The sky was still afternoon blue, but there was a gray tint to the air. "If she's out there to the northwest of town like we think, then she's closer to the fire than we are. Maybe we'll get lucky and—"

He stopped when he saw Edilio's skeptical look.

"Yeah," Sam said. Then: "I have to go after her. If I wait, then she uses my own power to kill kids. I have to try to take her down myself."

Edilio spread his hands as if to say, *But* . . . There was no but. It was the truth, and they both knew it.

"The only other alternative is, you know, to, um . . . deprive her of my power. It may give me a chance, her needing to keep me alive. That may give me an edge."

Again Sam was waiting to hear the counterargument. He was waiting to hear Edilio explain how wrong he was to believe that he had to die to stop Gaia. But that wasn't what he heard, or what he saw in Edilio's eyes.

"She's stronger than you are, Sam. It's like fighting yourself and Caine and Jack and Dekka, all at once."

"Yeah."

"Talk to Astrid about it."

"I already talked to Astrid."

"And she's okay with a suicide mission? Because I'm not. You go out there, go to win, huh? Don't go out there thinking you're doing us a favor by getting killed."

Sam sighed. "It's the endgame, my friend."

"Sam . . . ," Edilio began, but that was all he had, that one word, that one-word plea for a different solution.

"Take care of Astrid for me. Try to keep her safe and don't let her follow me."

"I haven't been very good at keeping people safe," Edilio said.

"No, man, what happened to Roger is not your fault or your failing. The grief is enough. It's enough. You don't need guilt on top of it."

Edilio looked grateful, but not like he believed it.

"Listen, Edilio, if she gets past me, she won't have the light anymore," Sam said. "You understand? But she will still be very dangerous. When I've fought Caine, the worst thing wasn't him dropping stuff down, because you see the arc of it going up then coming down, right? Him throwing stuff horizontally: that was worse because it was faster. Look out for that when . . . *if* . . . she gets here."

Edilio put out his hand and Sam took it.

"It's been interesting, hasn't it?" Sam said, trying for a smile.

"It's been a great honor to stand with you," Edilio said.

"Tell her I'm sorry I broke my promise," Sam said, so softly Edilio almost didn't hear. "Tell her I love her."

Sam didn't hurry. He knew where he was going. He wasn't happy about going there. No rush.

He walked the highway. How many times before had he made this walk? How many times had he passed this wrecked car and that overturned truck?

Someday if, when, the barrier came down, someone would clean it all up. The tow trucks would come. *Beep-beep*ing as they backed up to slip their lift beneath some battered hulk of a car. Maybe there were a few car windows that hadn't been broken, but not many. All the tires were partly or completely deflated. The gas tanks were long-since siphoned. Many of these cars had kept running until the gas was gone.

In some of these cars babies in car seats had died of starvation. In some of these cars kids had died when the driver poofed at seventy miles an hour. Would the CSI types have to come in and reconstruct it all? Would they identify the unidentified bones?

Someday families would try to come back only to find their home ransacked, torn up, sometimes reeking of human feces. There would be graffiti on their walls and trash stuffed in their toilets. And in many cases they'd find their homes burned down. Zil's fire had taken something like a quarter of the town, and other houses had been knocked down to make firebreaks.

People would marvel at the destruction and tut-tut and shake their heads because they wouldn't know what people had lived through in this place.

Those people returning to Perdido Beach wouldn't understand what desperate battles had been fought.

Yeah, sorry about pulling fuel rods out of the nuclear power plant and tossing them down a mine shaft. Why did we do that? Well . . . hah. You're never going to believe why we did that.

You say Coates Academy looks like it's been through an artillery duel? Well, in a way it has been.

Yes, there is at least one whisky still in the woods.

Yes, there are unburied corpses.

Those cat and dog bones? The ones that are charred as if someone cooked and ate a beloved household pet? Well . . . we got a little hungry.

Sorry about the graveyard in the town plaza. So damned sorry you can't begin to understand how sorry.

Sorry.

He was walking toward fire, into thickening smoke.

That was how he had crossed the line the very first time, so long ago, when an apartment off the town plaza had burned and he'd heard a cry for help. No one else had gone running toward the fire, so he had.

"All downhill after that," he said to no one.

That was the first burial in the town plaza. Sam had stepped up to try and save the nameless girl, and when he had failed, it was Edilio who had finally dug the grave and placed the marker. Edilio cleaning up after Sam's failures. That hadn't changed.

Battles avoided and battles joined. He had seen the rise of Caine and his fall. He had seen the threat from Zil's anti-mutant bigots grow and nearly destroy them all, and he'd seen Zil lying dead.

He'd seen Mary, good, sweet, decent Mary who looked after the littles, lose her mind under the influence of demons both internal and external.

He'd seen the zekes consume poor E.Z. He'd seen kids cough their own lungs out. He'd seen the bugs explode from a body half-eaten.

And how many dead? The little girl from the fire, she had been just the first. His first failure to save a life.

Duck. Good old Duck.

Thuan.

Francis.

How many of them? More than he could remember.

He'd seen the unknowns become pillars of strength. What a cliché that phrase was, but how else to describe Edilio? When the barrier came down he would probably be deported to Honduras.

Thanks for your heroism; now get out of the country, kid.

He had seen the weak become strong as granite. Quinn.

And Lana, what hadn't that girl been through?

Dekka, fearless, passionate Dekka, his right hand, his companion in battle, the sister he'd never had.

Through it all there had been Astrid. Difficult as always. Complicated as always. Superior, condescending, thoughtful, manipulative, beautiful, and passionate Astrid. The love of his life.

All worth it, just to have loved and been loved by her.

Coming down the road toward him was a flatbed truck. It was moving slowly but steadily. He could see that its wheels were not touching the road. It trailed smoke. The flatbed was piled with burning trees and tires and debris. It was an inferno that would have roasted any driver.

Gaia walked beside it, a hand raised to focus Caine's power and lift the massive truck.

She stopped, and the burning truck stopped as well. Gaia smiled.

"So," she said. "You're ready to die."

"Well, it was a short life. But it was a pretty good one," he said.

"I don't really want to kill you," Gaia said.

"I know. And I know why. But I'm not giving you a choice."

"Why fight me, Sam?" She had to shout to be heard above a sudden roar of the fire as a log collapsed on the others. Sparks exploded, fireflies to come drifting down on parched fields or continue to draft upward and maybe fall on the town.

Finishing Zil's work.

"Because you're going to kill my friends," Sam said.

Gaia shrugged. "They're a threat to me. I have a right to survive. Don't I? Don't all living things have a right to survive?"

"We're not here for a conversation."

"You know how many there are of me, Sam?" Gaia held up one finger. "One. Just one. I am the first and only like me. I am unique in the universe. Your friends? There are billions just like them."

She moved the truck forward and began to walk.

"There's no one like any of them," Sam said. "I doubt you can understand."

"Do you even know what I am?" she asked, mocking with a wry smile. "I was created to bring life. I was a seed sent out into the galaxy. But when I took root here, on this planet, all that changed. Is that my fault?"

Sam found himself taking a step back. He knew better than to argue. He hadn't come here for a debate. But he knew where this fight was going. And when the end is there, right there in front of you, is it so weak to want to drag it out for a few extra seconds?

"You're a killer. Killers lose their rights."

"Hah!" Gaia laughed. "Of course humans don't kill. You haven't slaughtered other species for food. Or wiped them out just for sport. You don't eat other creatures. Don't be ridiculous. What if I told you that you could join me, Sam? That you don't have to die."

She moved closer. Her movements were sensual, self-aware, calculated to mesmerize him.

"Look at me. I'm a human, too, aren't I? This is human." She gestured at her body.

"You've already killed whatever was human there," Sam said, but he was still talking and he was still moving backward.

"It will be human flesh you burn."

"It will be you, the gaiaphage, I kill."

"Do you think you'll kill me, Sam? I don't think you expect to. You came here to be killed."

"If necessary," he said dully.

"Let's see if it's necessary." Her hand came up, but Sam wasn't so mesmerized he was unready. He dodged left and the invisible punch only grazed him.

He fired with one hand, still moving fast to his left. But

showering him with sparks that stuck to his shirt and hair. The smoke billowed around him.

He choked and blasted randomly, blindly, all around him. Her cry of pain was the sound of hope. But he couldn't see what damage he had done.

Suddenly she was on him, bursting through the smoke, not with Caine's telekinetic power but with Jack's brute strength. Her hand grabbed his arm; he didn't resist, which would have cost him that arm, but leaped straight into her. Her own pull overbalanced her and she fell back.

With no other easy choice, he punched her in the face.

She pushed him off her and he flew through the air. He had time to see the burning logs and Gaia lying on her back, and then he hit the truck's cab, hard, bounced off, and lay winded on the ground.

Gaia was on him in seconds, leaning over him. "Come on, Sam, you can do better than that." Her hand closed on his throat. He could feel the immense power behind that grip. "No death for you. No, you're going to come along and watch."

She lifted him more easily than she'd have lifted a baby. There was a length of chain on the bumper of the truck. It was red-hot. He heard and smelled the flesh of her hands burning as she wrapped it around him, heard her cry out in pain but accept it just so she could hurt him. He screamed in agony as she laid the red-hot steel against him, as it burned through his clothing and seared his flesh.

"No glorious death for you, Sam."

He felt himself floating along above the ground, and then

Gaia had learned. She tracked his movement and t
missed.

He swept the beam of light horizontally and she
ily above it. Her invisible counterpunch didn't miss t
It knocked him twenty feet away. His lungs were en
wouldn't draw air, but he couldn't let her stop him,
way, not in a way that left him crippled again.

Win or die.

He rolled in the dirt as she laughed.

"I don't have to kill you, Sam. You do have to kill

He fired even as he rolled, and the result was a we
show of twisting green beams that singed Gaia's hair
erwise did nothing.

"We're too far from town," Gaia taunted. "Surely y
your last battle to be witnessed and admired. Beside
want my kindling to burn down to nothing. Come
let's go into town. I've never seen the place. I go to
nate. Don't you want to see?"

Sam jumped up, fired, but she dropped hard right
around his beam, and with effortless power lifted o
burning logs from the truck and threw it at him. It w
gering display of power. The log weighed tons.

No time to get out of the way. He fired with bot
and burned through the fire-weakened log. Two
separate torches blew past him, burning his skin and
his hair.

WHUMPF!

The log sections crashed behind him on th

he fell down a long, dark tunnel.

When he regained consciousness, he first felt the burns from the chain. Then the weight and strength of it, holding his arms tight against his body. He could move his hands, he could still fire his killing light, but he could not aim.

Floating. Wrapped in chains that stuck to his skin as they slowly cooled.

When he twisted his head, he saw Gaia walking down the middle of the highway.

Behind her the burning truck floated.

She noticed him stirring.

"Watch this," she said. She raised a hand and one log broke free from the flaming mass, rose in the air, and then hurtled like a missile across the parking lot to smash into the shattered glass and tattered banners at the front of Ralph's store.

"Fire is a very good distraction, don't you think?" Gaia said.

He couldn't speak. Whatever consciousness he had was almost a dream state, a hallucination.

"I realized, when I saw the forest burning, how fascinating the firelight is. It's beautiful, and people stare at it, don't they? It destroys things and kills people, but humans love it. Is it because they crave their own destruction, Sam? I want to understand your kind. I am going out into the wider world, and I must learn. But first things first. First, to escape this shell, this egg in which I have gestated, all eyes will be on the fire, all eyes blinded by the smoke, and when I walk out of here, out into your large world with its billions, no one will even see. It's the beauty of light, don't you see, Sam? It reveals, but it also distracts and blinds. It's even better than darkness."

"Don't do this," he begged in a choked voice.

He saw two people running from the burning grocery store. Some kids had been living there—skaters. The skaters loved it for all the smooth tile floors and the way the shelves and freezer cases could be turned into ramps.

Sam turned quickly to avoid looking, to avoid giving the two kids away, but it was too late.

Gaia stretched out her hand, and the nearest of the kids, a boy who insisted on being called Spartacus, came flying toward them, yelling in surprise.

He was twelve years old. He had hair down to his waist worked into mismanaged dreads. He wore a T-shirt that was more hole than cloth and oversized shorts.

"Watch the pretty light, Sam," Gaia whispered to him, right into his ear.

"No!" he cried.

"You've been a problem for me, Sam, right from the start. You were one of the first ones whose names I learned. I saw images of you in their minds, in the mind of the Healer, in Caine's mind, even distorted versions that Nemesis showed me sometimes. You defied me. Didn't you, you willful little boy?"

She was laughing, laughing at her own cleverness, laughing at the way Spartacus cried and begged and at the way Sam pleaded, at the way he turned his face away, at the futility of it.

Gaia grabbed Sam's head in the crook of her arm. She pried his eyes open with fingers dragging on his forehead. "Watch. Watch it all. Your light, Sam. Because you didn't have the courage to end your own life, did you? You wanted me to do it for you. The hero who missed his chance. Watch now, Sam. I'm going to slice him apart, and his every scream will be your fault."

"You're insane!"

"Compared to what?" she asked. "I haven't gotten out much."

The light burned from her free hand and like a power saw begun cutting into the boy's head, and he screamed and Sam roared and Gaia laughed, and Sam's hands were close enough, he could twist them just enough, and his own hands blazed with the green light cutting into Spartacus's heart.

Gaia cried out in ecstatic joy. She dropped the dead boy and with her telekinetic power twirled Sam around in the air like a top and laughed.

"Made you kill! Made you kill!" she yelled. "This will be fun."

She danced in a circle and shouted up at the smoke-darkened, spark-lit sky. "Too late, Nemesis, too late!" Like a child. Taunting. "Too late!"

"SHE'S COMING."

Edilio stood atop the town hall. It was the highest spot in the downtown area since the church was nearly leveled. Dekka was beside him, Jack and Orc just a few feet away.

She was coming with fire. Fire against a background of fire. She wasn't waiting for the Stefano Rey fire to reach town; she was bringing it, inspired by it.

A massive flaming torch of a truck floated at a stately pace down the highway, like some awful parade float. *Next up in the parade, ladies and gentlemen, the float from hell.*

Edilio raised binoculars and twisted the focus knob. What he saw made him catch his breath. A person floated before her, a person wrapped in chains.

He knew who it was. He couldn't see the face, but he knew.

Mary, Mother of God, if ever you were going to intercede, now would be a very good time.

The air was already hard to breathe for the smoke, and

now terror crushed the air from his lungs. He could hardly control his body. The gaiaphage was on the march and they would all die. All of them. Just like Roger, they would all die, no chance, no salvation, they would die die die die . . .

"Okay," Edilio said, tough, unflinching, because that's what the others all wanted from him. "Let's go do it."

He led the way, automatic rifle hanging from his shoulder, finger on the trigger guard, ready, scared. He trotted down the steps: *Don't miss, don't trip, Edilio; they're watching you, they're scared, they're so scared because they know it's over, they know death is here for them and there's no defense against it.*

Don't trip. Careful.

Out the front door, out onto the patio that overlooked the plaza. There were kids there, the few who hadn't yet run to the barrier, and yes, still some up in the windows with gun barrels visible.

You'll run when you see, he thought; you'll run and scream and so will I.

"Listen up," he shouted in a voice so calm it could not possibly be his. "Remember to make every shot count. Aim. Fire. Aim again. Fire. Keep that up until you run out of ammunition."

"Edilio!" someone cried out, but it wasn't a question: it was a slogan, it was a rallying cry.

"Edilio! Edilio!"

They shouted from their dark windows.

Like he was seeing her in a dream, he made eye contact

with Dekka, who nodded and said, "Edilio!"

Quinn appeared, carrying a gun. He was grim. A spark floated past his face, illuminating his eyes.

"There's a boat coming in," Quinn said.

Edilio nodded like he understood, but he understood nothing except that he had no power to resist what was coming.

Drake dragged her down Second Avenue, not seeming to have any plan or direction, really, just to drag her.

Astrid was in and out of consciousness, eyes misted red, hands scratching weakly at the powerful whip arm around her throat. A false night had fallen, a night that stank of smoke.

She must have passed out, because when she opened her eyes she was in a house. Vague, disjointed memories of footsteps on a porch, of a door kicked in, of herself hurled against a dining-room table.

Over her head a brass-and-crystal chandelier—much abused over the months—swung back and forth. Someone who had occupied the house at some point had hung Barbie dolls and action figures from the chandelier with bits of colored yarn. There was a smell of sewage to join the reek of smoke.

He threw Astrid onto the table, faceup. She gathered her strength and screamed, "Help! Help me! *Help me!*"

Drake came into view from behind her head, stepped around so she could see him and he could look into her eyes.

There was something odd and disjointed about him. The body didn't match the head. He was taller than he'd been, stronger, more muscled. His head was pale; his neck was tan.

A lizard's tail whipped madly, protruding from his brow, right between his eyes.

The windows glowed orange and red. The fire was coming. Endgame.

"Help me! Help me!" Astrid screamed.

Drake nodded in satisfaction. "That's good. That's very good. I've waited a long time to hear you—"

She rolled away from him, trying to get off the table, but his whip arm had her and dragged her back. She kicked and punched and none of it mattered. He enjoyed it.

He laughed.

She fell silent.

So he whipped her across her belly and she screamed in pain.

"Better," he said.

"You're a sick person, Drake. You sick creep!"

"Who, me? Hey, who was it who put whose head in a beer cooler and weighted it down with rocks? *I'm* sick?"

"Go ahead and kill me, because if you don't, when Brittney comes she'll let me go."

He cocked a pistol finger at her. "You know: I thought about that. I get a few seconds of warning before the change-over, so what I'll do is kill you as soon as I feel it coming on. But until then . . ."

He slashed at her again. Again. Again, and she tried not

to scream, but she did, she screamed: she screamed and he laughed.

"Sam will burn you to ashes!" she gasped out.

"That would be the only thing lacking now," Drake said, sounding genuinely disappointed. "I wanted him here. It would be way better if he could see. If he could watch. It's a hard thing to watch someone you care for being hurt."

She heard something there. Something.

"Who did you watch being hurt?" she asked, desperate to engage him, stall, distract . . .

"Really? You want to get into my head? Figure out what makes me *me*? You're not here to play shrink. You're here to suffer."

He slashed at her again. Astrid cried out. The pain was too awful to endure. She wished for unconsciousness. She wished for death. She sobbed quietly.

Petey.

Jesus.

Anyone . . .

But she felt no presence. Just the psychopath in the shadows cast by firelight.

"Gaia wanted me to bring you to her. So she could use you as a hostage. But I don't take orders from her anymore. I wasted too much time following. I followed Caine. I followed the gaiaphage. But she's not the gaiaphage, not really, not in that body, not with that face . . ."

"She's pretty," Astrid managed to say, gasping out each word. "Is that what you hate? Is that the sickness in you?"

Drake barked out a laugh. "Do you have any idea how many shrinks have tried their words on me? You think you can do better? It has to be some sickness, some syndrome, right? Put a label on it and everything will be all better." He laughed at the idea. "Are you as clueless as the rest of them, Astrid? It's simple. Here it is, here's the answer, Astrid the Genius: it's fun to hurt people. It's such . . . it's such joy, Astrid. Such joy realizing that all the power is yours, and all the fear and pain is right there, in your victim. Come on, smart girl, you know what it's called. You know the word for it. Come on, say it." He cupped his hand to his ear, waiting for the word.

"Evil," Astrid said.

Drake laughed, threw up his hand wide, and nodded his head. "Evil! There you go. Good for you. *Evil.* It's in all of us. You know that, too. It was in you. I saw it in your eyes as you looked down at me in that cooler. Evil, hah. We all want to have someone powerless beneath us while we stand over them." His voice had grown husky. "We all want that. We all want that."

He slid his whip arm over the painful wounds on her belly.

"I wish Sam was here to see. But he's probably dead by now." He sighed. "And if he's not, well, we'll tell him, won't we? We'll tell him every little detail.

"Be sure to scream," he said.

"You too," she said.

He looked at her, puzzled, his face inches from hers.

Astrid jerked her face forward, clamped her teeth down on Drake's nose, and bit down as hard as she could.

•   •   •

At Sheridan Avenue a group of kids broke and ran from a house. Gaia cut them down.

Sam turned his palms inward, toward himself. He couldn't turn them far enough to aim for his own head or internal organs. His only chance was to use the light to cut through a leg artery and bleed to death.

Better than watching his power be used to murder.

"If there really is a God, forgive me," he said, and clamped his palms to his thighs and . . .

The pain was searing. The beams of light burned into his thighs.

Gaia was on him in a flash. She twisted his hands away as Sam roared in pain.

Had he done it? Had he cut an artery? Could it be over now, please, please could it be over now?

"No, no, no, I don't think we can have that," Gaia said.

Sam struggled against the chains, struggled against her grip on him, but his strength was nothing compared to hers.

Gaia slapped him hard, a backhand blow that sent him reeling into a state that was neither conscious nor unconscious. He was vaguely aware of Gaia rewinding the chain, this time tightly binding his hands together so that they were palm to palm. This left his shoulders free, but he had missed his only chance.

He began to cry. He had failed. Finally, permanently, he had failed. And hadn't he always known he would? Wasn't that why he had resisted for so long becoming the leader?

Wasn't that why he'd been relieved, finally, to turn much of it over to Edilio?

He wasn't a hero. He never had been. School Bus Sam, the great myth that had caused kids to turn to him at first, that hadn't been heroism: it had just been quick thinking and self-preservation.

Everything he had done, it wasn't courage: it was all just a desperate effort to stay alive, wasn't it? In the end wasn't that all it was?

And now, failure.

Failure, and he would watch them all die, one by one, die because he had chosen life over heroic sacrifice.

Gaia had tired of levitating him before her as some kind of prize. She was angry now. She threw him twenty feet down the highway. He landed on his back and smacked his head against the concrete.

She ran up to him, laughing, and kicked him, crushing ribs and sending him rolling down the highway, chains clanking, crying like a baby, beaten.

"Aaaaahhhh!"

People running. Sam could barely see them through the smoke. Three girls who had never been anything important in the life of the FAYZ, three regular kids, Rachel, Cass, and Colby, three sisters who had never fought, never been in on any of the battles, had just kept their heads down and done what work they were given, now rushed madly, hopelessly, at Gaia with tire irons and clubs.

Gaia seemed startled. She raised one hand and froze them

in place. "Look at this," Gaia marveled. "Are they brave or stupid, Sam Temple?"

Sam blinked tears from his streaming eyes.

"Let them—" he started to say, but began to cough.

"I couldn't quite hear that," Gaia taunted.

Sam closed his eyes. Through his eyelids he saw a flash of green light. There were no cries. Just the wet-sandbag sound of bodies hitting the ground.

"Open your eyes, Sam Temple," Gaia said. "I cut them in half. With your light. With your power."

She pushed him with her foot to send him rolling.

"On to the rest. On to—" She fell silent suddenly. He opened one soot-streaked eye and saw that Gaia was looking around, nervous. Like she felt someone watching her.

"Where is the whip hand with my hostage?" she asked aloud. Then to Sam, as if he might have the answer: "Where is Drake with the sister of Nemesis?"

"Astrid!" Sam gasped.

"Hear me, Nemesis!" Gaia cried, choking then recovering. "Hear me! I have your sister!"

"I don't see her," Sam said.

"Never worry, Sam Temple: Drake will get her." But Gaia chewed at her thumbnail, a very Caine gesture Sam had seen before.

"You seem scared," Sam said.

Gaia snarled at him and raised her own hands as if ready to kill him herself. Then she laughed shakily. "Ah-hah. Trying to provoke me?"

But she was rattled. She had felt something. She had felt something she didn't like.

"Nemesis?" Sam asked her.

Gaia didn't answer. She was done playing games. She was done enjoying herself. She grabbed Sam's chain and began dragging him down the road, then broke into a run.

Caine and Diana docked the boat at the marina. The fire, which had been to the north, now seemed to be everywhere at once. Bursts of sparks rose high from the direction of the highway. The air was filled with ash, hard to breathe, hard to keep your eyes open. Impossible to believe that somewhere the sun was still shining.

"Should I tie off the boat?" Diana asked.

Caine didn't answer. He levitated himself from the boat to the dock. Then, with equal ease, he lifted the missiles in their crates and landed them safely on the wood planks.

"Give me a hand," Diana said. She held her hand up to him.

He looked down at her. "I don't think so, Diana."

"What do you mean?" she asked.

He raised one hand and pushed the boat gently away from the dock.

"What are you doing?" she demanded.

"Going out in style," he said.

"Caine. Caine. What are you doing?"

"There's no good reason for both of us to die."

"Caine, you're being silly," she said as firmly as she could.

"You know this is the end. I want to be with you. I don't want our monster child hunting me down and finding me at the end all alone."

He shrugged. "I know you asked Little Pete to take you. I know you offered yourself up."

"How? How did you know?"

He shrugged.

"But he didn't," Diana said. "He didn't, which—"

"Yeah. Well. He had a better offer."

"What?" The word came out as a sob. "Caine . . . No. No. We do this together."

"Nah, I don't think so," he said with strained nonchalance. "I think it will be like it is with Gaia. I think when Little Pete does his thing, well, I don't think I'll be around then. So I don't see how we do this together."

"Don't, Caine. Don't you do this," Diana pleaded.

"You have to understand, Diana: I'm not trying to be noble. It's just the only way I have to beat it. The gaiaphage. It thinks it has me. It thinks it owns me. It thinks it cracks the whip and I have no choice but to obey. And the pain . . ." He shrugged again. "So. So, we want old green-and-evil to be surprised when it finds out, right?"

"Caine, this is not what we . . . No. No."

He stretched out his hand and she rose through the air, almost as if she was flying to him.

They were in each other's arms, Diana shaking, Caine strangely calm.

"Sam's probably out there somewhere being his usual

heroic self," Caine said. "I can't let that boy save the world all alone. I'd never live it down."

"Don't do this, baby, don't do this," Diana begged as she stroked his face.

"Listen to me. I wrote something, back on the island. Two somethings, actually. One is for you to give to Sam, if he makes it out somehow, or Astrid, or someone, you know, trustworthy. And the other is for you. If you get a chance, you know, go and get them from the desk in that room."

"We're not beat yet, Caine," she pleaded. "We haven't lost yet."

"I was a king for a while. I wasn't a very good one. I wanted all kinds of things. I wanted, well, you know. Power. Glory. To be feared. All that good stuff. But you know what? When the gaiaphage did it to me, when she made me cry and grovel and beg for mercy, I realized: There's no end to this for me. There's no end to the FAYZ. If we get out alive, there's still no end. And what happens to me out there in the world?"

"No, you're wrong: they can't blame you for everything that happened."

He laughed. "Yeah, well, actually, they can. A king, a warrior, whatever I was, I want to go out in a blaze of glory. I've risen as high as I'm ever going to. And if I survive, I'm just going to end up as prisoner number three-one-two-whatever. You coming to see me on visiting days."

"But I will come see you. And I will wait for you."

"No," he said firmly. "I get my big finish. And you get your life. Move on, Diana."

"You're not fooling me," she said. "I know why you're doing this—"

"Because I want to win," he said.

"Yes."

"And because I want to write the end of my own story."

"Yes. And because you want redemption," she said raggedly.

He shrugged. "If that's what you want to believe."

"And because you love me."

Suddenly Caine was unable to say more. He waited, trying to master his emotions. They kissed, with Diana's tears running down his cheeks. Then, using the power he had, he pried her loose and gently deposited her in the boat, now drifting out of reach of the dock.

"Hey," he said. "Don't tell anyone about those last two, okay? You tell anyone who ever asks: right to the end, Caine was in charge."

He turned away quickly, lifted the deadly cargo, and trudged toward a burning Perdido Beach.

"Not yet, Little Pete," he whispered, touching his cheeks and feeling her tears on his fingertips. "Not just yet."

TWENTY-NINE
42 MINUTES

GAIA BURNED AND killed the length of the access road before turning right on Sheridan Avenue. Heading for the town plaza. At the corner of Golding she paused to attack the school.

She burned it in detail, firing the deadly light through long-shattered windows. She burned until the smoke began to billow and terrified kids who had sheltered there came running out.

Some made it.

Others did not.

She turned on Alameda, still carrying Sam by his chains, dropping him when she wanted both hands free to spread destruction.

"You definitely got the most useful power, Sam," she said. "I'm very glad you're still alive."

Many of the houses in the area were already burned, others had been knocked down, but a few still stood, and these

Gaia burned out. People fled like rats, leaping over fences, piling over mounds of rubble, and for Gaia it was almost a game, a shooting gallery.

People screamed and died. Or just died.

The counterattack came at the corner of San Pablo and Alameda.

Guns fired from the roof of the town hall.

BLAM! BLAM! BLAM!

Carefully aimed, but it was a hard shot in the smoke, with cinders in the air. Gaia fired back but was no more successful.

Gaia grabbed Sam in one hand and raised him over her head like a human shield. The firing from the rooftop stopped.

"Keep shooting! Keep shooting!" Sam cried.

"Shoot! Shoot! Shoot!" Edilio's voice. Sam couldn't see him. Was he behind the fountain?

Now again the firing started, but from a different angle, from the center of the plaza. Bullets whizzed past. Bullets pinged off concrete.

Gaia fired back with her free hand, but she wasn't hitting anyone, either.

It was a melee, a madness of guns blazing and light beams searing and all of it swathed in swirling smoke.

Edilio had cleared the streets—there were no cars for Gaia to toss around, nothing to grab and use . . . except for the rubble of the church. She dropped Sam, ran to her left, and as she ran . . . *disappeared.*

Sam knew immediately what had happened. Bug.

Somehow Gaia had learned about Bug. Had she been saving up for this moment? No, that would be insane. She'd have used the power earlier if she'd known. Someone had to have told her.

Drake?

But Drake was dead. Wasn't he?

With invisibility Gaia would regain the edge she'd lost with Brianna's death. Invisibility would leave Edilio's people baffled and—

"Paint!" Edilio roared before losing his voice to a fit of coughing. Then, recovering: *"Hit her!"*

Two kids hidden in the church's rubble threw balloons of paint. They splattered ineffectually on the ground. More were thrown from rooftops, and then from nothingness came the green light, killing one kid, burning the belly of the other. The wounded boy broke and ran.

But the deadly beams had revealed Gaia's location.

"Jack!" Edilio managed to gasp, and Jack rose from behind the fountain and bounded in a single jump from the fountain to the steps of the church. He spun, two spray-paint cans flowing, and yes, there! Just a swatch of red and a patch of white that gave away an arm and an impression of a torso.

The guns didn't need an order. They blazed. From the day care, from the McDonald's, from the roof of the town hall.

But now Gaia had broken timber and slabs of plaster and steel support beams to work with. Using her telekinetic power she threw a whirlwind of debris at the fountain. There were cries in the dark, and the firing from there stopped.

Then a bullet fired from the roof of the town hall caught her ankle, and she bellowed in rage and pain. The blood that sprayed was all too visible.

She snatched up a crossbeam that weighed hundreds of pounds and played her laser fire down its length, let it go, grabbed it with her telekinetic grip, and threw it through the front door of the town hall.

The firing continued.

Sam saw it and heard it from his position in the middle of the street.

Suddenly Jack was beside him. He lifted Sam in his arms and ran.

It was a bullet that caused Jack to fall. One misdirected bullet hit him in the lower back. His legs went out from under him. He dropped Sam, then fell atop him.

"Jack!"

"I'm okay. It's just . . . my legs. I can't move my legs."

Sam saw fear in Jack's eyes. Jack, who had never wanted the power he was given.

Jack who had never wanted anything but to play with his computers.

"Oh, man," Jack said.

He seemed to pass out for a moment, but then rallied. "Let me get you out . . . ," he said, and blood was in his mouth now, cutting off speech.

Jack, Computer Jack, as he had long been known, gripped the chains around Sam and pulled with all of his incredible strength.

He coughed blood onto Sam's chest.

A single link in the chain snapped.

And Jack was gone.

Sam squirmed, trying to work free of the broken chain. He saw Gaia, nothing but a creature poorly outlined in paint and blood, a human-shaped swirl within the smoke, raise high a steel support beam, ready to hurl it with Jack's strength.

Her arms bent, the beam fell, and she leaped out of the way and ran, as bullets flew, into the church.

Drake screamed. The sound of it, the wind from it, was in Astrid's face. She bit down as if she was hanging on to life itself by her teeth. She was.

Drake punched her in the side of the head.

She blocked him, softening the blows with one battered hand.

He tried to wrap his whip hand around her throat, but she was too close and he couldn't pull away, and her teeth were not just holding, they were cutting into flesh, ripping at him like a dog.

He tried to stand up, tried to get leverage, but he couldn't get distance, and now instead of blocking his blows she gripped his head with both hands and forced her thumbs into his eyes.

Drake bellowed and squirmed and beat at her, and her mind was swimming, the blows were taking a toll, bashing her temple; his whip was trying to lash at her exposed legs, but no, no, she wasn't going to let go, and her jaw was clenched with all the strength she had and her top teeth and bottom teeth were getting closer, closer, and Drake screamed curses, but he couldn't get away.

Her thumbs pushed his eyeballs, hard-boiled eggs, dug past them, dug around them, dug fingernails into the space between eyeball and skull.

And she was screaming, too: the words weren't clear, her mouth was full, and her jaw was clenched painfully, but it sounded just a bit like, "Die! Die!"

All at once, with a shake of her head, his nose ripped off.

Her thumbs were up past the knuckle; she felt the fragile bone cage crack.

Then, in one convulsive move, she pushed him off her. He rolled onto the floor, stood, and she backed away. She spit out the nose.

One of his eyes dangled from a thread.

The other oozed something like jelly from a split in the pupil.

Between them the lizard's tail whipped madly.

He swung his own whip, lashed the air, but blindly. He caught the chandelier, ripping loose some of the Barbies hung there.

He wasn't dead. She didn't have the power to kill him. He would regenerate: he would come for her again.

And then, there was Taylor.

The appearance of the golden-skinned girl, the anomaly-amongst-anomalies, just froze Astrid. It was utterly incongruous.

Taylor looked down at the lashing, screaming, losing-it Drake and said to Astrid, "Peter. He sent me. To save you."

"Thanks," Astrid gasped, and picked bits of Drake's nose out of her teeth.

"He's very weak. I think he only has minutes—"

"Little Pete? I asked him to take me," Astrid said.

Taylor shook her head, a too-slow, reptilian move. She seemed to be enjoying the way her hair flowed across her neck and forehead. "Not you. He is scared of you. Peter is scared of you. But he likes you."

"I get that sometimes," Astrid said. "Tell him thanks."

Taylor disappeared from the room. Astrid turned to flee, hesitated, picked up a chair, and slammed it down on Drake's head as hard as she could, breaking one of the heavy legs in the process.

Then she fled.

Somewhere close by, guns were firing.

The plan, such as it was, had worked.

Gaia was in the church. The idea had been that she would be drawn to the only debris she could use as weapons. The hope would be that she'd go all the way in.

And now Dekka sprang her trap.

Gaia stood, bleeding, visible now as she relinquished Bug's power of invisibility. She stood gasping from the pain, seething in rage, frustrated again, and surrounded, literally surrounded, by all the heavy, hard, sharp-edged debris of the semi-collapsed church.

Dekka was at the altar.

"You murdered someone I love," Dekka said, and raised her hands high. Thousands of pounds of wood and steel, plaster and glass, pews, roof tiles, and accumulated filth rose in a rush, a pillar of swirling junk.

Up and up, and Gaia rose with it.

Forty feet up and Gaia had recovered her wits well enough to take aim at Dekka, and then, just as Gaia began to fire, Dekka dropped it all.

WHOOOOMPF!

It fell and bounced and crashed and splintered with a noise like the end of the world.

Dekka jumped back to avoid being hit, but she still took a dozen small impacts from flying debris. She couldn't see Gaia, but she wasn't taking chances. She raised high the debris and dropped it again.

And raised it and dropped it again. Hammer blows.

On the fourth attempt Dekka saw Gaia floating above it all, bloodied, bruised, her clothing torn, her hair filthy, but not dead, very much not dead.

Gaia looked down at her, aimed, held Dekka directly in her line of fire, and laughed. "Very clever," Gaia said. "It almost worked. But I won't kill you. Not yet."

Gaia floated calmly down as the mess settled around her, slowly, under her control now.

Dekka drew a pistol. Gaia flicked it easily from her grip and sent it flying away.

"Anything else?" Gaia asked.

"You're getting weaker," Dekka blustered.

"Mmmm. So are all of you."

"You can't afford to kill me."

"No. But I can do this." Gaia used her father's power to raise a pew, a long, heavy oak bench, and blast it into Dekka's chest, pinning her against the altar.

Dekka lay still.

Gaia turned away, limping and in pain. Why was this proving so hard? She'd lost speed, now she'd lost Jack's strength, and worst of all, most dangerous of all, she'd lost control of Sam. He had gotten away, and he might come for her again. Or he might take his own life. Either way . . .

She had to heal herself and quickly.

Little Pete was doing something . . . something . . . she could feel it. She could feel his resolution. She could feel his anticipation. But she could also feel his ebbing strength.

So many left to kill. She would have to hurry.

The firing had stopped.

Edilio couldn't see much of anything, blinded by smoke tears, trying to make sense of a battlefield. All he knew was that the firing had stopped when Gaia disappeared into the church.

Then he saw Jack and Sam. Sam had rolled Jack over so that instead of the small hole in his back what was visible was the exit wound, an explosion of viscera poking out through his shirt.

"Jesus, Mary," Edilio said.

From the church came the loud crash of debris falling.

Edilio dropped down beside Sam. Sam was alive but looked almost as bad as Jack. There were burns on his body and arms. His shirt was tatters, a filthy, bloody rag.

Edilio began pulling at the chains.

"Edilio," Sam gasped.

"I got you, man," Edilio said.

"Do it, Edilio."

Edilio shook off the request, pretending not to know what Sam was asking.

From the church a second loud crash.

Voices above called out, "Edilio! What should we do?"

"Do it, man. I tried. I don't think I have the strength to try again, man: do it for me," Sam begged.

"Dekka's got her," Edilio stalled as he pulled the last chains away. The links tore at burned flesh as he pulled them free.

"She'll come out of there and—"

"Damn it, I can't kill you! You're asking me to commit murder!" Edilio exploded.

Sam stared. Nodded. "Yeah. Give me your gun, Edilio. I think I can do it with a gun. The other thing, though . . . It'll be easier with—"

"I can't do it," Edilio said, shaking his head, weeping.

"She's going to kill everyone—"

A third crash from the church.

"I'm going to go shoot her myself," Edilio said.

"Edilio!" Sam called after him.

Edilio spun around, stabbed a finger at Sam, and said, "I'll kill. I'll kill. That's enough. It's enough! I won't murder!"

"It's all the same," Sam muttered weakly, as Quinn appeared out of the smoke.

Edilio took two steps back, grabbed Quinn by the shoulder, and said, "He's not in charge. Don't listen to him. You understand? You listen to me."

Whether Quinn understood what was going on or not, he knew the power of conviction when he saw it. "Yes, sir," he said.

"Tell you what, Sanjit," Lana said.

"What, Lana?" he asked.

"See this?" She held up her cigarette. "This will be my last one. I promise."

Sanjit shook his head slowly. "What are you talking about?"

Lana looked around the shambles of a room. There were twenty-one victims: Some were dead and hadn't been cleared away. Others would live, for now, at least. There were more in the room next door. More still in the hallway.

Lana felt hollowed out. The endless hurry to save this one or that one, the sleeplessness, the soul sickness that came from seeing death and disfigurement, it was all finally too much.

And still she felt it. She felt its mind, its will, its glee as it killed.

She took a long drag on the cigarette and blew the smoke out, savoring it. "Last one."

"What are you doing?"

Lana put her hand on Sanjit's face. He made a tentative reach for the pistol at her waist. She was surprised. She pulled it out and handed it to him.

"No, not that," she said, smiling. "I don't think that's in me. Different fight I have in mind. The time has come. Listen to me, Sanjit. I'm going outside. Don't follow me."

She left then, walked down the hall, ignoring the pleas of the desperate, down the stairs, and out onto the lawn.

She took another drag, squared her shoulders, closed her eyes, and said, "This is going to hurt."

Gaia's goal was not a fight. Her goal was slaughter.

Kill them all. Kill every last one of them.

Gaia did not rush out to meet the guns in the town plaza. She blew out the remains of the back wall of the church and stormed onto Golding Street.

Time. She felt it slipping away, and it would take too long to hunt down the shooters right now, too inefficient. Kill more sooner, that was the right move. Kill more now.

Seconds and seconds and she couldn't run because there was a bullet in her leg and that leg did not want to run; it wanted to fold up under her.

Never mind, she would heal herself when they were all dead, and then, yes, there would be time, but her body, the body she had stolen, filthy weak sack of blood that kept leaking out, it was weakening, wasn't it? She could feel it. The blood leaking out of her. Had to stop and heal that, at least, had to stanch the bleeding.

She bent over and pressed her hand against the wound, hobbling down the street as she did, an awkward, laughable-looking creature.

And Nemesis was doing something, moving, preparing, wasn't he? She could feel him. He was a shadow of himself, weak, a ghost. Just die!

Just finally die, you stupid little boy!

The blood still leaked between her fingers. Why wasn't the healing working?

She reached the highway and there were people, kids, running in panic toward the brilliant lights of the barrier.

A burned-out gas station.

An overturned FedEx truck.

Panicked children.

"Die!" she roared, and fired after them. "Die!"

Her body woozy. And the healing . . . too slow. Why wasn't . . .

And then Gaia knew. She felt the mind pushing against hers, fighting her. Not Nemesis.

No, the *Healer*. Wrestling her for control of the healing power. Blocking her. Wanting her to bleed to death! Trying to kill her!

Gaia struck at her, invisible tentacles through the indescribable space that connected them. She saw the Healer in her mind, saw her face, her actual human face as though she was there on the road standing between Gaia and her victims.

Lana. Something was burning in her mouth. Smoke was coming from her nose. And she was unafraid. She was ready for the pain the gaiaphage could cause her.

Well, then, I wouldn't want to disappoint!

She saw Lana staggered by the lashings of pain, the burning thing falling from her mouth, hands pressed against the agony in her head, but fighting back, draining Gaia's strength, delaying, *delaying.*

With every last ounce of her strength Gaia struck at the Healer. She felt the Healer's pain, felt the Healer's weakening, and Gaia crowed, tilted her head back, and howled at the red-glowing sky in triumph.

Someone was shooting at her from behind a truck.

She rolled the truck over, crushing the shooter.

This time when she bent down to touch the bleeding hole, it sealed. The blood would no longer flow, but she could do no more; the healing power was ebbing fast as Lana pushed back again, fought Gaia for control.

How does she fight me?

Still time. Still time. Nemesis had not done it yet. Nemesis had not found his home. Not . . . just . . . yet.

And there it was finally: the barrier. It would mean showing herself. Not at all how she had planned this. Her body, her face, they would be revealed. It would make things much harder later, when Nemesis died and she walked free. But she had been stymied, attacked, burned, shot, hurt again and

again, nearly killed . . . No time for half measures. No time
for clever plans. Time to ensure that Nemesis died and took
this trap of a place down with him.

Like spooked cattle the humans gathered there. So many
of them. So easy to slaughter.

They cowered. They cried for mercy. It would be easy.

Gaia felt the peace inside her. She felt the joy of the moment.
She felt victory.

I don't need to heal if I can kill.

She raised her hands. Spread them wide apart.

And fired two beams of killing light. One to the left. One
to the right. Slowly she brought the beams toward the center.

The people screamed as the beams began to slice into
those on the left and right flanks.

They climbed over one another to escape.

Seconds and it would be over.

Connie Temple stood in the press of frantic parents and
hangers-on and thrill seekers who spread across acres of land
beside the barrier.

She had been worrying for days about what would happen
if the barrier came down. She'd occupied her mind with concern for the future, and with the gnawing guilt from fearing
that she might have sent her closest friend's daughter to her
death.

Now she watched the TV monitors on the satellite trucks
with mounting despair. They had showed satellite footage

of the spreading conflagration. They'd shown the video of a little girl ripping a man's arm off and eating it. They'd shown endless "interviews" with terrified, starving children. There had been long-distance drone video of something that looked like a monster made of stone and, in these last hours, what was undeniably a gun battle in Perdido Beach.

The whole world was watching. And the whole world was helpless. In the end it wasn't going to matter at all what she said or did or felt. In the end it would all come down to the kids in that awful fishbowl.

She thanked God the barrier had been opaque for so long: had she been able to see, had the world been able to see, the parents would have been driven mad.

She stood now just ten feet from the barrier. Almost within reach were children crying, screaming soundlessly, begging.

And just beyond them a lovely teenaged girl, with arms raised, who now fired bright beams of light. The dazzling green beams struck the barrier and passed through the transparent force field.

The people outside never realized their own danger until the left-hand beam burned through a National Guard Humvee.

And then, yes, everyone then knew that death was coming not just for their children, but for them, too.

Like a herd of panicked cattle they surged away from the barrier, screaming.

Connie Temple did not move. She couldn't. She had to watch this final slaughter. A witness, even if she died for it.

On the left and on the right, the first of the children inside burned. And the first of the adults outside screamed as hair caught fire and limbs fell severed to the ground.

And something large pelted down the hill, a monstrosity, a nightmare creature.

THIRTY

YEA, THOUGH I walk . . . valley of the shadow of death . . .

Orc was not a great runner. He weighed hundreds of pounds. His gravel legs were not quick.

His staff will comfort me . . . Angels and so on . . .

But the downslope helped a little. And the smoke didn't bother him so much. Maybe his throat was different.

I will fear no evil . . .

She didn't hear him coming.

The Lord is my shepherd . . .

A hundred yards left.

Her lights burned slowly toward the center, and she threw her head back and laughed and laughed as the crowd outside panicked and ran and died and the crowd inside crawled over one another like desperate animals to escape the slaughter and were cut in half.

Thou art with me. Not just thy staff.

Thou.

Orc hit Gaia like a truck.

She flew. Hit the ground facedown amid the panicked children. The impact rolled Orc into the barrier, squashing a girl beneath him. He hit the barrier and it sent a shock through him, so he jumped up, raging against it, searched for Gaia, saw her rolling onto her back, saw her face distorted with fury, saw her raise her hands.

He was off balance, trying to get to his feet, when she fired.

Both beams hit him mid-chest.

Orc collapsed like a puppet with its strings cut.

He lifted one massive stone fist to try and shield the patch of human skin that still covered part of his mouth.

People inside and out scattered in panic. The air was filled with screams.

Orc was on his knees. Two holes had been burned right through him. He looked at Gaia, who stood now, enraged, and advanced on him.

"I'm not scared of you," Orc said, slurring the words like in the bad old days when he was a drunk. "I'm going to dwell . . . I forget . . . forever."

Gaia advanced on him, but the crowd, the huddled, terrified mass, had used the distraction to break and run.

Gaia felt the fear creeping back in.

And then the missile exploded against the barrier.

Lana stumbled down from Clifftop. It felt like forever since she'd been away from that foul room, that now-terrible place.

She could see in the distance fire eating at the edge of

Perdido Beach. She tasted the smoke.

"Not much point quitting if the air's going to be one big cigarette," she muttered.

Her battle was over. She felt it inside. The gaiaphage had ceased to struggle against her. She had fought and won her own little war.

Suddenly Patrick came bounding up beside her.

"So, Sanjit sent you to look after me, huh?" She reached down and patted his head. "You and me, boy. You and me."

There came a loud explosion, a flat but powerful sound, just off to her right.

There would be people hurt by that kind of a thing.

For the last time, the Healer headed toward the sound of suffering.

The missile hit the barrier immediately behind Orc. His body took most of the blast.

It blew him apart. TV cameras caught the moment when a thousand little stones went flying like shrapnel. The rock was blown from his back and much of his chest, from his shoulders and most of his head. It was as if he was a mud-crusted shoe knocked against the wall. The mud gravel was knocked away in patches.

His internal organs were crushed. His eyes bled. For a terrible moment a body, the body of a young man, with pink flesh rising from still-stony legs, tried to push itself up off the ground. Surely just a physical instinct, surely not a conscious effort, because he could not be alive.

Charles Merriman, long known as Orc, tried to rise, and instead fell dead.

Orc's massive body had shielded Gaia from the worst of it.

She lived, still, but the shrapnel and the fire had stripped the skin from much of her body, a terrible mimicry of Orc's own destruction.

She was a creature of blood, red from head to foot.

But she lived still.

Sinder ran from the terrible scene. She tripped over bodies, got up, and ran some more.

She glanced back once and saw Orc hit.

She could hardly breathe for the beating of her heart and the sobbing that tore at her.

Her feet pounded earth, tripped, stood, ran, glanced back again and saw Gaia coming.

A beam of light shot past Sinder and she screamed. A girl to her right made a soft gasp and fell. The hole in her neck was smoking.

Feet on concrete now, the road, running. Clifftop! To the left, but uphill, and Gaia was coming, and another deadly beam of light, so close Sinder felt the heat of it on her cheek and cries and shouts and the sound of people gasping for breath, gagging in the smoke.

And suddenly, Caine rising up behind a wrecked car. He was holding something long and white.

The panicked crowd parted around him. Sinder ran on, glanced back, saw Gaia still running and firing, and Caine grim and steady.

"Damn," Caine breathed. "That is one tough monster Diana and I made."

The rest of the missiles were off to the side of the road in their crates. He kind of didn't think he'd get a chance to reload.

Edilio was there, unpacking a second missile, but nope, Caine thought, Edilio isn't going to get the shot, either.

Gaia saw him.

"You," she said.

"Yeah, me," Caine said, disappointed. "Well, I thought it was worth a try. Better than my backup plan."

"Your backup plan?" Gaia asked.

Caine nodded. And for a moment he hesitated, seeing Diana in his mind.

Diana.

A good final thought, that.

"Now, Little Pete," Caine said. "Right now."

Little Pete was ready, but he was still worried. Living inside a body had not been good for him. His brain had been his enemy all his life. And the only peace he had ever known was in this fading twilight unreality he had shared with the Darkness that called itself the gaiaphage.

But the gaiaphage had attacked him. The gaiaphage had

hurt him, even while crooning softly to Pete to just fade away.

Little Pete didn't remember much that his parents and sister had taught him back before. But he remembered that it is not okay to hit.

It is definitely not okay to hit.

Then he had seen the ghostly shapes of all the people starting to flicker and disappear. All those game pieces, all those avatars, just disappearing, and they were being destroyed by the Darkness, weren't they?

The gaiaphage wasn't just hitting Little Pete.

Which was wrong.

It was hitting other people, too.

He had tried to fight back using Taylor, but he'd been too weak to make her whole, and too weak to stop the slaughter.

And then he'd heard his sister calling to him. *Little Pete, take me and fight it.*

But he didn't really trust her very much.

Other voices had drifted to him, calling him through the emptiness, even as the Darkness tried to tell him no, no, Nemesis, just fade, fade into nothingness and be happy.

A girl he didn't know had called to him. *Take me. I deserve to die.*

But then had come the voice that said, *Come on, you little freak, wherever the hell you are, whatever the hell you are, let's get this done with.*

Pete had seen the scars on him, the fresh marks of the gaiaphage.

You and me. Blaze of glory, Little Pete. Blaze of glory.

Pete didn't know what a blaze of glory was, but it sounded good.

Now, Little Pete. Right now.

The Darkness was wrong. It was not time for Peter Ellison to fade away. It was time to hit back.

Caine had not wanted to feel it happening. He'd wanted it just to be over quick. Bam, over. But he did feel it.

He felt like maybe he'd stepped into a hot shower and was having that lovely sense of relaxation as the water warms the back of your neck, and you close your eyes, and you sigh away the night's bad dreams.

It was warm: that was the surprise. It was warm and it made him sigh. It was like . . . well, not exactly like anything he'd felt, but maybe closest to the way he'd felt after he made love to Diana, and lay beside her, and smelled her, and felt her breath on his cheek, and she would put a hand on his cheek and . . .

You're giving me a good memory to go out on, aren't you, Pete?

Well, good choice, Caine thought.

Huh. I can't feel my body, Caine thought.

Huh.

I . . .

Diana was wet and cold. She had finally jumped into the water and swum to the dock and pulled her battered self out of the water.

She had run as well as she could through smoke, through the streets toward the sounds of panic and death. She'd run into Sam. He was in the plaza calling for Astrid.

"Astrid! Astrid!"

He spotted Diana.

"Have you seen her? Have you seen Astrid?"

"No, Sam. Have you seen—"

They had heard the swoosh of the missile. And they had listened hopefully for the explosion.

For a second's time they had held on to hope. And then had come the sound of screams.

Sam looked half dead, but he took her hand, and she took his, and they ran toward the sound. Whether he was her protector or she was his, it didn't really matter. They were two scared kids, running the wrong way, running toward the sound of death, while fire chased them through the streets.

Gaia still stood. She still lived.

A million years in the blackness of space.

Fourteen years in a hole in the ground, growing, mutating, becoming the gaiaphage.

Not dead yet. The body it inhabited was beyond agony, but the gaiaphage lived, and it could still kill.

And there before her was Caine, somehow smiling. Not a cynical smirk: a genuine, happy smile.

And there, rushing up the road, Diana yelling, "No, Caine. No!"

Even Sam, still alive, excellent: her powers would be undiminished.

"Hello, Darkness," Caine said.

Gaia's face fell. Her bloody, feral grin faded to be replaced by lips drawn tight in fear. Her killer blue eyes widened as she looked at Caine who was no longer Caine.

"Nemesis," Gaia said.

THIRTY-ONE
11 MINUTES

A MILLION YEARS ago, and a bit more, a lifeless moon had been infected with a carefully structured virus. That moon had then been exploded, sending out countless fragments, seedlings, like the seeds of a dandelion, blowing across the billions of miles of space.

It was to bring life where no life existed. It was an optimistic gesture. But in one place, that hopeful experiment went terribly wrong. One seedling hit a nuclear pile on the planet Earth, and dragged shattered bits of human DNA into the crater.

Slowly the virus and the chromosomes and the radiation cooked up a monster. The virus spread, but instead of creating life it began to infect the very fabric of reality. It spawned mutations. It created its own unhinged version of evolution.

Some living things were affected, and others were spared.

One was especially vulnerable: a strange little boy whose own brain made him a prisoner, whose own mind made life painful and terrifying. Unbearable.

It would be a while before the gaiaphage began to suspect that it had unwittingly created its own nemesis. When the warping of physical laws sent the nuclear plant spiraling into a meltdown, that little boy, overwhelmed by sensory input he could not understand, sirens blaring and screens flashing warnings, created the barrier. In a flash of inconceivable power Peter Ellison simply removed all the noisy, troublesome grown-ups, silenced all that overload, and protected himself as best he could.

The gaiaphage's malignant effect was contained. The world had found its defense against alien infection. The antibody was a then-four-year-old boy with powers made possible by the gaiaphage virus.

Nature had found the way to defend itself.

And now, at last, gaiaphage and Nemesis stood facing each other.

"Why didn't you just . . . fade?" Gaia demanded plaintively.

"You hit me," Nemesis said. It was a little boy's voice coming from Caine's mouth. "And that's not okay."

Sam let go of Diana's hand, seeing Astrid ahead. He saw her blond hair from the back and almost wept with relief. But then he saw that she had been hurt.

"Astrid!" he cried.

But she held up her hand, silencing him. He looked past her then and saw Caine and Gaia, no more than a hundred feet apart.

Diana stepped closer.

"Diana, move back." Edilio, trying to get her to a safe distance.

Diana shook her head. "I don't think so, Edilio. He wanted a blaze of glory. He deserves an audience."

Gaia raised her hands, fury and fear on her blood-red face. Blistering green light blazed from them.

At the same moment, Nemesis returned fire, but his light came from every direction at once. It was a white light that shifted into blue and purple and red. It came down as lightning from the sky, a thousand thunderstorms.

The entire FAYZ burned as bright as a star.

Gaia's light hit Nemesis as she herself absorbed the awesome fire.

The girl and the boy burned bright and yet still fired.

And burned and still fired.

Their hair and clothing were gone.

Their flesh crisped.

Their eyes boiled out of their skulls.

And still the terrible light.

Their legs melted beneath them like candles. Holes appeared in their torsos. And only when they fell, each into a heap of glowing ash, did the light die.

"Well," Diana said, with tears running down her cheeks. "That was a blaze of glory."

There was a moment, a frozen, eternal moment, when no one breathed, and no one spoke.

Then: a sudden rush of wind. Wind! There had been no wind since—

"RUN!" Sam cried. "The fire! Run!"

Wind blew in like the leading edge of a hurricane, rushed into the disturbance created by the sudden disappearance of the barrier. The wind fed the flames, set small fires roaring to new heights, turned bigger fires into pillars of flame that shot high into the sky.

The population of the FAYZ, choked, terrorized, and battered, rushed in a wild panic down the highway. It was a stampede, and Sam was nearly swept along. But he held on to Astrid, held on to her and looked at her face and saw the bruises.

"Who?" he demanded.

"Sam, it doesn't matter; it's over," Astrid shouted to be heard above the roar of wind and fire.

"Who?" he demanded again.

"Drake. He wasn't dead. He may still not be dead. But Sam, there are police now, and—"

But Sam had broken free. He walked into the swirling smoke.

Astrid could barely breathe, but she would not let him walk away. Not when the end was this close. It was Edilio who left her no choice. He grabbed her around the waist and hauled her bodily down the highway until she stopped struggling.

"He told me to take care of you," Edilio said.

Those were the last words they could speak, as the smoke thickened, choking them, blinding them. They staggered on together, seeing nothing but glimpses of people rushing by, just following the ribbon of concrete beneath their feet.

Then the smoke lessened. The wind was blowing itself out, and a countervailing breeze now flowed from the south.

And then, there they were, Astrid and Edilio, standing at the edge, at the very end of the FAYZ wall.

And then through.

Out.

One hundred and seventy-one people—babies in arms, toddlers, kids—ran and stumbled into the arms of waiting parents. They ran to be scooped up by waiting paramedics.

Some kids ran, ran down the road, down the highway, screaming past the TV trucks, past the flashing lights of emergency vehicles, pushing and shoving through the well-meaning and the ill-intentioned alike because there was no safe distance for them, not until they could no longer hear or see any part of the place.

THIRTY-TWO
0 MINUTES

SAM FELT THE heaviness in his lungs lessen. His eyes were still on fire, but he was able to open them.

He didn't know where to look, only the person he was looking for.

"Drake!" he yelled. "Come out and fight me, Drake!"

The person who appeared was not Drake. Lana and Patrick stepped out of the smoke.

"The barrier is down," Sam said. "Fire's coming fast. Have you seen Drake?"

"Last I heard he was dead. But in this place . . ." She shook her head and looked somewhere between amused and resigned. "Sam, if the barrier's down, you don't have to do this."

"He hurt Astrid," Sam said. "She's alive. But he took her. He hurt her."

"And here you are the tragic hero, after all," Lana said dryly. She was unusually droll for Lana. The world was ending and she was being witty. "You may find you need this. And you know what? I think I'm done with it."

She slipped something heavy into the waist of his jeans, and then walked away with her dog.

Sam felt the butt of Lana's automatic pistol. Was it true? True that he didn't have to do this? True that he needed the gun?

"Drake!" he yelled.

He heard the town burning. Snap. Crackle. Pop. The heat was intense, right on the line between barely tolerable and not. It was like standing too close to a fireplace, feeling it dry your skin, and knowing that another five degrees and you'd no longer be dry: you'd be burned. There were sparks everywhere in the air. The whole town would burn.

"Drake!"

The whip slashed his back, a pain like being branded by a hot iron.

He spun, and Drake's fist smashed him in the face.

Sam went down on one knee, aimed his hands, and fired.

Nothing happened.

Drake seemed as shocked as Sam. He made a single, sudden laugh. "Not so dangerous now, are you, Sam?"

Drake struck again, and the whip burned across Sam's shoulders. Sam lurched forward.

"I had fun with your girlfriend, Sam," Drake said.

Sam tried again. But the light did not come. He was powerless. He drew the pistol.

"Come on, you know better than that, Sam, Sam, the hero

man. You know bullets don't kill me."

"Gaia's dead. The FAYZ is ended," Sam said, and leveled the pistol at Drake's face. "So I don't know what will work and what won't. Why don't we find out?"

But a line had appeared around Drake's neck. It was blood red, like a gruesome smile. Like the mark a hanged man might bear. It was widening, a gap forming between what had been Drake's neck and Alex's neck.

Drake hadn't noticed yet. He grinned and slashed Sam hard, landing the whip's blow again across his shoulder, curling around to tear at his back.

But when he retracted his whip arm, it was shorter. A foot-long segment had broken off. It lay like some nightmare worm on the sidewalk.

"No," Drake said, but the sound of his voice was weakened by air sucking in through his neck.

Drake tried to strike again, to bring Sam down, but his whip arm was limp; it barely moved. It was curling from the end, seeming to crisp like parchment held too close to the fire.

"I'll get out of here," Drake said in a fading whisper. "I will find her. And I will make it last for days, Sam. I'll make her scream, Sam. I'll make her—"

Sam's finger tightened on the trigger. It would be good to pull it. Drake was disintegrating before his eyes, and yet still, *still*, it would be good to pull that trigger. To feel the gun buck in his hand. To see the impact.

At that moment, as Sam stood poised between shooting

and not, Drake's head toppled off its grafted body and hit the ground.

One. Two. Three. Four. And the body collapsed.

The terrible whip arm looked like the skin a snake sheds during molting.

Sam picked up Drake's head. The eyes fluttered, as though there might still be life.

Sam walked stiffly up the steps to the church, where the fire burned hot. He forced himself forward into the heat, feeling the hair on his head turn crisp, eyes so dry he couldn't blink. And tossed Drake's head into the flames.

"Okay," he said to no one at all. "Now, I can get the hell out of here."

THE TOLL

THREE HUNDRED AND thirty-two kids between the age of one month and fourteen years had been confined within the FAYZ.

One hundred and ninety-six eventually emerged.

One hundred and thirty-six lay dead.

Dead and buried in the town plaza.

Dead and floating in the lake or on its shores.

Dead in the desert.

In the fields.

Dead of battles old and recent. Of starvation and accident, suicide and murder.

It was a fatality rate of just over 40 percent.

AFTERMATH 1

SAM TEMPLE WAS taken by helicopter to a hospital in Los Angeles, where there were specialists there in burn injuries. He wasn't consulted: he was found on his knees, obviously in shock, extensively burned. EMTs took over.

Astrid Ellison was taken to a hospital in Santa Barbara, as was Diana Ladris.

Other kids were shared out among half a dozen hospitals. Some specialized in plastic surgery, others in the effects of starvation.

Over the next week all were seen by psychiatrists once their immediate physical injuries were addressed. Lots of psychiatrists. And when they weren't being seen by psychiatrists, they were being seen by FBI agents, and California Highway Patrol investigators, and lawyers from the district attorney's office.

The consensus seemed to be that a number of the Perdido

survivors, as they were now known, would be prosecuted for crimes ranging from simple assault to murder.

First on that list was Sam Temple.

Astrid tried many times to phone him from her hospital room, but calls to his hospital were being blocked. No, the nurses explained each time, they could not get him to the phone. No, they could not deliver a message. Not their fault. Talk to the district attorney's office.

Astrid was able to visit Diana, who she found out was being cared for in the same hall, just three doors down.

Astrid walked slowly, cautiously, her body stiff from bruises and stiffer still from the bandages on her whip burns. They'd given her a cane to use.

She was not going to walk with a cane.

They'd offered her heavy-duty painkillers.

She'd rejected them, restricting herself to a few ibuprofen. The last thing she wanted was to be out of her mind, off in la-la land, when shrinks and cops and family were forever questioning her.

She had not told her parents about her own role in her brother's death. She had only told them that he had died a very good death.

Astrid had seen their pain. She had also seen their hidden but still-visible relief. They would not have to readjust to their out-of-control autistic son. That had hurt the most. But who was she to judge?

She found Diana's room. Diana was sitting in her bed

using a remote control to idly flip through the channels on the wall-mounted TV.

"You," Diana said by way of greeting.

"Me," Astrid said.

"Can't believe it," Diana said. "All this time. And there's still nothing on."

Astrid laughed and lowered herself slowly into a chair. "You know how they say hospital food is so awful? Somehow I'm not having that reaction."

"Tapioca beats rat," Diana said.

"I never minded rat as much as that dog jerky we were getting for a while. The stuff Albert had them flavor with celery salt? That was the culinary low point for me."

"Yeah, well, I had a lower low point," Diana said, sounding angry. Or maybe not angry, maybe hurt.

Astrid put a hand on Diana's arm, and Diana did not shake it off.

"How is Sam?" Diana asked.

"They won't let me talk to him. But they're going to release me in a couple of days. I'll find him."

"Won't your parents try to stop you?"

Astrid considered this, then barked out a laugh. Diana joined in.

"Oh, my God, we have parents again," Astrid said, wiping away a tear. "We're kids. We're teenagers again."

A nurse poked her head in. "Listen, ladies, it's not visiting hours, but there's someone here to see you."

"Who?" Diana asked.

The nurse looked left and right like she was afraid to be overheard. "It's a young woman. She seems very determined. In fact, I almost called the police because she scared me."

Astrid and Diana exchanged a look.

"Black or white?" Astrid asked.

"She happens to be white."

"Lana!" Astrid and Diana said in unison.

"You'd better send her in," Diana said. "You don't want to say no to Lana. That would be, um, reckless."

"And she's saved more lives than every doctor and nurse in this hospital," Astrid said.

Lana arrived a moment later, looking strangely clean, with her hair cut, and wearing clothing that was not stained or filthy or cut or patched together. She did not have a pistol. She did not have a cigarette.

"Oh, my God," Diana said to Astrid. "Lana's a girl."

"Yeah, hysterical. Cracking me up," Lana said with her very familiar, very hard-core snarl. "What, there's only one chair?"

"Who have you seen?" Astrid asked.

"I saw Dekka. She's with her folks. And if I said she wasn't happy about things, that wouldn't really begin to cover it. She wants to see Sam. Everyone wants to see Sam. Talked to Edilio on the phone. He's in hiding. Worried about *la migra* coming for him and his family."

"Edilio is in hiding," Astrid snapped. "Edilio has to worry

about being kicked out of the country. Our Edilio."

"He's got a volunteer lawyer—"

But Astrid wasn't done. "They should be putting up statues to Edilio. They should be naming schools after that boy—no, no, I'm not going to call him a boy. If he's not a man, then I'll never meet one."

Lana nodded approvingly, obviously enjoying and sharing in Astrid's outrage.

"And you, too," Astrid said to Lana. "No, don't even wave me off."

"Whoa," Lana said. "I had a power. I didn't make that happen. I used it. No big deal."

"I don't suppose you can still . . . ," Diana began, waving a hand toward Astrid's bandages.

Lana shook her head, not sadly, but with evident relief. "Nope. No, I cannot. I am no longer the capital 'H' Healer. I am Lana Arwen Lazar, period, *finito*. Just some girl with a weird name. I thought maybe I might miss it. Guess what? No. No, not even a little. You know what I do now? I eat. And I sleep. I throw sticks for Patrick. And then I do it all over again. That's my plan, for the rest of my life. Eat, sleep, play with dog."

"Have they got the shrinks all over you?" Diana asked.

"They tried," Lana said with a curl of her lip. "I don't see them coming back at me anytime soon."

All three laughed at that. But Diana grew serious. "Honestly? I don't mind the therapy much. I, uh . . . I don't know.

I just. It's okay. For me, anyway."

They fell silent then. The only sounds were of gurneys in the hallway, a child crying somewhere, a male and a female voice laughing flirtatiously.

Astrid looked at Lana, now leaning against the window, and Diana, lost in thought, and reminded herself that at times she had hated Diana. She had told Sam to kill her if necessary. And she had disliked Lana as a short-tempered bitch who sometimes abused her privileges.

She let her mind move beyond these two. Orc, who had been the first to kill in the FAYZ, the first murderer. A vicious drunk. But someone who had died a hero.

Mary. Mother Mary. A saint who had died trying to murder the children she cared for.

Quinn, who had been a faithless worm at the start and had been a pillar at the end.

Albert. She still didn't know quite what to think of Albert, but it was undeniable that far fewer would have walked out of the FAYZ without Albert.

If her own feelings were this conflicted, was it any wonder the rest of the world didn't know what to do with the Perdido survivors?

"Sorry, I kind of dragged the mood down," Diana said wryly.

"I'm going to write something," Astrid said.

"What do you mean?" Lana asked.

"I'm going to write about us. About all of it. Maybe a

magazine story, or, I don't know. Maybe even a book. But
what happened to the . . . No, wait. No, that's not even the
right way to start. I don't want everyone acting like we were
victims. I'm going to tell the story. All of it I know, anyway."

The other two girls looked at her, and to Astrid's surprise
neither of them told her she was being a fool.

"Might be a good idea," Lana conceded.

"Maybe," Diana said a bit more hesitantly. "It's going to
all come out anyway. One of us should tell the story. In fact,
Astrid, it should be you. Just tell all of it. *All* of it. The bad, the
worse, and the worst."

"And maybe one or two good things," Astrid said.

"One or two," Diana agreed softly.

Eight hundred and nine homes had been destroyed. Three
dozen businesses had been wiped out. Forty square miles of
forest burned. Nearly five hundred cars, boats, buses damaged, almost all unsalvageable.

The cost of it all, plus the cost of cleanup, lost revenues
from business, and the rest was estimated to be three billion
dollars. At a minimum.

Albert Hillsborough had come through uninjured. He had
come through famous. He'd been interviewed on CNBC and
by the *Wall Street Journal*. He'd been invited to a party at the
home of the chairman of Goldman Sachs. Important people
kept telling him they had their eyes on him.

Even his family treated him strangely, and the truth was,

he just didn't fit with his family anymore. He didn't fit, somehow, in the world of shared bedrooms and dinner-table discussion and school.

School. He knew he had to go. But really? He was going to be a high school freshman?

Really?

He rode now in the backseat of an SUV. There was a golden-arches logo on the side. Behind them a second SUV, and behind that two semis loaded with everything the modern filmmaker needed.

McDonald's had volunteered to pay for Albert's college if he would appear in some short videos about the importance to him of keeping the Perdido Beach McDonald's alive as long as possible.

All the way up from Santa Barbara, where his family now lived, he watched flatbed trucks hauling wrecked cars away from Perdido Beach. And in the other direction went the construction equipment. The cleanup was under way. It was like the aftermath of a hurricane.

But civilian cars were still not allowed on the highway. No one was yet allowed to drive through Perdido Beach: it was still too dangerous. They were still finding bodies, not to mention the occasional straggler. Just that morning an injured, traumatized boy had been found wandering in the forest, near death.

Helicopters buzzed overhead. Surveyors and news reporters and filmmakers. The National Guard camp was still in place. The flashing police and ambulance lights were gone,

and most of the TV trucks had moved on. But there were still
armed men scowling from behind sunglasses.

*Yeah, where were all you tough guys when we could have
used you?*

As they neared the edge of what had been the FAYZ,
Albert began to feel uncomfortable. He squirmed in his seat
and kept his eyes focused inside the SUV.

They'd assigned him a handler, a public relations person
named Vicky. She was a pretty young woman, a mother herself, she said, and so she felt for the kids, what it must have
been like. She had chatted with Albert on the drive up, and
every time she had said how she understood, how she could
imagine, how terrible . . . he had changed the conversation.

Now she noticed that his hands were fists and his jaw was
clenched tight.

"Is something the matter, Albert?"

"No. I'm fine."

"I can imagine that coming back here—"

"No. All due respect, I don't think you can imagine."

By the time they crossed the line, he felt his lungs straining. He was taking air in forced gasps.

He saw the first buildings, very few intact anymore, most
of them burned. And he saw, in memory, at least, himself
with the life oozing out of him from bullet wounds, months
earlier but so fresh in his mind. He remembered knowing
that death was very, very close. He remembered the certainty
that he would be extinguished.

"Would you like a bottle of water?"

He looked at the bottle. Stared at it. "I'm fine."

"Are you hungry? It's been a while since lunch."

Lunch had been at a McDonald's in Santa Barbara. It had been so clean. It had smelled like food. It had sounded happy and alive. In the bathroom, the toilet flushed. Water ran in the sink.

He had passed a trash can on the way back to his table and stopped just to look at it. It was full of food. Leftover burgers, the last few fries, smears of ketchup on cardboard. He'd had to hold back tears when he saw it.

"Candy bar?" Vicky asked, and held a Snickers out to him.

At that moment they slowed to turn off the highway and head cautiously, carefully, through recently bulldozed streets, toward the town plaza. That's where the McDonald's was. His McDonald's.

A candy bar. People had killed for less.

"I used to sell rats to starving kids," Albert said.

Vicky looked alarmed. "I wouldn't say that to the camera."

"No," Albert agreed.

"You did what you had to do. You're a hero," Vicky said.

It took a while to set up the equipment in the plaza. Albert would not get out of the vehicle. He made an excuse about enjoying the air-conditioning. About wanting to listen to the radio.

But as the afternoon wore on, they called for him to come onto the set.

The *set*.

They had cleaned it up inside. Not all the way, no, they

couldn't do that without weeks of work. But the debris, the filth, the pitiful decorations had been artfully rearranged. The service counter was gleaming incongruously. The menu had been uncovered and one panel replaced. The obscene graffiti had been cleaned off or painted over.

It was the sanitized version of the FAYZ.

He overheard the director talking to one of the cameramen. The cameraman was explaining that he couldn't get a good long shot on the exterior because someone had set up a fake graveyard right in the plaza.

"Kids just playing around, I guess, but it's morbid; we'll have to get rid of it, maybe bring in some sod to—"

"No," Albert said.

"We're almost ready for you," the director assured him.

"That's not a fake graveyard. Those aren't fake graves. No one was *playing around*."

"You're saying those . . . those are actually . . ."

"What do you think happened here?" Albert asked in a soft voice. "What do you think this was?" Absurdly, embarrassingly, he had started to cry. "Those are kids buried there. Some of them were torn apart, you know. By coyotes. By . . . by bad people. Shot. Crushed. Like that. Some of those kids in the ground there couldn't take it, the hunger and the fear . . . some of those kids out there had to be cut down from the ropes they used to hang themselves. Early on, when we still had any animals? I had a crew go out and hunt down cats. Cats and dogs and rats. Kill them. Other kids to skin them . . . cook them up."

There were a dozen crew people in the McDonald's. None spoke or moved.

Albert brushed away tears and sighed. "Yeah. So don't mess with the graves. Okay? Other than that, we're good to go."

AFTERMATH 2

THERE WERE POLICE guards outside Sam's hospital room. They stepped in occasionally to make sure Sam hadn't disappeared. For the most part they were nice enough. And the check-ins were less and less frequent.

Police and prosecutors were not allowed to talk to Sam without either his mother or a lawyer present. His mother, Connie Temple, was also on TV fairly frequently, talking up the just-formed FAYZ Legal Defense Fund. So he had long stretches of time when he was not being questioned by police, prosecutors, or parent.

He spent those free hours trying not to think too much. And yet thinking too much. There was a tsunami of memories waiting to drown him.

Video of the final hours of the FAYZ had done a lot to change attitudes about the survivors. People had seen the entire dome glow red with fire. They had video, lots of video, of Gaia. They had confirmed that the murderous teen they'd seen at the end was the same person as the child who had ripped a man's arm off. And eaten it.

Something about watching video of a murderous girl using lasers to slaughter children—and to kill three adults on the outside—had made people wonder whether the kids in the FAYZ deserved just a little slack.

Prosecutors did not believe in slack. They wanted an arrest and a trial. They had one target above all others.

At the moment that target was eating tacos his mother had brought in despite hospital orders against outside food.

"Oh, God, this is good," Sam said as juicy beef and crisp lettuce dribbled out onto the tray on his lap.

"Still not tired of eating?" Connie asked him.

"I will never be tired of eating. I'm going to eat until I'm huge. Food, hot water, clean sheets. At least I'll get those three in prison."

Connie pushed herself up out of the chair, angry. "Sam, don't talk that way."

He bit into a second taco. Chicken this time. "Mmm. They want someone to put away. They need a scapegoat. It's me."

"You're not being serious with me. I'm trying to treat you like an adult."

Sam put the taco down. "Are you? You're trying to treat me like an adult? Okay. Let's have an adult conversation, Mom. Tell me how I had a brother, but you kind of forgot to mention it. Tell me how that happened. A lot of bad things happened because of that."

"This isn't something—"

"He gave his life in the end. Caine. Your son. He's dead. You've seen the video."

"Yes. And I feel terrible—"

"Don't get me wrong: he was a bad person. Your son Caine. He was a very bad guy. You want a murderer? Well . . ." He stopped himself. "In the end, he gave himself up to Little Pete. He took the hit. Atonement, I guess. Redemption. Whatever."

"Then tell that to the district attorneys. Tell them it was Caine. There are plenty of other kids out there talking, putting it on Caine."

Sam pushed the food away angrily. He slid his legs over the side. His mother moved to help him, but he waved her off. "No. Don't. I'm fine."

He stood up. His legs were fine, at least. It was just the burns from the red-hot chain. It took so much longer to heal when you didn't have Lana. Half his body was covered in bandages and a webbing that held them in place.

"I want to see Astrid," he said.

"You know they won't let you talk to anyone, Sam."

"As soon as I'm better. They're not keeping us apart."

"Sam, you have more important things to worry about than your girlfriend."

He turned on her, suppressed anger now boiling up. "My girlfriend? Like we're talking about someone I dated? Like some girl I took to a movie?"

"I didn't mean—"

"Tell me. Tell me *why.*"

Connie looked around, spotted the pitcher of water, and

poured a trembling cup. "This isn't going to put me in a very good light."

Sam said nothing. He had waited so long to find out. Since the first surprise realization that he and Caine were brothers. Fraternal twins, born just minutes apart.

"There was . . . There were . . ." She took a sip, shook her head slightly, trying to get up the nerve, unwilling to look at him. "I was married. I was not faithful."

Sam blinked. "Caine and I were born at the same time."

"Yes. Yes. There was my husband. He worked at the power plant. He was a very intelligent man. Very . . . good-looking, kind, decent. But I was young, and I wasn't very smart about such things. I had an affair with a very different man. He was exciting. He was . . . forgive me . . . sexy."

Sam winced. The images this conversation was calling up were not ones he wanted to see. He was suppressing enough; he didn't need more.

"So there was my husband, and the other man. And when I realized I was pregnant, I also realized either of them might have been your father, or David's."

"David?"

"Caine. His adoptive parents gave him the name Caine. To me he was David. When your—when my husband died . . . when he was killed . . ."

"Mom. Did he die in the power plant?"

She nodded. "The meteor strike."

Sam looked at her. She tried to meet his gaze and decided instead to drink more water. Sam hesitated. Did he want to know? What good would it do?

"Why did you give Caine up? David. Whatever you called him."

"Maybe it was some kind of postpartum depression. I mean, I didn't think so, but maybe it was depression. Some kind of delusional state . . ."

Sam waited.

"He was evil. Sam, that's what he seemed to me. He was a beautiful baby. But . . . but I could *feel* something . . . some connection to a terrible darkness. He scared me. I worried I might hurt him."

"It was your husband who died in the meteor strike," Sam said, carefully not using the word "father." "The man I knew as Dad."

"Yes."

One question remained.

"Tell me this," Sam said, looking past her, out the window at the Southern California sun. "Caine and I don't look much alike. One of us must have looked more like your husband. And one of us must have looked more like the other man."

Connie Temple swallowed hard. She looked strangely young and vulnerable to Sam. He could almost see a teen mother there.

"David . . . Caine . . . was the spitting image of my husband."

"Okay," he said, feeling deflated.

"But it's not that simple," Connie said.

It was purely by accident that Edilio Escobar happened to see the TV report of a boy found wandering in the burned-out forest of the FAYZ.

He was eating. He'd been eating more or less without stop, because he couldn't focus on anything else, couldn't think about the future, or even tomorrow. He couldn't talk to his parents. His mother just cried a lot, and his father, well, his father didn't really want to know. His father had work. His father was not ready for stories of his son's life.

The truth was, as much as they loved him and welcomed him back, he was a liability to them. He was a big neon finger pointing at the family of undocumented workers.

They were living in a trailer in Atascadero. Too many bodies in too little space. It was clean, but it was also an overstuffed, hot steel box surrounded by other overstuffed, hot little boxes, many of them also full of people who did not need the attention that Edilio drew.

Edilio would have to figure something out. But he was exhausted. All the way down to the marrow, he was exhausted.

His mother kept the beans and rice and lemonade coming. *Someday, Edilio,* he told himself, *you will get tired of beans and rice and lemonade. But it won't be anytime soon.*

He looked up from the narrow table, saw his mother at the stove, then looked above her to see his automatic rifle wedged in atop the cupboards.

Full of food and hollowed out. That's how he felt. He was wondering if they could get away with selling the gun. Ought to be worth a hundred bucks or so. That would maybe take some of the strain off his family's finances.

He had not told his mother about himself, his personal self. He'd kept the stories simple. He'd answered the mostly clueless questions of friends and neighbors. He was polite, but not volunteering much. Not arguing when they came up with wild theories. Sooner or later it would all come out.

But he might not come out. It was one thing to be gay in the FAYZ—people had bigger worries on their mind than who liked who. It was another thing to come out to his family. And it would be still more difficult if he had to be openly gay in the completely unfamiliar, macho culture of Honduras.

La migra could come at any moment. There were plenty of people who didn't like the idea of Edilio as some kind of folk hero. Too many interviews with survivors had mentioned him as a leader in the FAYZ. He was conspicuous.

"I can't eat any more," Edilio said, pushing the plate away.

"You want to go out and play?" His mother posed the question in Spanish. She tried to speak English with him, but mostly she ended up back in her comfort zone.

Go out and play.

Despite himself, Edilio had to smile. Like he was a six-year-old. "No, Mama, I'll just see what's on TV . . ." And that's when he looked up and saw the video.

The video showed a helicopter landing in a clearing in the charcoal forest. A young man, a boy, at first running away, then caught by paramedics. Resisting. Then, it seemed, breaking down, before being finally led by kind hands to the helicopter door.

There was no audio: the TV had been muted.

Edilio's heart stopped beating the instant he saw the frightened figure. The video was shaky and poorly focused. The boy's face wasn't clear. But Edilio knew.

The chyron at the bottom of the screen said the unidentified survivor had been taken to a hospital just south in San Luis Obispo.

"I need to go to SLO," Edilio said.

"San Luis? *Por qué?*"

Edilio sighed. For several minutes he just couldn't speak. His heart felt ten times its normal size. He had given up. A voice in his head berated him: *Why did you give up, Edilio? After all that's happened, didn't you learn not to give up?*

He picked up a paper towel and pressed it against his eyes. He no longer felt as if he was on the verge of a heart attack. He felt, rather, that he might be on the verge of an uncontrollable laughing fit.

"Mama, sit down, okay? I have something kind of big to tell you."

Connie left after telling Sam all he had asked her to tell him. Not what he had wanted to know, but that's what happened when you got answers.

He sat in his hospital bed feeling winded. Feeling lost.

He wanted to talk to Astrid. He needed to talk to Astrid.

But what could he do? They were blocking his calls and—

"Really, Sam?" he demanded of the empty room. "That's all it takes to stop you now?"

The hospital was an older building on the University of Southern California campus, massive and imposing, but it still had windows that could be opened for fresh air.

An open window. Sheets. He stuck his head out and looked down. He was twelve floors up, but just two stories above the roof of a wing of the hospital.

He went into the tiny bathroom and removed most of his bandages. It hurt. He was not healed. And what he planned to do next would hurt even more. But the scabs probably wouldn't do more than leak a little. That was nothing: *Remember when . . . No, Sam,* he told himself, *don't remember when.*

He dressed in his street clothes, quickly wound the sheets into a loop, slid it over a pipe near the window, and without pausing to worry too much about it, swung out and slid down.

He pulled the sheet down after him. Then he bent over and let the pain subside. Yep. That hurt, all right.

He had left a note on his bed. The note said, *Poof!* He hoped the police guards would find it funny.

On the roof of the secondary hospital wing he could literally walk up to windows in the main building. He saw patients inside. One of them, an old man, waved. Sam waved back. A woman just stared. He smiled.

He found one window open. It was to a doctor's office. He slid inside and took a quick inventory. In the closet was a suit on a hanger. No wallet, no money, unfortunately. Frustrating. It was hard to do much here in the out there unless you had money.

There was a computer. It was password protected, but the password turned out to be "password."

"People did not get any smarter while I was away," Sam said with a laugh.

Now, the question was: Who would help him? And who could he find a number for? He only remembered one number from the old days, and what were the odds that Quinn had a phone? Or that it was the same number?

He opened a messaging app.

It's Sam. I need help.

He went on then, searching the office while waiting, expecting a notification that the message was undeliverable. He found five dollars in a junk drawer in the doctor's desk. Yay. The doctor wouldn't even notice.

There came a ding. A reply! It said, **Sam? Sam T?**

Hey, Fisherman, Sam typed. **I'm busting out of the hospital.**

The reply came quickly. **Obviously to go surfing.**

Sam laughed. Wow. Just how much would he love to be surfing right now?

Before he could answer, another message came. **On my way. Q.**

Quinn did not have a car and he was too young to drive. But he did have a mother who had already heard Quinn's account of life in the FAYZ.

"This is the same Sam?" she asked. "Our Sam? Your Sam?"

"My Sam," Quinn said.

"Get in the car."

Quinn kissed her spontaneously for that. It was an hour's drive. The Gaither family had relocated to Santa Monica, where his father had a better job than before. In fact, to Quinn's amazement they lived just ten blocks from the Santa Monica Pier.

Sam had instructed them to enter the parking structure, but not the one nearest the hospital. That one would be searched. Instead he'd given them the location of a parking structure adjoining a different campus building.

As instructed, they drove to the third floor, southeast corner, and honked their horn, just a couple of taps.

Sam emerged from a parked car and slid into the backseat behind Quinn.

"Dude," Quinn said.

"Thanks, Mrs. Gaither," Sam said. "I don't think they've even noticed I'm gone yet. But they may have, so I'm just going to duck down behind the seat."

"Don't you worry about it," Mrs. Gaither said. "This campus is wide open. We'll get you out of here."

They drove for half an hour and then, finally, Sam raised his head cautiously. Quinn tossed him a stocking cap. "Put that on."

They were on a freeway jammed with cars, doing a stop-and-go, heading north. Toward Santa Barbara. Toward Astrid.

Mrs. Gaither turned the radio on to NPR, and naturally

Quinn reached over to switch to a music station. But he was a little slow, and when he heard what was being reported, his hand froze.

It was a press conference. The voice speaking was calm, assured, audibly intelligent, and very familiar.

"My name is Astrid Ellison. A-S-T-R-I-D. E-L-L-I-S-O-N."

"And most of you know me." This was Todd Chance. "And you know my wife, Jennifer Brattle."

Astrid was seated between them. Between two of the most famous people in the world: the couple sometimes known as Toddifer. They were both beautiful, especially—from Astrid's perspective—Todd Chance. About fifteen years too old for her—okay, twenty years too old—but still and all a startlingly handsome man.

And Jennifer was cute. In her own way.

It was Jennifer who spoke next. "As you all know, our property, San Francisco de Sales Island, where we maintained a home, was part of the FAYZ. Our children, thankfully, are all alive and well and now at our other home in Malibu."

"We returned to the island just yesterday and found that it had been occupied during the time we were . . . away." And that seemed to be the end of her prepared remarks, because she looked beseechingly at Todd.

"The house is fine. Well, a little bit of a mess. And our yacht, well . . ." He pushed his fingers back through his mane of blond hair. "That's not the point, though. We're here to talk about what we found. I mean, two letters that were left in a desk in our bedroom."

There were eight TV cameras in the overly gold hotel ballroom where the press conference was being held. Microphones were mounted in front of Todd, Astrid, and Jennifer.

Astrid still wore a few bandages. And an amazingly clean cotton shirt and totally intact jeans and shoes. Shoes that had not been looted from some stranger's home. Impractical shoes you couldn't easily run in.

These are not fleeing shoes, Astrid had realized when she put them on.

"One of the letters was addressed to Diana Ladris, another survivor," Todd continued. "We've given that letter to her. It's private. But the other was addressed to us. To me and to Jennifer, which was a surprise, obviously. It's um . . . well, actually, we'll just have Astrid read it. She knew the boy who wrote it."

I knew him, all right, Astrid thought. I wanted him dead. And then this. The FAYZ continued to teach her lessons.

She picked up the photocopy of the letter. It was handwritten.

"'Dear Mr. Chance and Ms. Brattle. Sorry about the mess. Great bed. Loved it. As a matter of fact, loved the whole house. Actually, I tried to kill your kids when I found them here. Yeah, funny story. Maybe not funny, hah hah.'"

Astrid heard nervous laughter from the media people, or maybe just from the hotel staff who were hovering around the edges grabbing a glimpse of the Hollywood royalty.

"'Anyway, I missed and they got away. I don't know what will happen to Sanjit and that stick-up-his butt Choo and the rest, but whatever happens next, it's not on me. However . . .'"

Astrid took a dramatic pause.

"'However, the rest of what happened was on me. Me, Caine Soren. You'll probably be hearing a lot of crazy stories from kids. But what they didn't know was that it was all me. Me. Me me. See, I had a power I never told anyone about. I had the power to make people do bad things. Crimes and whatnot. Especially Diana, who never did anything wrong on her own, by her own will, I mean. She—and the rest of them—were under my control. The responsibility is on me. I confess. Haul me away, officers.'"

Astrid suddenly felt her throat tightening, although she'd read the letter many times already, and knew what it said. Rotten son of a . . . And then *this*.

Redemption. Not a bad concept.

Well, partial redemption.

"It's signed Caine Soren. And below that, 'King of the FAYZ.'"

It was a full confession. A lie: a blatant, not-very-convincing lie. But it would be just enough to make prosecutions very difficult. Caine's role in the FAYZ, and the reality that strange powers had actually existed in that space, were widely known and accepted.

Of course Caine had enjoyed writing it. It was his penultimate act of control. He was manipulating from beyond the grave.

"Now," Jennifer said, interrupting the long silence, "we want to discuss the deal we've just signed with Astrid to develop a book and then movie, telling the true story of the FAYZ." She began reading off a prepared statement. "'Astrid Ellison was a central figure, right from the start. She had long since earned the nickname Astrid the Genius, and . . .'"

And Jennifer went on, and then Todd, and Astrid smiled when it seemed appropriate, and made a humble face when that seemed appropriate, and her thoughts went far away, far from the ballroom and the cameras.

She didn't even realize that tears were running down her cheeks until she felt Todd offer her a tissue.

"Oh," she said. "Sorry. I was just . . . It happens some-times—"

And then she looked up, toward someone at the back of the room.

Diana's letter was much shorter. Just four lines.

> *Diana:*
> *I'm sorry for hurting you. I know I did.*
> *I'm most likely dead now, and I guess if there's any kind of fairness in the afterlife I'm probably in hell getting roasted. But if that's where I am, I want you to know, I still love you. Always did.*
> *Love,*
> *Caine*

She read the letter over and over again. Each time crying. Each time laughing.

●   ●   ●

The news networks and the local TV stations all led with the same footage. An obviously moved, very pretty young woman with blond hair and alert blue eyes looking up. Eyes widening. Stumbling a little as she pushed back her chair and went around the table.

Shaky cameras turning too fast, following her as she ran to a boy at the back of the room who pushed through the press of people to reach her.

The embrace.

The kiss that went on for a very long time.

AFTERMATH 3

FIRST THERE WAS Caine's patently false "confession." Then there was the fact that the FAYZ Legal Defense Fund racked up three million dollars in its first two weeks. Then there was a judicial panel that took statements from eminent scientists and concluded that the FAYZ was in fact a separate universe and thus not covered under California law.

Finally, there was a shift in public opinion following the involvement of the two popular movie stars, the McDonald's documentary starring Albert Hillsborough, the likelihood of a major Hollywood feature film, and the kiss seen round the world. Polls now showed 68 percent of Californians wanted no criminal charges brought against the FAYZ survivors.

The kiss alone would have wrecked the career of any prosecutor or politician who had anything bad to say about Astrid Ellison or Sam Temple.

The survivors by and large went on with their lives.

Three of them committed suicide.

An unknown number found their way to alcohol and drugs.

None were unscathed.

But most found a way to survive, as they had for so long alone. They rediscovered their families; they attended school and church; they attended counseling sessions. They walked through shopping malls in wonder. They were occasionally seen to break down crying in the middle of a grocery store.

The phrase "It's a just a phase" fell out of use.

Lana went to Las Vegas to live with her parents. They refused to let her carry a gun. She eventually got used to it. Her powers were gone. When she cut her hand while peeling carrots, she couldn't do anything about it. This caused her to laugh for a solid five minutes, during which her parents thought she'd lost her mind.

Dekka Talent's family took her in, still not happy about her "lifestyle," as they called it, but unable to summon the nerve to berate her. Dekka could no longer control gravity, except by virtue of being the most impressive person in any room she entered. Dekka made contact with Brianna's grief-stricken parents and told them about their daughter. They gave her a photo of Brianna, which Dekka framed and hung beside her bed.

Edilio Escobar was reunited with Roger. It was months before Roger recovered, but Edilio waited. During a routine traffic stop for a broken taillight a highway-patrol officer checked the IDs of Edilio's parents and announced that he would have to report them as suspected undocumented aliens. Then he recognized Edilio and insisted on putting out a call to fellow officers. Four other patrol cars pulled up, and it was made clear that as far as the CHP was concerned, they'd be damned if they would take any action against Edilio or his family. Edilio ended up signing autographs.

It took a while to organize a public memorial for the kids of the FAYZ. By the time it was held in Pismo Beach, California, many of the kids had scattered. But Sam, Astrid, Diana, Quinn, Edilio, and Dekka, as well as dozens of others, various celebrities, politicians, and locals, were there. Lana was not. She sent word that Patrick had an important deworming scheduled. Albert said he was busy taking meetings.

Sam was asked to speak and adamantly refused. He was mortally sick of being referred to as the hero of the FAYZ. Astrid had become the unofficial spokesperson for all of them, so she gave a short speech. In it she talked about Orc, Dahra, Duck Zhang, Howard, E.Z., Jack, Brianna, and Little Pete. Others too numerous to mention.

"There were heroes in the FAYZ. My little brother was one of them, although he didn't even understand the word 'hero.' And there were villains. Most of us were a bit of both."

Orc's parents did not attend.

Diana had been at loose ends since getting out of the hospital. She'd been taken in by parents of FAYZ kids but hadn't really had a place of her own.

After the service they grouped together with lemonades and iced teas in their hands, all of them dressed in "nice" clothing. None of them was armed. Not even so much as a spiked baseball bat.

"Nice speech," Diana snarked. "Are you going to play yourself in the movie?"

"The director considered it," Astrid said. "But it turns out I'm not quite the Astrid type. It was a somewhat surreal moment. *Koyaanisqatsi*."

That earned her a collective sigh and many rolled eyes.

"*I'm* not asking her," Dekka said.

"It means 'life out of balance,'" Astrid explained. "*Koyaanisqatsi*."

"And yet no one asked," Dekka pointed out.

"You guys hear about the camper?" Edilio asked. "Way up north of the Stefano Rey. Says he saw this girl. Golden skin. Saw her and then, poof. Not there."

"There are going to be stories like that for years," Astrid said. "The FAYZ will spawn a thousand legends and myths. Not to mention that it's screwed up the study of physics pretty well."

"It would be interesting, though, wouldn't it?" Quinn asked.

"Just a story," Sam said. He held up his hand. "Nothing there. All that is over."

They talked until the talk grew too painful. Then they hugged and went their separate ways, all but Sam and Astrid. And Diana. Sam took her arm as she started to leave.

"Listen, Diana," he said. "We have an idea. Astrid has all this Hollywood money now."

"Great for you. Now your girlfriend is smarter and richer than you," Diana teased. "But not quite as cute."

"Yeah, well, um . . . here's the thing. My mother and I . . . well. We aren't really close anymore."

"I'm sorry. There's a lot of that going around."

"And Astrid has to be down in LA a lot anyway. So . . . so my mother has emancipated me. That means I'm legally on my own. Legally an adult."

"Can you handle the responsibility?" Diana asked.

Sam grinned. "Well, it's tough. So much pressure deciding do I want pizza or Chinese food."

"Yeah, you're not good at making those life-and-death decisions."

"We have a place. The two of us. It's not far from Quinn's house, in Santa Monica. The school's not bad. The beach is right there. And it's crazy, but it's too big for just the two of us."

Astrid came over and said, "Have you told her?"

"I'm in the process."

Astrid sighed. "Come live with us, Diana. Don't argue. Just say yes."

Diana looked at the ground to hide her emotions. Then she said, "Would I have to be hearing you two going at it night and day?"

AFTERMATH 4

THEIR ROOM WAS furnished from IKEA. They had a queen-size bed, two nightstands, two dressers, and many lamps.

Sam still did not like the dark. But he no longer feared it.

They had a TV, two laptops, fast internet service, and two iPhones. Through the window came the sounds of traffic. There was a great deal of food in the refrigerator and the cupboards. The bathroom was well stocked with medicines. Enough to supply a small clinic.

Just in case.

They lay together under clean sheets and blankets having taken long, hot showers. Earlier they had gone to a Thai restaurant with Diana. Neither had eaten much Thai food before, but they were on the path now to being lifelong foodies.

Food. It was beautiful. The three of them had gone to a

Ben and Jerry's and ended up crying like idiots at all the ice cream.

Sam had still not shared everything with Astrid. He'd been holding on to the last of what his mother had told him, needing to make some sense of it in his own mind. But no matter how he turned the facts around, looking at them in this light or that, he still couldn't accept it all.

"I love you, Astrid," he said.

"Yes. I'm already in bed with you. You don't have to sweet-talk me." She put a cool palm on his chest and smiled.

"The gaiaphage," Sam said.

Astrid pulled her hand away. "Why are we talking about that?"

"Because my mom . . ." He sighed.

"Ah." She sat up, giving him a little room.

"I told you why she gave Caine up. She felt something was wrong with him. She felt guilty and believed he was almost a punishment on her. She gave him up for adoption to a couple who, unfortunately, also sensed something wrong. Or maybe they were just jerks, I don't know. Anyway, my mom said when his adoptive parents came to visit Coates, there wasn't much sign of affection."

"That would not surprise me," Astrid said cautiously.

"Anyway. I told you that she admitted to having an affair. I didn't tell you all of it. I asked her. It was silly to, but I had to know. Was my father my father? Who exactly was the man who died that day in the power plant?"

"I thought you might have asked her. I've been waiting for you to tell me. When you were ready."

"Stop thinking you're always one step ahead of me."

"Sam. Accept the fact that I'm always one step ahead of you."

He reached an arm around her and pulled her close again.

"So, according to my mother, one of us, Caine, was the spitting image of the man who died when the meteor struck. The man I thought was my father. The man whose DNA was absorbed and became part of the gaiaphage."

"That was the connection," Astrid said. "That's why your mother started to feel there was something evil in Caine. It was the gaiaphage."

"Except that it wasn't that simple," Sam said. "My mom went to work at Coates once she realized Caine was there, so close to Perdido Beach. She was a nurse, so she was able to get a blood sample. And she was able to compare the two of us genetically."

"Oh, my God," Astrid whispered. A step ahead.

Sam sighed. "It turns out, despite her having an affair, Caine and I were true fraternal twins. The human DNA that became part of the gaiaphage wasn't just Caine's father. It was from *our* father."

"You and Caine," Astrid breathed.

"My mother sensed Caine's connection to the gaiaphage. But not mine. We had the same connection. We had the same DNA. But Caine grew up without . . . you know. Without . . ."

"Without love," Astrid said. "All of his life."

"But not at the very end," Sam said. "At the very end he found it."

She put her hand back on his chest, then moved closer still to kiss his neck. "It's over, Sam. Finally."

"Yeah," he said. "I guess it is."

"Turn out the light, Sam."

Sam reached for the switch and turned out the light.

THE THANKS:

ANY BOOK, AND certainly any book series, involves more than the writer. Thanks to my lawyer and buddy Steve Sheppard, who helped me sell the series and was my consigliere throughout. Thanks to the wise Elise Howard, who acquired it at HarperCollins, and my first editor, Michael Stearns, one of the real good guys of publishing.

Thanks to Katherine Tegen, who inherited the series and embraced it and supported it and most of all put up with me. (Not always easy.) She's been a real friend. Love you, KT.

Thanks to all the publishers around the world who made Gone a hit in so many countries. A particular shout-out to Egmont Publishing and my many UK and ANZ fans.

As always, thanks to my wife, Katherine Applegate, for basically convincing me to be a writer, and our kids, Jake and Julia, just for being cool.

TO THE FANS:
Wow. We spent six books and three thousand pages together

in the FAYZ. Kind of amazing, isn't it? Worn out? I am.

From the start I wanted the Gone series to be like one single, long story. I wanted characters who would grow with you over time, characters who might make you mad or disappoint you, characters you might hate, and hopefully a few that you'd respect, and like, and even love. That required extra patience and devotion on your part. I hope you found it worthwhile. I hope you had fun. I did.

I'm not retiring from writing. There's the Magnificent 12, which I think you'll find funny—yes, even if you're supposedly "too old." None of my other teen series are an attempt to continue the Gone series; each is its own thing. But if you're looking for something to read, give them a shot.

I've enjoyed every minute I've spent with Gone fans on Twitter @TheFayz, on Facebook at www.facebook.com/authormichaelgrant, and at various visits around the United States and the world. You are a very smart, very interesting, very cool bunch of humans. It's been a pleasure entertaining you.

From me, from Sam and Astrid, Caine and Diana, Quinn, Edilio, Lana and Patrick, Dekka, Brianna, Albert, Computer Jack, Orc, Mary, Sanjit and Choo, Howard, Hunter, Little Pete, and all the rest (even Drake), thanks.

You are now free to leave the FAYZ.

MICHAEL GRANT has spent much of his life on the move. Raised in a military family, he attended ten schools in five states, as well as three schools in France. Even as an adult he kept moving, and in fact he became a writer in part because it was one of the few jobs that wouldn't tie him down. His fondest dream is to spend a year circumnavigating the globe and visiting every continent. Yes, even Antarctica. He lives in Northern California with his wife, Katherine Applegate, and their two children. You can visit him online at www.themichaelgrant.com.